A FRONTIER UNCLAIMED
BY ANY STATE,
THE PLAGUELAND DISTORTS ALL

The pain only came in the aftermath, in the wake
of turbulence caused by the crystals. And when it came,
it started small—a pinprick on her shoulder and a tiny burn
on her toe. But then there was another and another,
each small, but adding to the others until she was besieged
with a thousand pinpricks, ten thousand tiny burns.

Slanya had been trained to focus her mind,
to use the power of her thoughts against material pain,
and she tried to use it now, tried to concentrate
to keep the unity of her body and mind. But in the
wake of each filament, the onslaught of pain made it
impossible to focus, and her mind grew disoriented.

The elixir would protect her, would it not?
Gregor's concoction would keep her alive through this.
She had to trust him.
She did trust him. Didn't she?

The last segment of her right pinkie finger spun away
like a tiny fleshy mote. She watched it in silent fascination.
This time there had been no pain when the churning magic
had severed it from her hand. And as she looked down
now, she wondered in amusement at the blood.

ALL THAT'S CERTAIN
IS YOUR DESTRUCTION.

THE WILDS

FORGOTTEN REALMS

THE WILDS

THE EDGE OF CHAOS

Jak Koke

Wizards of the Coast

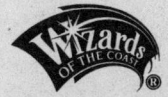

The Wilds
The Edge of Chaos

©2009 Wizards of the Coast LLC

Published by Wizards of the Coast LLC

FORGOTTEN REALMS, WIZARDS OF THE COAST, and their respective logos are trademarks of Wizards of the Coast LLC in the U.S.A. and other countries.

Printed in the U.S.A.

Cover art by Erik M. Gist
Map by Robert Lazzaretti

First Printing: August 2009

9 8 7 6 5 4 3 2 1

ISBN: 978-0-7869-5189-5
620- 25018740-001-EN

U.S., CANADA,
ASIA, PACIFIC, & LATIN AMERICA
Wizards of the Coast LLC
P.O. Box 707
Renton, WA 98057-0707
+1-800-324-6496

EUROPEAN HEADQUARTERS
Hasbro UK Ltd
Caswell Way
Newport, Gwent NP9 0YH
GREAT BRITAIN
Save this address for your records.

Visit our web site at www.wizards.com

To my beloved Karawynn
who finds reasons to live every day,
for which I am constantly grateful.

ACKNOWLEDGEMENTS

I owe a debt of gratitude to my brilliant and devoted editor,
Erin Evans, for her sharp eye, patience, and expert criticism.
The value of a good editor is inestimable,
and there is nobody I'd rather have editing my work.
Thanks also to the creators, writers, artists, and designers
of the Forgotten Realms universe. You have crafted and
developed a world full of wonder and complexity,
of rich history, riveting adventure, and exciting vision.
It has been a real pleasure playing in your world,
and I hugely appreciate the opportunity.
Appreciation also goes out to my awesome daughters,
Michaela and Claire, for their patience and for putting up
with too many weekend days without Dad.
I know you missed me, right? Didn't you?
And finally, for her generosity and support during the
difficult times arising due to novel deadlines, I am indebted
to Karawynn Long. Thanks, Sweetie. You truly rock.

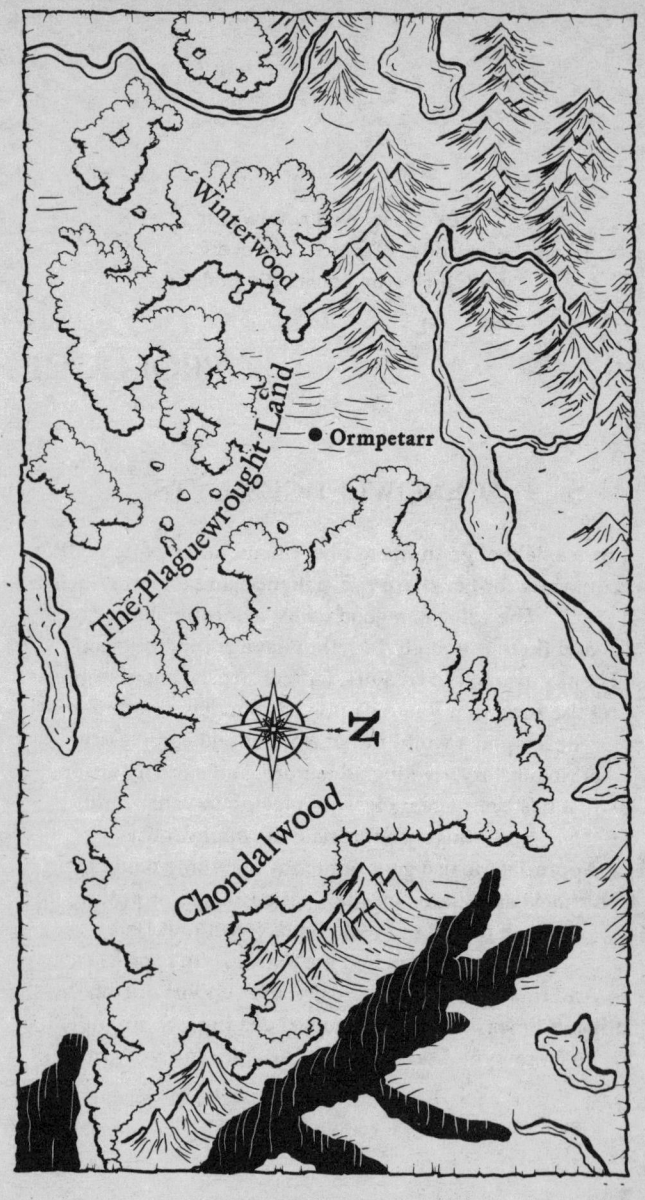

PROLOGUE

A flare of incandescent blue appeared and was gone, leaving darkness in its wake.

A flicker of light played against Duvan's closed eyelids. He turned and pressed his head into the burlap pillow. It could not be morning yet, and he didn't want to wake up to another day of tilling the fields.

When we are twelve, he thought, Talfani and I will run away and live with the elves at Wildhome. But that was two summers away, and now he needed his sleep. Papa would make him work hard in the morning. A quick glance across the room to Talfani's bed showed that she hadn't stirred in her sleep. Even the worst thunderstorms didn't wake her.

Another flash lit the night and cast sharp shadows on the walls of the small room he shared with his sister. Duvan slipped out of his low, wooden bed, instinctively checked the floor for scorpions, and went to the window. "Psst, 'Fani! Wake up! Something's happening."

Outside, the world was transformed. From the window, Duvan could see down the main road of the village, It was a moonless night, which would normally have been black as pitch, but there was a blue fire shimmering in the air.

Not just the air—in the ground too. Like a thin veil the color of spiderwebs, the fabric of the universe fluctuated in front of Duvan's eyes. He'd seen this once before: spellplague.

The remnants of the ancient unraveling of magic, spellplague storms were random and cruel. Striking without judgment the innocent and guilty alike, spellplague destroyed good and evil, lawful and criminal, young, old, human, elf, even the great and monstrous. To some it gave great power and ability, but to most it destroyed mindlessly and without bias.

As he watched from the window, the gossamer knife flickered its way through the left side of the street, and in a moment the houses there were splayed open like cloven fruit. The earth rent in the rift created by the spellplague's path, mud-brick and dirt flowing into the sky like an inverted waterfall of rock and trees and splintered wood, carrying people with it.

The earth shook around him, and he struggled to stay on his feet. But no sound came to Duvan's ears. Outside, people screamed and cried out in pain and terror, their faces twisted in fear as they ran. But their screams came to his ears as if from a great distance, muffled and faint.

They're all leaving, he thought. We need to get out too!

Abruptly, panic seized him and took hold of his limbs. He found himself running to the doorway. He had to get out!

"Talfani!" he yelled, and his own voice nearly broke his ears. She stirred in her bed.

"Duvan?" she mumbled. "What is it?"

He crossed the room and pushed aside the heavy blanket that served as a door. The imposing figure of his father met him there. "Thank the stars, you are all right," he said, looking first at Duvan and then at Talfani.

"All right?" Talfani was out of bed now.

"Spellplague has struck the village," Papa said. "Many lives are in danger, but you are safest here." The worry lines around Papa's olive-colored eyes deepened. "Stay here until I come for you."

Duvan felt his heartbeat slow a little. His breathing evened. Papa would protect them.

"Duvan," Papa said, "you are the elder—"

"Only by a quarter hour," Talfani protested.

"True, sweetpea. Still, I am putting him in charge should anything happen."

With a glance from Papa, Talfani bit back her retort.

"Duvan, you're in charge. Take care of your sister until I return."

Papa turned and slipped through the curtain, leaving only the smell of almonds and pipeweed.

"What do we do?" Talfani asked, and the tremble in her voice sent a chill through Duvan. Of the two of them, she was always the strong and defiant one.

"We wait," he said, turning to look his twin in the eye. "We stay and we wait."

And so they waited. They held each other against the upheaval when the ground ripped apart. They watched through the tiny window as the spellplague rampaged through their neighbors and the livestock running loose. They waited through the night and into the morning, breathing through their nightshirts when the dust in the air grew thick, and the metallic smell of blood pervaded everything around them.

Papa never came back.

By midday the storm seemed to have passed. No movement

outside. No sign of anyone, and the spellplague appeared to have receded to small pockets.

Duvan heard Talfani's stomach groan, and he realized that he was hungry too.

"I can't hear anyone," he said. "But my hearing is all messed up."

"It's gone quiet," Talfani said, and tears welled in her eyes. "Earlier I was praying to Selûne that the screaming would stop, and now it has. Now it has, and I'm more afraid."

Duvan took her into his arms. Talfani was his same size—tall enough to rest her chin on his shoulder—and her hair was as black as his, her skin the same deep brown tone. His eyes were black, though, while hers were lighter, and rare—golden yellow-brown.

"Selûne was not here tonight," he said. "She did not hear your call. The screaming stopped for another reason."

"I'm hungry," she said. "And I miss Papa."

"Me too, 'Fani. But I promised I would take care of you, and he said we should stay here." For the time being, she nodded and accepted that answer.

"Want to play tiles?"

Talfani looked at him, puzzled and surprised.

"To pass the time while we wait." They played for several hours, and no one came. It remained eerily still. Finally, they slept.

When he awoke, it was light again, and Talfani was in his bed next to him. His stomach was empty and growling. He nudged her. "We need food," he said. "I'm going to go out and find some. You stay here."

"No," said Talfani faintly. "Don't leave me alone."

So he stayed that time, and the next time she slept too. He waited for another day until his hunger clawed at his gut. And because he didn't want her to face what he suspected was outside the curtain of their room, he went when she was asleep.

"We need to eat," he whispered to her, all serene and peaceful against her burlap pillow.

No response.

"I will come back soon." He slipped from the bed and pulled on his sandals, then stepped to the doorway and pushed aside the heavy curtain.

Where before there had been hallway and the rest of their small house, now there was nothing but rubble and dirt, with sporadic patches of spellplague shimmering like will-o'-wisps among the destruction. Their bedroom stood alone, spared by the storm.

Duvan stood transfixed and uncomprehending. He took measured breaths, trying to fight down the panic. But it was his stomach that brought him back and reminded him of his need. He stepped through the doorway and caught one last glimpse of Talfani, sleeping and restful, before the curtain fell between them.

CHAPTER ONE

Commander Accordant Vraith suppressed a shiver of excitement. Everyone was here—her assistants and guards from the Order of Blue Fire, all the carefully chosen pilgrim volunteers, and perhaps even the sharn were watching from their hidden vantages, beyond the veil of the Plaguewrought Land.

Everyone was in place. The ritual could begin shortly—the ritual of borders.

Vraith stood at the edge of the world. On one side, a serene, sunny afternoon bathed a grassy field in bright yellow warmth, broken only by the shadows of a smattering of clouds and floating earth motes. Quiet and peaceful and ordinary.

One the other side, the world was ending. Behind the border veil that marked the edge of the Plaguewrought Land, everything was in upheaval.

The land beyond the veil was one of the few locations where the beloved wild magic—the anarchic, extra planar force that had changed Toril forever when it first tore asunder the rules and ways of magic—was constant and contained. Inside, unstable ground flowed at random up into the sky, or down, or sideways.

An ocean of blue fire—what the unenlightened masses called *spellplague* though it was only the remnant of that glorious event—surged and pulsed behind the border veil. Though no match for the Spellplague that had struck Toril a hundred years ago, the blue fire promised power unbound by the laws of nature. Raw power.

And in between—the border. The veil that separated these two worlds seemed fragile and hardly up to the task of holding in the most powerful force in all Faerûn, but it nonetheless managed. The border stretched up into the sky, like an undulating, prismatic curtain—a translucent sheet blowing in a wind, covered in an oily sheen that reflected a rainbow of light.

Borders existed in all worlds—edges of nature that formed the margins between darkness and light, between heat and cold, between order and chaos.

Between life and death.

And it is time to move this one, Vraith thought. Time to give the blue fire a little more room. Against the backdrop of the Plaguewrought Land, Vraith drew herself up and prepared to address the pilgrims who had been chosen for her first ritual. As an elf of diminutive build, Vraith had to work to maintain the aura of authority she commanded.

Whatever her size, they could not deny her magical prowess. That was her power. That was what she brought to the Order of Blue Fire and its secretive masters. This ritual would be her glorious ascension. Her rapture.

This endeavor's success would not only be a triumph for her, but for all involved. For the volunteers, to be personally accompanied and baptized in the spellplague by one of the leaders of the Order of Blue Fire was an honor, to be sure. But no exposure to the spellplague was without risks. And when Vraith had explained the risks, these five pilgrims had seemed unconcerned. Perfect.

If all goes well, she thought, their devotion and commitment to the cause will be rewarded. Vraith knew that, for it had been promised by a sharn, a true prophet of the Blue Fire, that had come to Vraith in a dream.

Hadn't it? Vraith was sure it had . . . in its oblique and awe-inspiring way.

"We are ready," she said, raising her voice to an evangelical pitch. "Pilgrims, gather around me." She spread her arms wide as if she would embrace them all.

The pilgrims approached, each garbed in simple white robes. They had been chosen for their devotion as well as their constitution, for this ritual would tax their physical endurance.

Vraith took each pilgrim one by one, placing them in a tight semicircle next to the border veil. She avoided looking at their faces as she arranged them. Their identities didn't matter to Vraith—they were pieces in a game. Pawns, interchangeable and easy to lose for the greater good.

When each of the pilgrims was in position, an arm's length apart, the five of them forming a tight half-circle with end points nearly touching the border veil, Vraith carefully unsheathed a ceremonial dagger from its jeweled scabbard. The dagger's razor-sharp blade shimmered with blue magic. Beyond the semicircle stood the guard contingent, ready to keep the peace or fight any creatures that might appear.

"May the Blue Fire burn inside you, each one," she said as she made a small incision in the palms of their hands, one by one. "May you find your rapture."

Inside the veil, chaos ravaged the land. Outside, the mid-afternoon sun shone warm The sound of the surging plagueland was a muffled roar behind the veil, and the late-summer smell of the blue fire leaked through: decaying flesh and rotting oranges.

But the blue fire itself remained contained within. Like a caged beast, the spellplague remnants raged inside the Plaguewrought Land, its pale blue and white energy like sheets of gauzy lightning. Wild and alive, that power spoke to Commander Accordant Vraith, urging her to set it free of its bonds, for the blue fire would purge all of Faerûn of its weak and frail. In the wake of the baptism by spellplague, only the chosen survived and were made stronger for it.

"Take the hand of the person next to you," Vraith said. "Palm to palm so that you become bonded to each other through blood—a single, unifying thread."

The pilgrims complied, seemingly entranced.

A deep, throbbing ache resounded in Vraith's sternum as her spellscar activated. The world shifted in front of her eyes, colors fading to red and black as tendrils of magic—invisible to all but herself—snaked forth from Vraith's chest and touched the threads of the pilgrims' souls, starkly evident now to her enlightened vision.

Vraith started the ritual, weaving the filaments of these souls into a new curtain, something matching the mesh of the border veil. her assistants brought forth powdered metals, bottles of swirling residuum, and dangerous salts that burst into flame as they came into contact with Vraith's magic. It was a delicate and exhausting spell, lasting hours as she painstakingly crafted a new border and tied the souls of the pilgrims into the shifting, prismatic membrane that held back the blue fire.

Vraith rejoiced in her work, nudging the edge of chaos just a tiny bit. The plaguelands surged and crashed like an angry ocean of raw magic behind the veil, and now that raw, blue fire leaped from pilgrim to pilgrim.

Come on, Vraith thought. Hold fast.

But the life force of the pilgrims flared brightly and guttered out. Each unit lasted mere moments. Not enough time to finish the ritual. Not enough time for anything but burning and death.

Vraith felt, more than heard, the screams and terrified cries of agony as the pilgrims came apart, burned from the inside by the chaotic fire. As she came out of her casting trance, Vraith disentangled herself from the frayed threads of the spell she had woven. She recoiled as the border curtain collapsed back to its previous spot.

A wave of exhaustion weakened her knees, and as her spellscar diminished, the wind was knocked out of her. Struggling to breathe, she looked over the aftermath. What a failure!

At her feet, the remains of the pilgrims still smoked and smoldered. Inadequate, she thought, and weak! Vraith stepped away from the bodies and composed herself. After a minute her breath returned, and she yelled, "Get them out of my sight!" The venom in her voice surprised even Vraith.

As Jahin, the genasi wizard who currently served as captain of the guard, moved to obey her, Vraith took a few deep breaths. The noxious aroma of singed flesh coiled in the air, contaminating it. She needed to think. How had the ritual failed? It was the first test; some degree of failure was to be expected. But the deaths of all five pilgrims was catastrophic.

These pilgrims were too frail. The blue fire was discriminating of course—it would not spare just anyone. She couldn't count, it seemed, on the pilgrims lasting long enough for the ritual to complete. If only there were a way to give them strength so that they could remain exposed to the blue fire a little longer without dying.

Vraith drew herself up and turned away from the remnants of the pilgrims. The entourage of Peacekeepers—the Order of Blue Fire militia—was busy cleaning up the smoking remains, but she didn't have to oversee that. And as she walked toward her carriage, Vraith's mind was already concentrating on the next test ritual, on how she would change things.

She turned to her assistant, Renfod—an ebony-skinned human cleric in the pale blue robes of a Loremaster Accordant of the Order. His short, graying, black hair receded over his forehead, and cataracts dulled his brown eyes a little.

"We need to pay a visit to the monk," she said.

Renfod arched his brows. "Brother Gregor?"

Vraith nodded. "He's been working on something. The pilgrims whisper he has a potion that will grant them safe passage through the Plaguewrought Land."

"Gregor hasn't been eager to join the Order," Renfod said.

Vraith climbed into the coach and sat on the blue silk cushions. At least she was permitted some degree of comfort in this otherwise revolting backwater of a place. "We don't need him to join the Order," she said. "We just need enough of his draught to protect our volunteers." She gestured toward the blackened remains on the ground.

Renfod grimaced. "Quite so," he said. "And yet, such reliance on an unbeliever is risky."

"You leave that to me," Vraith said. "I am all too familiar with such risks."

Renfod leaned in close, his masculine odor almost palpable as he whispered, "Indeed you are."

Vraith smiled at the remembrance of their intimacies. He had used her for advancement, and she had been quite willingly used.

Renfod stepped back from the carriage and said, "As you wish, Commander. We shall persuade the monk to join in our cause. I am sure he will be made to understand our need."

"Duvan?"

From the recesses of his consciousness, Duvan felt someone shake his shoulder.

"You said to wake you when the manticore flew off. It's gone now."

Chills from the dream memory shivered across his skin as he came awake, dreams of the Blue Fire fleeing his mind. It had been more than ten years since his village had been hit by the plaguestorm, and still it haunted his dreams. His unfortunate decision to leave Talfani to find food made him shudder with anguish. He missed her still.

Duvan yawned and tried to shake off the remaining images of nightmare death from the cobwebs of his mind. "Thank you, Beaugrat. Get the climbing gear ready."

Duvan heard the plate mail-clad warrior retreat and begin barking orders to the other hirelings—Seerah and the mage whose name Duvan could never remember. Duvan wasn't good with people, which was why he'd let Beaugrat pull the team together. Beaugrat was a part of Tyrangal's security force, and though he was new, he knew to listen to Duvan.

Brushing dirt and jungle insects off his black leather pants and tunic, Duvan stood and stretched. Duvan had tanned all of his leather himself, and he had inlaid the hide with fragments of broken dragon scales, which Tyrangal had managed to obtain for him. The result was remarkably supple for its strength, despite the armor's current travel-worn state.

Stepping through the jungle undergrowth and out into the bright sunlight, Duvan squinted as he approached the edge of the Underchasm. Even the dense Chondalwood foliage receded slightly from the cliff's edge as if the thick jungle growth, normally a force of nature so daunting and formidable, knew when it was overmatched.

Shading his dark eyes with his hand, he stared out over

the cliff's edge. The jagged hole in the world was narrow here, the span speckled with motes—the islands of rock that floated in the air like stone clouds. Duvan could see the other side in the misty distance to the north. The bottom, on the other hand, could not be seen. The chasm merely disappeared into darkness far below.

It's not really bottomless, Duvan reminded himself. The chasm ended in the Underdark—the homeland of the vile and truly monstrous, including the cities of the drow. Luckily, he wasn't seeking the bottom. Not nearly. If Tyrangal's maps were accurate—and they always were—there had been a citadel here, just along this edge.

There were telltale signs of an ancient structure along the ground by the cliff edge—mason-cut flagstones and a ruined stone wall pulled apart by years of jungle overgrowth. But the actual citadel had fallen into the Underchasm, landing on a ledge below where they now stood.

Duvan grabbed the rope he'd earlier tied to a sturdy banyan root thicker than his waist. He tested its fastness and, satisfied that it held secure and fast, he leaned out over the cliff edge and looked down. The citadel was still there, clinging to a ledge about two or three hundred feet down. The tower hung precariously on the broad ledge, its top jutting at an angle out over the fall.

Earlier, however, a manticore had been circling nearby, eyeing its territory for intruders and prey.

"Excellent," he said. "Are we all ready to drop down?"

There was murmuring among the hired help behind him.

Duvan pulled himself back from the edge, pushing his long black hair from his face. "Well?"

Seerah, the pale, blonde woman in worn leathers, grinned. She didn't speak much, and when she did, her northern dialect was difficult for Duvan to follow, consisting mostly of curses in a language that he only partly understood. She wore a crossbow on her back and a short sword at her hip.

As Duvan considered Seerah, the third man asked, "Do we really have to go down into the chasm?"

Duvan stared at the man who had spoken. Black eyes met his for a second before looking away. "Yes," Duvan said. "I know it sounds crazy, but it's really not. We're just going to the ledge to search the citadel tower."

He regarded the slight and aging man. His deep brown skin was almost as dark as Duvan's, and he was shorter than the woman next to him. Of the three, Duvan had pegged him as the most dangerous. His robes and the wand lashed to his belt named him a spellcaster even though he hadn't yet performed any obvious magic.

Beaugrat scowled down at the man as if disgusted by his hesitance. Taller and heavier than Duvan, Beaugrat had a reputation for being quite the brawler in a scrape. His large frame carried plate armor as easily as Duvan wore his leathers. There was a custom-crafted gap in the right pauldron. It allowed the deep and jagged spellscar in Beaugrat's flesh, which emanated heat, to cool in the air.

Duvan glanced at the spellscar, noting the blue tinge to the semitranslucent muscle there. A spellscar was caused by exposure to spellplague remnants. Only the extremely lucky escaped from the plaguelands with a spellscar. More often it caused another condition: death.

"Very well," the sorcerer said. "If we're all going down, I will go too. But just as far as the ledge."

A few minutes later, Duvan and company were rappelling down the cliff face. Hot wind, laced with moisture, whipped up out of the Underchasm, carrying the smell of decay. Duvan looked up for a second as he let the rope slide under his hands to allow a controlled fall.

Above him, the bodies of his three hirelings descended with various degrees of awkwardness. He just hoped none of them fell on him. Making sure his feet were steady and solid against the pitted and jagged cliff wall, Duvan pushed off and rappelled down. Then he turned his attention to the approaching ledge below.

Thick wisteria vines covered the pitted black rock of the cliff face, runners from the jungle above seeking to invade the Underdark miles below. Pushing off of the black basalt, Duvan's boots crushed green leaves and fluted purple flowers. Wind cooled sweat on Duvan's neck as he let himself slide deeper into the chasm.

The cliff fell away as far as he could see, disappearing into blackness miles below. Pocks and hollows marred an otherwise sheer wall, but according to the old maps that Duvan had found in Tyrangal's library, the treasure he sought should be in the ruins of the citadel perched on the ledge below.

The citadel below had long ago been part of a larger castle, according to the map—a castle belonging to one Baron Ryseleth at the time of the Spellplague. Built from granite bricks as tall on one side as Duvan, the structure looked only tenuously intact, having since mostly fallen into the chasm.

Slipping down along the rope, Duvan surveyed the ruins. The base of the main tower clung to the cliff face like a mushroom to rotting wood. The top of the tower canted dangerously, jutting away from the cliff wall like a finger sticking out over the chasm.

Duvan touched lightly down on slanted flagstones that used to be a courtyard. Up close, the ledge was much less substantial than he'd assumed from above. He tested his footing on the stone surface. The rock was damp with the windblown spray of the waterfall on the far side of the chasm, but vines and roots interlaced through the flagstones and provided purchase as well as structural support.

"Baron Ryseleth," Duvan said, "what a charming home you have. I presume you won't mind me taking a souvenir or two."

It looked to Duvan as though about half of the original citadel had fallen away, but as the central tower remained, he figured their chances were good. He would just have to find Ryseleth's own offices. The rest of the treasure hunters slid to the ledge beside him.

"Come on," Duvan said, creeping across the courtyard to the archway that led into the crumbling tower. Ivy formed a disorganized crisscross weave up the side of the tower, blackening the large blocks where the vines had anchored themselves.

Behind him came the sound of stone grinding against stone. Turning, he saw Beaugrat and Seerah stumble off-balance as the flagstone under them loosened and shifted. Seerah leapt lightly to the side and landed on a more solid flagstone, but there was nothing agile about Beaugrat. He fell to his knees and waited for the rock to stop shifting.

Duvan looked up at the tower, leaning precariously out over the abyss. "You'd better hang back here, Beaugrat," he said. "Seerah, you stay with him. The sorcerer and I will explore the tower." To Duvan's disappointment, the other man merely nodded, showing none of his earlier eagerness.

Pausing just outside the entrance, Duvan listened for the sounds of the manticore or other creatures whose intentions would be less than charitable. He also took a moment to check the masonry for the telltale signs of embedded traps. This building hadn't been created as a vault, but checking for snares and triggers had saved him from pain or death on numerous occasions.

Even though Duvan did not fear dying, he *was* afraid of pain. Oblivion was far preferable than torture.

No danger here. Duvan slipped inside and waited in silence and darkness for his eyes to adjust to the dim light. When they had, he and the sorcerer made a quick tour of the four rooms at the base of the citadel.

One of the many things Tyrangal had taught him was how to

make a quick assessment of the value of things. Duvan's mentor and benefactor, Tyrangal was an unusual, copper-skinned woman of remarkable influence in the city of Ormpetarr. It was at her behest he had traveled across the Vilhon Wilds to the Underchasm, in search of Baron Ryseleth's citadel.

"Let's head up," he said, finding nothing of value in these rooms. He sprinted up the spiraling stone steps, coming to an abrupt halt when he came across a hole in the wall where a chunk of the tower had fallen away to reveal a fathomless drop into darkness below.

Duvan made sure the sorcerer had caught up before deftly skirting the opening and showing the man how it could be done. Up and up they went, until they found what must have been the baron's offices. "We must be nearly to the top," he said. "We're looking for anything of value, but particularly any tomes or scrolls."

The remains of purple velvet curtains still hung on the walls, tattered and moth-eaten. A quick scan of the remaining desk revealed nothing more than rusted styli and mold-eaten parchments. No books or scrolls of value here.

A sudden roar from outside sent a shiver up Duvan's back. The manticore, from the sound of it, about two hundred yards to the south and slightly above them, likely riding a thermal out of the Underchasm. Duvan just hoped it wasn't headed for this ledge.

"This place is cleaned out," the sorcerer said. "Ransacked years ago, probably before it fell into the chasm."

"Unfortunately true." Tyrangal had been wrong. Still, if the book was going to be anywhere, this was the room it'd be in.

Duvan decided to make a thorough check for secret compartments and hidden doors the baron might have kept his treasures in. He ran his fingertips along the stone walls, ceiling, and floor, searching by touch and by sight. There was a window that looked toward the cliff face and through which shone the midday sun. A thorough search would take some time, especially since decay and time had cracked and crumbled the stones and masonry to the point that any unusual feature might just be a product of age and not design.

Outside the manticore roared again, closer this time. Too close.

Abruptly, the sky darkened as the great winged creature filled the window. Immediately, Duvan signaled to the sorcerer to hide, and while the man cast a quick spell, Duvan slid into the shadows of the tilted room.

As the mage faded from sight, Duvan fought against the natural instinct to panic. His heart leaped into his throat, but he focused on calming it and on taking steady, silent breaths. In moments, his calm returned, and he was hidden from sight. Both of them were hidden.

The creature was too large to fit through the opening, even folding its huge batlike wings. Spotted brown and black fur covered its great catlike body. Black spikes protruded from its spine and, most dangerously, from the stinger bulb at the tip of its tail. The creature bent its neck and stuck its head through the window.

Duvan had seen live manticores from a distance before, and Tyrangal had shown him a preserved head once. That one was larger than the one in the window here, but all things equal, Duvan preferred the dead one.

The head was hideous; its vaguely human face and eyes made all the more monstrous by the flat snout and the wide mouth full of dagger-sharp teeth. Head swaying to and fro, it sniffed the air.

Then, just as abruptly as it had appeared, the creature took flight, and with three heavy beats of its dragon wings, was gone. Duvan held perfectly still, his senses alert against the possibility that the creature would return.

Crouching silently in the shadows, straining for any telltale signs of movement, Duvan caught the impression of a panel in the corner of the long-deposed baron's office. Something odd in the curve of the rock floor, an ever-so-slight deviation in the smoothness of the stone, drew his keen attention.

He ran his fingers over the stone. There was an indentation there—too even to be a product of nature. He probed the edges. Definitely artificial. He pressed down on the small panel.

The panel slid down into a recessed compartment, revealing a hollow space beneath. Duvan peered inside, checking for spring-loaded traps and symbols that would indicate magical warding. There was nothing . . . except a rusting iron handle embedded in the wall of the compartment.

"You had best remain hidden," he whispered to the still-invisible sorcerer. "Just in case that beast returns."

He tugged on the handle. In front of Duvan, a large stone shifted from the wall with a horrible screech, leaving about a three-finger-wide opening. He pulled the prybar from his pack and expanded the gap. The stone was on some sort of rail system, but the iron had long been rusted and yielded begrudgingly. But finally, Duvan could see what was behind—a hidden cache, undiscovered and filled with treasures.

Resting on top of a pile of ancient coins rested a heavy tome—a thick book covered in tough leather that looked like wyvern hide. Gilt Elvish script and platinum filigree decorated the cover. It matched Tyrangal's description perfectly.

As he slipped the tome into his pack, the tower shook violently, knocking him over.

Behind him, the manticore slammed into the window arch, sending rocks flying into the room. The floor beneath him lurched as the tower groaned from the extra weight. The sun went dark again as the creature hit the wall once more, trying to dislodge the rocks around the window. Their chances of killing a creature of such size and power were slim to none.

Most of the time, Duvan preferred to be alone; everything was just better that way. But now he wished he'd brought more help. This was exactly the situation where a group of minions would come in handy. But alas, it was not going to happen. All he and the invisible sorcerer could do now was run and hope to not die.

"Run!" he called out. "Back down."

With no cleric in sight, death held an uncomfortable degree of finality to it. Never his first choice.

For Slanya, staring into the blazing funeral pyre, death was a doorway to another realm. The flames danced their primal destruction on the pile of dead bodies—pilgrims who'd uprooted their lives to come here to Ormpetarr in search of promise and power, only to end up as fodder for this fire.

Slanya sensed madness lurking in the chaos of the fire, an unbound wildness raging just beyond the veil of flame. Behind the line of stones that clearly marked the edge of the fire pit, Slanya felt the heat coming off the burning bodies. It burned her skin even from this distance.

Despite her strict adherence to an ordered and controlled life, Slanya sometimes felt like a moth attracted to the allure of the fire. She never stepped through that veil into chaos, but some tiny part of her, in the very recesses of her mind, wanted to abandon all caution. The wild dance of the flames tempted her, daring her to approach.

"Sister Slanya?"

Slanya shook her head and stepped away from the fire. She took a deep breath, wrinkling her nose at the smell of charring fat and muscle. What had she been thinking? Death was not a wild and chaotic event. Kelemvor judged all souls who came through the veil. He balanced all the deeds of their lives and guided them on to the next stage.

"Sister Slanya," came Kaylinn's voice again. "Brother Gregor asked to see you."

Slanya turned to look at her friend and superior. Kaylinn stood a full head shorter than Slanya, although she was not unusually short by any means; Slanya was taller than many human men. Where Slanya was tall and lithe, Kaylinn's hips were wide and her breasts full.

Both their heads were shaved except for the characteristic sidelock, but while Kaylinn's was long and auburn, Slanya's blonde lock barely reached her shoulder. She kept it wrapped with the thinnest of white leather straps.

Kaylinn and Slanya each had a tattoo depicting the sign of Kelemvor—a skeleton hand holding a set of scales—at the base of the skull where it met the spine,. Where Kaylinn's was inked in simple blue, Slanya's blue outlines had been filled with red and green and extended down her spine to to the spot between her shoulder blades.

"Yes, High Priestess?" Slanya asked.

Kaylinn dismissed the formality with a wave of her hand. Even though she was the head of their order here in Ormpetarr, she governed more by friendship and example than by dictate. Kaylinn's nurturing demeanor gave her a comforting manner with the sick and dying, and she had a wealth of healing power granted to her by Kelemvor. While Slanya also prayed to Kelemvor to grant some small powers, her skills were predominately in combat and body control.

Slanya gave Kaylinn a slight head bow. "Thank you for that news, sister," she said, then turned away from the fire. Already the pile next to the pyre had grown by a few additional corpses. That afternoon's dead, to be burned tomorrow.

"Brother Gregor is in his study," Kaylinn said.

"Do you know what he wants?"

Kaylinn exhaled a laugh. "Nay," she said. "But I do know

that he's meeting with that elf woman from the Order of Blue Fire."

The Order of Blue Fire was a sect devoted to studying the remnants of the Spellplague. Most of the members she'd met seemed likeable enough, but she was the first to admit that she didn't really understand why they were so devoted, so fanatical about the Spellplague and its remaining effects.

"I wonder what that's all about," Slanya said, lowering her voice.

"I'm sure Brother Gregor is just trying to help more pilgrims," Kaylinn said.

Gregor was an alchemist of exceeding skill and power. He was not devoted to Kelemvor as were the majority of the priests and monks in the temple complex of Ormpetarr, but to Oghma, the god of innovation. Though, if Slanya allowed herself the thought, he seemed more devoted to his own ideas than anything else. His laboratory was filled with strange smells and noises at all hours of the day and night as he produced elixirs to test on the waiting pilgrims. Rumor was that one of these elixirs could prevent the changelands from causing illness and death.

That's why they all came, masses of these desperate pilgrims, young and old, rich and poor, living and dying. They all wanted to increase their chances of surviving the exposure, to live through the baptism by blue fire that would give them their scar—and with that scar, their new power.

Sometimes the ability was minor, but most of the time the ability transformed the lives of those who survived. Most of the time, their spellscar gave them access to power and ability that would otherwise take years of training.

And yet, only a tiny fraction of pilgrims survived the journey past the border of the Plaguewrought Land where the spellplague thrived. The vast majority of them simply vanished, consumed by the blue fire, and were never heard from again. A tiny few survived exposure, and of those many grew sick or were hideously transformed. These ended up under Kaylinn's care, and quite a few found final rest in the funeral pyre.

"I need to tend to the dying," Kaylinn said, then made her way toward the healing tents.

Glancing back at the fire pit, Slanya no longer felt the allure of the flames. Ah well, there were worse places she could be. Here, she could work to better the lives of others and ensure the justice of their passage into the realms beyond the veil of death.

Some people would consider working with the dead and dying to be taxing and heinous duty, but Slanya liked it. People on the edge of death were more real, more immediately themselves as they saw the horizon of their life so close. Many were full of regret; some were consumed by guilt and wanted nothing more than to confess. Few were ready to meet Kelemvor. Slanya liked helping them make peace with their lives and prepare for their journey.

Slanya slipped into the quiet of the monastery. She moved quickly and silently past the central courtyard where a group of monk brothers and sisters sat in a meditation circle. Mind and body are one. That was the first lesson a monk learned, but it was one that needed to be learned and relearned, for it had many levels.

The daily construction work had stopped, and the sun had dipped—nearly time for the evening meal. Slanya loved this time. She liked the quiet, the peace, and above all the precise timing and regularity. Order meant knowing exactly what to expect. Adherence to law was one of the founding principles that defined a monk's being and allowed her to realize unity of mind and body and derive power from it.

Next to the disorder of the city of Ormpetarr and a stone's throw from the untamed wildness of the Plaguewrought

Land, the temple complex of Kelemvor was a sanctuary. The structure and arrangement of the monastery—the *peace*—made this her home.

The bright afternoon gave way to shadows and darkness in the hallway between the small chapel and Gregor's study. The silent corridor was punctuated only by the muffled sounds of voices. People were talking in urgent tones, and if Slanya concentrated, she could just make out what they were saying.

"I do not want a repeat failure," a woman's voice said, possibly the Vraith woman from the Order of Blue Fire whom Kaylinn had spoken of.

"Of course not, Vraith." That deep voice belonged to Gregor—Kaylinn's right hand and the man who had intervened when Slanya was just a child. Intervened and saved her.

Slanya approached the door, acutely aware of the empty hall. She lingered for a moment, silent and listening. All her life she'd had the ability to be quiet and unobserved. As a child, before . . . before the accident with her aunt that had left her an orphan, she'd honed the skill to be present without being noticed. Drawing attention often led to pain.

From the other side of the heavy wooden door, Gregor spoke again. "I am committed to the well-being of all pilgrims to the Plaguewrought Land who seek exposure to spellplague."

"Yes. Yes, of course," said the other. "We also have our ideals—similar to yours, in fact. Do you think you can help?"

"Perhaps if you gave me more details about the ritual—" Gregor began.

"The ritual is vast and complex," Vraith said. "And I am not about to reveal the secrets of it. However, I can tell you that the key component involves weaving the life threads of sentient creatures together and igniting this new pattern with spellplague from the border veil.

"The pilgrims I use are volunteers, of course, and selected based on their health and vigor. The ritual magic weaves the threads of their souls into a combined entity—a tapestry that matches the mesh of the border veil. So far, none of the volunteers have survived long enough to finish the weave.

"Brother Gregor, our plan requires that these volunteers survive this ordeal. I've heard rumors that you are passing out a potion to pilgrims seeking exposure to the blue fire. These rumors say the potion guarantees their survival."

"Well, the elixir doesn't guarantee anyone will survive." Slanya could hear the excitement in Gregor's voice. "But pilgrims do survive exposure longer. I can show you my charts if you'd like. The results of my latest trials have been phenomenal."

"No, that won't be necessary. I'll trust you." Vraith's voice grew smooth. "So how can we obtain some of this magic elixir?"

"This ritual of yours," Gregor asked, "it doesn't kill the pilgrims, does it?"

"No, no. Although during the ritual, the volunteers' exposure to the blue fire is prolonged. If they can survive that, they can survive the ritual."

"And," Gregor continued, "the purpose of this ritual is . . . ?"

"Imagine being able to create barriers to the plaguelands," Vraith said. "Imagine if we could replicate something like the border veil anywhere we wanted. We could contain the storms and the outbreaks . . ." Her voice trailed off, and there was a scuffling of feet from the room beyond.

Slanya's eyes had adjusted, and the corridor was much brighter now. She felt more conspicuous, more vulnerable in the open hallway. If somebody were to come in . . .

Calm down, she told herself. Breathe. She took a moment to center herself, anchor her body and mind together.

"You make a powerful argument," Gregor said.

"Excellent! If this next ritual proves successful," Vraith said, "we will need thousands more doses. The festival is a few days away. Can you provide that many?"

The festival? Slanya considered for a moment. Vraith must be referring to the Festival of Blue Fire. Thousands of pilgrims were gathering in and around Ormpetarr that tenday to participate. It was one of the reasons the numbers of sick and dead had increased.

Gregor said, "I will need more reagents to produce that much. But I'm already working on getting more."

"How long will it take?" Vraith's benevolent tone gave way to one of commanding urgency. "If the next test works, I'll want the elixir ready to distribute."

"Several days at least," Gregor said. "One of the ingredients is very difficult to acquire."

"Get started right away. This is critical." The sharpness in Vraith's voice made Slanya wince.

When Gregor spoke again, there was a warning in his tone. "Let me do my job and you do yours. I am provisionally committed, because this ritual of yours seems to be the key to containing spellplague. That is a worthy goal, and one which can make a profound change in the world. But do not take that tone again with me. I do not take orders from you."

"Can you create more elixir or not?"

Gregor paused. "Yes, I don't expect it to be a problem."

Vraith's tone was back to sweet and peaceful, "Perfect. I'll let you get to it then."

Abruptly there were footsteps and the sounds of movement. They were headed this way, toward the door where Slanya was standing. Getting closer.

Slanya's heart shot into her throat, and in her panic she

missed the next part of the conversation. She was about to be discovered, and the punishment would no doubt be the switch across her back. Memories threatened to overwhelm her.

Stop it, she told herself. There were no punishments like that in the monastery. That fear came from a long-ago life she hardly remembered. That was in a past that could never hurt her again.

And with that thought, some of the adrenaline fog lifted. She focused and relaxed her breathing, calmed her heart. And she knew what to do.

She knocked on the door. After all, she had been summoned. She was *supposed* to be on the way.

The door opened almost immediately, revealing Gregor with his silver-dusted black hair and neatly trimmed beard. A patch over his left ear where, his spellscar had bleached his hair and skull to the pale, milky blue color of moonstone lay bare.

Gregor gave Slanya a warm smile, "Ah, Sister Slanya, prompt as usual. Thank you for coming."

Slanya's heart warmed slightly at the sight of Gregor's pleasure with her, and then she became aware of how irrational her response to Gregor was. She wanted to please him; she had held a special affinity for him ever since he'd saved her; he'd judged her and found her worthy. She knew that her reaction was less than objective, but it didn't hurt anyone but herself.

"I am just escorting our guests here, including Commander Accordant Vraith of the Order of Blue Fire, to the gates."

Gregor indicated a diminutive elf woman holding a wooden box, who radiated power and confidence. "Just 'Vraith' is fine," she said with a slight nod.

Gregor continued, "Our business has concluded. Please walk with us."

Slanya stood to the side as Gregor and Vraith stepped into the hallway, followed by four others who apparently did not merit introduction. Vraith wore sky-blue wizard's robes, which shimmered in the dim light, the embroidered Order symbol of a flaming blue iris glittering on her heart. Her blonde hair was cropped short in back and straight across her brow in front, giving her an angular look.

Two of the four others, well-muscled human men in plate armor displaying the Order symbol on their chests, flanked Vraith and walked just slightly behind her. Trailing in the rear was a dwarf woman with curly red hair and glowering eyes under bushy red brows. She sported pale blue clerical robes, a faded copy of those worn by Vraith, bound at the waist by a white rope.

Next to the dwarf walked a genasi woman, wearing the bright robes of a wizard, which served to accentuate the aquamarine color of her skin. The genasi looked to be a mage to Slanya's eyes, and considering the hydra-shaped spellscar that seemed to drip like a liquid crystal stain over her left ear, she was bound to be quite a dangerous one.

Slanya brought up the rear, grateful that her anxiety hadn't been noticed. She would wait until she was called upon. Following Gregor and Vraith out into the late afternoon heat of the monastery courtyard, Slanya listened as their conversation shifted from business to superficiality.

"Your orders have accomplished a great deal in the short time you've been here," Vraith said. "You've built the bulk of your temple in such a short time. It's most impressive."

Gregor smiled and nodded, apparently appreciative of her compliments. After a few more moments, they were at last out through the main entrance and standing in the shadow of the billowing black cloud rising from the funeral pyre off to the right.

"Brother Gregor," Vraith said, handing the wooden box

to the dwarf cleric, "thank you again for undertaking such important work."

Gregor nodded.

"I look forward to your attendance at our ritual tonight, and I am hopeful that with your elixir we shall be successful."

"I wouldn't miss it," Gregor said.

Vraith smiled. "Perfect." Then with a slight bow, she said, "May the Blue Fire burn inside you."

The elf priestess turned and picked a path through the vast disarray of pilgrims' tents, which filled the fields between the monastery and Ormpetarr's main gates.

Standing next to Gregor, Slanya looked over the broad plain. The camp outside the monastery sprawled like an infection, and all attempts at establishing organization among the tents had been futile. So many new pilgrims arrived every day.

Slanya glanced across the distance at the wild city into which she rarely set foot. Unlike its ancient namesake, modern Ormpetarr was a frontier city—ruled not by a hierarchical leadership or a figurehead but governed instead by a loose alignment of power brokers.

A blue-brown haze cut a swath through the city. This was the veil—the Plaguewrought Land border that the pilgrims came here to cross, if only briefly. There was a steep drop-off just through the hazy veil, and rumor said that the terrain inside the changelands was as inconstant and volatile as a storm-wracked ocean.

The once-mighty city told of a rough history, of a glorious past now worn down by the ravages of time and the Spellplague. Ormpetarr may have once been a monument to order and to the rule of law, but the monument had shattered, and the only order or law that had arisen from the wreckage was survival of the cunning and the strong. "We are here to help establish order on the edge of chaos," Kaylinn had told her, "where it is most needed."

But Slanya, who preferred the quiet and ordered life in the monastery, found it hard to avoid openly gagging from the smells drifting across the fields—the aroma of food cooking mingled with the charred smell of the roasted dead from the funeral pyre. And beneath it all was the summer stench of the Plaguewrought Land itself, like rotting flesh crammed with sour oranges.

The vast encampment was no more than a disorganized jumble of tents and makeshift shelters that served as a refuge for the grotesque plaguechanged who had come for hospice care. It was also a last stop for pilgrims without the means to afford lodging in Ormpetarr.

Pilgrims! To purposefully expose the sanctity and wholeness of their bodies and minds to the destructive chaos of the Plaguewrought Land—it was insanity.

Slanya shook her head, chiding herself for the derision she felt for the pilgrims. These people came from all over the world in search of improvement, and most of them met with death or illness. She should admire their courage.

Still, as much as she tried, the most she could summon for them was pity. The lucky ones walked away alive, with some unforeseen and unearned magical power to counterbalance some physical or emotional deformity. And, she thought, the very lucky ones die quickly and in little pain. They go to Kelemvor.

Gregor sighed. "So very many souls come here looking to better themselves," he said. "It is part of our mission now to help them accomplish that goal."

Slanya nodded.

"And in that light, I have an important task for you," Gregor said. He wasted no time getting to the point. "This task will require you to face chaos beyond anything you've ever experienced."

Slanya felt a chill despite the afternoon sun. Over the years, Gregor had changed from the nurturing father figure who'd rescued her off the streets when she was a girl. He was no longer the man who had brought her into the fold, who had mentored her, who had treated her like his own daughter for so many years. Was that man still there behind the obsession and the fervor?

She believed he was, for she saw the old Gregor come out sometimes. His frequent acts of kindness and his thoughtfulness for her well-being were evidence, were they not?

Still, he had been altered somehow, and Slanya could pinpoint the exact time it had happened. A little over a year earlier, Gregor had reported that spellplague had manifested in his chambers. They had lived far north of the Vilhon Wilds in Impiltur. Gregor claimed that spellplague had appeared and given him a vision. Then it had marked him with the spellscar he now manifested on his head.

He'd fallen ill for a month. And when he'd recovered, Gregor had told her that the spellplague manifestation had given him a new mission.

Gregor then proceeded to convince Kaylinn, and together they uprooted the temple's clerics and monks and led them south to the Vilhon Wilds and Ormpetarr, to rebuild their monastery and offer aid to those who sought the Plaguewrought Land and those who died in its borders.

In light of his recent conversation with the leaders of the Order of Blue Fire, Slanya worried that Gregor's new mission had become a dangerous obsession—one that was about to involve her. She looked over at him. "What must I do?"

"You must leave the temple complex and travel past the border and into the Plaguewrought Land."

CHAPTER TWO

Reflexes borne of a thousand escapes brought Duvan into hyperawareness. The humid air clung like a heavy blanket on his skin, and his breath quickened as he crouched in the shadows of the leaning citadel tower. Duvan watched as the manticore ripped away more brick from around the widening window. The beast grinned, exposing needle teeth.

It was almost upon them.

The creature stretched its membranous wings and took brief flight, only to crash back down against the tower. Abruptly, the floor under Duvan's feet shifted as the tower beneath him groaned under the manticore's impact. Its wings sent gusts of wind through the ever-widening window arch, causing dirt and dust to swirl up in the room around Duvan.

"Run down!" he called to the sorcerer who had remained invisible.

A quick glance at the treasure cache told him that besides the tome that he'd come for, there were also a large number of valuables worth taking, many more than he had time to get. Without hesitation, he scooped up an armload and dumped it into his backpack, paying no heed to what it contained.

That would have to do. Now to get out of—

The window frame's masonry exploded, showering Duvan with rubble. The creature burst through the wall, landing in a crouch in the center of the room and deafening Duvan with a load roar. Throwing his backpack over his shoulders, Duvan darted for the door and the stairs that would take him down and out.

The manticore brought its tail around and flicked it, sending a sharp spike hurtling toward Duvan. The thing might not kill him, but it would hurt, and it would certainly slow him down enough that the creature could catch him and eat him.

Duvan's awareness grew clear as he watched the spike. He dodged to the side and the spike whizzed past him.

A low grunt came from behind him. Turning, Duvan saw the sorcerer reappear. Surprise showed on the man's face, and it drained of color as Duvan started toward him. The manticore tail spike protruded from the sorcerer's chest. He slumped to the floor as a dark stain of blood spread over his robes.

The man would die.

"I'm sorry, friend," he said, "but I can't tarry."

The sorcerer merely lay there losing life by the moment.

From behind him came the snick of the manticore's tail snapping again. Duvan didn't hesitate; he sprinted out the door. He was halfway to the stairs when the floor shifted again, tilting from sloped to vertical. Duvan fell and landed against the wall which was now the floor.

Duvan's mind raced. He had to get out before the tower tore completely away from the cliff face. Sky showed through the wall of the baron's offices where the stones and masonry around the window hole had crumpled away, leaving only the empty network of woody vines.

The manticore had lost its footing when the tower had tipped, but was now angling toward Duvan again for another attack.

Duvan mentally catalogued his weapons: twelve throwing daggers in a bandolier across his chest, three of them coated with a paralytic poison; his single-shot crossbow at his hip; twin stiletto daggers in thigh scabbards; a pouch with flash powder.

There is no way I can kill that thing by myself, he thought.

The tower groaned and tilted farther so that the ceiling was coming around below him. Duvan danced along the leaning wall, keeping a precarious balance—but keeping it nonetheless.

The beast behind him huffed as the rotating wall sent it sprawling. Duvan took a glance back to see its shadow go reeling. The darkened shape of large membranous wings stretched across the stone wall as it used them to right itself.

Taking advantage of the few seconds' reprieve, Duvan scanned for a way out of the tower. Going down the stairs was no longer an option; the tower was jutting nearly horizontally out from the ledge. All he found was a stone wall—breaking apart to be sure, but with holes and cracks too small for him to fit through.

His gaze passed over the floor, wall, and ceiling, growing more desperate when all he saw was stone and more stone. Getting trapped inside the tower would mean certain death when the tower hit bottom.

Behind him, the manticore finally righted itself and

jumped for a closer position to Duvan, then clung to the door frame that was the only thing separating Duvan from being killed and eaten. He hoped, at least, it would be in that order.

A flash of light, up and to his left, caught Duvan's attention. A small slit window, previously too narrow for him to squeeze through, had widened a little. Duvan didn't know if he could get through, but it wasn't as though he had an abundance of choices at the moment.

He sprang for the wall and jammed his fingers into the cracks between the stones. Scrabbling, he pulled himself up, then swung his feet onto the window's sill.

His feet found purchase and pushed him higher. Using the grip of his right hand as an anchor, he swung across and extended his left arm to reach for the edge of the small window slit. Outside, thick wisteria vines stretched and snapped as the tower's extra weight proved too much for them to support.

It was coming down.

Behind him, the monstrous creature turned and flicked its tail again. This time Duvan wouldn't be able to dodge. Through sheer force, he lunged up and into the narrow window. The tail spike would hit him, he knew. But he still might be able to escape.

The spike hit, and Duvan felt the impact. But the deadly needle didn't touch him; instead, it penetrated his backpack and stopped, blocked by something inside.

That was lucky.

The window opening was tight, and the stone scraped rough against his skin as he squeezed through. In seconds he was out—and hanging off the side of a crumbling stone tower that stuck out over the abyss. Just the place he wanted to be.

If he got on the top of the cylinder, he might make it back to the ledge, assuming it was still there. A glance to the cliff face showed him that Beaugrat and Seerah had already started climbing back up to the jungle.

Oh, how he longed for level ground.

Inside the building, the manticore launched itself at the window. Not the smartest move, as it was nigh impossible that it would actually get through. Duvan climbed away from the opening anyway. He'd been wrong about the manticore's demolition skills once.

After pulling himself to the side of the tower that was most horizontal, Duvan half crawled, half scampered down the structure. The manticore battered itself against the stone behind him, but this time the baron's construction held together.

Duvan was about halfway to the ledge when several thick wisteria vines snapped and the tower's weight grew too heavy for the remaining vines. It started to fall from under him. His stomach lurched into his throat with the sudden freefall, while his mind raced. Was this the end? The long fall to oblivion?

Nothing he had in his pack or on his person could help him now. There was his glideskin—a triangular patchwork of wyvern leather and pegasus feathers that he'd made as an apprentice. He might be able to use the glideskin to slow his fall, but it was buried in the bottom of his pack.

No time to get it out. There must be another way.

The vines holding the tower to the jungle above snapped one by one in front of him. In a flash he realized that if he held on to the right one—a vine still connected to the jungle—he could make it.

He grabbed one and held on, hoping that the vine he held was attached above and not to the tower. The rock beneath his feet crumbled away as he climbed the knotted vines.

The old citadel fell away below him, and the echoing roar of the creature inside it faded and was gone.

Duvan gripped tightly to the vine as he crashed into the pitted stone wall where the tower had once clung, slamming his shoulder and nearly jarring his grip free. He bounced off but was able to twist around to get his feet in front of him to brace the impact of the second hit.

After he stopped swinging, Duvan found purchase on the cliff face. He took a moment to calm himself and get his bearings.

He was about thirty yards below what was left of the ledge where they'd first landed, where the end of his rope still hung. Most of the ledge was gone now, and what remained looked precarious. The flagstones hung loose, and if they came free they could fall right on top of him.

Duvan climbed carefully up the network of vines to the ledge and found a section that felt solid. He spent a moment taking stock, giving himself a quick once-over. No injuries. He had his haversack and all of the prizes he'd taken. The tome that Tyrangal had sent him to get was still inside it, as was the manticore spike that the book's heavy cover had managed to stop.

There was a hole in his pack, but that could be patched, and the heavy book had saved, if not his life, then at least a good deal of pain.

Duvan had to smile. All in all, things were looking good.

He decided to keep the manticore spike, which as about the size of his forearm and very sharp, with hundreds of small barbs along its length. He winced at what could have happened to him had the spike impaled him the way one had the sorcerer.

Duvan took his time making the climb back to the top. No need to hurry it. The manticore was gone, and he would emerge from the Underchasm relatively unscathed, all things considered.

When he reached the top, he flopped over the edge and lay on his back, breathing heavily. A wave of exhaustion washed over him as he rested and thanked the gods he'd made it out.

"Thank the gods you survived," came Beaugrat's deep voice. "Did you get what you came for?"

Duvan grinned, but there was something in Beaugrat's tone that raised Duvan's hackles. "Certainly."

"Very impressive," Beaugrat said, running his fingers through his blond hair. "I must say, I thought you were going to die when the manticore landed on the tower."

Duvan looked over at his two remaining lackeys. The ranger, Seerah, had her crossbow aimed directly at Duvan's chest, while Beaugrat himself drew a huge two-handed sword. This could be bad; Duvan hated crossbows.

"What do you want?"

"Actually, all the loot you're carrying will do just fine," Beaugrat said. "Give it to me."

"Or what?" Duvan asked, pushing wearily to his feet.

"Or we kill you."

Standing below a reddening sky in the monastery courtyard, Slanya tried to retain her calm while absorbing this new request. Leave the monastery? All right. But travel to the changelands? And go past the border where the changeland was rampant? That was impossible to accept.

"I can see that this is a surprise for you," Gregor said. "Follow me and I will explain." Putting his arm around her shoulder, he guided her into the chapel. They crossed the mosaic inlaid in the chapel floor, a skeletal hand holding a balance—Kelemvor's scales—and walked into the alchemist's laboratory.

The laboratory was Gregor's domain, and Slanya rarely visited it. The smell of sulfurous powder mingled with the aroma of crushed red-bark leaves. One whole wall held racks of crystal vials that contained purified ingredients for Gregor's concoctions, each labeled with a glyph. Another wall housed floor-to-ceiling shelves filled with books and scrolls, and a door leading to what Slanya assumed was a storage room, although she'd never been through it. On the third wall, coal burned in a narrow oven, and an iron ring bolted to an elaborate stand held a ceramic cauldron over the fire.

In the center of the room was the workbench, perfectly organized like everything else. Racks of cleaned vials stood to one end, ready to be filled and distributed to the next wave of pilgrims headed for the changelands.

"Our need is simple," Gregor said, closing the door behind them. "We must make more elixir to protect the pilgrims who will participate in the Festival of Blue Fire. I originally planned for a few hundred, but Vraith claims that we may need enough for thousands."

Slanya nodded. The influx of pilgrims had increased over the past few tendays, and many of them seemed to be waiting until the festival to visit the Plaguewrought Land.

"We only have a few days to make a great deal more, and our supply of plaguegrass is depleted."

Plaguegrass—tall, brown grass that grew inside the borders of the Plaguewrought Land—was the key component to the elixirs that Gregor concocted to help the pilgrims survive exposure to the spellplague.

"You are the only one I can trust to get this done," Gregor said. "You have proven that you can accomplish difficult tasks."

Yes, Slanya thought. I am the one who gets chosen for such tasks. She had been in charge of the team sent to scout this location for the monastery. She had been the one sent to negotiate with the Order of Blue Fire for access to this land. When Gregor or Kaylinn needed someone for a special purpose, Slanya was their first choice.

And truth be told, she liked it. Because, while performing funeral rites and advanced meditation formed the bedrock of her existence, sometimes the routine grew monotonous and tiring. Still, routine was better than a suicide mission.

"We need more plaguegrass." Gregor said. "The small quantity that I originally obtained from Tyrangal is depleted. I have completed the preventative for the spell-sickness, and now I need to make a lot more so we can save all these people."

Slanya looked at Gregor. The passion in his face showed strong and clear. He truly wanted to help these pilgrims. "The formula works?" she asked. "You're positive?"

His ability to create new concoctions was uncanny, coming partly from his comprehensive knowledge of the effects of herbs and animal parts. But he claimed that his genius came primarily from his spellscar, that his exposure to the spellplague had granted him a lens through which he could *see* the effects that potions would have on people.

A smile broadened on his face. "Yes," he said, nodding happily. "All the testing was worth it, don't you see?" He rubbed his hands together. "And now all I need to do is make enough to protect all pilgrims going to the changelands. But for that I need more plaguegrass—lots more plaguegrass."

"Why can't you get more from Tyrangal?" Slanya asked. "Why do you want me to risk my life to go into the changelands?"

"Your life will not be at risk, my child," Gregor said. "I have enough of the elixir to protect you while you complete the task. And unfortunately Tyrangal has no more plaguegrass. Neither does anyone else. It only grows inside the Plaguewrought Land. It's quite amazing that she had some to begin with."

Slanya stood at balanced readiness and waited for him to continue. She had made her decision; she would go regardless of the risk. She had never been inside the Plaguewrought Land, but the benefits to those who came into contact with the spellplague would be immeasurable.

And despite his recent obsessions, Gregor had saved her life and had given her everything. She trusted him and would do whatever he asked.

"I have two doses of the elixir left," he continued. "You will take them with you, and they will protect you from the spellplague remnants."

Slanya nodded.

"I need someone I trust to do this for me," Gregor said, putting his hand on Slanya's shoulder. "Vraith has offered to help, but I don't want the Order of Blue Fire involved. Just between you and me, I'm not sure I trust their motives, and I'd rather they stay ignorant of the elixir's ingredients."

"Very well," she said. "When do I leave?"

"Tomorrow," Gregor said. "First thing in the morning, you will meet with Tyrangal."

"Tyrangal herself?" Slanya did not follow the gang politics of Ormpetarr, but even she had heard of the secretive woman who commanded a sizable fighting force to keep the peace. She had a reputation for ruthlessness and cunning.

"Yes," Gregor said. "I have spoken with her, and she's agreed to help. Someone who works for her has been inside the changelands and will act as your guide."

Slanya blinked. Everything was happening so fast. "I'll need to get my things prepared."

Gregor nodded. "Yes, but hurry. I've arranged for you to meet with Tyrangal. She's expecting you at dawn."

"Whoa, whoa," Duvan said, circling carefully away from the cliff edge. "Let's talk this over before anyone gets hurt." He continued his slow sideways walk to put his back to the jungle.

"The only one who might get hurt is you," Beaugrat said.

"It's two against one. You're tired and, frankly, look like you've been through the Nine Hells."

As the other man spoke, Duvan gathered detailed stock of the situation. Beaugrat and Seerah stood slightly apart with the horses behind them. No getting to the horses without going through the two of them. Smart.

He could run for the forest; that might be his best bet, if he could get the crossbow off him. The ranger clearly wanted to shoot him. The setting sun's light made her pale skin and blonde hair seem limned in blood. No uncertainty showed in her eyes; she clearly hoped he would try something so she could pull the trigger.

Duvan cursed himself for not seeing this coming. He rarely trusted anyone, but Beaugrat had been one of Tyrangal's men. And over the years he had come to trust Tyrangal. But now, this riffraff could kill him here and take all his possessions—including the book he'd risked his life to get for Tyrangal. In fact, they would be stupid to threaten that and not do it.

The main question on Duvan's mind was, would they kill him even if he gave up the treasure?

Not that giving up the book was even an option. At least not a permanent option, but he might be able to use it as a delaying tactic until he could figure out a way to kill them. He'd made a promise to deliver the book to Tyrangal if he found it, and Duvan never backed down from a promise.

Kill or be killed. It was a strategy that he'd often lived by, and one which had served him well. The other strategy he liked was "run or be killed." So, he mused, it was decision time: fight or flight?

"I didn't find much," he said, more to buy time than anything else. "Just a few things, most of them worthless." Duvan took another step, adjusting his posture so that he'd be ready if an attack came.

"We'll just see about that," Beaugrat said. "Hand over your sack."

"I think you know that's not going to happen."

A predatory grin spread across the big man's face, reminding Duvan eerily of the manticore. "Seerah," Beaugrat said, "on the count of five, if he hasn't given over the haversack, put an arrow in him."

"Now hold on." Duvan put on his most reasonable expression. "Drop this mutiny, and I promise I'll pay you double what we agreed."

The sun had set and dusk was nearly here. Not many shadows to hide in if he could get away, but the waning light would make it difficult to distinguish shapes. Under the jungle canopy, this would be perfect for invisibility.

"That's a very generous offer," Beaugrat scoffed. "But we seem to have the advantage here."

Duvan held up one hand. "Hold it," he said, taking a step back toward the relative safety of the deeper jungle. "You do understand that you can't take Tyrangal's property. She won't allow it."

"Tyrangal's power is waning, Duvan. Soon the accordants of the Blue Fire will reign." Beaugrat's voice had grown dreamy and reverent.

Duvan edged one more step back. If he could get close enough to dash—

"Stand still, or Seerah will shoot you."

Duvan stopped and gave a conciliatory nod in Seerah's direction. The ranger smirked back. Yes, she would shoot, Duvan knew. Any hesitation on her part would be brief. But while she was distracted with the exchange, her aim drifted ever so slightly—down and to her right.

Now! As soon as he formed the thought, he was in motion. His left hand, held in front of him to signal "wait," served as a distraction for his right hand, which was already in his flash powder pouch. A smooth motion pushed a pinch airborne, and with a flick of his fingers, two of his rings chimed together, one flint and one steel.

Duvan dived right as the spark ignited the dust, blinding in the dim light. And by the time the ranger brought her crossbow back to where his chest had been, her quarrel missed him by a good six inches.

He hit the ground and rolled once, then used the momentum to hop back on his feet. They would expect him to bolt into the jungle, and that *would* be the prudent thing to do—try to lose them amid the dense undergrowth, wait them out, then later make his way back to Ormpetarr on foot.

Instead he decided to attack, quickly and decisively. An enemy dead was always better than him dead.

Duvan plucked one of his paralytic-coated daggers from his sash and flicked it with dead-on accuracy toward the shoulder gap in Beaugrat's plate armor. Before that dagger landed, Duvan hurtled the next dagger, also coated with poison, at the twisting torso of the ranger. He finished his throws while both were still dazed by the blinding flash.

The first dagger was aimed perfectly and flying too fast for Beaugrat to dodge. It hit home, buried deep in the fighter's spellscar, and should have dropped him mid-motion. Instead, the dagger vanished in a burst of blue fire.

The second dagger wasn't aimed quite as well, but Duvan could tell it was enough. The point barely made it through the skin of Seerah's thigh. But that would be enough; the poison would eventually lock up her muscles. The ranger was already stumbling, and after a moment she lay still on the ground.

Instinct prompted Duvan to dive to his right again, and he'd learned to trust that feeling. Just in time, too, as one of Beaugrat's steel-covered gauntlets, barbed with sharp extensible spikes, swept past Duvan's cheek. If it had been any closer, it could've taken his three-day stubble with it.

Duvan stood, now having circled so that he was between Beaugrat and the horses. Taking on the barbarian directly would be folly; Duvan would be giving up any advantages he had and would be playing into the other man's hand.

Beaugrat wore plate armor and was no doubt at least half-again stronger than Duvan. The openings in his armor were limited to his face and the spellscar.

But Duvan was faster, more agile, and smarter. Well, he hoped he was smarter. That would be determined by the outcome.

Beaugrat gave a quick glance at his fallen cohort, and it registered on his face that she was out of the game. She would be dead shortly if an antidote wasn't delivered.

"You should've taken the deal," Duvan said, breathing heavily in the humid jungle air. "Now it's even odds, and you're about to go down."

Beaugrat grinned again. "I don't think so," he said. Then he extended his arms and pressed his wrists together, palms out toward Duvan. Immediately, his right arm erupted in gauzy blue-white flames. Spellscar.

"My master and I were hoping it would not come to this," Beaugrat said, "but I see no choice now."

"Your master?" Duvan said.

"Not that it matters to you anymore, but the Order has plans for Ormpetarr and the changelands. Tyrangal has been a consistent impediment and is standing in the way of unity and progress. She must be eliminated."

Duvan spread his arms. "All right, but what does that have to do with me?"

"We've been interested in you for quite a while, Duvan. You are Tyrangal's darling, but we can't figure out why. She sends you to find things, but we don't know what they are and why she wants them. You are a mystery, and we don't like mysteries."

"I am happy to fade away. Disappear."

"Enough talk," Beaugrat said. "Time to die." The fire engulfing his arm shot from his hand toward Duvan. The big man screamed in rage as the blue energy fire swirled like a tornado around Duvan.

But it did not touch him. It did not affect him.

Duvan felt a weakening in the base of his gut, like the whole of his being was transforming into liquid. It was a feeling he'd had before, many times—a feeling which brought back flashes of torment at the hands of the elves—memories of long, painful nights caged inside the plaguelands.

Duvan had always tried to keep his resistance to spell-plague secret. It had been the source of more pain in his life than anything else. The fire's energy dissipated the closer it got to Duvan, all of its potency gone by the time it reached his body.

Beaugrat lowered his hands, his eyes going wide in disbelief. The big man's shoulders and back slumped from the exertion.

It was Duvan's turn to grin. His gut and body felt solid once again, and he sized up his angle of attack.

Abruptly, Beaugrat lunged directly for Duvan.

By reflex, Duvan sprang sideways to dodge the onrush. He simultaneously drew one of his daggers from a scabbard on his thigh.

Beaugrat, however, didn't attack. He kept running, past Duvan and into the cluster of horses. Duvan looked on as the big man pulled himself, plate armor and all, up onto his war horse.

Duvan watched the barbarian ride off, and decided not to go after him. Their paths would no doubt cross again, and Duvan would deal with Beaugrat then. The present crisis was past, and that was all that mattered at the moment.

"Kill me," said the ranger, Seerah, in her northern dialect. "It's burning me up on the inside."

Duvan looked over at her. She had dragged herself a few yards, although it wasn't clear where she'd been trying to get to. The skin around her mouth and eyes had turned blue; it was too late to administer the antidote. Seerah would be dead shortly.

Duvan had miscalculated. "I'm sorry it had to be this way," he said. "Life comes and goes. Death will take me one day, just as it has taken you and your sorcerer friend down in the chasm today."

"Not my friend," she croaked. "Just—" She gave the hint of a shrug. "Just someone else from the Order."

The Order? Duvan wondered. Beaugrat had also mentioned the Order. The Order of Blue Fire concerned itself with the running of charitable works in many cities and towns. It was headquartered in Ormpetarr, though, and held a comparable amount of power in the city to Tyrangal.

"And Beaugrat?" Duvan asked, retrieving his dagger from the dead mage. "Was he your friend? Was he part of the Order?"

"Order, yes," she said. "But . . . not my friend." Her breath came in shallow gasps. "He left me here to die alone."

Duvan nodded. "He is a coward," he said. "And you are not alone. I am here to bear witness to your passing. May you find something better on the other side."

Her eyes showed deep gratitude as he cut her throat to relieve the pain. Or maybe he imagined it. He didn't know what awaited her on the other side. But Duvan knew for certain that prolonging her pain was cruel, and contrary to what some people believed, he was never cruel.

He built a fire and burned the ranger's body, first sifting through her belongings for things of value that might make his life a little more comfortable. She wouldn't need them where she was going.

Duvan did not rush, but he wasted no time, for he didn't want to be here if Beaugrat came back with friends. Somewhere on the periphery of his awareness, he was starting to realize that letting Beaugrat live had been a mistake. A big mistake.

The Order of Blue Fire was a powerful organization in Ormpetarr, and Duvan was now quite squarely on their hit list.

CHAPTER THREE

The night swirled around Gregor, spellplague traces flickering like blue and white ghosts. He couldn't look directly at the remnants of spellplague—at the hell of chaos that was the core essence of that energy—without losing exacting control over his body.

The blue fire was pure and random violence, destruction in its most wild and primal form. For Gregor, whose entire life had been about achieving and maintaining control, such force in close proximity caused an uncontrollable nausea to flow through him. Vertigo teased the edges of his mind.

In the presence of Vraith and her entourage from the Order of Blue Fire, however, Gregor was determined not to show any outward signs of discomfort or fear. His invitation to be here, he realized, was more than a courtesy. He supplied a critical component to make this ritual possible, or so they hoped. But it was certainly clear that Vraith wanted him to agree to what they were doing, to support it, and perhaps even to devote his resources and those of the monastery to it.

Gregor was flattered by the attention, and if this ritual worked, the possibilities for containing spellplague across all of Faerûn would make it all worth it. But his informal arrangement with Tyrangal would make working with Vraith risky. He didn't understand exactly why, but the two women—probably the two most powerful figures in Ormpetarr—did not get along.

Squinting to avoid swirling dust particles in the air, Gregor stood at a safe distance and watched Vraith perform the trial ritual. Even three hours after the sun had set, the wind was warm and fickle. It switched direction seemingly at random, kicking up sand and dirt in the process.

Gregor stood with a small group of observers, about thirty yards from the sharp drop-off that marked the border to the changelands. The sky above was dappled with high, gray clouds and darker spots where motes floated silently. The sky seemed positively serene compared to the ground, which Gregor felt could buckle and shake at any moment, and it was only the knowledge that the border had been stable for nearly a hundred years that allowed him to remain calm.

There was a veil of sorts at the cliff—an almost imperceptible translucent curtain that held the storm of spellplague in check. Vraith had told him that she'd been studying how the border worked, and how that magic might be manipulated—controlled even.

Vraith took the pilgrim volunteers and spaced them out evenly in a semicircle facing the border. Gregor counted nine of them, and each held a vial. His elixir would hopefully be able to help the pilgrims maintain the integrity of their bodies against the wild nature of the spellplague.

"Drink the elixir," Vraith commanded, her voice like slate. "It will protect you."

This would be her second trial, Vraith had claimed. The first one had failed because the blue fire killed the pilgrims before the ritual could be completed. Gregor hadn't asked how they had died, those pilgrims, but he suspected that it had been fairly painful and gruesome.

The pilgrims who came back sick from their pilgrimage to the border of the Plaguewrought Land were only exposed to tiny amounts of spellplague—mere brushstrokes on the canvas of their souls. Many of those were ill for tendays and often didn't survive even that much exposure.

Gregor did not understand the pilgrims who came to the Plaguewrought Land. Too often, they were unpredictable and driven by unquantifiable forces—it wasn't logical or even comprehensible for them to risk the integrity of their bodies and their lives by purposefully seeking exposure to the spellplague in hopes of gaining a spellscar and the ability that went with it.

His spellscar had happened by accident. He had not sought it out, and it had nearly killed him. He understood the power that came with the spellscar—the incredible clarity and vision he now had with potions and alchemical concoctions. Still, he would counsel none of these fools to follow his path.

In front of him now, Vraith had started casting a complicated and powerful ritual. She held a small, bejeweled dagger in her hands, pressing its shimmering blue blade to the palms of each pilgrim to make small cuts.

"Join hands now," she instructed. "Blood to blood, you will form a seamless entity."

The pilgrims happily obliged. Under her spell, Gregor presumed, they would do almost anything.

"Now, take one step forward in unison."

Fascination and dread welled inside Gregor as he watched the half-circle move toward the border veil. The pilgrims at either end of the arc nearly touched the spellplague that undulated like liquid fire on the other side of the veil.

Abruptly, wispy tendrils snaked out from Vraith's chest like red-tinged fog. Standing outside the ring, the wizard's eyes went milky, and her body swayed in rhythm to her chant. The red tendrils snaked through the pilgrims and wove them all together with their magic. Vraith sang in a language that Gregor did not know. Her voice rose and fell, rose and fell, and as she sang, the acrid odor of the Plague-wrought Land in summer swelled until Gregor felt he was going to retch. He clamped down on his gag reflex, using all his self-control to remain stoic and anchored.

The veil moved, then the swirling magic inside the border jumped to the nearest pilgrims. Like flames to tinder, the blue fire leaped from pilgrim to pilgrim, burning through their bodies. Their clothes evaporated. Their hair and skin glowed with translucent energy of the palest blue. Like the finest gauze, spidery and ethereal, the spellplague engulfed the semicircle of pilgrims.

The vision returned then, the vision he'd experienced when the spellplague had first come to him, haunting him like it always did. Gregor reached out for support as his head split in pain for a moment. The world vanished around him. Even the stench was gone.

In his vision, Gregor walked through a landscape of flat green fields covered at regular intervals by archways of blue fire. The spellplague was under perfect and exacting control, forming a lattice threadwork of geometric patterns through the flat, grassy plain.

Here was the possible future—one which was organized and controlled. One in which wild magic interwove with the plane in knowable and predictable ways. No more random and irrational tragedies.

Just as suddenly as it had come, the vision faded, and Gregor found himself back at the trial ritual. This was first step to achieving that vision, one possible way that the changelands could be ordered.

The veil that marked the border of the Plaguewrought Land shifted then, moved to encapsulate the new bulge and the pilgrims with it. That border had not moved in years, but Vraith had moved it.

"Now!" Vraith screamed. "Break the circle now!"

The pilgrims let go of each other and flung themselves out of the border—inside which the earth was already collapsing and breaking up, flying into the sky like an inverted waterfall of rock.

Or most of them did. Gregor caught sight of two who didn't make it out in time, whose bodies went flying up with the earth, and who did not come down. They disappeared into the vastness of the Plaguewrought Land.

Clerics rushed to the pilgrims who had made it, examined them, and pronounced them all alive. Not well, but alive. They would require healing for many, many days, and might not make it.

But they had survived the initial exposure, every one. The elixir worked!

Vraith would certainly want more for her full-scale ritual. Much more. All that rested on Slanya now, and the guide Tyrangal said she could get.

Gregor smiled broadly. His head pain was gone, and he felt renewed. His path was clear.

Letting the blanket that served as a curtain fall into place behind him, ten-year-old Duvan stared at what remained of his village. The houses and barns had been leveled and burned to the ground by the spellplague. Smoke still rose from the ashes. Partial skeletons and scattered bones littered what remained of the single road.

Duvan staggered away from the house, razed except for Duvan's small room. Some of the bodies were more fully recognizable as people. There was Trelthas, an older girl who had just announced her intention to marry Erephus. Duvan had liked her, and there she was providing a fertile bed for maggots.

His stomach heaved at the stench coming from the corpse, and his knees buckled. He vomited bile, the acid burning his throat.

When the nausea passed, he wiped the tears away angrily and continued his search. He found no one alive and many more bodies, all maggot-riddled and decomposing.

Everyone was gone, including Papa. He searched for Papa's body, but he never found it. What he did find was a food cache, near one of the huge holes in the ground, over by what was left of Elder Lindraut's barn. Duvan stared into the jagged scar in the ground and caught sight of the food cellar about ten yards down.

One wall and part of the ceiling had been ripped away like the skin of an orange, and inside he could see shelves of dried fruit, hard bread, and bottles of wine. As with other places in the destroyed village, here and there, patches of the blue gauzy web still flickered like the last clinging remnants of fire to a cinder. There were several small but active patches down in the scar, between him and the store of food.

Still, this was the only food he had found, and his hunger drove him to get it. He climbed down the jagged rock wall, managing to avoid the pockets of spellplague, and slipped into the cellar. He found an empty burlap sack and filled it with as much food as he could lift.

Then he climbed back out. He'd always been good at climbing. He hurried back to Talfani to share the food. "Hey, 'Fani!" he said, pushing the heavy blanket aside. "It's eating time!"

Talfani rolled in the bed and stared up at him, her tired eyes full of grief. All color had drained from her face, her normally dark skin pale and her lips almost translucent. Clearly she'd been exposed while he had been searching for food.

Talfani's illness had worsened after he'd come back with food. He'd tended to her over the next few days as she faded away. He had tried to save her and care for her as best he could. He remembered it like it was yesterday; her soul's light had dimmed, guttered, and then finally, when it went out, it was a relief for her.

But for ten-year-old Duvan it was no relief. He could not bear it. Talfani had been a joined soul—his twin. He had depended upon her, and with her gone it was as though half of his spirit had been ripped away. When she finally gave up and let go of her body, young Duvan had stopped eating. He'd stopped caring and had just lay with her emaciated corpse for days or tendays. He had no recollection of time passing.

Duvan might've died back then, but for a travelling company of elves bound for Wildhome. They had wandered up to see if they could salvage anything. Ageless and graceful, these noble people had saved Duvan from the wreckage.

He had always wanted to run away and join them, but when they had finally come for him, he didn't care. He never forgave them for rescuing him . . . and for what they did to him after.

Lying on the ground, Duvan shook himself and yawned. A hot wind gusted through his hair, drying the sweat on his forehead, and cut the humid jungle air. A magic ring—one of Tyrangal's treasures—had brought him halfway back to Ormpetarr before depositing him and his horse in a clearing in the middle of the Chondalwood. He had ridden the better part of the remaining distance in the last day, but he still had some time to go before he reached Ormpetarr.

Tendrils of memory clung to him like spider silk. Duvan angrily wiped his eyes as he saddled up his horse. Selûne was high, and it was hardly midnight, but if sleep meant the same nightmare remembrances, he'd rather ride than sleep.

Duvan finished packing his saddlebags and mounted up. He spurred the horse into motion and pushed out in the deep blue dark of the half-moon, as the horse slipped as fast as it could toward Ormpetarr, Tyrangal, and the completion of this botched mission.

Not home, Duvan thought. I have no real home.

But he did crave a deep, sound sleep and a long, hot bath. All in the company of his favorite girl—the inestimable Moirah. Well, Duvan thought with a chuckle, she actually *was* estimable; he knew exactly how much she charged.

Still, as the night landscape moved under his horse's hooves, Duvan felt safe in the anonymity of the darkness and silence. Night meant shadows and obscurity. Other creatures, emboldened by the darkness, prowled in the grass and scrubby trees that covered these moonlit hills. Wild and alive, an untamable and primal energy swirled around him.

Duvan rode all night, and by the time the sky had begun to lighten, he was passing caravans of pilgrims headed south to Ormpetarr. He skirted them in the dim light but did not stop despite their jubilance and offers of food and drink. He wanted nothing more than to reach Ormpetarr and melt into the arms of his temporary lover, his rented friend. Moirah's attentions were what he needed after this journey, before he reported to Tyrangal. He knew that the tall, strange woman would want him to deliver the recovered tome as soon as he could. But she knew his habits and his needs, and she would wait for him.

Tyrangal understood him better than any other person. They had a mutually beneficial business arrangement, although sometimes Duvan wondered why she had chosen him. Of all the available people, she had sought him out.

It had been Tyrangal who had finally given him liberty when she took him away from the Wildhome elves, many years after Talfani's death. The same elves who had saved him from wasting away next to Talfani's corpse had taken him to their alien and beautiful forest city—and had never let him leave their velvet prison.

Duvan shuddered. He would never trust a Wildhome elf again, and he would always hate clerics of Silvanus. Rhiazz-shar had forever spoiled their reputation in his eyes. The young elf priestess had come to him when he was outcast and ridiculed. She had comforted him, befriended him, and lured him into trusting her. Duvan had loved her, and she had abused his love.

Finally, as the sun was growing low again, he came over the last hill and stared down into the valley that housed Ormpetarr. Half of the old city had been destroyed by the Spellplague long before Duvan's time. That half still lay behind the hazy veil of the Plaguewrought Land border.

Looking down into the valley, Duvan marveled at the proliferation of tents and makeshift shelters. Pilgrims were arriving and staying in numbers he'd never seen before.

Ormpetarr consisted of a central thoroughfare surrounded by a bustling merchant district with the Changing House just to the side closest to the border. To the city's south there was the only recently-built stone building—a temple complex of all things. And crammed cheek by jowl across the spaces around and in between were hundreds upon hundreds of pilgrims' tents. Ormpetarr was a boom town. Lots of coin to be had, but wild and quite dangerous. Just the sort of place where people like Duvan thrived.

He grinned and made his way through the gates and into the city. One of Tyrangal's guards—he recognized the guard's burnished red chainmail—hailed Duvan.

Duvan waved the man over. "Well met," he said.

"Well met, sir," the guard said. "You've returned?"

"Yes, and I have news for Tyrangal, for her ears alone. Tell Tyrangal that the 'scarred man she hired, Beaugrat, is a spy for the Order."

The man's eyes went wide. "He passed this gate no more than an hour ago, sir. Looked tired. Nearly fell off his horse."

"Too bad he didn't," muttered Duvan. He jerked his head in the direction of Tyrangal's abode. "Go, now."

The guard bowed slightly, then turned and made his way along the road that led up the hill. Tyrangal lived in an old stone mansion overlooking the city. The better to keep an eye on its inhabitants, Duvan supposed. Duvan would pay her a visit later in the day, but first he wanted to get some dreamless sleep. There was only one person he knew who could help him with that.

Thus, a few minutes later, as the sky grew light, Duvan found himself the sole patron of the Jewel. He sat at the polished wood bar, whose numerous knife and burn scars were more of a testament to its less-than-savory clientele than to its age.

Duvan ran a hand through his shoulder-length black hair. He needed a bath, he knew. The dirt of the road stuck to him like dried sweat, and his leathers were permeated with travel grime and the blood of the past evening's events.

A bath and a shave, he thought. Now that would feel good.

Duvan downed the last of his ale. Moirah could help when she got in. Ah, Moirah. "Another tankard, Pritchov," Duvan said.

The half-orc nodded and slid a freshly filled tankard down the bar to him.

Duvan sipped the ale. Not as bad now as the first half-mug. The Jewel didn't have the best food and drink, but they made up for it in the quality of their other offerings. He set a silver coin on the bar. "Just keep 'em coming, Pritchov. At least until Moirah gets in."

"I'm here." Moirah's voice was the perfect growly blend of raspy and sweet, like honey over toasted seed-bread.

The stale-beer-and-piss-pot odor gave way to jasmine perfume as she approached. If he weren't already intoxicated, she would have done the job at one sighting.

Moirah was a slight woman with an elf's build and raven curls. Her dark eyes gazed dreamily at Duvan. It was a look, he knew, that was either calculated or drug induced. Still, he pretended there was some sincerity. Their interaction was a performance, a dance, and a business exchange. He rarely let himself lose his edge, but when he did, he went all the way.

Duvan found himself smiling, his gaze tracking over Moirah as she walked toward him. Her slow saunter agonized him. Her over-red lips and her eyes said, "Come and get me." But Duvan waited. He'd played this game before, and she had to dictate the pace. Slow was good, he knew. Slow was exceedingly good in the end.

Gauzy blue and purple silks wrapped her body, layered enticingly to hide all the most desirable parts. Her navel was showing, and below it was her spellscar, nearly translucent, trailing down and disappearing into the sash at her waist. That scar, and the ability that came with it, was a good part of why Duvan always asked for Moirah.

She reached the bar and pulled his head down to breathe into his ear. "I'm ready when you are," she whispered.

Duvan looked at Pritchov. "No interruptions," he said, lifting his pack. Then he let Moirah lead him by his belt down the hall and into a room.

Slanya awoke well before dawn, donned her travelling leathers, ate a quick breakfast, and left the temple on foot. She walked past the hospital tents and the smoldering funeral pit, heading into the city. Gregor had said that Tyrangal was expecting her at dawn, and she intended to be prompt despite her doubts.

Chances were slim that the guild leader would know of anyone willing to guide her into the changelands, let alone someone capable. Slanya figured such a guide didn't exist. Who would be stupid or desperate enough to risk his or her life like that?

Slanya skirted the main thoroughfare, which was already awake with locals and eager pilgrims. She fought down a surge of disgust. These people sought power and uniqueness but were unwilling to work hard for it. Greedy for their spellscars and whatever abilities that came with them, the pilgrims risked their lives for an instantaneous transformation.

Sighing, Slanya reminded herself that she was here to help the pilgrims, not to pity or despise them. Fools would always exist, would always hasten their own deaths. Such was the way of things. If she succeeded in gathering more plaguegrass for Gregor, perhaps the elixir would help give some of them a second chance.

Slanya walked up the ancient road that led north out of Ormpetarr and up toward Tyrangal's mansion—away from the Plaguewrought Land. Slanya had never been to the changelands before, nor had she seen the border from closer than the city's main thoroughfare. It was danger enough living so close to the edge of the wild magic.

Tearing her gaze from the border veil, which stretched up into the sky, Slanya passed through the once-grand city gate and out of the city. The cool pre-dawn light cast the city walls and structures in deep indigo and cobalt.

Tyrangal's home stood just up the hill from the northeast corner of Ormpetarr and was easily the most expansive and commanding building in the whole city. As she climbed up the winding road toward the mansion, Slanya realized that she was being watched. She caught glimpses of burnished red armor—members of Tyrangal's Copper Guard, which kept peace in Ormpetarr as well as protected Tyrangal's interests, whatever those were. But nobody approached or detained Slanya. The benefits of making an appointment, she presumed.

Slanya passed through an old iron gate hanging crookedly on rusted hinges. Then she picked her way across an expanse of pitted rubble and collapsed stone buildings. Huge craters gaped where house-sized chunks of earth had been uprooted.

The smell of soot and blackened pitch mingled with the odor of brine blowing in from the dry mud flats on the far edge of the ruins. Ormpetarr had been a lake town in its heyday—a bustling commercial port. But the huge lake had dried up decades earlier, drained into the Underchasm like the seas themselves.

Finally, Slanya reached the doors of Tyrangal's mansion. Gargoyles leered down from the gutters and cornices of the clean and sturdy masonry. A gemstone amongst trash, Slanya mused—and a well-protected gemstone at that. She knocked on the carved wooden door that towered in front of her, filling a stone archway at least three times her height.

The door opened to reveal a high-ceilinged vestibule. "Please come in, Sister Slanya." The voice was melodious and deep for a woman's. "I won't bite, I promise."

Feeling drawn forward, Slanya stepped inside. And before she realized it the door was closing behind her, plunging the room into darkness. "I have had brief communication with your Brother Gregor," came that musical voice again, seeming to harmonize with itself. Slanya wanted to listen to it for hours.

The light filtering in through the high windows did little to allay the darkness in the room. Slanya hesitated while her eyes adjusted. Soon she found herself fascinated by the room itself. The marble floor was inlaid with a mosaic of a dragon, the sinuous likeness crafted from many tiny shards of polished copper. The stone walls held paintings and alcoves for statues, but there was no order to them. Too many valuable pieces crammed cheek by jowl together.

Slanya pursed her lips in distaste. The display conveyed not beauty or elegance, but excess and wealth.

"Mistress Tyrangal," Slanya said in the direction of the voice. "Thank you for meeting with me."

Tyrangal stepped into view from the shadows. "Please just call me Tyrangal—no 'mistress' necessary."

Slanya was tall for a human, but Tyrangal stood a head taller. She wore a rust-colored silk robe embroidered with runes that Slanya couldn't read. Tyrangal looked older than Slanya, but how much older Slanya couldn't say: the other woman's face had a timeless quality. The most striking thing about Tyrangal, however, was her hair. Hanging straight down to the backs of her knees, it shimmered a strangely metallic auburn in the dim light.

"Certainly, Tyrangal," Slanya said, gathering her wits. She had no reason to be intimidated, but the thought did her no good.

"Can I offer you nourishment?" Tyrangal asked.

"Thank you; I have eaten already this morning."

"Ah, but do you not desire to try new things? Curiosity, Slanya, and new experiences are what keep us alive."

"Certainly," Slanya said. "But my matter is of some urgency to Brother Gregor, and I would do well by him to conduct our business first."

A smirk flickered across Tyrangal's features—amused and predatory all at once. "Very well," she said. "We shall start with business. What can I acquire for you?"

"I need a guide into the changelands."

"You wish to become spellscarred?"

Slanya shook her head. "No. Brother Gregor has perfected an elixir that can protect the exposed from getting sick and dying. One of the ingredients can be found in abundance only inside the borders of the Plaguewrought Land."

"So this guide would have to travel into the changelands with you and help you find and gather this ingredient?"

Slanya shrugged. "Does such a person even exist?"

"Well," Tyrangal said with a coy smile, "it turns out that I know someone qualified to do just that."

"In truth?" Slanya hadn't believed anyone would be foolish enough to do that, even for the kind of coin Gregor was willing to pay.

"In truth." Tyrangal's tone was playful. "Although, in truth, if I were lying—which I have been known to do from time to time—you would not be able to discern it from truth."

Slanya considered. She would have to trust Tyrangal on this. "You have a good reputation."

Tyrangal laughed, and it was a melody of the gods to Slanya's ears. "Yes, dear girl. Trust in society comes from a collection of opinions. I like you."

Unsure how to take that, Slanya remained quiet.

"There are some things that you should know," Tyrangal continued. "One, the journey will test *you*. Two, *you* have a good chance of dying. And three—"

"Are you trying to scare me into not going?"

"Not at all. Not at all," Tyrangal said. "These are just things I can tell. I can also see that you've never been inside the border of the changelands."

Slanya nodded. The statement was true enough, although she suspected she'd be tempted to agree with whatever that wonderful voice told her, true or not.

"If there is an order, purpose, or logical organization to the Spellplague's destructive force, then I know not what it is," Tyrangal continued. "The changelands are the one place in Faerûn where the rules of law are always changing, where nature follows no patterns and the only constant is chaos."

Tyrangal paused, her smirk gone. Her golden eyes shone yellow in the morning light. "That seems like a dangerous place for someone who holds tight to an ordered world."

Slanya remembered the funeral fire from yesterday, the allure of the flames oh so close. All the fires from her past came to her mind, and the temptation of losing her control rose up in her in that remembrance. Yes, there was something to Tyrangal's assertion.

"I understand," Slanya said. "And thank you. But you need not concern yourself with me."

Tyrangal smiled. "I'm not 'concerned,' but I do like to give my customers the full benefit of my knowledge. You're paying for these warnings. Perhaps they will help you prepare."

Slanya nodded. "Thank you. What was number three?"

"Three, you will find the guide is a bit . . . wild and unruly."

Slanya gave a confident smile. "That, I think I can handle."

Tyrangal appraised Slanya carefully. "I think you might, at that," she said.

"So where might I find this guide?"

"He is currently out on a task I have given him. I expect him to return to me by tonight or tomorrow."

"That long?" Slanya asked. "With the Festival of Blue Fire in two days, we need vastly more elixir than we can currently make. Otherwise hundreds of pilgrims will get sick and die."

"Well," Tyrangal said slyly. "I do happen to know that he's arrived back in Ormpetarr, but he hasn't personally paid me a visit just yet. Not his style to come to me right away. He attends to . . . other needs first."

Slanya frowned. "I'd like to speak with him as soon as possible. If he's in Ormpetarr, I shall seek him out."

"I don't recommend it; he will return when he is ready. Hurrying him isn't likely to speed your departure any, and it certainly won't win you any favors."

Shifting from foot to foot, Slanya considered her options. She could ignore Tyrangal's counsel, or she could wait.

"However," Tyrangal continued, "I can see that you feel you cannot sit idle. So for your own sense of accomplishment I will tell you this: His name is Duvan, and you will likely find him at the Jewel—the festhall and gambling house across from Finara's Inn on the main thoroughfare."

"Thank you," Slanya said, wanting the interview to be over. "I shall seek him out."

"Be careful, young cleric," Tyrangal said. "Duvan is a feral beast on his best days, but he is truly the only person who can accomplish what you seek to do. I have considerable influence over him, but he is completely free to make his own choices. I advise against angering him."

"Your counsel is very much appreciated, Tyrangal. If my need weren't so pressing . . ."

"But I see that it is. You may go, and may the gods watch over you."

Slanya took her leave and headed back down into Ormpetarr, her gaze studiously avoiding the gut-heaving swirl of the border veil. And by the time she'd made the walk back down the hill, through the gate and into heart of Ormpetarr, the sun had fully risen.

Beneath a cloudless sky of palest blue, peppered with

motes flowing out from the changelands, the thoroughfare bustled with activity. The cobbles and flagstones from the city had pitted and become uneven, replaced with dirt and mud. Wooden shop fronts and businesses of all kinds lined the thoroughfare while merchants with wagons and carts, tents and tarps crowded the streets. Under the vigilant gaze of Tyrangal's guards and the Order of Blue Fire Peacekeepers, merchants plied their wares to the crowd.

Slanya insinuated her way through the people, heading for the Jewel and its reportedly seedy clientele . . . including her guide. Not for the first time, Slanya wondered what she'd gotten herself into. This Duvan character sounded uncivilized and potentially dangerous.

Ormpetarr drew all races and all professions. It was a magnet for adventurers, danger seekers, and those on the extreme edge of reason. Dwarves and elves worked side by side with humans, halflings, and genasi. Order was intermittently enforced, and yet everyone seemed to operate under similar basic understandings. Still, there wasn't enough of a social contract for Slanya's comfort. In the monastery they learned about the interdependence of the different parts of society. Kaylinn required all her clerics and monks to acknowledge this interdependence and make explicit their agreement to maintain the order.

The rules of commerce and social convention in Ormpetarr were more haphazard and arbitrary than Slanya was comfortable with. For all her helpfulness, Tyrangal wielded her Copper Guard like a weapon, and the only group powerful enough to thwart their influence was the Order of Blue Fire.

Slanya didn't know all the ins and outs of the city's power struggles. This absence of the rule of law was certainly unfair to the newcomer pilgrim, who could easily get fleeced by predatory swindlers and street vendors.

The Jewel was in an older wooden structure in the center of the town, across from the main inn and down the street from the Order of Blue Fire's headquarters. Slanya entered through the swinging doors and stood alert and ready.

"Welcome to the Jewel," came a deep voice from the darkness to her right. "I'm guessing you're not here for a drink, and you don't look like you'll be buying our usual services . . . although we are discreet if that's what you're looking for." The voice held an amused edge. Slanya's eyes had adjusted enough to the dim light in the room to see the voice's owner, a large half-orc wearing an apron and tending the bar.

"Or maybe you're here for a job?" Slanya glanced left toward this new voice. Leaning against a post was a middle-aged dwarf woman wearing makeup and brightly colored, fancy clothes. "You're a mite threatening," the dwarf continued, "but not unattractive . . . and the bald, tattooed-scalp look would attract a whole new clientele!"

The bartender laughed. Other than the two who had greeted her, the Jewel was predominately empty. A small group of halflings and humans spoke in hushed tones in one corner, and there was an elf in scarred black leather standing at the bar.

Slanya felt her face start to redden, but she concentrated to make it not show. "I'm here looking for a human named Duvan," she said. "It's important."

"Duvan is here," said the bartender. "But he's, ah . . . indisposed, if you know what I mean. Knowing Duvan and Moirah, he will be here all day, and maybe all night as well."

The dwarf woman spoke. "You'd best come back tomorrow, girl. Unless you fancy a drink, a rattle and roll, or a turn in one of our comfy beds. I guarantee they're more comfortable than the burlap and straw you're used to."

Slanya took a slow breath to avoid the anger she felt rising. Anger was the enemy of self-control. All of her identity and abilities required control of her body and mind. "Not that I don't appreciate the offer and the advice, but I need to find Duvan now. I can't wait until tomorrow."

"It's your funeral," said the bartender.

"All life is," Slanya said. Stepping into the hall, she started opening doors.

A knock sounded on the chamber door.

Commander Accordant Vraith rolled over and went back to sleep in her darkened bedroom on the top story of the Changing House. Her wide bed was luxuriously appointed with down-stuffed pillows and silk bed linens.

Such comfort befitted a person of her stature, and she wasn't about to relinquish her privileges just because the Order had assigned her to this pit. Working at the very edge of the Plaguewrought Land was supposed to be the highest honor, but Vraith hated it.

She was only here to make her chances of rapture—of absorption into the sharn—more likely. Once she'd followed through on its prophecy and had completed the rituals then she would be truly transcendent. She could escape this grubby mortality completely.

Ever since the spellplague had appeared to her on thirteenth birthday, hovering like a ghost of blue fire in her dormitory room at the wizard academy, she had wanted to merge with it. Ever since the spellplague had touched her, blossoming a spellscar in her chest, Vraith had pursued a singular agenda.

She would learn and work, manipulate and coerce, struggle and create to achieve her goal. Whatever it took, Vraith would do it. Her passion was unmatched, her dedication unparalleled.

Vraith was convinced that when her ritual expansion

of the Plaguewrought Land succeeded, the sharn—creatures of pure chaos and power—would see the benefit of her contribution and welcome her into their immortal essence.

Only when she had become part of that godly communal consciousness would her rapture be complete. Only then could she escape this dingy backwater.

The knock sounded again, more insistent.

What could the perpetrator be thinking? she wondered. She had a reputation for quick anger and decisive justice for those who disobeyed her commands. And one of the reasons she had cultivated that reputation was so that her sleep would not be interrupted.

Vraith slipped out of the silk sheets. "This had better be important" she said, standing in the cool dark.

"My apologies, Mistress Vraith," came the muffled reply. "I have urgent news."

Vraith had trouble placing the voice at first, primarily because she was expecting Renfod or one of his lackeys. Standing naked in the darkened chamber, Vraith's small body gathered energy. Wrath was a great source of power, and Vraith knew how to use it.

She walked to the door and opened the small viewing square in the top of it. "What is so important that it justifies waking me?" she snapped.

"I am sorry." Beaugrat cowered on his knees outside the door. "I needed to speak with you right away."

Vraith's spellscar seemed to burn in her gut. Looking down on her nakedness, Vraith watched her spellscar, which formed a jagged, deep black line from her sternum to her crotch. Her abdomen glowed slightly red with the scar's activation, and suddenly she could see Beaugrat's soul, the spirit energy of his life force.

Red tendrils wisped out from her spellscar and intertwined through the door with the threads of Beaugrat's soul. She probed his being and understood the weave of his life energy. One magical tug and he would be dead.

"Go on," she said. "Explain."

"Tyrangal's pet. Duvan." Beaugrat's speech came haltingly. "He seems to be immune to the Blue Fire."

That got Vraith's attention. Such a power could be devastating to the Order and to her plans. "How do you know?"

"Our team went with him as instructed," Beaugrat said. "We lost the sorcerer, but Seerah and I tried to take the items that Tyrangal had sent him to get."

"You failed to get the items?"

"Yes. The rogue is very resourceful; he killed Seerah, and when I tried to kill him by summoning the Blue Fire . . ." Beaugrat gestured at his shoulder spellscar. "It had no effect."

Questions swirled around Vraith's consciousness. Was this true immunity or just resistance? Was it an active power that needed to be invoked, or an innate aspect of this person? Did it require components? Speech or motion? Did it come from a spellscar?

Too many questions and not enough answers.

"We need to capture this person, Beaugrat. For now, I will overlook your failure to acquire the items. Your new task: assemble a team and bring Duvan to me. We need to discover the extent of this ability."

Beaugrat bowed his head. "Thank you for your lenience, Commander. I will capture him today."

"Use whatever means necessary. This is important, but I do not have time to deal with it myself."

"Of course, Commander. May the Blue Fire burn inside you."

Vraith closed the view window and latched it. Her scar throbbed below her sternum, and she sank to the cool floor. She needed rest to prepare for the next stage of the ritual; she couldn't allow anything to get in the way, certainly not some no-account rogue.

Soon she put it out of her head and slipped back into her bed. It was possible that he didn't even know what he could do. Tyrangal might know, and that was some cause for concern. But the boy himself was no threat. Soon this wrinkle would be ironed out. If this Duvan proved a threat, he would be eliminated. Simple.

CHAPTER FOUR

In the small room at the Jewel, Moirah danced with Duvan. Their choreography started with playful gestures, discreet and calculated steps. He wanted her, but she dictated the tempo. She gave the instructions, and he obeyed. She took care of him—a tease of the tongue here, a tender caress there. And he played because he knew the game was rigged; she would give him what he wanted in the end.

The deliberate progression of their flirting into passionate embrace allowed Duvan to lose himself. Moirah freed him from his worries, letting him unleash the wild animal inside him as he rolled with her, as he pressed her into the bed beneath him. Her magic urged him to lose himself. Nothing else mattered and he took her as she wanted him to, as she begged him to, as she willed him to.

Her spellscar magic controlled him and set him free. Free from making decisions. Free from his nightmares. Free from his thoughts of remorse, regret, and anger. And, ultimately, free to rest in peaceful bliss.

Moirah made all the decisions and held him safe, and he loved her for it. In that instant, he loved her. In that isolated moment, she was all that mattered. All that made sense.

"Now," she commanded.

And with her permission explicitly granted, he lost the last vestige of control. His body and mind were one in feral heat. Primal, animal sex washed away all his cares and concerns.

The perfect moment stretched on and on . . .

Interrupted by a knock on the door.

What in the Nine Hells is that? Duvan thought. He'd clearly said no interruptions. He felt the ecstasy drain away, leaving a void for anger to fill. This was the not the freedom he craved, the rest he so desperately needed.

"Ignore it," Moirah breathed. "I'm sure it's just a mistake. Whoever it is will go away."

Duvan turned back to her, so calm and beautiful beneath him. In the silence that followed, he drifted slowly back into her embrace. He relaxed into her arms and felt the anger start to give way to contentment.

Abruptly, the bedroom door opened. "I apologize for the intrusion," came a woman's stiff voice. "But I need to speak to Duvan about a matter of some urgency."

His hope for peaceful rest vanished as he glanced over at the offender. Tall and lithe, wearing light combat leather, the woman's proud nose and thin lips reminded him of his old lover from Wildhome—Rhiazzshar. Same arrogance. Same condescending voice.

Rhiazzshar had broken his heart and had manipulated

him. She had used him, and he hated her. He could not allow Rhiazzshar to capture him. He would fight her.

Rage flooded back into him and took control. He'd get rid of this intruder, this enemy. Duvan sprang from the bed and rushed at the offender. Unconcerned about his nakedness, he shouted at her as he ran across the room, "Get out!"

If she was surprised or startled, she showed no sign. Her face was unreadable, and her expression did not change. She stepped very deliberately to the side to avoid his rush. There was a weapon in her hand, he suddenly registered—a wooden staff or stick of some sort. But she didn't use it.

"I come to enlist your service, Duvan," she said. "Not to fight you."

"Just get out!"

The infuriating intruder was now farther from the door, her movements light and calculated. "We need to leave today," she said. "I'm prepared—"

Duvan had closed in on her, pinning her between himself and the wall. This intruder would pay for her interruption. Then he could rest, finally.

Duvan punched the woman, aiming first for the face, then the gut. With a rapid movement of her head, she dodged his fist. His punch to her gut went wide as her staff came down hard on his forearm, deflecting his blow.

He missed! Duvan could hardly believe it. He rarely missed.

Rage pushed him into a flurry of blows, each one dodged or blocked or deflected. Every strike landed on the wall or her staff. He had her cornered, but he couldn't hit her.

Some logic filtered past his rage. She was fast, he granted her that. He prided himself on being fast, but she might be faster. Yet perhaps she was just better trained.

Other details registered. This wasn't the Rhiazzshar

he remembered from Wildhome. This intruder was human and not elf. Her tunic sported a different clerical symbol—a skeletal hand holding scales. Not Sylvanus. Instead of long mahoghany hair, her head was shaved save for a shoulder-length blonde sidelock, carefully wrapped with strip of white leather.

His rage lessened.

Watching her dodge his attacks, Duvan realized that her senses were attuned, focused on his body and his eyes. She knew what to look for and how to react. Her response was logical and predictable . . . which meant that she could be defeated.

"I thought I knew you," he said. "I thought you were someone who's done me great harm."

"We've never met."

"I realize that now," he said. "Still, I'm not going with you." He started a punch to her gut, but changed it at the last second to strike her neck.

She started to block the attack, and he saw surprise in her face when she realized that it wasn't going to work. At the last instant, she managed to shift her position and take the brunt of the blow on her shoulder instead.

She used the momentum of her movement to dive left and gain some distance from him. The close call with the last blow must've fazed her. Still, she did not return his attacks.

Duvan pressed forward. If she wouldn't leave, he might have to take her down. Then he could pin her, tie her up, and drag her out of the room.

"I'm tired of this, but I'm not leaving," the woman said. "My matter is urgent, and you are the only one who can help."

Duvan found himself falling as she swept his legs out from under him. Then her weapon was arcing toward him.

"But I am tired of this fight," she said.

His head exploded in pain from at least two blows in rapid succession, and then inky blackness seeped in from the edges of his vision and the fight was over.

Slanya bounced to her feet, still at the ready in case the other person—the woman—came after her. The woman, however, appeared to be no threat. Huddled in a ball up against the headboard, the petite young human had covered herself in pillows.

Slanya saw that the woman was shivering. Afraid.

Slanya gave the woman the warmest smile she could muster, considering the incredible awkwardness of the situation. At Slanya's feet, Duvan's naked body lay slumped, unmoving for once. Their initial exchange had not gone as she'd hoped.

Slanya loosened the ties to a pocket sewn into her pants and pulled out a gold piece. "Apologies for the interruption." She tossed the coin to the woman. "Here is for your trouble. It should be enough to cover whatever he owed you for your services."

Black curls shook as the woman emerged from the pile of pillows to catch the gold. Her shivering seemed to have vanished. She gave Slanya a flirty smile. "Yes, this'll do."

"You'll be so kind as to leave me alone with him for a while," Slanya said.

"He'll be angry when he wakes," said the woman, slipping into a silk robe and gliding across to the door.

"No doubt, but I can handle him."

The woman nodded. "I'll leave you two alone then."

"Thank you."

The woman closed the door behind her.

Duvan stirred slightly as Slanya lifted him to the bed. The room smelled a stifling and pungent mix of odors that

Slanya found distracting. She used the bed linens to secure Duvan's wrists and ankles to the bed posts.

He was thin and wiry with compact muscles. She could admire his fitness while at the same time marvel at how poorly he seemed to treat himself. The numerous scars that traced light strokes on his chest, arms, and legs told of a hard life. Slanya made a quick count as she appraised his dark skin: twelve that she could see, and she guessed there were more on his back.

Duvan's dark, unbraided hair grew straight and long, and his face bore only the faintest hint of the scars on the remainder of his body. He had no tattoos that she could see, nor any piercings. And no visible spellscar either. Slanya was surprised to find that as long as he was lying unconscious and quiet, he was handsome, in a rugged, unshaven way.

Slanya sighed. She'd prefer an ugly but polite guide any day.

Duvan came fully awake a few minutes later, his fore-head wrinkling from the pain in his head. Slanya watched as he took careful stock of his situation. His demeanor was wary, and she was glad that she'd restrained him. This was a much more dangerous man than the anger-driven brute earlier.

"I will release you after we have spoken," she said. "After you have listened to my proposal."

She could see him weighing the options. He could undoubtedly escape from the bonds she'd tied. He'd likely done that sort of thing numerous times. But he was trying to figure out if he could do it before she knocked him out again.

"It's not worth it," she said. "You are quite vulnerable, as you can see." She gestured at his exposed privates with her staff.

Duvan grimaced, then nodded.

"One of the leaders of the monastery of Ormpetarr has developed an elixir that prevents people who are exposed to the spellplague from dying."

"Sure he has," Duvan said with a snicker.

"But," Slanya continued, "he has run out of a crucial component. And he needs more, much more, before the Festival of Blue Fire begins."

"So?"

"He has given me the task of heading into the Plague-wrought Land and bringing some back."

Duvan let out a harsh laugh. "Well, you're not nearly as smart as you look."

Slanya ignored the insult. "It's important."

"More important than not being killed by spellplague?"

Slanya narrowed her gaze. "Do you know how many pilgrims die of spellplague sickness every day? Nine in ten just burn up instantly, and as for the rest . . . Well, have you seen the tents full of the dying? The funeral fires?"

Duvan asked, "Why should *I* care?"

"If you've ever been with someone sick from spellplague exposure, you'd have more sympathy."

He started to retort but stopped and glared at her. What had she said, she wondered, to break his shell?

After a moment he said, "These people come here by choice. They do not deserve my sympathy or yours."

"What if we could help everyone who's exposed? Prevent suffering far and wide?"

"A fantasy," he said. "I've seen what the changelands can do. I've seen it. You and your elixirs can do nothing to stop it. It's too late."

Slanya wasn't sure what he was talking about. "Too late for what?"

A pained expression flashed across his face, and he turned away. "Nothing," he said. "Don't talk anymore about it. In fact, don't talk to me anymore."

"Believe me," she continued, "if there was anyone else who could help us, I'd have never come. But Tyrangal told me that you were the only one who can safely guide me into the changelands."

"Tyrangal sent you?" Duvan's tone drained of animosity.

"She's serving as a broker for your services," Slanya admitted.

"You should've just said so." He relaxed into the bed. "We could've saved all this bickering."

Slanya cautiously stood upright, still wary. Duvan's body language and temperament had changed completely with the mention of Tyrangal.

Duvan held his free hand out to her, empty. "You seem to know who I am. May I ask your name?"

Slanya stared at the man's hand. It was clearly a conciliatory gesture, but she could hardly trust him now. "My name is Slanya," she said.

"Well, Slanya, could you untie me? I can get free on my own, but you seem like you're in a hurry."

Duvan sized up his companion as he dressed and walked out of the room. The human cleric could hold her own; he had to give her that. She'd had some good combat training, and he found himself respecting her. Still, he wasn't sure he believed her story. He wouldn't trust her until he had Tyrangal's word.

He led Slanya out into the thoroughfare. "Let's go this way," he said. "Short cut."

Slanya's brow furrowed in disbelief. "Of course it is." But despite her wry tone, she followed.

Duvan angled away from the Changing House building so as to lower the chances of running into any members of the Order of Blue Fire who might be looking for him.

Still, there was no place in Ormpetarr truly hidden from Order eyes.

As he and Slanya made their way through the crowd, Duvan avoided eye contact with anyone. They passed the inn—operated by a member of the Order—and then skirted around the counting house—owned and run by Tyrangal and the Copper Guard. There was no law in Ormpetarr, and normally Duvan liked it that way, but the Order had started mounting patrols to persuade the darker elements to vacate the town.

Problem was that it was the Order who decided what elements were good and which were unacceptable. As soon as they decided that Tyrangal and her Copper Guard were in the dark faction, then the delicate balance would erupt into open conflict.

Many townsfolk had joined the Order and paid their tithe just to avoid being hassled. Duvan didn't have contempt for those who did. It was the cost of business in Ormpetarr. Still, he hated bullies.

No sign of Beaugrat. Duvan surreptitiously patted his chest to reassure himself that his daggers were ready for action if need be.

Gliding beside him, Slanya remained quiet. She held herself with a ready confidence, wary and alert. Which was good—if Slanya were telling the truth, Tyrangal would have his skin for supper if he let something happen to her.

Slanya seemed content to walk in a wary silence as they passed out of the city and up the hill. They passed the ruined gates which marked the entrance into the 'burn zone,' as Tyrangal called it, a wide swath of destruction that surrounded the mansion.

Duvan suspected that Tyrangal purposefully kept this burn zone area around her mansion devoid of other new structures, making it more imposing and difficult for people to come visit her. No one just happened along here.

Duvan knew that Tyrangal had guards and sentries posted among the remnants of ancient masonry and sculpture that had once been part of a broad garden. Duvan knew where the hidden posts were, most of them, and he knew many of the Copper Guard too, but not all of them.

He led Slanya along the old flagstone path across the burn zone, until finally the two of them came to Tyrangal's ornate door.

"Come in," rang Tyrangal's mellifluous voice, and Duvan complied, noting that Slanya could no more resist the voice than he could.

Once inside the ornate and cluttered house, Duvan's eyes still adjusting to the dim light, Tyrangal stood before them, radiant in her red finery. "Were you able to recover the tome?"

Duvan nodded, then slung his pack from his shoulders and pulled out the book. "I had quite the time getting this before the esteemed baron's last bastion fell into the Underchasm forever."

Tyrangal accepted the tome gingerly in her small hands. She muttered something under her breath, casting a spell as she examined the thick hide cover.

Slanya stood perfectly erect next to Duvan. No sign of her earlier rush to get moving on her journey was in evidence now. Duvan understood that; you didn't hurry or interrupt Tyrangal. He'd learned that over the years.

Despite her luxurious appearance, Tyrangal was one of the most accomplished thieves he'd ever met. She'd rescued him three years earlier from the Wildhome elves—from Rhiazzshar and her ilk. Tyrangal had taken him under her wing, had continued his training in thievery, in combat, in climbing and falling and countless other things.

And in return, he acquired things for her. The sorts of things she sent him after were esoteric and bizarre: a vial of powder negotiated from a nomadic merchant in Murghôm;

an amulet containing a metallic liquid at its heart, recovered from a treasure casket in prison dungeons underneath Alaghôn in Turmish; a cache of wine barrels floated from a sunken galleon in the Sea of Fallen Stars.

Duvan never asked questions about why she wanted these things. He didn't really care, and Tyrangal would never tell him anyhow. She paid him enough that he didn't need to ask questions. Besides, he thrilled to the challenge.

He had done the occasional job for other collectors in the past, but like a child to fire, he always returned to Tyrangal. He owed her so much, and he loved the work she gave him. Can't stay away from the intensity, he thought. It was the only thing that made him feel alive.

Tyrangal looked up from her examination of the tome. "You have done well," she said.

Duvan smiled. He was embarrassed to admit it, but he wanted to please Tyrangal. He had wondered on occasion what it would be like to kiss her, but he had never dared to try.

"I will need the ring back as well; it won't work where you're headed next."

"Of course," Duvan said, and handed the teleportation ring to her. Enchanted jewelry and other magical items often misfired or just didn't work in the Plaguewrought Land. The ring would be just as likely to explode or turn into a swarm of moths as it was to work properly.

"I received word that things did not go exactly as planned."

Duvan scowled. "There are spies among the Copper Guard," he told her.

"The Order is getting bolder with their infiltration."

Duvan nodded. "I should never have let Beaugrat hire the team. I should have screened them myself."

"Yes; then you would have had but one mutineer." Tyrangal's gaze was intense, but not disapproving. "Tell me, did Beaugrat or any of the others get a look at the tome?"

Duvan shook his head. "No. The other two are dead anyway, and I chased Beaugrat off when he tried to take the book."

"Did he know what he was trying to take?"

"I don't think so."

"Excellent. Tell me the whole story."

Duvan sent a questioning glance in Slanya's direction. "In front of her?"

"In a manner of speaking," Tyrangal said, her hands reached out and brushed the air in front of Slanya's chest. The cleric went into a trance, staring straight ahead where she stood. "She cannot hear us now."

So Duvan told her the whole tale. He relayed how they found the citadel barely hanging from a ledge down in the Underchasm, and how they'd descended to search it. He described the battle with the manticore, and the secret compartment he narrated the sorcerer's demise and the tower's plunge into the darkness, until finally, he told of the mutiny and Seerah's death, Beaugrat's spellplague attack and cowardly escape.

"Beaugrat's spellscar created blue fire?" Tyrangal asked. "Are you certain?"

Duvan nodded. "I'm quite familiar with it."

Tyrangal gave a laugh, although Duvan wasn't trying to be funny. "I suppose you are," she said, and then added, "And he realized that his attack had no effect on you?"

"Yes, I'm certain of it."

Tyrangal frowned. "That is unfortunate. I fear you will be sought by those who would use you for your talents."

Duvan looked away. It was convenient for Tyrangal to tell others he was clever or lucky, but she and Duvan knew the truth: he was resistant to the spellplague, and his resistance extended to anything and anyone near him. A blessing and a curse, as spellscars were, though in his case the curse came more often by the hands of those who had stopped seeing him as a person and only saw him as a spellscar to harness.

Duvan shuddered. His years at Wildhome threatened to come flooding back over him. He tried to focus on the here and now, on Tyrangal and this new mission. He needed sleep; dreamless rest would help him focus.

"Duvan," Tyrangal demanded his attention. "Be exceedingly careful. Avoid the Order and get out of town. Take Slanya." Tyrangal touched Slanya's chest again. "Duvan here has uncanny luck avoiding the threats of the changelands. He is the only person I know who has survived near-exposure to spellplague without getting spellscarred."

Slanya came out of her reverie and nodded her nearly-bald head. "He seems like the ideal guide for my journey. Well, except for the trying-to-kill-me part."

"Oh?" Tyrangal said. She looked enquiringly at Duvan.

Duvan smirked. "Yeah," he said. "That was a misunderstanding."

"I presume," Tyrangal said, "that it won't happen again."

His smile grew. "As long as she gives me no cause," he said. "Besides, she can take care of herself."

"Excellent," Tyrangal said. "Sister Slanya has my full approval. And her quest is an important one, even though it is probably more dangerous than any I have sent you on previously. It is your decision whether to go or not; I will not exert my influence on you in that regard. However, it would be a convenient way to stay out of potential mischief for the time being."

"Yes, Tyrangal, I will—"

"However, I request that if you agree to take it, you promise to see it through to the end."

Duvan nodded. "I promise," he said. "If I accept the job, I will see it through."

Slanya looked at him. "Will you do it, then?"

"What's the arrangement?" he asked Tyrangal.

"You will get triple your normal pay," Tyrangal said. "One third up front and the balance when you and Slanya return with the plaguegrass load."

You *and* Slanya—he looked over at the priestess. Solemn, but under that stern face she was worried. At least she was smart enough to know it wouldn't be easy.

"So," Duvan said. "When do we leave?"

Walking next to Duvan with the high Vilhon sun beating down on them, Slanya found herself sweating in the heat. For some reason that wasn't yet completely clear to Slanya, Duvan wanted to avoid discovery by the Order of Blue Fire. So they had decided to skirt around the city on their way to the monastery, where they would pick up their supplies and head out to the Plaguewrought Land.

Gnarled trees and tall brown grass surrounded the disused trail on either side. Through the foliage Slanya could see glimpses of some ruins off to their left—perhaps an ancient military tower, its once-strong structure no more than discarded rubble now.

A stony mote floated like a low cloud above them, and as it drifted to eclipse the sun, it cast a wide shadow that blocked the searing heat. Slanya was grateful for the reprieve, even though the close proximity of the motes made her nervous. Sometimes, the small ones fell out of the sky.

"We must hurry through this area," Duvan said, keeping his voice low. "If we are being pursued, this is the best place to—"

The sound of approaching hooves interrupted Duvan.

Slanya glanced around. "You were saying?"

"Hide!"

Slanya barely noticed Duvan disappearing into the tall grass and ducking behind a pile of stone rubble. And as she moved off the path and crouched down in the shadows of a ruined wall, her eyes lost track of him. She concentrated and tried to find him again.

Yes, there he was: just across the narrow track in the shade of a large flagstone. It was right where she knew he'd been all along, but if she looked away, even for a second, she had a hard time finding him in the tableau of shadows and shapes.

The riders approached at a rapid canter from the direction of the Tyrangal's mansion. Slanya picked out four of them, coming directly for her: three human men she didn't recognize and one red-headed female dwarf in blue clerical robes, tied at the waist with a braided white rope. The dwarf had been part of Vraith's party when she'd visited with Gregor. Within moments they drew reins in the path next to her.

"We can see you, cleric," said a large man in dull plate armor. "And our quarrel is not with you. I'm Beaugrat from the Order of Blue Fire. We're looking for a man by the name of Duvan."

Behind the man, an archer with a pockmarked complexion nocked an arrow. Next to him was a thin skeleton of a man with the air of a pilgrim.

"The criminal was recently seen walking with you," said Beaugrat.

So they haven't seen Duvan yet, she thought.

Slanya stepped out into the open, standing ready. She gripped her staff loosely, prepared to swing it. "Good morning to you—"

Beaugrat swung down from his horse and stood facing her. He wore a heavy suit of armor and a huge sword on his back.

"Criminal?" Slanya took stock of the other three. The archer and the pilgrim hung back on their horses. The pilgrim wore leathers but seemed uncomfortable in them. The archer brought the bow up, the ready arrow aimed at her. The dwarf cleric merely looked on, her dark eyes set in a ruddy face. The Order of Blue Fire symbol of a flaming blue eyeball, was embroidered on her robes.

"Yes," Beaugrat said, "he killed two respected members of the Order and is wanted for questioning and enlightenment."

Slanya winced. Enlightenment was not something that could be imposed upon someone by an external force. Despite the fact that Gregor had forged ties with Vraith, the more Slanya learned of its practices, the less she respected the Order of Blue Fire.

"My meeting with Duvan was brief. I don't know where he is at the moment."

Beaugrat stepped closer, prompting Slanya to lift her staff. "If he submits without a fight," the man said, "you have nothing to fear."

Slanya drew up to her full height. She was taller than Beaugrat, and although the man outweighed her by double, she managed to look down on him. "I do not want to fight you, sir," she said. "But you will find me a formidable opponent. There is also a formal alliance between the leaders of my monastery and Commander Accordant Vraith of your order. Any aggression toward me would jeopardize that, and such an act would meet with punishment from above. So, in that light, Beaugrat, I suggest you look elsewhere."

For a passing moment, Beaugrat hesitated, his face revealing his confusion. Then he threw his head back and laughed. "I'm afraid you don't understand," he said. "Just tell me where Duvan is, or we will be forced to kill you."

Without warning, the bowman on the horse behind Beaugrat grunted. Slanya looked up to see his face stricken into a frozen grimace of pain. He toppled sideways off the horse, his arrow springing free from his grip. The wayward quarrel plunged into the hindquarters of Beaugrat's riderless horse. The black stallion reared and bolted.

Slanya saw Duvan's shadowy form approaching Beaugrat from behind, moving fast. Go, go, she urged silently. On the periphery of her vision, she noticed the cleric make a pattern with her hands, drawing power from her god. That would not do.

Slanya leaped sideways, closing the distance, and struck three rapid blows to the cleric's head and neck, aiming for the specific spots she knew had a high chance of stunning the dwarf. Two of the blows landed, and the dwarf slumped unconscious mid cast.

A quick glance told her that Duvan was fighting with Beaugrat. Duvan lunged, touching the tip of his dagger blade to the exposed part of the big man's neck. Beaugrat's huge gauntleted hands tried to lock down on Duvan. They failed as the smaller man snaked out of his grasp and danced away.

Not dead yet. Which was good, because she needed him.

Slanya darted at the pilgrim in leather armor. The man made a slow attempt to draw the unfamiliar sword on his waist. But he was clearly not trained for this sort of activity and had come along as a tourist or voyeur. His mistake. Two strikes of her staff later, and the pilgrim lay on the ground, disarmed and knocked out.

Slanya heard the distinct sound of a large sword being drawn from its sheath. She turned to see Duvan and Beaugrat circling each other. The big man swung the huge sword in broad arcs that prevented Duvan from getting in close. Duvan, for his part, was keeping a good distance, dodging and feinting to keep the barbarian off-balance.

Slanya purposefully made noise as she approached. "You'd do yourself a favor to leave," she told Beaugrat. "Your companions cannot aid you."

Beaugrat took his eyes off Duvan to glance at what remained of his group. When he turned back, there was a brilliant flash of light in Duvan's vicinity, blinding Slanya for a second.

She caught the sound of metal glancing off metal and saw one of Duvan's throwing daggers skitter across the hard dirt.

Beaugrat swung his sword in huge arcs, backing toward the other horses. He grabbed the pilgrim's chestnut mare and swung up. "I'll be back for you, Duvan," he said, riding off. "And you, too, priest." He rode off toward the city.

Slanya looked over to find Duvan standing over the dead body of the archer. He was breathing hard and taking stock of the situation.

"I had things under control," she said, feeling the anger driving her words. "Fighting is not always the best option."

Narrowing his eyes, Duvan said, "You're welcome."

Slanya blinked, unperturbed.

"He was going to kill you!"

"No," Slanya said. "He would've realized that he couldn't attack me without angering his superiors. Then he would've left us alone. A peaceful solution."

"Um, not likely," Duvan scoffed. "Beaugrat is driven by revenge for his wounded pride. I don't practice revenge myself, and I suspect you don't either, but unlike you, I do understand it. He would never have given in to a logical argument."

"Perhaps not," Slanya conceded. "But there's more to this attack than simple revenge. The Order of Blue Fire is interested enough in you to spy on your activities. Think about it: what do they want from you? Boiling it down to revenge is a dangerous oversimplification."

Duvan was quiet for a minute, then he nodded. "You're right; they want me for something."

When he didn't elaborate, Slanya decided to let the issue drop. For now.

"I'm sorry that you got caught up in my business, Slanya. This was certainly not your battle."

Slanya shrugged. "I am not worried," she said. "They attacked us, and we held our own." In truth, she'd found the fight exciting. "We should get going."

Nodding, Duvan drew a dagger from one of his leg sheaths and kneeled by the unconscious body of the dwarf cleric. He started to press the dagger to the cleric's neck.

"Stop!" Slanya said. "There will be no more killing."

Duvan looked up at her, his eyes wide in stunned disbelief. "You're not serious. If we leave her and that scarecrow alive, they *will* be back after us, and they might kill us the next time. Or worse."

"Perhaps," Slanya said, her voice measured. "But what they have done to us does not deserve death, and it is not our role to mete out this level of justice. Death will come to them on its own time."

A scowl crossed Duvan's face as his brows narrowed. He stood up and sheathed his dagger. "You knocked them out, so I will respect your wishes here," he said. "But you're being naive, and your decision now could cost me later."

"You can't kill the whole world, Duvan," Slanya said. "You can't even kill those who may do you ill in the future. That is not your role in the universe, and it goes against your responsibility to society."

"I don't want to kill the *whole* world, Slanya," he replied, and his scowl gave way to an all-too-attractive grin. "I just want to kill these here. They are the threat. Your ethical code is just one way to approach things. One *idealistic* point of view. In the real world where I live, I've found it prudent to eliminate threats when the opportunity presents—because there may not be another chance."

CHAPTER FIVE

Sweat prickled on Duvan's brow as he gathered up the rest of his throwing daggers. He removed a blade from the dead archer's back and wiped the blood on the archer's linen shirt.

"We must hurry," Slanya said. "Beaugrat may return with reinforcements."

Duvan squinted in the bright sun, trying to see his companion's face clearly. "Beaugrat will be back, yes," he said. "But he's too much of a coward to attack when we're expecting it."

"When will he come for us?"

Duvan pulled out some rope to bind the prisoners. "Sometime when we're already beaten down or otherwise occupied. Sometime when he thinks he'll have a clear advantage."

"That would be highly unethical," Slanya said.

Duvan rolled his eyes. For someone so talented and well trained, Slanya was very idealistic about how people acted in the world outside her temple and its grounds. Tyrangal must be punishing me for something, Duvan thought.

He helped Slanya bind and gag the two assailants that she'd knocked out. It was foolish not to kill them; Ormpetarr was small enough that it would only be a matter of time before he crossed paths with these two again.

"They'll just die out here anyway," he said.

"Bind them to each other, but not to anything else. That should give them a chance, but they won't be able to follow us."

"All right," he said, too tired to argue. She had defeated them, so as far as he was concerned, she held their fate.

Slanya peered at him. "Are you agreeing with me?"

Duvan smiled at her. "Let's just say, I'm not disagreeing for the moment." When he was sure the pilgrim and the cleric were tightly bound, he swung up onto one of their horses.

"What are you doing now?"

"Leaving. Taking the horses with us. I hope that's not a trick question."

"Help me get this one onto his horse," she said pointing to the body of the archer.

"Just leave him here. Scavengers will get rid of the body."

"No," she said. "He needs a proper funeral—a ceremony to celebrate his connection to the living and the dead."

Duvan gave her a blank, disbelieving look. "What?"

"Everyone deserves—"

"Yes, I heard you, and there again, I agree with you, but we don't have time for 'a proper funeral.' It's not like it's going to matter to him."

Slanya scowled. "It will matter to those who cared for him," she said. "And it's important. Either we take the body with us to the temple, seek out his loved ones, and give it to them, or burn the body here and now."

Duvan shook his head and considered arguing. However, if past experience were an indicator, this stubborn cleric would not be swayed. Arguing would just waste more time. He considered leaving. These sorts of disagreements were why he almost always worked alone. But he had promised Tyrangal, and he wouldn't back out of that promise.

Duvan sighed. "All right. You're in charge," he said. "If you insist on a funeral, then we should do it here and now. The fewer people who know what happened here, the better."

Slanya nodded, then turned to the body of the dead archer. She knelt down and straightened his garments.

Duvan swung down from the horse and helped her prepare the fire. He dragged the corpse through the tall grass to the ruined guard outpost. Crumbling rock walls would hold vigil to his passage, and weed-pitted flagstones would be his bier.

The man's clean and well-mended clothes told a story of aristocratic upbringing. He had a callused right hand, so he was well practiced at bowmanship. His face was round and boyish—the son of a merchant, maybe, who ran away to the changelands for his spellscar. Or perhaps he was an Order of Blue Fire recruit from a faraway land, moved here recently. He smelled of soap and perfume, but that was overwhelmed now by the iron tang of blood that leaked out beneath him. And that, in turn, was overwhelmed by the smell of his voided bowels.

There is no dignity in death, Duvan thought. He rifled through the saddlebags and found a small skin that smelled of fire oil. He doused the body with it.

Slanya bowed her head over the corpse. "May Kelemvor judge you well," she said, "and guide your passage through the Fugue Plane to wherever next you land." She stepped back and nodded to Duvan.

Striking the rings of his right hand together to ignite a

spark, Duvan lit the fire. He stepped back as the oil caught. First the flames were yellow and the smoke billowed clear, but soon enough the flames turned orange, then red. The smoke rose in gray clouds, turning to black as the man's flesh caught and his fat ignited.

Staring into the flames, Duvan remembered many burnings. Too many people gone to fire—the gossamer flames of blue fire. He saw his papa's dark ruddy face beneath a black beard, always stern. And always right . . . until he wasn't. Until he was gone. Spellplague. So many dead. And Duvan the only witness to their passing.

But that was another life, another existence. He had often wished he'd died along with everyone else, and perhaps he had. His death had not been due to fire, but to the loss of everything he knew. After Talfani had finally succumbed, leaving him alone among the decomposing corpses, Duvan had gone as cold inside as drifting snow.

He knew he'd gone cold hearted, and yet he didn't care. It was better that way. Ice couldn't be hurt. Imperviousness to emotional pain was far better than compassion.

As he watched the fire consume the flesh of this unnamed archer, he saw Talfani's face in the fire. It had been a gossamer fire that had taken them all, but she—his sweet sister—had lingered on, sick and suffering.

Steeling himself, Duvan grit his teeth and forced away the memories. Since Talfani's death years earlier, he'd shunned friendships. No reason to risk pain. Even Tyrangal was not a true friend, although they understood each other. Perhaps Duvan would miss her, ever so slightly, if she were gone.

"Good-bye," he whispered into the flames engulfing the dead archer's corpse. "I did not know you, but I hope that your continuing journey be not alone, but among friends."

Standing in the heat of the rising sun, the sharp sculptures of ancient crumbling masonry like twisted sentinels around them, Slanya reflected on Duvan's words. They struck a chord inside her. For all that he lacked in civility, there was a vestige of compassion in this wildman.

The fire caught on the dead man's clothes soaked in oil. Slanya resisted watching at first. But the flames drew her, and she stared into them. They glowed like sunlight through an open doorway—a gateway to a realm of chaos and light, a portal into a wild universe, abandonment of reason and law.

Involuntarily Slanya took a step toward the funeral fire. The searing heat coming off of it stung her skin, and she felt water rising in her eyes.

"We should leave now."

Duvan's voice snapped her from her trance.

"It's not safe to stay here any longer," he said.

Not safe, she thought.

Flames licked the body in front of her, leaving blackened and blistering trails. The smell of burning fat brought her back to her childhood, back to her memory of the event.

The vision was always the same. Evening had come to the city and the cacophony of the sprawl had finally quieted. Aunt Ewesia's breathing had slowed, and she had started to snore—asleep in her rocking chair.

It was the only time little Slanya could relax. The only time she knew that she wouldn't get in trouble.

In the vision, she looked down on her younger self. Little Slanya in her stained dress was six years old with blond hair flying out in tufts from the braids that tried to keep it organized. She watched in her mind as little Slanya finished removing the linens from their drying line next to the fire, folded them, and put them away. They had to be folded just so, or she would have to do it again when Aunt Ewesia discovered her failure.

When little Slanya returned from the bedroom, Aunt

Ewesia was on fire. Alarmed and frightened even then that she would be punished for this accident, young Slanya blanched and she held her breath. Aunt Ewesia's clothes blazed, but she awoke slowly despite that. The infusion she drank to put her to sleep every night worked too well.

And then, the fiery behemoth that had been her aunt heaved itself from the chair, screaming like a thousand banshees, making the hair on Slanya's skin stick straight out. Aunt Ewesia lurched toward Slanya. The flames had ripped through the cotton and wool of her clothing and had started in on her skin.

Slanya felt her breath catch as she watched her younger self run from the groping, screaming demon. Later she was ashamed that she had run. Later she would tell the other orphans that she had tried to help, but couldn't stop the fire. But she hadn't tried to help; fear had gripped her, and she had run away from the beast of flame and anger.

"Can you ride?" Duvan's voice shook her from her reverie.

Slanya squeezed her eyes closed to block out the fire. She held her breath to avoid smelling the burning body. She waited until her heart's frantic beating slowed and some semblance of calm returned to her.

Then, nodding to Duvan, she took the reins of the pilgrim's black mare. Slanya straightened and stretched her back. "I'm ready," she said, climbing up into the saddle.

Riding the dead archer's horse, Duvan led them expertly through the rubble away from the pillar of black smoke that rose from the burning body. He headed away from the old outpost and along the path that led around the city to the monastery.

After a minute of silence, Duvan spoke. "Thank you for standing by me back there," he said. "It means a lot."

Slanya's face wrinkled into a puzzled expression. It had never occurred to her to run.

"Not many folks have fought for me," he added.

"Well, I couldn't very well lose my guide, could I?" she said, but regretted it as soon as the words escaped her lips. Here he was expressing true gratitude, and the least she could do was accept it.

"I suppose not," he said. "But thanks all the same."

"You have been alone all your life?" Slanya asked.

He considered the question for a moment. "Yes," he said, but Slanya could tell there was more than he was letting on. "For the most part, I don't play well with others."

"Well, I'd say we made a good team back there."

Duvan glanced over at her, his dark eyes examining her face. Perhaps he was looking for a lie or exaggeration, but if he saw anything he gave no indication. After all, Slanya had been serious, and at least on one level had been telling the truth. As far as the fighting went, they *were* a great team.

"Yes," Duvan said. "We do make a good team."

That made Slanya smile, not least because something in his tone and expression told her that those words had rarely, if ever, escaped his mouth before.

Duvan dismounted just outside the temple complex, amid the stench of the afflicted. Tents full of dying pilgrims surrounded the unfinished stone structure.

He didn't understand the pilgrims. Why would anyone come here by choice? Why would they leave a comfortable life full of friends and family? And for what?

Perhaps they just didn't realize that of all the possible outcomes of spellplague exposure, emerging alive with a spellscar and a wonderful new power was by far the least likely. Most just died instantly—burned up before they had a chance to scream.

And of those who came out alive, a good many were doomed from too much exposure. They grew sick, while death lingered around them, their bodies riddled with the chaos of the Plaguewrought Lands.

Duvan wondered if anyone would come if they'd been told what it was really like instead of the propaganda disseminated by the Order of Blue Fire. *Travel to the Plaguewrought Land to be touched by the divine fire. Spellplague will give you power and change your life forever!*

He imagined bards would attract smaller crowds with lines like, "Want pain and death? Visit the Plaguewrought Land."

Monks and monastery clerics of Kelemvor moved among the sick and dying, providing comfort and aid. Also scattered in the mix of tents and grass mats were Order of Blue Fire volunteers in their pale blue robes.

"Lots of Order around, Slanya," Duvan said. "Why is that?" He knew his tone was suspicious, and he didn't care.

"Nothing nefarious, I assure you," Slanya said. "They come to ease the pain of the sick and dying. Most of them are unskilled, but they can clean up excrement with the best of them."

"But clearly your monastery has dealings with the Order," Duvan said. "That may or may not be cause for alarm."

"These volunteers don't come inside the monastery," Slanya said. "I know of only one formal arrangement, and that's for a supply of Brother Gregor's elixir."

Duvan scrutinized Slanya's face. Not lying.

"Let's just get our supplies and move out," Slanya suggested.

Duvan nodded his agreement.

"Sister Slanya," said a short cleric, bald except for a long auburn sidelock. Duvan caught sight of a tattoo at the base of her skull, in the same location as Slanya's—the scales of Kelemvor in simple blue ink. "Gregor has your supplies ready."

Slanya nodded. "Thank you, High Priestess."

The cleric turned to Duvan. "I am Kaylinn, head of the monastery."

Duvan gave a head bow. "I am glad to meet you," he said. "I'm Duvan."

Slanya interrupted, "We should get these horses to the stables."

"I'll take the horses," Kaylinn said. "Brother Gregor will meet you in the chapel anteroom; that's where your supplies are."

Slanya gave a slight bow. "Thank you."

The stench of dying pilgrims and smoldering bodies lessened as they made their way into the monastery. Here Duvan breathed a little easier. If he wasn't careful, the smell that floated on the summer air in the Plaguewrought Land would trigger painful memories.

Looking around, Duvan noticed how clean and ordered things were inside the monastery. The walls were white and scrubbed, the appointments spare. Most of the halls had stanchions for torches or candles, but there was no art or decoration of any kind, save for a simple mosaic of Kelemvor's skeletal hand holding his scales of death.

Duvan also noticed how quiet the monastery was. Scores of clerics and monks moved about their business—doing construction work or writing scrolls or even practicing combat training—in near silence.

Duvan found it eerie. The silence made him ill at ease and alert.

Slanya led him through mostly bare corridors, furnished by an occasional wooden table or chair. Their boots clomped on the washed tile floors. They came to a wide doorway and stepped into a small, empty room with a broad wooden table in the middle.

There was an assortment of supplies on the table, and Duvan immediately started to inspect the goods. Even though he suspected that the monks had laid out too much to carry, Duvan didn't set anything aside. There was plenty of food, and he loaded a portion of it into his own pack. He double-checked his other supplies to make sure he was ready. For Slanya to have a chance of surviving, they'd have to be in and back out of the Plaguewrought Land in less than a day anyway. Still, Duvan always went prepared.

Out of habit, he catalogued the contents of his backpack— extra leathers, weapons, poisons and powders, a sharpening stone, his glideskin, rope, food, oil, soap, and water. Checking Slanya's pack, he noticed that she seemed well prepared too. Including—

He pulled out a black cloth pouch cinched at one end with a braided rope. It was valuable, he could tell. Opening the pouch, he looked into a black void, but when he reached inside, he felt several objects that could not actually be inside, including a tarp and two bedrolls.

"That's a bag of holding," said Slanya. "We'll use it for collecting the plaguegrass."

"Nice," Duvan said. He'd never seen one before, as expensive as the magic pouches were; the fact that these clerics would risk sending one along meant that this mission was very important to them.

"Well met, Brother Gregor," came Slanya's voice from the doorway. "This is Duvan."

A slender man, middle-aged but fit, his cropped black hair split by a tuft of silver growing from where his spellscar cleaved his skull stood in the doorway. Duvan stared at him and wondered what it was like to be touched by the storm of the spellplague remnants in the middle of his head.

"We owe you a debt of gratitude, young sir," Gregor said, making a slight bow in greeting.

Duvan paused, unsure of the proper response. "I will do my best to keep us both alive," he said finally.

"And I'm happy to say that you shall have help in that regard," Gregor said. "My protective elixir is a great discovery indeed."

Duvan said nothing.

"It's incredible! It allows someone to be exposed to the Plaguewrought Land and survive. So far I've raised the survival rate twentyfold!" Gregor had a huge toothy grin on his bearded face. "Compared to the control group. Even a layman can appreciate those numbers."

Duvan stifled a shudder. "Control group?"

"Yes," Gregor said, unconcerned. "Some of the pilgrims got a different elixir that we hoped would have no effect."

And all of those must have died, Duvan thought. Died thinking that maybe they'd have a better chance.

"How many pilgrims in this control group died?" Duvan asked.

Gregor's eyebrows arched. "The same number who would have died without any elixir. Spellplague exposure results in death most of the time, on average. It actually depends upon the amount of exposure."

"The control group didn't know their elixir was false, I assume," Duvan said.

Gregor nodded. "For the results to be unbiased, they cannot know. The vials are labeled by color and—"

"So you give them false hope," Duvan said, feeling his anger rising. "They think they have a better chance and throw away their lives."

Gregor pondered for a moment. "You are clearly a passionate soul, Duvan." The monk's tone was calm and measured. "The truth is that all of these pilgrims were intending to 'throw away their lives' before they came to me for the elixir. I would argue that hope is what drives many of these folks to risk their lives at the border of the changelands. Almost all of their hope is false, and I am certainly not adding significantly to it."

Duvan scowled. Some people held the belief that false hope was better than no hope, but he didn't buy that. Still, he said nothing.

"Anyhow, back to the immediate need," Gregor went on. "The thing we're paying you to help us obtain . . ."

Duvan nodded.

"Plaguegrass is a key ingredient," Gregor said. "And we're out of it. So we need to replenish our supply if we're going to save more pilgrims. Slanya has the last two doses of the working elixir."

So it's all right then, Duvan thought wryly. Experimenting on pilgrims is a good thing because you discovered a potion that works.

"This is plaguegrass," Gregor said, holding a long stalk of yellow grass. The stem glittered where flecks of crystal grew. "Take it with you so that you'll know what you're looking for. You shouldn't have any trouble finding it once you're past the border."

Duvan took the stalk from Gregor, then turned and put it into his pack. "I've seen this before," he said. "We'll bring back plenty."

"We can save so many lives," Gregor said, his black eyes flashing. "Imagine no dying pilgrims. Imagine a world where the remnants of the Spellplague cannot kill."

Duvan shivered. He could not imagine that. It was perilous to imagine that, because it meant dropping his guard. Fantasy. Underestimating the destructive force of the gossamer blue fire was a step on the path to annihilation.

"It takes great hubris," Duvan said, "to think that the changelands can be controlled or mitigated."

Gregor's smile evaporated. "I suppose it does," he said. "But one does not accomplish great deeds without a little hubris."

"Fairly spoken," Duvan admitted. "But in my own experience, efforts to control spellplague have always met with disaster."

The look of puzzlement on Gregor's face nearly brought a smile to Duvan's. "You've been involved in such efforts?"

But Duvan's mind was far away, crouching in a cage of adamantine on a vast and stormy plane inside the Plaguewrought Land, shivering with cold. And waiting for his love, Rhiazzshar, to come and let him out and give him his reward.

"Duvan?" Gregor said. "Are you with us?"

"Just for the record," Duvan said, "I'm going to help you because Tyrangal has given you her endorsement. But personally, I don't condone the use of pilgrims or anyone for such experiments, regardless of the possible outcome."

"They were all volunteers, I assure you," Gregor said, unfazed. "All well-informed volunteers."

"We should be going," Slanya said, interrupting.

"Yes," Gregor agreed. "Quite right, quite right."

Duvan nodded, glad Slanya had changed the subject. He finished loading the packs and lifted his to his back. Time to be moving along. Slanya donned the other pack, then bowed slightly to Gregor.

Duvan merely strode away without a good-bye. Gregor might be paying him, but he didn't have to like the man. They exited through the main gate, heading south on foot. Duvan planned for them to skirt the city, keeping to the east, and intersect the border of Plaguewrought Land.

Gregor climbed up onto the balcony and watched Slanya and her guide slowly pick their way through the tents. He gazed over the encampment pilgrims, many of them sick and dying, past the ever-belching funeral pyre to the city walls, and beyond those, to where the gauzy veil that marked the border of the Plaguewrought Land rose up into the sky like a curtain.

"May your journey be easy and fruitful," he whispered at the retreating figures. "The salvation of many depends on it." With the approaching Festival of Blue Fire, his elixir could save many lives, provided he had enough plaguegrass.

When they had disappeared from view, Gregor found himself looking back at the encampment. The sprawling tent hospital was an eyesore, and despite the best efforts of the monastery's monks and clerics, it was filthy with excrement. With more than ten plaguechanged or sick pilgrims for every monk, the logistics were overwhelming. So it stank, and when the wind blew just the wrong direction, the stench infiltrated the monastery.

In fact, one of the reasons that the funeral pyre was so near the temple complex's walls was because the smoke was far more pleasant than the reek of decay, refuse, and feces. Choosing between the lesser of evils was not Gregor's preferred mode of operation, but in these times and in this location, it would have to do.

Gregor turned from the balcony and retired to his study, using the peacefulness of the monastery to center himself. Abruptly, the images came to him. They always came when he least expected it and took over his mind.

In this vision, Gregor walked at the head of a large crowd of pilgrims, part of a small group that led them into the Plaguewrought Land. There were hundreds of pilgrims, each one drinking Gregor's draught, his perfect concoction. They formed an arc in front of a wave of blue fire, which raced like wildfire toward them.

The pilgrims formed a wall with their bodies, catching the wave of spellplague, and as they moved to complete the circle, capturing it. Containing the chaos. Bringing order to the Plaguewrought Land's wildness.

His elixir kept them alive. His creation made it possible for ordinary people to help make sudden spellplague storms and appearances harmless. He was rendering the most wild and chaotic force in all of Faerûn impotent. The vision faded, leaving him feeling euphoric and wanting more.

The visions seemed to be coming from outside him. And they weren't a prediction of the future, he knew, but more of a divine guidance, the hand of Oghma providing direction. The visions helped shape his decisions, showing him what to strive for and which path to take. They had started sometime after he got his spellscar, after that morning he had awakened with a cloud of spellplague hovering next to his simple bed, back before he had come to Ormpetarr. The visions had started subtly, like waking dreams. Over time, they had grown in strength and frequency.

As he reached the door to his study, he saw Kaylinn approaching. He took a deep breath to compose himself. "Yes, Priestess?"

Kaylinn gave a short bow. "There is a group here from the Order of Blue Fire," she said. "They want to speak with you, and they're quite demanding."

Gregor noted Kaylinn's tone. She was suspicious of the Order. "Have they said or done anything offensive?"

Kaylinn's look softened a bit. "Not really. Just arrogance, perhaps. As much as they claim to strive for the betterment of all people, they aren't guided by the same principles that we are. I find their charitable activities to be more self-serving than altruistic."

Gregor nodded. Kaylinn was a very astute observer and her judgment had been a good guide for both him and the monastery for years. "I understand," he said.

"I advise caution in your dealings with them, Brother Gregor," she said, concern on her face. "I don't profess to understand the intricacies of your projects, and you have always been trustworthy, but don't let yourself be manipulated."

"I am exercising great care in this," Gregor said. "But I envision a great revolution in how people regard the changelands. No longer will they fear them. No longer will their loved ones disappear without warning, or worse, end up as plaguechanged monsters. I am on the verge of achieving that vision, and unfortunately collaboration with the Order of Blue Fire is required for me to proceed."

Kaylinn frowned. "Collaboration is a good thing," she said. "But do not be blinded by your vision. Ends do not justify means, Brother Gregor."

"Of course," he demurred. "Thank you for your sagacity. As usual, your view is wise."

The high priestess gave a small smile. "I worry about you," she said. "You have been . . . distracted. I worry that you're driving yourself too hard."

Gregor gave his most earnest smile. "I have never felt this clear-headed," he said. "And I am close to the end. We are doing great good here on the changelands border."

"That's true," Kaylinn said, with a nod. "Very well, I will stop worrying. Where will you meet them?"

"In here is fine, but I can escort them back."

"No, no. I'll get them."

"Many thanks."

After Kaylinn left, Gregor opened the ledger which showed the numbers and mortality rates of the pilgrims who had tested the latest elixir. Gregor paged past all the other experiments. Hundreds of pilgrims had been tested, and five different elixirs, their data compared with that of the false elixirs.

The last formula had a twenty-onefold increase in survivability, while those taking the false elixir fared in the usual range. Gregor smiled. Numbers didn't lie.

The door opened again. Following Kaylinn came the blonde elf—Vraith, slim and looking even more delicate in silky, sky-blue robes. Behind her clomped a huge human wearing shiny plate armor with a section of his right pauldron cut out to reveal a spellscar.

"Well met, my friends," Gregor said. "I think things went successfully last night, no?"

Vraith gave an abbreviated bow. "May the Blue Fire burn inside you." The human stood a pace behind her in deference, and he did not speak.

"Last night went quite satisfactorily," Vraith said. "But that is not why we've come."

Oh? Gregor thought, and he wondered what brought this arrogant priestess down out of her nest of followers. What he said was, "How can I be of help?"

"A young man was seen with one of the temple's clerics this morning," Vraith said. "We need to know where he is."

"A young man? What does he look like?"

Vraith's eyebrows arched up to disappear into her hairline. "You don't know of whom I speak?"

"Perhaps I do," Gregor said. "And perhaps I do not. Many people matching the description of 'young man' pass through and near the monastery every day."

Vraith gestured to the plate-clad human. "Beaugrat, describe this Duvan person."

Beaugrat stepped forward. "Duvan is dark skinned, of average height and sinewy. Very quick. Black hair, black eyes, and a day-old beard. He is known to work for the head of the Copper Guard, Tyrangal."

Gregor kept his face implacable. "And what is your business with this man?"

Vraith said, "He has committed offenses against our members and is wanted for questioning."

It was Gregor's turn to be incredulous. "Offenses? What offenses?"

Beaugrat said, "He killed two members and stole their property."

Gregor laughed. "Sounds like he's wanted for more than questioning."

"Do you know where he is or not?" Vraith asked, her tone darkening.

"I do not," he said, dodging the question. "But I may have valuable information concerning his whereabouts."

"And do you plan to tell me, or do I need to have you questioned as well?"

Behind Vraith, Kaylinn raised an eyebrow at Gregor. The half-elf's tone and attitude had been pushing at him the whole time, and he finally snapped. "I will not be commanded in my own home, Vraith," he said, his own tone growing fierce. "We work together, and together we can accomplish much. Apart . . ." He let the implied threat hang in the air.

Vraith stared at him, her pale gray eyes as hard as slate behind her translucent blonde lashes. She seemed to be weighing the merits of arguing with him or defying him some other way. But finally, she averted her gaze. "Yes, yes," she said, waving her hand. "Solidarity and cooperation and all that. It's very important that we find this man."

Now we're getting somewhere, Gregor thought. "All right," he said. "We may be able to come to an arrangement. But first you will tell me the true reason you seek this man."

CHAPTER SIX

Under a bright afternoon sky, Duvan guided Slanya toward the border of the Plaguewrought Land. It was a journey he'd taken several times before, but the path he chose was a little different each time.

"To be honest with you, Duvan," Slanya said, "I'm nervous."

Duvan regarded his companion. Slanya took sure and confident steps; no doubt she'd trained intensively. She also seemed to have some measure of the body control that monks were famous for. She'd demonstrated quick thinking as well as enviable discipline.

All of which would mean nothing in the face of the changelands.

"You shouldn't be nervous," Duvan said. "You should be afraid."

"I'm not afraid to die."

"Really?" Duvan had yet to meet anyone else besides himself who did not fear death.

Slanya shrugged. "My death will come as everyone's will. Why should I fear that? If the cause is right and I am true to myself, then my death will have meaning, as will my life. Kelemvor will welcome me, and I will pass on to the next life."

Duvan remained silent as they passed into the shadow of a large mote which hung precariously low in the sky. Large motes tended to be stable, but Duvan had seen smaller ones sustain damage as they passed through the border veil. Quite a few of those lost their buoyancy and plummeted to the ground. In fact the terrain along the border was littered with boulders and the deep furrows they had made upon impact.

Around him, the gentle hills gave way to steeper ones, the grassy knolls replaced by bare rock dotted sporadically with tenacious weeds. The faint sensation of the disturbance in the Weave the Plaguewrought Land caused made the hairs on his arms stand on end. The faint odor of oranges and decaying flesh drifted occasionally on the warm wind—the sour and sweet stench of the plaguelands of the Plaguewrought Land in summer.

"Have you ever been very close to the changelands?" Duvan asked. "I know you understand what they can do, but if you haven't experienced living plaguelands, it's likely to be a shock."

Slanya looked at him, her eyes narrowing. Perhaps she was trying to figure out why he was asking the question. "I have seen it from afar, through the border veil. And I have prepared myself by talking to many who have been exposed. I believe I know what to expect."

Duvan nodded. "Nonetheless, I think you should let me go in alone."

"No."

Duvan pressed on. "I can find the plaguegrass as easily as we both can, probably faster. Nobody goes very far past the border. The pilgrims merely wait near the edge or just inside until they are exposed, hoping for a minimal wound."

"I will not let you go alone."

"Most people don't go inside for more than a few minutes, and I've only been deep inside once . . ." Duvan trailed off. The nightmare journey of his one and only trip across the changelands came back to him in staccato flashes. Gossamer scythes of blue fire burned precise cuts across the land. Dirt, rock, and plants obliterated all around him.

Duvan had walked into the hell wanting to be taken by the fire, but it wouldn't take him. So far it never had. "There are some stable places in the Plaguewrought Land, but those areas are only temporarily safe. Eventually all the landscape bleeds and burns. I seem to be charmed or cursed when it comes to changelands," he said. "I seem to be able to avoid the effects, so to stay safe you must stay near me."

"I will be safe," Slanya said. "Gregor's elixir will protect me." Her tone was matter-of-fact.

Duvan snorted. "I highly doubt that."

"You heard what he said: the chances of survival are dramatically improved."

Duvan laughed. "I heard it, but that just means you'll be able to survive for a third of an hour instead of dying immediately. We'll need longer than that."

"Well, I trust Gregor."

Duvan shook his head. "He's using you. I bet he's done it before, too, and because you have faith in him, you agree to being used."

"I owe him my life," Slanya said. "That doesn't mean that I'll throw it away for him, but it does mean that he has earned my trust. He has never let me down."

Duvan guided them up out of a ravine and onto a sunny

slope, heading south. "Blind faith will be your undoing, I fear," he said. "The Plaguewrought Land is wild beyond anything you've ever experienced. It abides by no rules, no laws."

"I don't see how—"

"Spellplague cannot be tamed by a draught," Duvan said flatly.

Slanya was silent for a few moments, and Duvan was content to let the conversation drop. If she was determined to go with him inside the borders of the Plaguewrought Land then at least she would do so with her eyes open.

"There are people behind us," Slanya said after a long silence.

Duvan had noticed that too. "Likely pilgrims. Likely dead soon."

"So you hate pilgrims as well?" Slanya asked.

Duvan glanced over at her to try to read her expression, which was wrinkled in dismay. "I don't hate anyone," he said. "I do think that many pilgrims are greedy and misinformed, and that they have a high likelihood of dying."

"You don't approve of following one's beliefs?"

"Not if those beliefs will get you used or killed."

Slanya was about to retort when she stopped herself. Duvan watched in amazement as she concentrated and willfully evoked a change in her demeanor. "Very well," she said. "Despite the fact that you express yourself cynically, and I have a more optimistic view, I think we are mostly in agreement concerning the pilgrims."

He had to admit he was impressed with her restraint.

"But what if those folks are from the Order and have come to take you in?"

Duvan had considered that. "If they threaten us, we will kill them." He smirked. "Or knock them out, as the case may be."

"Why is the Order after you, anyway? Did you kill two

of their members, like Beaugrat said?"

Duvan shrugged. "I killed one of them because she and Beaugrat turned on me and tried to kill me," he said. "The other one was eaten by a manticore."

"Ugh," Slanya said. "So that's why the Order wants to take you in?" Slanya asked. "It seems like a lot of trouble for a misunderstanding."

"That must be it," Duvan said, although he suspected that Tyrangal was right: the Order of Blue Fire wanted him for his resistance to spellplague. Just like Rhiazzshar, they wanted to use him.

"Is there any other reason they'd be interested in you? Have you done anything to make them want to interrogate you?"

Duvan lied easily. "Not that I can think of."

"Don't you think it would be a good thing to find out? If you know what they want and who wants you, then you might be able to thwart their plans concerning you and avoid future incidents like the one this morning."

Duvan blinked at Slanya. "Why hadn't I considered that?" he said, his tone mocking.

Slanya recoiled from his sarcasm as though she'd been slapped. "You don't have to be an ass," she said. "I was trying to help, because frankly you seem to need some of it."

"Look, Slanya, I'm sorry." And he was too. He felt bad for lying to her. "There is very likely another reason that the Order wants me, but I don't talk about that reason to anyone. It's not personal."

"Maybe they're interested in why you're so lucky around the spellplague," she mused. "Like, how can you have been inside the Plaguewrought Land a number of times and yet you have no spellscar?"

Duvan sighed. She was going to figure it out sooner or later. "I am spellscarred," he said. "But my scar is completely hidden."

"Oh? What does it do?" Slanya asked.

"I can't tell you," Duvan said. "Like I said, I don't talk about it."

They walked along in silence for a while, before Slanya continued. "Well, regardless, I think you need to find out why the Order is after you."

"Yes, well, that sounds like a good idea, but I can't do it."

"What do you mean?" Slanya's eyes grew wide. "It's not that hard. You make a plan, ask some questions, do some counterspying. Maybe interrogate someone. It seems like you'd be good at those things."

Duvan snorted. "I don't even know where I'm going to be living two days from now. I *never* make plans past a tenday."

"By Kelemvor, why not?"

"Why think about anything long-term when I might be dead any moment?"

Sweat cooled on Slanya's neck as she walked next to Duvan. Gravel crunched beneath her leather boots, and she relished the shade provided by the large mote overhead. The fall morning had grown hot, but her sweat was more from nervousness than heat.

Slanya had always met challenges head on. She had always been able to make a quick and impartial assessment—a logical analysis of the obstacles in her path, acceptance of what she could not change. But she found that the prospect of going into the Plaguewrought Land was provoking an unusual reaction in her—apprehension and fear.

She tried to concentrate through this unfamiliar feeling. She concentrated on the conversation with Duvan. Here was someone whom she did not immediately understand, someone intriguing. Slanya sensed pain in Duvan's words. Real pain, not embellished or fabricated. Slanya suspected that he might even be downplaying the pain he truly felt behind the words.

She looked over at the young rogue, expertly picking a path up an ever-steepening rocky slope. "You *want* to die?"

"No," Duvan said. "Although sometimes I don't want to *live* either. But it doesn't really matter what I want, does it? I merely acknowledge the fact that we have a limited quantity of tendays. We all pass through the veil into death's realm sooner or later, and none of us know when that will be."

Slanya nearly winced. Such hurt and loss behind those words. She found herself intrigued. What was this man's story? Would he open up to her? "What happened to you?" she asked. "What led you to such a belief?"

"You have a different take on it, no doubt."

She sighed, allowing the sidestep. "I do," Slanya said. "And so do most people. We make plans about the future and strive to achieve goals. Do you have any ambitions?"

Duvan was quiet.

Slanya let him consider. She noticed that the group behind them had veered off to the east. So they weren't following them after all. Just some pilgrims heading to a different border spot. Slanya knew that there were several popular places for the pilgrims to go.

"My goals are all short-term. Eat, survive the day, share a bed. All immediate goals, except for the missions that Tyrangal sends me on; I have a long-term goal of repaying the debt I owe her, so I strive to achieve those missions."

"Do you owe her a great deal?"

Duvan nodded. "She would say that I owe her nothing. I certainly don't owe her any coin, but I am in her debt nonetheless. She saved me, freed me."

"I'm curious," Slanya said. "Why do you not make long-term plans? Don't you want to accomplish something big or build something—a family or a homestead even?"

"I just don't think about that."

"Why not?"

Duvan let out a laugh. "Because I've learned that making such plans is a waste of energy. Because I see no reason to plan or hope for something when it can all be taken away in a heartbeat."

Maybe the straightforward approach would work. "Duvan, have you ever told anyone about what happened to you?"

For a moment, she thought he might deny that anything had happened. But he didn't. He just stared at her, the muscles in his jaw clenched. "It wouldn't make any difference," he said. "It would just bring back the—"

Slanya jarred some rocks loose on the hillside, and they skittered down the steep slope. She caught her balance and waited, but Duvan had grown silent and would speak no more.

"It helps to tell someone you trust," she said.

Duvan snorted. "Perhaps, but that cuts the number of possible confidants for me to . . . let's see: zero!"

"I can see that," Slanya said. "I'm sorry."

"I don't need your pity."

Slanya sighed. Maybe if she reached out to him with something personal, then Duvan would be able to talk to her. Partly, she was curious about him because he was an enigma, a mystery. What had happened to make him so fatalistic and without hope?

And partly, she felt that despite their unfortunate first encounter, she enjoyed his company. He was challenging and fun to be around. Or maybe she just wanted to save him like she saved all her patients, helping them come to peace with their lives before they died.

She decided to trust him with her story. She would open up to him, and perhaps he would reciprocate. Confiding in someone was therapeutic.

As they continued their ascent of the long, stony slope,

Slanya told Duvan of her life before the monastery. She opened herself up to him, telling him of the hard life she'd had without parents, of living under the strict rule of Aunt Ewesia.

Under the warm afternoon sky stippled with hundreds of rocky motes flowing up and out of from the changelands like an inverse vortex, Slanya unraveled to him the story of losing Aunt Ewesia to the fire.

"I remember hating her," she said. "Not all the time, of course. But sometimes I did. Sometimes I wished she were dead. And after the fire, which I thought for the longest time was my fault, I regretted those feelings."

Duvan's black eyes narrowed on her, but he said nothing.

"She was my only kin," Slanya said. "I don't know what happened to my parents; Aunt wouldn't talk about it. So after the fire, I had no one."

Duvan listened intently without responding.

"Kaylinn and Gregor took me into the temple complex to raise me, and I've been there ever since." Slanya considered her next words. "The monastery was exactly what I needed—an ordered environment where the rules were always the same."

A gust of breeze carried the smell of carrion. The strong odor made Slanya wrinkle her nose. "I know that I wasn't a very well-behaved child at first; I hated everyone, and I felt guilty for not dying in the fire. I was headed on a track to become a criminal or an evil person before they rescued me."

Duvan was silent for a long stretch as they switched back to traverse across the slope on the opposite tack. The top of the long hill neared, the tenacious weeds and scrubby trees were all that remained sprouting here and there from the loose rock.

When he spoke finally, his tone seemed distant and overly harsh. "Can you remember details about the fire? What color was the nightgown you wore? What glass did your aunt use for her infusion? What did she say when she was on fire?"

Slanya said, "I don't see what those have to do with anything."

"Can you remember?" Duvan repeated.

Slanya's fists clenched, and she tried to see her memory in her mind's eye but couldn't. Why couldn't she? Surely she was wearing the same nightgown she always wore, but what did that look like? What about the other details; where had they disappeared to in the recesses of her mind? "I confess that I'm not sure," she said finally. "It'll probably come back to me eventually."

"I'm sure it will."

"I'm not lying," Slanya said, aware that she was being defensive. "And I don't know why you're asking me those questions."

"Listen," Duvan said, "I believe that you were in that fire. I think all of what you told me happened. But I've been through trauma, and it's never as clean as what you described."

"Clean?" Slanya was appalled. "You think that was clean?"

Duvan nodded. "Look, I would never diminish what happened to you by claiming it's not true, but to me, your story sounds polished, whitewashed."

"No, I—"

"That might be the healthy thing to do, Slanya," Duvan said. "Perhaps it's better than the alternative." His voice trailed off as if remembering something. "But it's not the truth."

"The truth," Slanya said, trying to calm herself and really consider what Duvan was saying. "That was what happened. That's how I remember it."

"And maybe you remember it like that in order to organize your feelings about that traumatic event. I did that for years, but it does no good in the long run."

Slanya bristled. "Perhaps the truth is in the stories we tell ourselves."

Duvan looked at her, his dark eyes filled with sadness. "The truth is that life cannot fit into organized structures and stories. The truth is that the world is wild, and above all, chaotic."

They rose above the crest of the hill just then, and the far side dropped away precipitously, sloping steeply down and down and down. Slanya's hold on the world loosened a bit at the sight, for there just ahead was the border veil—a gauzy, fluctuating wall that rose up into the sky.

Through it and beyond the cliff, Slanya caught a vision of a nightmare panorama—a world of flux and plasma, stretching off into the distant horizon. Blobs of earth and sky, of fire and crystal, fused and parted in a constant roiling dance.

That way lay madness, Slanya knew. And yet she was drawn to it, for here was raw wild energy. Here was the fire and the salvation.

Slanya dug into her backpack, removed one of the vials of elixir that Gregor had provided, and quaffed the entire contents. The oily liquid slid down her throat, and the strong taste of anise made her wince.

Duvan led her right on through the veil, and as she stepped willfully across the border behind him, part of her mind broke, her iron lock on an organized world cracked just a little, aching to dance with the forces of chaos ahead.

Duvan felt an electric prickle pass over his skin as he passed through the border veil and carefully picked his way down the incline. The slope here was steep, but at least it was passable without using rope.

In front of him, the land splayed out like an open, festering wound—a scar gushing otherworldly light and motion. The very bedrock was unstable, a dangerous undulation of earth and light.

Duvan couldn't help but be impressed every time he saw this awesome sight. The changelands were the most raw and widespread wild magic infection in all Faerûn. No wonder people made the pilgrimage here.

Duvan checked to make sure Slanya was close behind him. He derived no pleasure from arguing with her. And perhaps he was projecting his own hardships on her, but the way she told of her aunt and the fire—relaying the story as if by rote—and her lack of details, gave him the impression that she had told this story over and over until it had become her truth. It seemed too pat, too clean and ordered to be the whole truth.

What had she really gone through? he wondered. What had she really endured?

"We will need to stay close together for the rest of the journey," he said. "The instability of this place can uproot the earth anywhere, and we don't want to be separated."

Slanya nodded solemnly, clearly stunned by her first sight of the changelands.

Duvan considered saying something, but he refrained. He'd give her some time to adjust. He had visited the border numerous times, and the sight always brought him to his knees in awe. She should be allowed some adjustment time.

"I'm a little dizzy," she said.

"Don't look into the distance," Duvan suggested. "Too disorienting. Nobody is used to the solid ground in flux like this."

Slanya nodded.

"Pick a spot on the ground just ahead and focus on that," he said. "Glance up frequently to make sure there's nothing dangerous approaching, but always come back to the spot just ahead. That should help with the vertigo."

Slanya took a slow deep breath, her face waxy and sallow. "I'll try that."

The ground moved, started dropping ever so slowly. Abruptly, Slanya fell to her knees behind him. Clutching her gut, she vomited on the shifting ground.

This was going to be a long trip.

Climbing back up to her, the shale surface slipping under his feet, Duvan put a hand on her back. "You all right?"

"I'd say the answer to that is pretty obvious," she said, but her tone was wry.

"I hate to say this, but we have to keep moving. And this is just the beginning of this sort of thing. You can do this."

Slanya stared at him for a moment, focused her attention on him. Then she gave the barest hint of a nod. "Give me just a moment," she said. The ground shifted again, and Duvan found that he was already starting to get used to it.

A high-pitched screech pierced the air off to his right, and he glanced over to see a wave of spellplague ripping up the landscape. It seemed like the sound of the universe tearing. Gusts of foul wind laced with fume and needle-sharp rocks blew over them.

"I hope your moment is up," he said, yelling to be heard over the din. "We need to keep moving!"

He tugged Slanya to her feet, and she rose at his insistence. She followed him as he plunged down the slope, choosing a path perpendicular to the approaching wave. Her eyes were locked on the ground just ahead, and she'd gotten control of her breathing. Quite remarkable.

The blue shimmer passed by them like a ripple in the fabric of the world, a few body-lengths away. And in its wake, the ground lurched and buckled. The air crystallized and swirled in the vortex created by its passing.

Duvan gripped tightly onto Slanya's hand, determined not to let go. He brought his other arm up to protect his eyes. Tossed into the air by the heaving ground, they flew airborne.

He did not let go, and when the two of them came crashing down, landing hard and skidding down the slope, he still hung on. He was determined not to lose her. Tyrangal liked her, and despite her previous isolation from real-world issues, Duvan found himself concerned about her. He would do his best to protect her until their mission was fulfilled. He'd given his word.

They rolled down the slope and skidded to a stop next to a small patch of spellscarred bushes. How anything could grow in here always amazed him. And as he watched, the bushes doubled in size, then dried up, withered, and died.

The silence that followed left his ears ringing with the screech of the passing wave. And for the moment, they were in a small pocket of calm.

For the moment.

"You all right?" he asked, getting to his feet and brushing the rocks and debris from his hair.

"I think so," she replied. Her voice quavered at first as she stood next to him and took stock of herself. "Yes, I seem to be all here."

He laughed. "Corporeal unity—always better than the alternative."

She gave an amused snort. "Agreed."

"Let me see if you've got any splinters," he said. "The shards are so sharp they can be difficult to feel, and if left they'll work into the skin. You don't want that. Believe me, I know from experience."

"Good to know," she said.

And as he examined the exposed skin on her face, he discovered that he was touched somewhat by her story about being orphaned when her aunt had died in the house fire. Despite his dubiousness about the telling, Duvan felt sure there was a good deal of truth behind her story. Perhaps he understood her; he too had been orphaned.

Perhaps she could understand him.

He removed three shards from her face and neck. "Please check me," he said.

Her head was close, her measured and even breath on his face. She smelled of lilac soap.

She pulled a shard out then looked into his eyes. "I—I think that's all of them."

Duvan looked away, but the look of concern or connection or whatever it was that passed between them stayed with him. He'd only ever felt that kind of connection for one other person—his twin sister, Talfani.

This look was fleeting and perhaps only imagined after all. "We'll wear gloves and goggles and face scarves from here on in," he said, and he heard traces of anger in his voice. Anger at what? he wondered, but now that he was aware of it, he recognized that he *was* truly angry.

"Done," she said.

"Thank you."

"I owe you my life," she said. "I should thank *you*."

At her gesture of appreciation, he felt the anger well inside. Why did she have to be so kind? Why did he care so much?

It was infuriating.

In the privacy of his office, Gregor scratched absently at the white hair over his spellscar and stared at Vraith. "You seriously believe this young man could be . . . what did you say? 'A threat to your entire order'?"

Vraith gave a tight smile. She had sent her entourage into the courtyard while she and Gregor spoke of more sensitive matters. Kaylinn had excused herself. "I said he could be a threat to our operation—our plans for the ritual. It depends on what we discover about his powers."

"He seemed to me to be unconcerned with the affairs of the Order," Gregor said. "More interested in relatively petty activities, really. I wouldn't concern myself with him." Gregor didn't despise small-time thinkers, but he certainly had no deep respect for them either. He was going to make an impact on this world; he would achieve greatness. Of that he was certain, and those who had no aspiration for deep impact on the world—for greatness—deserved little respect.

"I don't take chances," Vraith said, her tone serious. "Not when it costs me almost nothing to avoid this risk. We need to discover if his ability is controllable and how much power he has over it. His power is a threat, and we need to determine how much it has the ability to derail our plans."

Gregor nodded. He didn't really care about Duvan as long as he got his plaguegrass. Though he did worry about Tyrangal's reaction if she learned of his complicity in helping the Order capture Duvan. He would have to do something to prevent her from finding out.

Still, it would not do to anger Vraith at this time. The Order of Blue Fire had its fingers in too many affairs in Ormpetarr. This situation would require finesse and diplomacy. Outright defiance had the potential for dire consequences.

"Duvan and one of our clerics left this morning on an important mission for me," Gregor said.

"Where did they go?" Vraith asked.

"The Plaguewrought Land."

"When—"

"And I am not certain when they will be back," he continued, cutting Vraith off. Gregor was growing annoyed at being treated like a subordinate. "But it will be no later than noon tomorrow."

Vraith frowned. "I'd rather not wait that long," she said with a sigh. "But I see that I will have to. Very well, I will send Beaugrat and a party to scour the border. When they come out, we will take them by force."

"I just need what they're carrying," he said. "They're gathering a vital component of the resistance elixir."

Vraith gave the slightest of nods.

"I would also like to have my monk, Slanya, unharmed and brought back safely. She deserves nothing less."

"We only need the rogue—Duvan," she said. "And your continued participation, of course, in the plans ahead."

Gregor nodded. "As long as we are in agreement about the plaguegrass and Slanya."

"We are."

A grin spread across Gregor's face. "Perfect," he said. "I am excited about the festival. As soon as Slanya returns, I will have everything necessary to manufacture a batch of the elixir—enough to accommodate the thousands of pilgrims necessary."

"Excellent."

"We have an agreement then," Gregor said. "Send your men after them, and you can do whatever you want with the rogue. I don't want to know about it."

Vraith snorted. "It's insincere to get squeamish on me now," she said. "I'm sure you've done worse to thousands of pilgrims by exposing them to experimental elixirs. We're just going to test the extent of his ability."

Gregor bristled. Vraith's comparison was unfair and grossly inaccurate. Not only would the results of his research save vastly many more lives that had been lost, but every single pilgrim who had taken his elixirs had done so *willingly*. Vraith was not offering Duvan a choice here.

Vraith gave a slight bow. "May the Blue Fire burn inside you." And without waiting for a response she turned and walked from the room.

Gregor followed. In the courtyard Vraith commanded her man, Beaugrat, to mount up and head out in search of

Duvan and Slanya, with clear instruction to return them both here to the monastery when he found them. "Do not let them escape," she said.

The sky lightened in the east just as they rode away south. Perhaps it was all for the best, Gregor thought. This way the Order would owe him a favor, and their partnership would be that much stronger. The arrangement would even be good for Slanya, because she'd likely get back faster and in more comfort.

In fact the only one who stood to lose from the arrangement was the rogue, Duvan, and his preferences mattered little in this. It was unfair, perhaps, but he would simply disappear, and for all important parties, that was for the best.

The only backlash for Gregor would be if Tyrangal learned of his involvement in Duvan's capture. He couldn't afford for the powerful woman to be his adversary. If only there was some way he could absolve himself of complicity in Tyrangal's eyes or mitigate her anger.

This was a delicate dance. Gregor hoped his skills were up to the performance of it.

Letting his anger fuel him, Duvan picked his way down the steep incline and deeper into the Plaguewrought Land. He kept silent, focusing instead on the task at hand: survival.

The bare rock of the landscape gave way to a grove of rapidly growing maples. Duvan picked a quick path through the grove. Saplings grew into trees, and soon they were arching overhead, branches budding green leaves, turning yellow, and then raining down in a vermillion shower around them.

Slanya looked up from the fixed point on the ground. "It's beautiful," she said.

"Stay close," Duvan said, breaking his silence. "It may

look beautiful now, but it could change into something dangerous at any time."

As they continued through, the trees aged around them. They shrivelled and died. Undergrowth of vines and bushes rapidly filled the space. Duvan took Slanya's hand and pulled her. Fueled by the remnants of the Spellplague, this undergrowth could easily grow fast enough to trap and suffocate them.

The pungent odor of decaying plants and humus rose around them like a palpable tide of death. Duvan headed left and up a slope that seemed to be rising as they ran. Leaves and rotting vegetation deepened until they threatened to suck the two down into the muck.

Duvan scrambled up the slope, finding footholds easily. Slanya seemed be struggling to match his pace, but she managed it—a fortunate thing. If they stopped they'd be trapped.

"Will you know how to get back out?" Slanya said.

Duvan nodded. "Of course I will."

Slanya followed him step for step as they snaked further into the changelands. He kept his eyes open for plaguegrass, but so far there was no sign of the elusive plant. Duvan marveled at the level of trust that Slanya put in him, amazed that she did not question his choices.

Perhaps her faith in the elixir was so strong that she felt protected. The thought of such blind trust in anything so experimental angered him, and he wanted to get her to question it. But he held his tongue. Even if it provided no additional protection from the changelands, at least it reassured Slanya and helped her avoid panicking.

Staying calm was critical in negotiating the dangers of the Plaguewrought Land.

Duvan took them over hills and through the rapidly shifting landscape. Spellplague was ubiquitous in here, all around them, but there were waves and pockets of blue fire, where its intensity was far higher. Duvan tracked these by sound and sight and smell, but also by feel. His stomach grew heavy when remains fo the Spellplague stirred like stormclouds, filling him with a gut-churning irritation.

"Can you feel that?" he asked.

"Feel what?"

"The spellplague—a flare of it is off to our right, moving toward us."

Slanya shook her head. "I have no sensation of it," she said.

"You'll become attuned to it," he said.

"I doubt it," she said. "If it were possible to attune myself to something like that, my training would make it simple for me to focus. You have a gift."

Duvan scowled at her and guided them away from the approaching wave of spellplague. It wasn't visible yet and seemed to be passing underneath them. Suddenly the fire changed direction and rose up toward them.

The earth heated up around them.

"Run!" But every way Duvan turned, he felt the blue fire. Finally, he stopped running and crouched next to Slanya. "It's all around us."

The sky darkened to a deep purple as the smell of burning rock smoldered into the air. The ground beneath their feet started to drift upward.

Slanya covered her ears as the screech of rock against rock crashed in on them. A spiderweb tendril of blue fire spun into existence around Duvan and Slanya.

"Stay close," Duvan said. "Do what I do." As long as she remained within about ten paces, his spellscar would keep her safe from the blue fire. And if she wanted to attribute that to Gregor's elixir, Duvan would just have to hold his tongue.

Duvan's stomach felt like lead, and the hairs of his back and arms stood straight up. The tendril of spellplague arced toward them, snapping like a whip . . .

And dissipated just as it was about to hit them, vanished like a puff of smoke in the wind.

The storm seemed to howl with frustration, and underneath them, the ground shifted. Another whiplash of spellplague struck at them. More gut churning, but now Duvan was moving. He didn't see what happened behind them as he led Slanya in a run away from the spellplague wave.

The earth beneath their feet lurched and rumbled as Duvan dodged the hottest flares. The tilting earth made him stumble, and Slanya fell to her knees behind him, but soon they were back on their feet and heading farther and farther from the surge of blue fire.

The ground seemed to be lifting slowly now, floating upward perhaps. They ran across a narrow patch of hot, dry desert, then down a trail into a shaded cleft. At the bottom of the cleft, Duvan led Slanya across a mossy creek, the rocks slippery from the green growth and dewy moisture.

He reached out to her, and she grabbed his hand. He did so at least as much for his own benefit as hers. The stream's water misted into the air like rainy fog around them, and for a moment they existed only in a white cloud, drenched and cold and unable to see. But her hand was still in his.

Together meant that she'd be safe. He'd promised to keep her safe.

Then the cloud gave way as they pushed through and up a short incline, emerging to sun and the smell of wildflowers. Warm breezes dried the dew from his forehead and neck as he led them into the tall grass of the meadow.

"Look," Slanya said. "This meadow is filled with plaguegrass!"

The grassy field ended abruptly, Duvan noticed, at a cliff. The shifting ground and the sensation of rising was clear now. They were on a mote, a large one to be sure. "Get as much as you can now," he said. "This meadow might not be here much longer. Beyond that edge there is nothing but a long fall."

Slanya's eyes widened as she gazed out over the rim of the cliff. The ground below, dotted with flares and wisps of blue and white spellplague, receded quickly. "By the gods, how do we get off of this?" Slanya said.

"We don't," Duvan said. "We're too far up now, and the plaguegrass is right here. We'll have to wait until it floats back down."

The mote they were on was a good three hundred feet above the rest of the land. And it was rising. Fortunately, it seemed to be heading toward a swath of the changelands that was relatively stable, for the moment. Duvan breathed a little relief; it looked like they'd have clear sailing on still waters, for a short while at least.

Ahead, however, they would run into trouble. If the mote stayed on course, it was headed directly into the center of the changelands. Still a good distance away, but definitely in their current path, was what Duvan recognized as the vortex of a spellplague storm.

A dark blue sky streaked with purple made the backdrop for a swirling whirlwind of destruction. Gossamer threads of white and blue entangled with flames of red and yellow in an angry and wild display of raw nature. It was beautiful and terrible, awesome and indiscriminately perilous.

And they were heading directly into it.

CHAPTER SEVEN

A hot, grassy meadow stretched out around Slanya, an illusion of peace in this landscape of unpredictability and turmoil. Beyond the edge of the meadow-mote, she knew the Plaguewrought Land boiled with the rising blue fire.

Still, the smell of flowers and the warm tranquility of the meadow in the hot sun lulled her. The peace of the here and now was a pleasant anomaly. A vision of how life could be, how life should be despite the larger landscape of danger and chaos. It was too easy to forget the world beyond—the world that would rapidly intrude without warning.

"It's going to be calm for a little while, I think," Duvan said, shading his eyes from the last rays of sunlight slicing down through the clouds and the constellation of smaller motes above them.

Looking over at Duvan, so confident and reassured amid the surrounding hysteria and flux, Slanya thanked Kelemvor for Duvan's presence. The man could be infuriating and pig-headed, but he was proving strong and knowledgeable. Indispensable. Slanya would be dead without him. Right now he was staring into the distance, his brow knitted in consternation.

Duvan's black eyes sparkled in the light. His broad nose and boyish face were at odds with the three-day beard and straggly mane of hair. When he turned to look at her, his gaze was gentle. "Gather up as much as you can while we have time," he said. "I'll try to figure out how to get us off this rock and out of here."

Slanya tried to quiet her mind, but in the recesses of her consciousness a little girl couldn't stop screaming. She needed the quiet seclusion of the temple to order her mind and regain control over her body. Or perhaps she just needed to surrender to the fire. Maybe she could let chaos overtake her, move inside her.

How good would it feel to give in and let all her control go? Could she abandon her hold on order and still survive? She had no real idea, but the temptation to lose control surged up inside her like never before.

Focusing on the ground in front of her, Slanya knelt down into the dewy grass. Her knees dampened from the moisture, and the heavy smell of grass and earth filled her nostrils.

Grab. Pull. Bag.

The long, translucent, yellow stalks came easily out of the ground, roots and all. Rich dirt clung to the rhizomes as Slanya shoved the grass into the magic bag of holding that Gregor had given her for carrying it. The bag would hold all the plaguegrass they'd need for a long while.

"How much time do we have?" she asked.

Duvan stood and looked out past the edge of the mote—the rim of which dropped off to the shifting ground far, far below. "Not sure," he said. "The good news is that we seem to be in an eddy of spellplague for the moment. It's not too strong or too fast."

"And the bad news?"

"We're heading away from the border and into the most intense blue fire I've ever seen."

Slanya let that sink in. She fought against the dread welling up inside her. Stronger changelands. Wilder and more chaotic—pulling them toward madness. Slanya was not afraid of death, but she did fear insanity. Accept what comes, she told herself, but the words rang hollow.

Grab. Pull. Bag.

The plaguegrass gave off a sweet smell when the stalks broke, reminding her of the herb garden back at the monastery. She used the smell and the manual labor as an anchor. Focus on the here and now, she reminded herself.

The last rays of the sun dimmed to darkness, and the blanket of night stretched over the sky above them. The high clouds overhead were thickening. Their gray bellies glowed blue and red, flickering with the reflection of the turmoil of the fires below.

Grab. Pull. Bag.

The repetition was calming. Slanya lost herself to the act of harvesting the plaguegrass. There was plenty of light to continue to work, and she was happy to lose herself in the rhythm of the task.

"I need food," Duvan said suddenly. "Need to figure out a way off this mote."

The edge in his voice was less than reassuring, but eating was a good idea. They needed energy to keep going.

Grab. Pull. Bag.

As she worked, Duvan gathered up what looked like dried wood and piled it up at the inner edge of the meadow. She wondered at first what he was doing, but it soon became clear that he was building a fire. What do we need a fire for?

she wondered. None of the food they'd brought with them needed to be cooked. A campfire was unnecessary—a waste of energy.

After about a half hour, she was finished filling the sack, her knees were soaked through, and her hands were numb and icy cold, covered with tiny scrapes from the sharp edges of the grass. Duvan's fire didn't seem so wasteful anymore.

Slanya stood up and brushed dirt and dry grass from her legs. She felt centered and focused for the first time since they'd entered the Plaguewrought Land. And famished.

"Come and eat something," Duvan said.

"Thank you," she said, walking over to the fire. She warmed her hands, relishing the tingle as the flames nudged away the chill from her fingers and palms. When they were sufficiently warmed, Slanya helped herself to the dried rations and fruit they'd brought and sat down on the ground across the small blaze from to Duvan. "I think we have enough plaguegrass."

Duvan nodded. He swallowed his bite, then said, "Good. Unfortunately, I don't see how we can get off this rock any time soon. Perhaps you should've hired a wizard instead of me."

Laughing, Slanya said, "No, I can see now that you were the clear choice. Despite your inability to magic us back."

"Well," he said, his dark eyes soft in the firelight, "we could be stuck on this mote for a long time."

Sitting there talking to him, the fire a warm glow next to them, Slanya felt herself relax. The searing screech of the heavens and the earth below faded to background, and all that mattered was the here and now. Her mind could contain this moment and make sense of it.

"Do you always assume the worst will happen?" Slanya asked.

Duvan smiled. "Yes, I suppose I do. In my experience the

worst is more likely to happen than the best, and it's far better to be prepared for the worst."

So cynical, she thought. But there was practicality in that way of thinking.

"For me, being stuck doing nothing is worse than death," he said.

"There's not much we can do right now."

"True, but if we're stuck up here for hours or days . . ." Duvan let the idea linger in the air.

There were scars on this man's soul, Slanya could see that in sharp relief now. But what had happened to him? He kept his past bottled up inside. How could he have turned out so bitter and jaded?

"The clerics and monks of my order sometimes spend tendays doing nothing more than meditation and training," she said. "Learning how to master oneself."

"I'm no cleric."

Slanya laughed. "Clearly," she said. "But my point was that perhaps you could learn something from me just as I have learned from you."

"As far as I can tell, I have taught you nothing."

"Well, you many not think so," Slanya said, "but your calm has helped me cope with the randomness of the changelands. While you may be a tempest in the city, you're like a rock in this stormy sea. Just being in here has helped me understand more about chaos—and fear it far more—than I ever have."

Duvan looked her, the lines of his face bunched in puzzlement. His eyes reflected the fire as the sky continued to darken overhead.

"I am intensely uncomfortable with so much chaos," Slanya continued. "But with your guidance, I have been able to stay sane in the midst of it. I consider that a gift."

Duvan seemed to absorb her words, but his face was impassive. His blank expression was neither questioning nor dismissive, as though he merely accepted what she had said, but had no opinion of it. At least not yet.

Slanya stared at this enigmatic man, his strong, dark features limned in the orange glow of the fire. She wanted to heal him if she could, help him heal himself.

"All right," he said. "Although it feels like a stretch to me. Now, what would you teach *me*?"

Slanya smiled. "Simple things at first—breathing and meditation. But with those will come mind balance and perhaps the discipline to confront your demons. The ultimate goal is peace with yourself."

Duvan frowned. "From where I stand, I don't see the benefit of inner peace."

She laughed. "Well, it's liberating. Healing your scars and wounds will help you resolve your past. You are a remarkable person, Duvan, capable of so much. But you are held back by . . . I'm not sure what—guilt or regret, perhaps? Discipline can emancipate you from that, by resolving issues instead of burying them."

Duvan's eyes narrowed. "And why do you care so much?"

It was an appropriate question and one that had already occurred to Slanya. "Balance," she said. "Because you've helped me."

Duvan seemed to accept that, nodding.

Looking across the fire, its temptation dulled at the moment, Slanya watched Duvan's dark shape. He was gazing into the glowing orange coals, his expression melancholy.

And of course he had saved her life. She had trusted him, and he had lived up to that trust. He had proved himself worthy. That too was a gift.

"What happened to make you so cynical?" she said.

Duvan remained quiet, but his expression in the firelight grew soft, pensive. And beneath, Slanya thought she detected some vulnerability, which was immediately endearing.

"By telling someone," she said, "by sharing your story with another soul who will not judge you but will simply listen and validate what has happened to you . . . by doing that you take the first step to resolving it."

"It can't be resolved away," Duvan said.

Slanya nodded, but she wasn't ready to back down just yet. "Maybe not, but talking about it can let someone else share the burden." She stared directly into his eyes.

He held her gaze for a moment then shook his head. "I can't lose it," he said. "And you don't want to share this burden. You have no idea what you're asking."

"Lose it?"

"This cannot be washed away," he said. "Like you've done with your past."

Slanya bristled at that. "I have not washed away anything," she said, then admitted, "Although it is possible that my memory of what happened isn't accurate. But then yours might not be either."

Duvan snorted. "And how would you know?"

"Exactly," Slanya said. "It's what we remember and the lessons we draw from those memories that are important."

"No disagreement there," he said.

She thought back to the fire in her aunt's house. There *was* more to the story than what she had revealed to Duvan, but even beyond that, some of her recollection of it was fuzzy, the details indistinct. That bothered her.

"To be honest," she said, "I don't remember everything about the night of the fire—about my Aunt Ewesia's death."

Duvan's dark eyes glimmered in the firelight. "I sometimes wish I didn't remember, but I can't help it."

Slanya shivered and moved a little closer to the fire. "What happened?"

"I don't want talk about it," he said.

"I will trust with you with my story," she said, "if you trust me with yours."

Duvan chuckled. "Convenient," he said, "since you don't even know your complete story."

Slanya smiled. "I will try to remember what really happened, but in any case, I never claimed the deal was fair."

Duvan's dark, grinning face reflected firelight for a moment before growing somber. And then, against the backdrop of the approaching storm—the sound and the fury of which surpassed every other phenomenon of Slanya's experience—he surprised her when he began telling his story first.

"Until I was ten, I lived in a small farming village with my father and my sister, Talfani. My mother had died giving birth to us. I never knew her. Talfani and I were inseparable."

Standing, Duvan brushed the dust from his leathers and walked around the fire. The sky had darkened to a midnight blue, laced with threads of vibrant purple and punctuated by occasional explosions of blue. He noticed that the mote had stopped rising, which was good because the air was already cold enough up this far. But they were still floating toward the 'plague storm, caught like a leaf in a whirlpool. And soon they would be in the midst of a spellplague storm as nasty as Duvan had ever encountered.

He knew well that the mote could descend any time so the best option was to wait.

For the moment.

"We lived in a small house on the edge of the village, next to our fields and the olive orchard we tended. Talfani and I shared a room and the chores, helping Papa with the fields."

The mote had found an island of calm in the turbulent sea of chaos. Over the edge, Duvan could see boiling destruction.

Explosions of molten rock and flickers of crisp blue magic punctuated the swirling plaguestorm. Pinpoints of light far, far below what could be ground level shone like stars in an upside down world. Perhaps he was seeing down into the Underdark.

"I was awakened one night by a light—a glimmer of the palest blue. There was the overwhelming stench of the plaguestorm, although I didn't know what it was at the time." Duvan turned to look at Slanya, "Do you know that smell— the rotten oranges and corpse odor—that only comes in late summer and fall?"

"Yes," Slanya said.

"I remember the smell vividly. I remember that it was the end of summer and the harvest had gone into full swing. Everyone was happy. Harvesttime was a good time for the village."

Slanya remained silent, listening attentively from across the waning fire. Her pale skin reflected red in the light of the campfire, and her fine features seemed frail against the violence of the storm. Slanya sat crosslegged with her hands resting in her lap, her sideknot hanging delicately by her ear with the end just touching her shoulder.

Duvan had wanted to tell someone this story—the true events of what had happened—for years. And he had tried a few times, but people *never* understood. People never wanted to understand.

Slanya seemed different in that regard. And perhaps his story could help her to realize that cynicism and mistrust was the only way to make it through life. She was far too trusting, especially of Gregor, who Duvan thought was vastly overestimating the efficacy of his precious elixir. Gregor was playing with Slanya's life and lying about it.

Duvan shook his head. There was nothing for it but to leap into the telling. Duvan had to just take the plunge if he was going to go there at all.

And with a deep, bracing breath, he did.

"I woke up Talfani—she could sleep through anything." Duvan gave a weak laugh, remembering. "Papa came in and told us to stay put until he returned for us. And if I had known that he would never come back, that I'd never see him again, I would've hugged him and begged him to stay with us.

"We waited for over a day for our father to return, waited until we were so hungry we had to have food. He had left me in charge. I was the elder, you see, by just a quarter hour. Talfani hated that. So I slipped out when she was asleep to go find food." Duvan paused. The fear and loss threatened to pour over him. He took a deep breath.

"Everything was destroyed," he went on. "Everyone was dead or had disappeared. The entire village brought down to rubble, except for the part of our house that was the bedroom I shared with Talfani. Deep ruts cut into the ground from where the blue fire had plowed under buildings and bodies. Nobody else had survived. All that I'd known was gone.

"I found food and returned to find—"

Duvan's voice broke, and he fought back the tide of emotion. He took a breath.

"Talfani had grown pale and sickly. She died over the next few days. I had a chance to say good-bye to her, but her slow, lingering death was agony for both of us. And when she passed, I had nothing left for myself. I just lay down next to her and hoped death would also come for me."

Duvan stopped pacing and stared into the red depths of the fire. "And I might've had the opportunity to meet your death god if a group of Wildhome elves who often came to trade with us hadn't been wandering near. They found me, cleaned me up, and took me to their settlement in southern Chondalwood.

"You'd think that living with elves would be wonderful, full of merriment and joy. The wood elves are remarkable and noble, fair and fey. But they are also extremely secretive and insular. For years, after I recovered from the physical trauma of what had happened, my life was good.

"I had everything I could want except my father and sister back. The elves took me in, not as one of their own, but as a guest outsider—*n Tel'Quessir*. I participated in their customs and rituals. I learned their ways, but I was teased mercilessly by my peers. There were things I couldn't do. But it was a life of luxury compared to my previous one. I often felt guilty for having survived encountering spellplague and ending up in an easier lifestyle.

"They taught me a great deal. How to climb. How to hide in shadows. How to move quickly through the forest and leave almost no trace. How to fight. I was not automatically adept at any of these things, but I wanted to fit, so I learned the skills as best I could, until I felt I had succeeded."

Slanya's gaze was riveted on Duvan as he spoke. Her face was somber in the firelight, as she waited for him to continue.

"If I had been paying attention to such things," Duvan went on, "I would have noticed that I was never allowed to go on any trips outside of Wildhome, except on the rare circumstance that the chieftain went abroad. And even though I was a ward of the clerics of Silvanus, I was required to go with the chieftain whenever he traveled.

"I was not at all sure why at the time, but they considered me good luck."

Duvan looked away from the fire. Their mote was still caught in a tightening spiral, moving toward a hurricane of spellplague. They were closing in on the storm's outer arms. Perhaps their path would miss the center completely. Perhaps they'd veer wide and slingshot back around. Only time would reveal that. Duvan predicted he'd know the answer in less than an hour.

"So when I was thirteen," he said, looking back to the fire, "the elven clerics of Silvanus, with the consent of the chieftain agreed that I would be invited to become a full adult member of their society. This was something I had been hoping for. I immediately accepted and was prepared for the flame-etch ceremony.

"The clerics created the symbol of a tree on my chest—nature and harmony with the trees and all that—representing Silvanus. They used metallic inks, blended with some materials that were supposed to attract the blue fire on the edges of the Plaguewrought Land, to etch the symbol on my chest.

"They spent days teaching me how to approach the spell-plague pockets. I needed to get close for the etching to work, but not so close that the spellplague would kill me.

"On the morning of the ceremony, I walked naked to the Plaguewrought Land border, searching for the white gauze. I found it easily and danced toward it, eager to have my scar and join the Wildhome elves as one of their own—or as close to one of their own as a n *Tel'Quessir* could ever be.

"But the edge of the changelands wouldn't reach out and burn the symbol of Silvanus into my chest as it should have. So I pressed in a little farther, toward bluer fire. And just then, a wave of intense spellplague pulsed along the border veil as it sometimes did."

Duvan took a breath, remembering the event like it had happened yesterday. "They screamed at me to run out. To dodge and flee. But I wanted to join them so badly. I couldn't figure out what had gone wrong, why my etching hadn't activated. All I could feel was my gut grown heavy and liquid.

"And then the surging wave of blue fire washed over me and blotted out the world. And in its wake . . ."

Duvan remembered the young elves and the elders yelling at him to run away. The fire would kill him or change him into a monster. He remembered feeling . . .

"Nothing," he said. "Nothing had changed. My gut slowly

returned to normal. My chest etching remained untouched by the spellplague, and I emerged unharmed.

"After that my life took a completely different course. A more treacherous and sinister course."

Slanya stared silently into the fire. Her own history of chaos flickered on the edges of her memory. Elusive.

She looked up, watching Duvan carefully as he paused in telling his story. He had packed and repacked their backpacks, had organized the firewood, and he kept looking out over the edge of the mote at the swirling vortex ahead. Now he paced, having nothing more to occupy his attention while he considered how to continue.

After a minute, Duvan went on, "They were surprised that I emerged from the Plaguewrought Land whole and untouched. And soon after, it became apparent that some of the elves were afraid of me. I was already a social outcast because of my race, but now I was alien.

"Boys and girls died during the fire-etching rituals. Not all, of course, but a goodly number. The rest were marked by the changelands—etched. Nobody came away untouched. It had never happened before.

"I found myself shunned. Friends I had worked so hard to make avoided me. Everyone whispered about me as I passed. They didn't know what to do with me. And then Rhiazzshar came to me and made everything right. She was a young priestess of Silvanus—very beautiful, very kind. She befriended me and held me while I cried in her arms. I was desperate for some affection, and she was very comforting.

"Rhiazzshar told me that the others were afraid of me, that they didn't understand why the changelands had had no effect. She wanted to know if I knew. But of course I had no idea. She said that we had to find out why so that we could convince the others that I was no threat. Then I would be accepted, perhaps even regarded as a hero.

"I asked her how I could do that, and she suggested I start by seeing what my limits were. How long can I resist the Plaguewrought Land? Is it just avoiding me, or am I impervious to it?

"I considered what she said, but I was afraid to try any of that. She held me and said it was all right."

The emotion in Duvan's voice tore at Slanya's heart. Rhiazzshar had clearly meant something to him. She also realized that Duvan was revealing a great secret about himself. His ability to avoid the effects of the changelands wasn't luck at all, and it was only partially rooted in knowledge. If what he had told her was true, Duvan was resistant to spellplague.

Around them, the sound of the storm had grown—a keening, scratchy wail, like an orchestra of sand rubbed on tin, punctuated by the booms of earth cracking apart and smashing together. It was close now, and Slanya needed to not think about it. So far, this mote had been drifting through a patch of calm, but it felt like it could pass into the storm at any moment.

"I fell in love with Rhiazzshar. She was my coming-of-age, really. After my failed fire-etching ceremony, she and I spent all our free time together, mostly isolated from the others. And the elders allowed it, which I suppose should have given me warning signs. But I was blissfully in love.

"Finally, one day, lying in bed after making love together, she convinced me to go back through the border veil. To be fair, I wanted to know what the limits of my ability were. But I wouldn't have gone without her encouragement.

"At first I just went in for a minute, and then it was two, then five, until I was remaining inside the border of the changelands for an hour or longer, just coming out when

I got so tired I couldn't see clearly. And while the blue fire didn't seem to be able to touch me, exposure to it made me exhausted.

"Every time when I would come out of the Plaguewrought Land, Rhiazzshar would hold me, caress me, and make love with me. We got into a cycle, and eventually I started to suspect she was manipulating me. I didn't see it for such a long time. A woman like that can blind a man. Plus she was my only friend, and if she wasn't really my friend, then I had no one. That prospect was too terrible to believe.

"I had to know for sure. So I decided to stop going in. I hadn't tested the full limits of my spellplague resistance, but I knew enough to be content for a while. Rhiazzshar wasn't happy with that decision. At first she tried to persuade me to keep learning more about my abilities, and when I refused, she tried harder. Her methods of persuasion were very enjoyable." Duvan laughed wryly. "But when it became clear to her that I wasn't going to keep testing myself, she changed. She told me that she wished it hadn't come to this, that our pleasant fantasy could have continued indefinitely. But the safety of Wildhome and the Chondalwood was paramount. They needed to understand my ability fully. They needed to make sure I was no threat, and to find out how they could use me to protect them.

"At first I was hurt. Betrayed. But I didn't fully comprehend the extent of the betrayal until later. My life changed completely yet again. Rhiazzshar kept coming to see me, but we were no longer lovers. I learned that she had been keeping a record of my excursions in the changelands—a log of my exposure.

"The experiments continued every tenday or so. They put me in a cage and pushed it across the border then left it there—longer and longer each time, until I was inside the cage swallowed by the Plaguewrought Land for three days."

Duvan gritted his teeth in firelight. "Rhiazzshar said she

was sorry. She said she still loved me, but that she loved her people more. She came to me several times. And at first I just wanted company, I needed caring, and so I accepted her. But over time, I hardened and grew jaded, cynical, and solitary. She never offered again.

"About a year later, I think, a burst of blue fire destroyed part of the cage. I had learned how to control my ability, just a little. Some things near me are protected, and with practice I had learned how to extend or shrink the area within limits. I shrank it as much as I could and huddled in a corner of the cage, and when the wave of spellplague came near me, it vaporized the opposite side of the cage.

"I walked out and into the heart of the Plaguewrought Land, straight into the hell that you've now seen with your own eyes." He gestured toward the center of the storm vortex that they drifted toward.

Slanya wiped away a tear and felt the urge to reach out to him, to offer some comfort, but she didn't know how. The fire had died down, but Duvan stoked it with more wood. Slanya was glad; the air was chilly this far up.

"That journey across the changelands was a nightmare. I was alone. I was weak. I was confronted with an unknown chaos. Once again, I didn't care if I lived or died. Quite frankly, I expected to perish."

Duvan paced at the edge of the halo of firelight. "But an unexpected thing started to happen; I started to feel the faintest stirrings of hope. I had escaped my long captivity. Perhaps I could remain free. Perhaps I could reinvent myself. I had no idea how I would accomplish that, and it seemed so distant, so remote, that it was nigh impossible. But that dim ray was still there and growing stronger each day I survived.

"Several times I nearly fell through the perforated fabric of the world and into the Underdark. Ultimately, however, I made it across. I was scraped up from a number of falls, and bruised from many a battle with the changelands, but otherwise whole."

Duvan gave a wry laugh. "After I passed out of the Plaguewrought Land, I was starving and weak, so parched that I nearly died of thirst. And ironically, it was a group of feral elves who found me. They gave me food and water. They had been searching for me, so they could take me back to Wildhome."

"Oh, no!" Slanya blurted out. Her chest hurt in sympathy for him. "I'm so sorry." It had been a long time ago, but she understood that level of futility. She understood. She'd spent a long time planning to escape from her aunt, only to be caught again once she did, returned home, and punished with beatings.

Duvan stopped his pacing and glanced at her. "Thank you," he said. "When I realized who had found me, I lost all hope. And frankly, I started looking for opportunities to end my life." He began pacing again, like a caged beast, at the edge of the firelight.

Slanya was silent, staring at the deep orange-red glow of the coals, watching the occasional spark fly on the waves of heat up into the sky. Suicide was not anathema to her. Kelemvor wasn't unambiguously opposed to it. Under the right conditions, a life could be ended voluntarily and by choice. Still, in her philosophy those circumstances were very narrow.

"The elf group camped on the edge of the Chondalwood for several days, waiting for me to recover a little before taking me back to the forest city." Duvan's voice seemed to drift out of the darkness. "However, early on the second evening someone came with a group of armed fighters—Tyrangal and her Copper Guard.

"Tyrangal had gotten news, she told me later, of a human who was resistant to the plagueland's effects. She had spies in Wildhome apparently. And while she hadn't been prepared to take on the entire elven city, she was perfectly willing to go up against a small reconnaissance group. The elves were charmed by her golden tongue. They were also afraid of her, so they eventually left without me.

"Tyrangal took me back to her mansion and offered me a place of distinction in her organization. She offered to continue my training: weaponry, woodcraft, mastering my spellscar. She helped me in so many ways. I had never met anyone like her.

"I stayed for several months before testing out my freedom. Tyrangal had told me that I could come and go as I wished, but she had also made the argument that she could protect me more effectively if I stayed close. Eventually I needed to make sure I really was able to leave."

Duvan approached the fire with some more sticks. He started breaking them and setting them on the dying fire. "She let me go," he said. "I wandered for months, mostly thieving to make my way. But I was on my own! I was anonymous and not bound to anyone. I traveled north from port to port for the better part of a half-year.

"Eventually I returned on my own, and Tyrangal welcomed me back. She said that she had a job for me, that it would be challenging and lucrative. Would I take it? Obviously, I accepted. I've been with her for a few years now, but I am free to make my own choices, and the benefits have been quite substantial."

Duvan stood in silence for a while, staring into the fire, his story seemingly at an end.

Duvan's tale had brought back cascades of memories for Slanya. Her own childhood had been filled with manipulation and horror. Aunt Ewesia had not only been strict, she used to change the rules arbitrarily and punish Slanya when she broke them.

Slanya understood what it was like to never be able to win. She had never known when she was doing something that would get her the strap or the paddle or the hot iron on the backs of her thighs. Slanya shuddered with the remembrance. How could she have forgotten about that?

"Thank you for sharing your story with me," she said.

He gave her a solemn nod.

"Now, I can help you share your burden."

Duvan glanced up at her. "What?"

"What you've been through was horrific," Slanya said. "But you don't have to be alone with your pain."

"Exactly how can you help share my burden?"

Slanya sensed danger in his tone but felt she should explain. "I can sympathize with what you went through."

The keening of the storm suddenly grew louder, and wind gusted around them. Blue The gauze of clouds above flickered blue. The storm was closing in on them.

Duvan seemed unfazed. "You think you understand what I went through by hearing me tell it?"

"No, I don't *fully* understand," Slanya said. "But I do know you better. And I feel confident that if you'd met different people after the attack on your village—if you'd met people who had nurtured you instead of exploiting you—you would have been able to trust them and they would have taken care of you."

"And what? Losing my twin sister to a spellplague storm would've been easier for me? Finding out my true love was using me would have been all fine?"

Slanya knew the question was a trap, but by Kelemvor she was *right* in this. "No, but living with those losses and betrayals would have been less traumatic."

Duvan's sadness had grown into full anger now. "You think everything can be solved by order and a society based on trust, but it can't. Some things can't be solved."

Slanya was about to say something but a loud crack from the plaguestorm filled the air. There was a brilliant flash and when her eyes adjusted to the light, Duvan was gone.

No, there he was, walking away. She watched as he strode out of the light cast by the fire and passed into darkness.

Into the storm.

The air rang like a thousand tiny bells around Duvan. He didn't know where he was going and he didn't care. He just needed to get away for a moment. He needed to escape Slanya and her persistent prodding, her false compassion.

He needed to escape his memories.

There was a reason he'd never told anyone the full story. He couldn't bear to remember it. He felt guilty for surviving the attack on his village. And he hated himself for succumbing to Rhiazzshar's manipulation.

Talfani's face, ashen and hollow, filled his mind. Her green eyes dull from fever and milky from the burns. That was how he remembered her—how she haunted him.

Where did you go, 'Fani? Duvan had hoped for years that she had gone to a good place in her next life, but the more he saw of the hardships that the gods allowed to happen, or—if some were to be believed—even caused to happen, Duvan was more and more convinced that there was no hope of anything better after life. Nothing but the end of living. Death was perhaps not a door at all, but an end.

Duvan fought the urge to run. He wanted to flee straight into the storm, until the storm grew so intense that it took him finally, or until he fell off the edge of the mote. Death, whether it was nothingness or something brand new, would be a welcome relief from this agony.

At least perhaps he wouldn't know what he had lost then. Oblivion would be an improvement.

But he did not run. He did not flee. He couldn't get too far from Slanya. Even now, as he circled the camp, hiding in the shadows, he made sure that he was still close enough to shield her from the blue fire.

A gossamer blade of spellplague sliced up the ground right in his path, approaching like a fiery scythe harvesting the sick earth. Duvan ducked his head and clutched his roiling gut. His stomach grew heavy and seemed to melt as the wall of blue fire passed over him.

He felt nothing in its wake.

The night swirled around him—a maelstrom of power and light, underwritten with a cacophony of violent grunts and belches as the land itself groaned with pain. The wild magic was angry tonight, and the universe protested.

Duvan tripped and fell forward. He instinctively tucked and rolled, coming back to his feet. He took a moment to steady himself and regain his balance on the undulating stone. Part of the mote had fallen away here, and he now stood at the very edge.

Far below him, the blackness of the Underdark yawned. The land was perforated by hundreds of holes, the spaces created by a haphazard lattice of solid land and drifting motes the size of cities.

Spellplague tore the universe in twain here at the center of the changelands. For that was where they were, certainly. Duvan had never been here before, to the place where it was said that the gods themselves could not come without fear, and that pantheons of darkness battled those of light.

Duvan didn't know what to believe. He knew with certainty, however, that were he to take one more step and hurl himself into the abyss that he would die and would bid farewell to the pain of living.

But so too would Slanya die. Almost certainly, she would not make it back out of the changelands alive without his protection. And Duvan had made a vow—a promise to guide her and protect her if he could. He had told Tyrangal he would do his utmost to keep Slanya safe.

Slanya had gotten to him, he realized suddenly. She had cared and had offered to hear his woes. And he had trusted her, just for a moment, and that moment had felt wonderful. That moment had dissolved in a flash, but he was happy to have had it.

Duvan took one long, slow breath.

And yet, Slanya was no Rhiazzshar. She could not really understand him. Her assertion that she could sympathize was too dangerous to entertain. But she wasn't malicious. She wasn't manipulative.

He exhaled.

Slanya was being a friend.

Duvan knew then that he couldn't abandon Slanya. That she cared for him was part of it, but more than that, he felt connected to her. She didn't understand him half as well as she thought she did, but despite their short time together, she knew him better than anyone else in all of Faerûn. She knew him, and she still wanted to help him.

Duvan carefully took a step back away from the edge of chaos. He turned and looked back toward the campfire, at Slanya's silhouette huddled by the flames looking around, no doubt for him.

He knew he should get back, but he needed a few more moments alone. Just a little longer. To calm himself.

Abruptly, a wave of nausea washed over Duvan. His stomach lurched and grew heavy. Suddenly blue flames lit up the ground and air, stirring both like a titanic, prowling beast, waiting to strike.

Duvan saw Slanya glance around her, frantic, like frightened prey. She didn't deserve this. He had to make sure she was safe.

Spellplague struck the ground under him. Like thousands of earthworms, tendrils of blue gauze ate away the earth beneath him. The rock crumbled and fell away.

Duvan fell. Holes opened up in the mote's foundation. Through them, he could see the air beneath the mote. He dived toward what looked like solid ground to his left.

When he hit the rocky earth, he tucked and rolled, somersaulting back to his feet. Duvan used the momentum to run. Behind him, the blue fire chewed the ground like meat. A short burst of speed, and Duvan found himself on safer ground, at least for the moment.

Panting, Duvan got his bearings. Where was he? Was he actually safe? Yes, seemed to be for the moment. Good.

Where's Slanya? he thought.

Abruptly, dread filled him. His flight to safe ground had taken him away from the campfire. Slanya was far outside his protection now. With the plaguelands erupting so close, she was sure to be exposed. And that much exposure could easily kill her. He needed to get back.

He needed to get back *now*.

After Duvan disappeared, Slanya instinctively moved closer to the fire, not for warmth but a need for protection. She knew that the fire could not protect her from anything in the spellplague storm, but it felt safer.

Spellplague lit up the air around the camp. Like a spiderweb, strands of magic hung glowing in the air. The small cocoon that had been their camp grew smaller and smaller until Slanya felt the universe coming apart around her.

Chaos.

Tiny filaments of shimmering magic sliced through the air and the ground and the haversacks. And Slanya. In their wake they left a vortex of randomness. There was no pain as they cut through her, only the sensation of dissociation between her mind and her body.

The pain only came in the aftermath, in the wake of

turbulence caused by the crystals. And when it came, it started small—a pinprick on her shoulder and a tiny burn on her toe. But then there was another and another, each small, but adding to the others until she was besieged with a thousand pinpricks, ten thousand tiny burns.

Duvan would return. She had never seen him so angry, but she felt strongly that he would come back, that he would not leave her alone. Although even with his ability, what could he do against anything this intense? She did not know, but his companionship would be a comfort now.

Slanya had been trained to focus her mind, to use the power of her thoughts against material pain, and she tried to use it now, tried to concentrate to keep the unity of her body and mind. But in the wake of each filament, the onslaught of pain made it impossible to focus, and her mind grew disoriented.

The elixir would protect her. Gregor's concoction would keep her alive through this. She had to trust him.

She did trust him. Didn't she?

The last segment of her right pinkie finger spun away like a tiny fleshy mote. She watched it in silent fascination. This time there had been no pain when the churning magic had severed it from her hand. And as she looked down now, she wondered in amusement at the blood.

So unpredictable. So incomprehensible.

Screeching leather on steel filled the air, and Slanya was suddenly upside down, floating. How was it possible? It was as though the storm had picked her up and was examining her like a trapped insect before squashing her. Slanya found herself floating toward the campfire, which had grown to the size of the monastery funeral pyre. Blue mist and white fog burned gauzy sheets across her vision.

Was it her imagination or did she smell burning bodies? An intricate weave of palest blue gauze blanketed the camp, permeating all things. Slanya could not help but breathe it in—inhale disease and exhale fire.

The rational, objective part of her mind knew that this was too much exposure. Pilgrims to the changelands tried for the briefest of touches—a kiss of spellplague, an oblique lash of blue fire.

But this . . . this was like bathing in it. Drawing it in, spellplague permeated her whole being, and she could not run. She could not escape or withdraw. She had to endure, merely endure the choking and the disintegration.

The campfire's yellow and red flames belched black smoke as they beckoned to her. Give in, they said. Abandon reason.

Slanya listened. Why not? She had lost, so why not embrace the changelands? Twisting in the air as she floated, Slanya danced. Whirling and spinning and throwing herself in writhing, acrobatic circles, Slanya took in the pain and the chaos. It was the true power of nature, and she could not force it to make sense. She felt her mind unhinge, and she did not care.

If Kelemvor meant for this to be her time, then she would celebrate.

Slanya watched, detached, as she reached into the fire with her maimed hand and moved the flames. Her arm lit up and with amusement she waved it around in her dance. The entire camp was ablaze in glorious yellow and red, with constellations of tiny blue electric balls unraveling pale strands throughout Slanya's personal sky.

Abruptly, her world went dark, and Slanya felt herself falling . . . falling.

Was death coming?

She wondered if she should be afraid. Most people were afraid of dying.

In fact, Duvan was the only person she'd ever met who did not fear dying. Where had he gotten to?

The truth was that at this moment, Slanya had no fear. Something told her that she was ready, that she had prepared for death, and that Kelemvor would have a place for her in the City of Judgment.

Blackness and silence filled her senses until she knew no more.

CHAPTER EIGHT

Slanya!" Duvan yelled into the swirling darkness. He forced himself to sprint, back toward the campfire. Fear of what he would find clamped down on him as he ran. Swirling wind and dust pelted him with needle sharp fragments of stone. Pale blue threads lit up the night around him like ball lightning, itching at the periphery of his sight.

Duvan sped back the way he'd come. Or so he thought. It seemed to be taking too long to find the camp. The changelands were tricky and shifting. Rule number one was to never separate. He shouldn't have left the fire.

But she had made him so angry. Nobody can understand what it was like to lose a twin like that. If he'd stayed with Talfani, maybe she'd be alive now. It was his fault that Talfani was gone.

Just as it would be his fault if something had happened to Slanya.

Duvan slowed his frantic, headlong crashing through the swirling darkness. "Slanya!" he screamed. "Slanya!"

But no answers came through the howling wind. No voices reached his ears, save the growling, mocking laughter of the storm.

Maybe I've lost her too, he thought. Maybe I've given her to the storm.

Ribbons of blue fire seared the air around him, but none touched. In the flashing, eldritch light Duvan caught sight of red embers and the square shadows of two backpacks in the blackness.

He ran toward the fire, stumbling over a dark lump. "Slanya!"

She lay motionless and silent, curled into a fetal position on the rumbling ground at his feet.

"Slanya?" he gasped. "Slanya, can you hear me?"

She said nothing in response, but he saw that her body started making gentle rocking motions. "Alive," he breathed quietly. "Alive."

But when he saw the web pulsing inside her like veins of blue light, he gasped. Not again, he thought. This is not happening again.

Duvan had lost one soul under his care to spellplague, and it had devastated him. It had, in fact, defined his life. And even though he knew that to be true and knew that he should move on, he could not simply shed his guilt and his responsibility. His failure had led to Talfani's death, and now it would result in Slanya's.

No, he told himself. No, it would not.

"Slanya," he said, not sure if she could even hear him. "I'm going to get us out of here if I can. If we stay here you will surely die, and I won't let that happen."

The gentlest hint of a nod from Slanya indicated that

she'd heard him. He took quick stock—she looked physically whole. There were no major wounds he could see. There was blood coming from her right pinkie finger where it had been cut at the last knuckle.

Duvan grabbed a bandage from his pack and strapped it around her finger. It would help stop the bleeding, at least. That was the only part of her condition that he had any treatment for.

Tiny, translucent blue stars of magic twinkled at hundreds of points on Slanya's skin. But Duvan could do nothing to address it. Slanya would have to mend herself. Duvan found himself hoping that Gregor had not been lying, that his elixir would save Slanya from the funeral pyre.

He quickly assembled their things, stowing all of Slanya's gear inside his own backpack. He would also have to carry her, he knew. They had to get out of the Plaguewrought Land before Slanya grew any worse.

"I am going to carry you," he said. "We're just going to the edge of the mote for now. I have to see where we are and where we're headed."

Duvan put his pack on backward so that it rested on his chest instead of his back, then lifted Slanya across his shoulders and stood up. She was larger than he was but weighed about the same.

The rim of the mote was no more than forty or fifty paces away, but he didn't want to take the chance of losing Slanya. When he reached the edge, he lowered her to the ground and stared out at the maelstrom.

Their mote seemed to be caught in an ever-tightening vortex, spiraling down.

Duvan watched another mote ahead of them reach the center of the vortex and plunge down abruptly and disappear into the fabric of the land.

Time to vacate this mote, Duvan decided. But how?

He considered the glideskin in his backpack. If he'd been

alone, using the glideskin might have been ideal for flying off this rock and drifting down on the gentle winds. But he wasn't alone and the winds were far from gentle. Slanya's weight in addition to his own would be too much for the glideskin to hold for long, even in ideal conditions. This storm was far from ideal, and falling here would mean death, or worse, surviving and landing in the Underdark.

An entire realm of vile and hostile creatures, the Underdark could be more dangerous than the Plaguewrought Land. Duvan had heard enough from Tyrangal to know that he did not want to go there, ever. Armies of drow elves, cities of mind flayers, hungry beasts—even Tyrangal wouldn't travel the Underdark. Duvan and Slanya would never make it back to the surface alive.

Duvan had failed Slanya once already, like he'd failed Talfani years ago. But this time he was going to get her some help in time to save her. He liked Slanya, and he wasn't going to let her die.

Duvan looked out over the distance and watched for opportunities. In the purple and blue light, Duvan saw patches of what looked to be relatively solid land masses below. They might be able to lower themselves down with a rope.

No—a quick calculation showed they were most likely too high up for that. At the limit of their rope, they'd still have a long fall. Too long to survive, even with the glideskin.

Then an idea came to him. It was incredibly risky and would take exacting timing, but with luck and skill it could be accomplished. Every few minutes, a smallish mote would shoot across the storm, its trajectory bent by the pull of the vortex.

The fastest motes avoided getting caught by the vortex. Instead they sped out of the center and into calmer sections of the Plaguewrought Land.

Duvan didn't know if he could do it, but catching any

one of those fast motes would probably be safer than staying where they were. The mote they stood on was destined
to be crushed and torn apart while being hurled into the
Underdark. Not his first choice.

Lying down next to Slanya, Duvan used leather straps
to secure the cleric to his back. She was heavy enough that
the straps would leave marks in her skin. But it was the
only way he could move her.

When she was as secure as he could make her, Duvan
struggled to his knees and then pushed up to his feet. Breathing hard and feeling the burn in his legs and back, Duvan
went about the business of scanning the sky for incoming
motes. He tried to find one big enough to hold them, but that
also would fly close enough to theirs so that they'd have a
chance of crossing to it.

A short wait later he found a prospect arcing across the
plane of the vortex like a comet. It was larger than many
of the others, but far, far smaller than the one they were
on now. It might be moving too fast, but Duvan knew they
had few options.

First however, they'd have to move. He watched the
smaller mote's trajectory and tried to estimate the rotation
of their current mote. They needed to be on the opposite
side of their mote.

Duvan checked to make sure the leather straps holding
Slanya were secure and tight, then he began the trudge out
across the rock. Most of the vegetation had been stripped
off by the storm, so it was a little easier to move, but the
flashes of light made it hard to see holes and jutting stones.
Duvan caught his foot on a rock as he ran—he stumbled.
He struggled to keep his balance and sank to his knees.

Slanya groaned in his ear. A good sign. She was still
alive, at least.

But he did not fall. Duvan smelled the iron tang of blood
mingled with the faint odor of lilac soap from Slanya's skin.

He recovered his footing and pushed. Hopefully there was still time.

The smaller mote was almost to them by the time he reached the other side. He was still pulling out the rope and grappling hook when it whizzed by and disappeared into the distance.

Chagrined, he watched the mote vanish. One chance gone.

The night wore on, and it looked as though they would have no choice but to ride their mote through the vortex, when he saw another possible opportunity. This time a very small mote hurtled toward them. Tiny, Duvan thought, but perhaps large enough. This one was traveling very fast.

It's not like we have a surplus of options, he thought wryly.

Duvan predicted that this tiny mote would pass by extremely close. No need for him to carry Slanya very far this time. He took a couple of narrow leather strips from his backpack and lashed the wrists of his fingerless leather gloves so that they wouldn't slip off his hands. The gloves might just save his palms.

Then he readied his rope and grappling hook. The other mote would pass below them, so he lowered the rope down and swung it so that, as the speedier mote passed by underneath, the hook would catch.

The rope sped through his glove-clad palms. "Time to go," he whispered to Slanya. "Our coach has finally arrived." Duvan tightened his grip on the rope as he watched it draw taut. Even so, his arm nearly ripped from its socket as the rope pulled him and his burden—Slanya and pack and all— over the edge of the mote.

Wind blasted his face as they fell, his hands sliding on the accelerating rope. Duvan gritted his teeth and held on with all his strength. Even through the reinforced leather of his gloves, he felt the heat of the rope. Finally, just when he thought his strength would give out, they came to a stop, swinging like a pendulum beneath their new mote. They sped through the loud and chaotic night.

Duvan folded his legs and feet around the dangling rope, entwining himself with it so that he could use his legs to hold them while he rested his arms and hands. The leather straps that held Slanya's unconscious body to him chomped deep gouges in his shoulders, but he could hardly feel that over the burn in his hands.

Taking quick stock of their situation, Duvan realized that they couldn't remain where they were for very long. They were flying through the sky, tethered by a black filament of rope three hundred feet below the mote. Even if Duvan could hold them there for the duration, the chance was great that they'd slam into something—the ground or another mote or who-knew-what.

So after a few minutes' rest, Duvan stretched his thumb muscles. He laced his fingers together and cracked his knuckles. He could climb anything on his own, but this load was unlike any he had borne before. He massaged his palms, alternating between the left and the right until much of the burn and ache had receded for the moment.

When he was ready, Duvan started climbing. Hand over hand, he ascended the rope, using his entwined legs as support. Slanya's body was canted awkwardly, slightly off-center and heavier on his left side. His muscles burned from the effort, especially his left shoulder.

"We're going to make it," he said, not sure if he was trying to reassure Slanya or himself. Wind dried sweat on his face as he climbed. Far below, the ground was a dark expanse illuminated in patches by dim blue fog. It seemed mostly solid to Duvan.

Above them, past the small, dark silhouette of the mote at the top of the rope, the black and purple sky was cleaved in twain. Through the gash flowed a swirling hurricane of blue galaxies and fiery red motes of fire. Pure chaos and the Nine Hells could not have been more frightening.

It took over an hour and several rest stops along the way, but finally Duvan was able to pull himself and Slanya up over the ledge and onto the stone surface of the mote. There was just enough level ground for them both to fit lying down.

Duvan made sure that Slanya was fully on solid earth, then he tied the rope around them and collapsed. And as exhaustion took hold of him, he realized that they were headed back north toward the border, roughly in the direction of Ormpetarr.

"I did it," he said. "I got us off that mote."

Slanya said nothing in response, and perhaps she was already dead, strapped to his back. But for now, he was too exhausted to do anything but lay there with the grit of gravel against his cheek, and stare out at the approaching horizon.

They were far from safe, he knew. But at least they still had a chance. At least, for the moment, they weren't in imminent danger of being sucked though a hurricane of blue fire and vomited into the Underdark.

Duvan knew there was a huge array of things that could still go wrong, and that he should get up and start dealing with them. But he was too exhausted to move. Too tired to even think about moving. Those problems would have to wait their turn.

He needed to rest. And if something killed them while he was recovering, then so be it. Duvan closed his eyes as his exhaustion overcame his pain and pulled his consciousness down into the sweet dark numbness of oblivion.

Gregor felt the last drops of the thick liquid on his lips and swallowed. The oily potion tasted of bloodbark and lavender. He immediately found the small cot in the corner of his lab and lay down on it.

In moments, his awareness was out of his body, slicing through vaporous walls and ghostly objects. The magic of the potion allowed him only limited time, but his awareness could move fast.

Gregor's awareness moved past the throngs of pilgrims in their tents and wagons and through Ormpetarr's city walls. He skirted the thoroughfare, noticing that the veil on the border of the Plaguewrought Land was milky and opaque in his mind vision, like a cataract.

Gregor moved away from the border, back out of Ormpetarr, and up the hill to the ruins outside Tyrangal's mansion. There was a haze surrounding parts of the burned-out structures.

The hard stone of Tyrangal's mansion was woven with a magical latticework of some sort of warding—protection from clairvoyant spies and extraplanar intruders. Gregor admired the order of it, the beauty of the perfect crisscrossing web of shining copper light.

No matter. He had done this before.

Gregor pushed his awareness up to the entrance and focused. *I seek audience with you, Tyrangal*, he said through his mind. *I have important news.*

A small opening formed in the latticework of protective magic, and Gregor's awareness moved inside.

Tyrangal seemed to uncoil in front of him like an elegant and shining metal snake. The form she had chosen to display to him was difficult to identify, so brightly did she shine. But her movements were sinuous in the smooth way she turned and rose to face him.

Gregor felt, more than saw, Tyrangal's smirk, but it seemed more like the smile of a cobra about to strike a mouse who dared get too close. Gregor knew she was just trying to make him afraid of her, and he laughed inwardly. It was working.

Well met, young monk, she said sleepily. *To what do I owe the pleasure?*

And he heard the danger in her words. Do not waste her time was the subtext. Do not wake her from a nap for no good reason. Do not make her angry, for she is powerful and can destroy you. What he said was, *I have news that your . . . friend, Duvan, is in danger. The Order of Blue Fire wants him for 'questioning.'*

In this form, Tyrangal's head reared at the news. Gregor did not know what Tyrangal was—human wizard as she most often appeared, or something else entirely—but one thing that he knew for certain was that she was immensely powerful. In any case, she was a force to be respected.

Vraith? she asked.

Yes.

Tyrangal snorted derisively. *That elf is ambitious beyond caution. I've watched her rise too fast in the Order. She is not as powerful a wizard as she would like everyone to believe, but she's charismatic and knows the ancient art of manipulation exceedingly well.*

Gregor remembered the ritual from the night before. He doubted he'd seen a ritual that powerful before. It seemed clear that Tyrangal underestimated Vraith.

Her spellscar is also a problem, Tyrangal went on. *She has some sort of ability to see and manipulate the essence of creatures. Have you noticed? That is the true source of her power, and like virtually everyone who gains access to great power quickly and without proportionate cost and training, she abuses and misuses hers.*

Certainly, Gregor said, knowing that Tyrangal was on his side.

In fact, Tyrangal said, *one of the reasons I have supported your work, Gregor, is because you seemed different. You have a great ability, but you have been mostly cautious in its use. For over a hundred years, I have seen the evidence. The great danger of obtaining a spellscar is that the 'scarred lack the wisdom to use their abilities conscientiously. With great power comes great responsibility. Do not forget that.*

Of course, Gregor said. Normally, a part of him thought, he would have rankled to be lectured this way. But there was something about Tyrangal . . . something about her voice . . . *I have been exceedingly careful with mine.*

True, Tyrangal said, *for the most part you have. What else do you know about Vraith?*

Gregor smiled. Confiding in her was exactly the right thing to do, he thought. It would feel so good to share this information, any information, with her.

Go ahead, came the melodic voice. *Tell me everything that happened.*

He told her of the ritual on the border of the Plaguewrought Land, how his elixir allowed the pilgrims to survive long enough to move the border. He still wasn't sure of how the elixir worked—more tests needed to be done—but it was clearly powerful.

A rush of warmth filled Gregor. Confiding in Tyrangal was exactly right. She would be happy with him, and her approval was critical. He needed her to like him. He told Tyrangal everything, for she was his ally and she needed to know.

Somewhere in the back of his mind, Gregor had an inkling that she was using magic on him, charming or persuading him to tell her things. But, no—he pushed that suspicion aside. Tyrangal was his friend. He *wanted* to tell her. Gregor didn't do things he didn't want to do.

Gregor told her of his visions. That Vraith's ritual would help achieve control over spellplague storms outside the Plaguewrought Land. With this magic, all of the blue fire in Faerûn could eventually be tamed!

And after he was done, Tyrangal spoke. *Of course she wants Duvan,* she said. *He could harm her. But she must not get him. She must not be allowed to complete the next ritual.*

Gregor frowned. *Vraith's magic would organize and contain plaguelands,* he said. *It would create order from chaos.*

Tyrangal's golden eyes flashed. *This ritual might be able to accomplish that, young monk,* she said. *But Vraith and the Order of Blue Fire will not use it for containment. I guarantee you that that is not their plan.*

What does she intend then?

A hint of anger was evident in Tyrangal's voice, *Vraith will use this ritual to move the border of the Plaguewrought Land, to expand the total area of these plaguelands. Of that I am sure. The Order wants to increase the blue fire's reach, and if they gain control over the border, they will eventually be able to unleash the spellplague contained within.*

She continued, *I have been monitoring the border, and it has been stable for a hundred years now—not the longest time, but long enough to indicate that, barring some major magical catastrophe, it's unlikely to move. This is a good thing. This is a necessary thing for the survival of most creatures.*

I didn't know what Vraith was planning, Gregor said.

So now that you do, Tyrangal said, her words dripping with honey, *you will refuse to make the elixir for the festival. She must not be allowed to proceed with a larger ritual.*

That sounded reasonable to Gregor. If he didn't supply the elixir then Vraith couldn't perform the ritual.

Perhaps.

All those pilgrims were already gathering in the valley, all preparing for the festival. Even without the elixir, they will all be heading to the Plaguewrought Land. Vraith might or might not try to proceed without enough elixir to protect the pilgrims, and if she did proceed then all those pilgrims would die. If she didn't proceed, then most of those pilgrims would die anyway.

Gregor shook his head. *No,* he said. *There must be another way to stop her. If I don't make the elixir, then thousands of pilgrims will die. I can't be responsible for that.*

Tyrangal's anger was like the lash of a whip. *You will not supply her with the elixir. Trust me: you do not want me as an enemy.*

I trust that, Gregor said. *I don't want to be your adversary.* He felt Tyrangal's charm dissipating fully. *But I cannot have the deaths of thousands on my conscience when I know that I can prevent it. I will make the elixir to protect the pilgrims. That is why I came to Ormpetarr, and that is what I will do.*

That decision is regrettable, Tyrangal said. *I have supported your quest to perfect the elixir because such knowledge is critical to diminishing the impact and power of the spellplague in Faerûn. I have provided you with knowledge and with Duvan's services.*

But there's a reason it's called a plague, Tyrangal continued. *And if Vraith succeeds in her ritual, she will be set to wreak far more havoc and cause countless more deaths than a paltry few thousand pilgrims.*

There must be another way, Gregor said. There *must be a way to save the pilgrims.*

Your concern for the pilgrims is disingenuous, monk, Tyrangal sneered. *You were fine sacrificing pilgrims to serve the greater good when you were experimenting on them. As long as you were going to be the hero, it was all right to lose a few hundred or a thousand 'volunteers.'*

Gregor cringed at the anger in her voice. *I'm sorry,* he offered.

You're not as sorry as you will be if you enable Vraith's plan, Tyrangal said.

But I can't oppose her; the Order is too powerful. They will make me pay a high, long-term price.

Then you have a decision to make, Tyrangal said. *You are fortunate, actually; you get to choose your enemies. Most people don't have that freedom.*

Gregor's awareness snapped back across the distance. He was in his own body, his heart pounding and his breath coming in gulps as a sheen of sweat chilled his skin.

Gods, he thought, what have I done?

Duvan woke to wind whipping across his face and the red glow of the sun shining through his closed eyelids. He could feel the sun's heat slowly roasting him.

Duvan's lips cracked as his tongue—dry as a dusty road itself—pushed through his glued-together lips and tried to wet them. I need water, he thought, breathing in hot air as dry as a desert wind.

There was a waterskin attached to his backpack. His backpack was still on his chest. Slanya was still on his back. She lay beside him, unmoving. The makeshift leather straps that he'd used to attach her to his shoulders had dug so deep into his flesh that the muscles burned at the slightest movement.

First, he thought, untie the straps so that he could move.

His hands protested, pain shooting down the muscles of his fingers and forearms with the very smallest effort. But after repeated attempts, he had managed to detach himself from Slanya and his backpack.

Second, sit up.

That step proved to be far more difficult and painful. His could barely move his arms; they felt dead, numb and heavy. Yet he needed to sit up. He kept trying and falling down, trying again, only to fall down again. But Duvan knew he needed to drink, and he knew that the more he moved, the more the ache would fade. Mobility would come back.

Eventually, Duvan had propped himself against the squat boulder.

Third, drink.

Duvan rested with his back against the hard stone. He struggled with the straps, but eventually he managed to detach his waterskin from his pack. The liquid inside was warm and bitter, but it quenched his thirst ever so slightly. It wet his mouth and throat. He resisted the urge to take a second drink. Who knew how long they'd need to make it last?

Duvan examined Slanya, sprawled in an unnatural position next to him. The gentle rise and fall of her chest meant she lived. Good.

Her unconscious, open-eyed stare was partially protected from the sun by the shadow of the squat boulder. One of her arms was pinned awkwardly behind her back and looked broken, but when he checked it he found that not one of the bones was fractured.

She was anything but whole, however. Duvan had never seen anything quite like the network of spellscarring that pervaded Slanya's body. Usually someone with so much exposure died instantly.

Duvan carefully straightened Slanya's back, which had been severely twisted. He closed her eyes and propped her feet up as he'd been taught by the Wildhome shaman who had trained him for a summer. He dribbled some water from the skin onto Slanya's lips and held her mouth closed.

"Come on," he said aloud. "You can't die. Not after I was being so nice to you."

Duvan had learned rudimentary healing skills during his imprisonment at Wildhome. He carried some oils and ointments to help healing. They would help protect Slanya's skin from prolonged exposure to the sun.

"I'm never nice," Duvan said. "You should know that about me. I don't like caring about people." He spread healing salve over the skin of Slanya's face and skull.

"But," he said, "I'm going to tell you a secret: I like you.

You remind me of—of people I cared about in the past."
Talfani. Rhiazzshar. "Not that things worked out so well
with them," he continued wryly. One he allowed to die, and
the other betrayed him.

"And since I do care, I will bend the world for you. I'll
even try the superstitious and stupid, just on the belief that I
don't know everything, and perhaps something I don't know
can help."

With that thought hanging in the air, Duvan rummaged
through Slanya's belongings. He knew she must have some of
Gregor's elixir left. Maybe it would help her after the fact. Maybe
Gregor's alchemy could save Slanya when he couldn't.

Duvan found the last flask of the elixir in her smallish
pack, which he had stuffed inside his own. The crystal vial
was nearly empty, but surely the shimmering liquid was a
single remaining dose.

He parted her dry lips and poured the contents into her
mouth. He hadn't felt such a strong bond for anyone since
Rhiazzshar. Perhaps it was because he felt responsible for
her well-being, as he had felt for Talfani's. The symmetry
was uncanny, and that had to mean something. Slanya
did not deserve to die. She was a good person. Better than
he was, that was for sure. She wanted to help people. She
wanted to make Faerûn a better place.

When he'd done all he knew to do for her, Duvan made
the heroic effort to stand up. He needed to survey their new
mote. But painful as it was, getting to his feet proved easier
than he'd expected.

Smooth rock, covered in places with sharp gravel, the mote
was small, perhaps only a handful of paces across. The boulder
that had been shading them took up a chunk of the level land
near one side. And the whole thing was moving fast, heading
almost due north from what Duvan could tell.

The mote was flying lower than the previous mote, but
high enough that he could see the Chondalwood far off to

his right, like a dark stain against the dusty green hills in the distance. High enough, hopefully, to clear the cliff wall at the border.

They hadn't left the changelands yet, but they were out of the vortex, which is what Duvan had hoped would happen. There was no food or water on this mote, however, and his stores were almost out.

There was also no shade except for the table-sized boulder. But at the rate they were flying, Duvan estimated they'd reach the border of the changelands before midday. The challenge then would be to figure out how to get safely off a mote moving at such speed.

Once they passed through the border veil, this mote would be relatively low to the ground so the fall might not kill them. But what the mote lost in altitude it made up for in velocity. This hunk of rock was moving mighty fast.

Duvan sat on the boulder and watched the approaching edge of the changelands. It seemed like they should be there any minute, and he knew the border zone would be concentrated with more intense blue fire. He had to be ready.

Wind buffeted his face, cooling him as he dug into his backpack and removed his glideskin in case they needed it. The sun shone high in a pale sky as he prepared his grappling hook for another throw—it never hurt to be ready for everything.

Due to the height or the distances or his misjudging of their speed, the border never seemed to get closer. Several times, he thought they were almost to the border veil, but then another quarter hour passed without the edge of the changelands nearing visibly.

This is a wild ride, he thought as the sun arced farther across the sky. One I will never forget. How many people can say they rode an earthmote through a spellplague storm?

Sometime later, he said, "Hang in there, Slanya. We're almost out of here. Almost home."

"Duvan?"

Slanya stirred. She rolled over and coughed up blood.

"I'm right here," he said, instantly at her side. "We are nearly out of the changelands. Everything is going to be all right."

Slanya gave a pained smile. "That's an outright lie," she said.

Duvan laughed. He was just so relieved to see her awake. "Yes, you're right. I am lying. I have no idea what's going to happen."

After seeming to be perpetually on the horizon, the border veil loomed suddenly large and imminent. The heavy, liquid tugging of nausea in Duvan's gut told him that the blue fire was particularly intense.

The mote plowed through the border veil, exploding into normal light. There was a bone-rattling *boom*, and then stability and order were abruptly restored. Duvan's skin stopped tingling, and his gut settled. The air smelled of humans and genasi and dwarves, of livestock and feces and the fires of the dead. It smelled like home, and Duvan felt grounded here. A feeling of rightness pervaded all of his being.

The mote, however, didn't act like all was right in the world. Duvan felt a shudder, deep and resonant, in the rock beneath them. The passage through the border had weakened the stone.

A large hunk of the mote tore away from the rest of it, spinning away like a satellite island in the air. The mote split into two, neither piece large enough to hold altitude. Below them, the ground just outside the border was grooved from years of fallen motes. And apparently, they were on one.

Its magic stripped away, the mote lost buoyancy and started to fall.

Pain.

Slanya's entire being was pain. It was as if she stood in the center of the funeral pyre and burned. As if she let herself, mind and body, be consumed by the razor-sharp licks of the flames, her skin blistering and blackening, her eyes boiling.

Slanya found herself rubbing the bandage over her right pinkie. Dried crusts of blood peeled away as she scratched at it. Even Slanya's intensive training could not cope with the anarchy that had been wrought upon her. She struggled to take stock of herself, but nothing was familiar. She was no longer the same.

Slanya tried to maintain diligence, starting with her hands and focusing on every inch of her body. Her mind recognized parts of her arm and chest and leg, some familiar fragments of herself, and she tried to use those fragments as an anchor from which she could rebuild her sense of self.

A cleric's mind and body were a conduit of her god. She called on Kelemvor to help cure her, and perhaps he would help save her.

Or he could call her to him. She needed to prepare herself for both possibilities.

"Slanya," came Duvan's voice like a rock in a surging sea. "We are going to have a big problem in a minute."

Can they get bigger? she thought.

Slanya felt the ground falling away, sending her stomach into her throat. I guess they can, she thought. She rolled over and vomited, clutching her gut and heaving.

She was dimly aware of Duvan above her, his quick, sure movements reassuringly decisive. He reached down for something—a large triangular piece of leather. Then he lashed the corners to himself, securing his gear and donning his pack.

He is saving himself, she thought. He's leaving me to save himself. Slanya's heart leaped in panic. By Kelemvor, he's abandoning me to die.

Then Duvan was lying down behind her, intimately close to her, cradling her. His proximity felt good, reassuring. He smelled of earth and sweat; his presence exuded confidence. If anyone could save her, he could.

Duvan reached around her, threading a thick leather strap under her arms and across her chest. "I'm tying us together," he said. "I don't know if our combined weight will be too much for the glideskin, but it will be much better than doing nothing. Doing nothing means crashing to the ground."

Slanya nodded. Warmth filled her; she was touched by Duvan's gesture. He wasn't leaving her to die alone. He hadn't left her before when she was sick. "Thank you," she croaked, coughing. "Thank you for saving me."

"Purely selfish of me—I need someone to argue with."

She tried to smile, but it came out as more of a lopsided grimace.

"Besides, you stood by me, which counts for a lot. Only one other person has stood by me, ever."

"Tyrangal?"

He nodded. "But for now, you're not saved yet. Thank me fully when we're both on the ground, alive and well."

Slanya shook her head. "Don't be so stubborn. I'm thanking you now, in case I die and can't thank you later." She needed to express her gratitude. She'd been betrayed and lied to by Gregor, who'd promised his elixir would protect her. Instead, she'd found trust and friendship in this rogue.

"You won't die," Duvan said. "I'm not letting that happen."

"Good to know," Slanya said, smiling. "I really appreciate it." And in that moment she felt a surge of euphoric affection toward Duvan.

Duvan laughed then said, "However, this may hurt a little. Hold on."

Above her, Duvan unfurled the glideskin. Slanya heard

it catch the wind like a kite. Duvan held on to the leather straps attached to each corner. The glideskin used magic and air to stay aloft, but it was only built for one.

Suddenly, the leather straps that held her to Duvan came taut, digging painful rows into her waist and shoulders. At her back, Duvan grunted from strain, and Slanya watched as the mote fell out from under their feet as they lifted off.

The straps held tight as she hung suspended from Duvan, who hung suspended from a wide triangle of leather. Her vision was fractured and uneven, and her body seemed to be dissociated from her mind. This was something alien to her, but she willed herself to be calm, to breathe evenly. Slowly.

Below her, the mote grew smaller against the massive, unyielding landscape. Autumn had nearly taken complete hold. Browning grass covered the rolling hills and plains as far as she could see. Away to their left was the dark line of a road, and a geometric, angular shape that had to be Ormpetarr.

Slanya knew they might die any minute, and the urge to confess overwhelmed her. "I need to tell you something," she said, her voice insistent. "In case we die."

Duvan huffed in her ear. "I'm sort of busy here."

"You were right about the story I told," she said. "It was too glib, too organized. The truth is that my aunt used to beat me with a belt, if I took too long washing the dishes or stacking the firewood. She used to burn the backs of my thighs with an iron if I broke a mug or spilled the chamber pot."

"Hells."

"The truth is, I wanted my aunt to die. I hated her and wanted her dead."

A gust of wind buffeted them, and they suddenly rose and turned. Duvan shifted his weight to steady them and keep their gliding descent steady.

"I forgive you," Duvan said through teeth gritted from exertion.

Slanya watched as the mote crashed into the rocky hillock

below, breaking apart in an explosion of sand and pulverized stone. They would not have survived that. Duvan's glideskin might not save them, but at least it gave them a chance.

Duvan whispered in her ear, "You should try to forgive yourself."

Abruptly, they fell. Slanya's stomach leaped to her throat, and her breath caught. But, grunting and straining, Duvan managed to right them one more time. He seemed to be aiming them for the ground about five hundred paces out. Still, they were moving far too fast for a survivable landing. Slanya hoped Duvan could slow them down before impact.

Otherwise, they would meet Kelemvor together.

"Take it from me," Duvan said with a laugh, "and do what I say rather than what I do: forgive yourself."

Slanya knew he was right. And yet, she didn't know if she could. She still hated Aunt Ewesia. She still despised how she was treated, and the only way she had been able to move on was to rewrite her own history—to structure her past in such a way as to blur the horrific things.

Duvan moved again, nosing the glideskin up to try to get the air to brake them. The glideskin creaked and fluttered, shaking violently for a second before Duvan regained control. But they'd slowed a little, and by the time they were a staff-length off the ground, Duvan had brought their speed down to a horse's gallop.

Slanya was grateful for Duvan's forgiveness and understanding but found no other relief. Every time she thought about what had happened to her in that tiny row house with Aunt Ewesia, she felt the past slip away until she was thinking about the fire and Gregor and not what had happened before. She could not forgive herself for what had happened. She could not even remember all that had happened.

The ground sped by beneath her. Dark rocks and tall, brown grass almost within reach if she stretched her arms.

This close to the ground, the obstacles grew larger and larger; they passed by faster and faster the closer they got.

Duvan angled the glideskin up slightly again to slow them down and they almost stalled. Five yards up now, maybe lower. Perhaps even low enough to survive. Slanya put her arms over her head to protect it as they dropped the final distance. She brought her feet into her chest to form a fetal crouch as they hit.

Landing in a skidding, sliding heap, Duvan curled himself around her. Her stomach heaved as they lurched and bounced, but she felt protected and safe in Duvan's embrace. When they finally came to a dusty stop, she wiped the dust and grime from her eyes before opening them again. Her muscles ached, and there was deep burning pain where the leather straps dug into her.

But they were out of the Plaguewrought Land. They'd made it! Solid and unchanging ground was beneath them. The rules of order and magic were consistent and predictable. The air smelled of harvest and dry grass and burning fields.

All in all, despite falling out of the sky, Slanya felt better than she had since entering the changelands.

Behind her, Duvan groaned. "I think my leg is broken," he said.

Duvan's left leg throbbed in agony, crumpled underneath the combined weight of Slanya and himself. He'd felt it snap when they had impacted—a sharp, shooting agony in his shin. Even with the glideskin, the collision had been too hard.

The sharp pain had mostly edged into the background, replaced by a deep throbbing in sync with the beating of his heart. Something wet and sticky slicked his leg, and he feared he was bleeding, but he couldn't turn to see how

...ach. Sweat prickled on his brow, and he felt lightheaded and cold. Injury and trauma could have that effect, he knew. It had happened to him before.

He did not want to pass out.

In the tall grass, Slanya rustled next to him. She was alive at least. Not gone yet.

"Don't move," she said.

Duvan laughed grimly. "That's easy advice to follow."

"I hear horses, and I'd prefer not to have unwanted company right now."

Duvan listened for horses; he hadn't heard any. But focusing now, he realized that his ears were filled with ringing, and all sound was dulled through that noise. "How do you know they won't help us?"

"If they're on horseback, chances are they're road agents or maybe wealthy pilgrims. Either way, they're unlikely to help us."

"Cynicism from such a trusting soul. I'm impressed."

Slanya rolled over and coughed. Still considerably unwell.

Despite her advice to remain still, Duvan unlashed the leather straps and edged himself carefully and slowly out from under her weight. And although he desperately wanted to sit up and examine his leg, he remained supine. Sitting up would increase his risk of blacking out, and that would only slow them down.

When her coughing had subsided, Slanya whispered, "They must've seen us; they're approaching."

Duvan decided that he needed to risk a look and propped himself up on his elbows. Sun burnished, grassy fields rolled out around them, but he couldn't see any horses.

No, wait. There they were, straight south, a group of five or six horses and riders. They seemed to be riding quickly, directly toward Duvan and Slanya's location.

The silver glint of plate metal shining from one of the riders seemed familiar, but before he could place it, a wave of sparks rippled across his skin. The edges of his vision darkened.

Duvan lowered himself back down, and slowly the darkness retreated. *I must be bleeding more than I expected,* he thought.

Next to him, he felt Slanya rustle and try to stand. Escaping the Plaguewrought Land seemed to have given her renewed strength. "I am too weak to mount a fight," she said. "And you're in no condition for one either."

Duvan had no argument to that.

In moments, the riders were on them. One of them dismounted and removed his plate helm.

"Sister Slanya," came a familiar voice. "So glad to have found you."

"What do you want, Beaugrat?" Slanya said. Duvan heard the warning in her voice, but the whole exchange seemed to be coming from a great distance away.

"We want to help you back to your monastery. The Order of Blue Fire has reached an agreement with Brother Gregor, and we have guaranteed your safe return."

"What about Duvan?"

Her concern brought a smile to Duvan's lips. He concentrated on the sun warming his skin, on the feel of lumpy earth and grass against his back. His leg throbbed, and he knew he'd lost a lot of blood, but he needed to pull himself together.

"Duvan will be taken care of as well," Beaugrat said.

Duvan checked himself for daggers. He catalogued two on his chest and one in the scabbard strapped to his right thigh. He took a breath and waited. There would be an opportunity, perhaps, for him to use the daggers.

He opened his eyes to assess the situation. Beaugrat towered over a brave, but obviously weakened, Slanya in her torn and dirt-encrusted leathers. She stood leaning to the left as though not quite sure of the ground.

In the blurry background, Duvan could make out four others on horseback, but despite the effort he wasn't able to identify their strengths and weaknesses. He smelled horses and something else he couldn't identify. Like burning metal. Something was wrong with his mind.

Beaugrat said, "The Order will guarantee he makes a full recovery."

"I'm certain you will," Slanya said. "How about this for a deal: You give us a ride back to the monastery where we can heal up. After that you can talk to Duvan as much as you'd like, as long as it's all right with him."

Beaugrat said, "Let's see . . . No!"

Duvan heard the sound of swords being drawn, metal on leather, and the cocking of a crossbow. Slanya said, "You don't want to fight me. I've had a pretty bad day, and I'm not in the mood to let you live."

Beaugrat laughed. "Well, it's true that I don't want to fight you," he said. "But we outnumber you, and you're both sick or injured. You have surprised me in the past, which is why I'm not taking chances this time. Cedril, now."

Duvan heard the crossbow spring, and the quarrel made an unusually faint sound as it hit something solid. His mind imagined a lightweight bolt, perhaps hollow. From Slanya's gasp, he presumed it had hit her. There was movement around him as Slanya attacked. Duvan grabbed for his dagger, but his hands never closed around the hilt.

"Don't worry, the poison isn't deadly. It will only put you to sleep for a short time."

"How kind of you." Slanya's sarcasm brought a wry smile to Duvan's lips. But then her words slowed and stopped. Duvan heard her body collapse to the ground next to him.

"What about him?" The voice floated on the air, but he couldn't tell who was speaking. "He doesn't look so well."

"He looks dead," Beaugrat said. "Like we're going to be if that Copper Guard contingent catches us out here."

Unconsciousness inked over Duvan's vision before he caught the answer to the question. And then he was falling into the pit of night that yawned beneath him.

Was this what death was like?

CHAPTER NINE

Gregor stood on the balcony and shaded his eyes to look across the valley and south along the dirty road coming over the dull green hills. The sun burned overhead, its light fading and leaving the sky a bruised color in the distance where the Plague-wrought Land changed all the rules. The odor of charred flesh drifted over from the funeral pyre on the ground below. Gray smoke was all that was left of the afternoon's dead.

With luck, Slanya would return soon with the plaguegrass, and the funeral pyre could be extinguished. The elixir would stop the procession of dead and dying.

"Come home, young one," Gregor whispered to her. "Come home safe."

For years after Slanya had come to the monastery,

Gregor had cared for her as if she were his own child. He had been the one to take her from the orphanage. He had been the one to choose her—the neglected and abused girl. The sole survivor of a tragic fire.

It was the policy of the temple complex to take in children who could benefit from rigorous training, meditation, and adherence to a life of the religious orders. Ideal children showed great internal fortitude and strength of will. They demonstrated passion and the potential for great power. But above all Gregor chose young children who would feel enormous gratitude and obligation.

There had been something about Slanya, a fire inside her, a thirst for knowledge. He saw himself in her, or so he thought at the time. He saw a defiance burning deep in her soul that appealed to Gregor and made them the same in their passionate pursuit to impact the universe.

The young Slanya had needed so much more than the orphanage could ever offer. But Gregor knew that if she was able to maintain her studies, she would be eternally grateful for the opportunity that he'd given her.

Gregor had been a young monk of about twenty when he'd taken her in—young and idealistic and brave. He had fallen smitten with the angel with the smudgy face and dirty, blonde hair. So cordial and proper on the outside, little Slanya's manners were belied by mischievous eyes and sly glances.

Standing on the monastery balcony, gazing across the field for sign of her return, Gregor smiled. Young Slanya had taken to the monastery life with difficulty. Originally he'd imagined training her to be his assistant, to embrace the life of a monk of Oghma, but the discipline proved too much for her wayward mind. After she'd run away the third time, only to return a few days later, Gregor gave her over to Kaylinn.

Kelemvor had room for her, and the orphaned young woman found her place within his orders. Slanya took to the care of the dead and dying with unusual focus, and Gregor's influence over her faded somewhat after that. He still cared for her, still checked in on her, but his child of choice had moved on for the most part.

Gregor sighed. Such eventualities always came with the passage of time, he supposed.

Scanning the horizon, he caught sight of horses as they crested a hill to the southeast. And after a brief wait, he could tell that they were the team Vraith had sent out. Beaugrat and his companions.

Gregor strained to see if there were other riders with them, but they dipped into the shadow of another hill before he could discern. When they emerged into the light, however, he did see that one of the horses carried two people, and another horse dragged a makeshift wooden travois upon which someone had been strapped.

Excellent! Gregor thought. Now to see if they've got the plaguegrass with them!

The recent meeting with Tyrangal weighed on him. He didn't want her as an enemy, but he wasn't convinced that she was right about Vraith and the ultimate intentions of the Order. His vision was so strong, and it had come to him again later that night. The vision showed him hope and a future to strive for—a Faerûn where all the pockets of spellplague were stable and mapped. Ordered. Contained.

It was worth the risk to let Vraith continue with the ritual. Gregor would reevaluate after tomorrow's festival. And in the meantime, he would have to watch out for Tyrangal; he did not really know the extent of her power. He didn't doubt that she could be a formidable adversary, but as yet she had not made a move against him. Wait and see, that was his plan. Be ready and prepared for whatever might come.

A few minutes later, Gregor descended to greet the travelers. In the lead, Beaugrat drew reins and slid from his saddle. Behind him rode a red-headed dwarf cleric, a halfling rogue, and what looked like a pair of human wizards. Quite the party to capture one thief.

Slanya slid woozily from her saddle. Her puffy, red face was burned, though she did not seem to notice. She came to him. "Brother Gregor, you must—" She doubled over and heaved up blood-streaked bile.

"Blessed gods!" High Priestess Kaylinn stood in the doorway to the courtyard, flanked by two of her clerics. She came up next to Gregor. "You are ill, Sister," she said to Slanya. "We must get you to the infirmary." Kaylinn nodded to one of the clerics, Edwaif, who stepped up to support Slanya's weight.

Slanya tried to resist, but Gregor could sense that she was weak. "Duvan—?" she began.

"Duvan will be taken care of," he said. "Did you find the plaguegrass?"

Slanya nodded. "In the bag."

Beaugrat handed down the small leather pack that Slanya had carried with her. Gregor opened it and found the bag of holding inside. Loosening the braided silk cord, Gregor looked inside.

The odor of fresh cut grass, humus, and dirt lingered in the air with an undercurrent of sour oranges. Reaching in, Gregor grabbed a fist full of the wet plants. Such a quantity would not only allow him to inoculate all the pilgrims at the festival, but supply him for many years to come. Slanya had performed exceedingly well.

"Not that it matters now," Slanya said. "The elixir does not work."

Gregor stepped back as if he'd been slapped. How could she lie thus? The data clearly showed that it did work. "Hush, child," he said, keeping his tone positive. "You are delirious."

"I still have my wits," Slanya said. "The elixir may have helped some, but it did not provide adequate protection."

"You're alive, aren't you, Sister?"

"I'm alive because Duvan saved me. With just the elixir I was deathly ill. It does not work!"

"Nonsense! I never promised that you wouldn't get sick, but clearly it did save you from dying. Argue as much as you like, but you're living proof that it works, and soon all these pilgrims will be like you." Gregor's sweeping gesture indicated the entire field of pilgrims.

Beaugrat turned his horse. "We will be going now," he said. "You have what we agreed on?"

Gregor nodded. He was sorry to give Duvan up, but the man was not his concern. His delivery to Vraith was a small price to pay for the salvation of thousands upon thousands of pilgrims.

"Wait!" Slanya tried to turn, but she was weak. Her knees gave way, and she collapsed into Edwaif's supporting grip. "Where are you taking him?" she asked.

Beaugrat ignored her and led his small party away toward Ormpetarr with an unconscious Duvan bound to the travois behind the dwarf cleric.

Gregor looked at Kaylinn. "Shouldn't she be taken to the infirmary?"

"What are they doing with Duvan?" Slanya protested. She tried to stand, but Edwaif refused to let go. "Gregor?" She coughed. "You said he would be taken care of."

Gregor sighed. "An agreement had to be made, child," he said.

"But what are they going to do with him?"

"I don't know," Gregor said honestly. "I'm sure they will heal his wounds." But while he didn't really know exactly what Vraith had in mind for Duvan, Gregor could hazard a guess.

"Their cleric already mended his leg," Slanya said. "The better for the Order to experiment on him, isn't that it?"

Gregor startled. Slanya held a new bitterness and cynicism in her tone and demeanor. This was not the same Slanya who had left the monastery two days ago. He would have to be careful with her, but that did not mean he would be dishonest.

"I'm sorry," he said. "I hate to be a party to such suffering. You must believe me that your efforts—and his sacrifice—will mean a great many pilgrims will be safe."

Slanya glared up at Gregor. "No, they won't," she said. "And now, you have given Duvan to the Order without a fight."

"It was the right decision. I have you and the plaguegrass. If I had made no deal, the Order would have those in addition to Duvan."

"But they're going kill him."

"No," Gregor said. "They merely want to subject him to various magics to see how strong his resistance really is."

"Torture him, you mean?"

"I advise you not to let yourself be limited by semantics," he said. "This is for the good of us all."

"Enough," Kaylinn said. "We will discuss your actions later, Brother Gregor. Slanya, we'll speak as well, but you need to rest. Now."

Slanya's whole body seemed to sag from exhaustion. "All right," she said to Kaylinn. "Thank you, but I do not need to rest."

Kaylinn said, "You know you do. Let wisdom guide you. Choose to take action when you can be effective. You must gather your strength."

Slanya glared at Gregor. "If harm comes to Duvan, I will not forgive you," she said.

"I am sorry, my child," Gregor said. "But I had no choice."

Besides, Gregor thought, I warned Tyrangal about Vraith's plans for Duvan. Gregor was certain that he'd gone above and beyond any measure of the call of duty. He owed Duvan nothing, and the rogue was no longer his problem.

And as Kaylinn and Edwaif led Slanya away to the infirmary, Gregor turned his attention to the plaguegrass and the elixir. He needed to get to his lab and get started; the elixir would take hours to brew, and the festival was tonight!

Rhiazzshar's sly, angled face glowed with ecstasy above Duvan as she moved her hips against him. Her amber eyes stared down into his. Her mahogany hair fell around his face, smelling of freshly crushed pine needles. "I love you, Duvan," she mouthed. "I love you."

I love you . . . That persistent honeyed lie hung in the air.

Then it was gone, snatched away by the howling, swirling maelstrom. He huddled in his cage, cold and exposed, his knees pulled into a tight ball as purple threads of lightning struck around him. Rhiazzshar's image dissipated like a betraying phantom in the storm, leaving him alone at the mercy of the Plaguewrought Land.

Just before she disappeared, her face above him changed. Her hair was replaced by a head, shaved except for a blonde sidelock. Slanya's serious expression admonished him. "You should've seen this coming," she said, her voice hollow and ghostly.

Duvan came awake to voices above and around him. He kept his eyes closed and tried to get a picture of his predicament before revealing that he was awake. He lay flat on his back, and his skin and hair felt as though they had been washed.

The smell of peppermint soap wafted from his body, mingling with the tallow and tar smells of candles and torches. That meant that it was either nighttime or this room was underground. The surface beneath him was hard like wood or stone.

Where's Slanya? he wondered. What happened to her? His dream flashed through his mind, and he couldn't help but wonder if she'd handed him over to the Order.

No—suspecting Slanya of betrayal was his own paranoia at work. Slanya was nothing like Rhiazzshar. Still, the elf's betrayal made him question everyone's loyalty. Perhaps it always would.

His leg seemed whole again, although without inspecting it visually and testing it out, he could not know for sure. He could feel a breeze on his toes and legs, which meant he no longer wore his leathers. Instead, a lightweight fabric covered his naked body.

In fact, he felt better than he had in months—clean and shaved, not hungry, not tired, and no muscle aches. Whatever powerful magic they'd used to heal him, it had worked brilliantly. His skin tingled slightly, but otherwise he felt perfect.

Well, except for the slight itch in his mind that he couldn't quite figure out. Every time he tried to focus on it and pin down what it reminded him of, the niggling irritation slipped away, defying recognition.

He'd felt this particular sensation before. Someone was scrying him, eavesdropping on what was happening to him.

"He is awake." The voice was low and scratchy, but melodic. The speaker was female and standing about three paces off to Duvan's left. The accent was faint, but decidedly northern, perhaps from Waterdeep or Neverwinter.

Duvan opened his eyes to a torch-lit room with an arched stone ceiling, the amber-colored bricks streaked with soot stains. He immediately counted four people in the room, although there could be more behind him.

The woman who had spoken was an elf, slight of build, and she had short-cropped blonde hair. Duvan guessed she was in charge. Standing closer to him, just to his right, was a dark-skinned human man in white clerical robes wearing a pendant that bore the symbol of the Order: a stylized, flaming, blue eyeball. The man's milky cataracts gave him a reptilian look.

No sign of Slanya. Hopefully, she was spared this indignity. *I don't really suspect her of betraying me, do I?*

Behind the cleric stood Beaugrat, his plate mail polished to a silver shine. The big man's eyes were on the blonde elf. And behind Beaugrat, by the archway that led to the stairs, stood a single guard—a spellcaster by the looks of her loose-fitting silk clothing. This guard woman was genasi, her skin the color of the ocean, and she had a spellscar that manifested as flowing tributaries across the hairless, aqua skin of her skull, just above her pointed ears. Duvan could not tell by a quick glance what sort of spellcaster she was, but she would no doubt be powerful.

The blonde elf spoke, her voice like silk-covered glass shards, all smooth but with a sharpness underneath. "It is good to see you are whole and alert, Duvan. I am Commander Accordant Vraith."

Duvan realized abruptly that his hands and limbs were not bound, but even so he could barely move them.

"You are our guest here," Vraith continued, "until we decide to let you go. And I assure you that your mundane escape tricks will not work."

"You have an interesting definition of *guest*," Duvan said.

"You should see how we treat intruders," Beaugrat said with a laugh.

"Enough!" Vraith's eyes fluttered as though she wasn't quite in control of herself. "We are going to conduct some tests, Duvan. These tests may pose significant danger to your body and mind, but they are necessary. And we have our best healer here to ensure that you will be able to endure them indefinitely."

"You know," Duvan said, "while that sounds incredibly

inviting, I think I'll have to pass this time. I really do have someplace else to be."

Beaugrat gave a chuckle at that.

Vraith, however, failed to see the humor. "Let's begin," she said.

Beaugrat grew serious then pressed his wrists together, palms facing Duvan. Gauzy blue flames ignited from the big warrior's shoulder spellscar and sheathed his arm and hands.

Duvan took a slow breath. Hadn't he been here before? This was a waste of time.

Beaugrat concentrated and focused. The translucent energy gathered into a ball of twisting folds near the big man's hands, then shot forth like a spray, directly at Duvan.

Duvan watched as the flames dissipated before they hit him. He didn't want to flaunt his ability, but other than the challenge of escaping this place, which seemed highly unlikely without help, he was bored.

Gasps and whispers came from onlookers behind Duvan. He could not turn to look, but he heard two more people in the room.

"This was as we expected," came Vraith's voice. "Let's try a stronger dose."

Beaugrat nodded then took a deep breath. He gathered a larger ball of gauzy flames and sent them lashing out at Duvan again. The light flashed searing white this time, casting the room in sharp shadows.

The familiar melting gut feeling triggered inside Duvan's abdomen. And again, the wild magic weakened and faded before it could touch him. The coherent burst of white disintegrated into an ineffectual mist when it neared Duvan, then vanished completely, dissipating into nothingness.

More murmurs and gasps from the gallery.

"You know, I could save you some time," Duvan said. "I have been thoroughly experimented on already."

"Hold off for a moment, Beaugrat," Vraith said. After a relieved nod from the plate-clad warrior, she stepped slowly up to Duvan. Her blonde eyebrows narrowed as she looked down on him. "When was that?" she asked.

"A few years ago." Duvan's mind flashed on his tenure in the Wildhome cage, huddled against the elements inside the border of the Plaguewrought Land, miserable and waiting for Rhiazzshar to come take him out.

"What can you tell us?" Vraith asked.

"I can tell you the extent of my ability," Duvan said. "I'm sure we can come to some agreement."

"Why would I trust you?" Vraith said. "You work for Tyrangal, and she has been less than cooperative."

"I am a man of my word."

The faintest of smiles tugged at Vraith's thin red lips. "Oh, perhaps you are," she said. "But then again, if you weren't, you'd say the same thing."

"True," Duvan admitted.

"We both know how this is going to go. You are not in a position to negotiate at the moment." Vraith's hint of a smile faded completely, and she retreated to stand back out of the way.

"I could agree to stay far away from your operations," Duvan offered. "I could agree to help—"

"Beaugrat," Vraith said, ignoring Duvan. "Resume the testing. More power this time."

Lashing blue-white fire struck out at him again. Then once more. Over and over, with increased intensity, each successive attack. Each time, he felt no hint of an effect. Nothing.

Finally, Beaugrat collapsed to his knees with exertion. "That's all I can do."

"It's enough," Vraith said. "He is immune to the Blue Fire."

Duvan sighed. "I could have told you that and saved poor Beaugrat some embarrassment."

Ignoring Duvan, Vraith said, "Let the next stage of tests begin. Guraru, you're up."

A dark figure stepped out from behind him—a dwarf with a brilliant red beard intricately plaited down his portly front. The dwarf nodded, the dry brown skin of his balding head stretched over his skull like aging parchment. "Let's try some heat," he said. The dwarf muttered an incantation so softly that Duvan could not hear the words, while at the same time his hands traced the lines of an invisible glyph in the air.

Suddenly Duvan was on fire, his skin blistering and blackening from the heat. Agony took hold of him, his whole being burned. Duvan clenched his jaw, trying to resist the urge to scream. He didn't want to give them the satisfaction. But he felt like he was being drowned in a vat of boiling oil. His skin singed and blackened. His eyeballs seemed to melt in his head.

He gave in. He let out a guttural scream that was at least as much anger as it was pain. This dwarf must be stopped. Duvan would happily kill him to make the pain go away. Duvan would kill them all. He screamed and screamed, and he wished he could pass out from the pain.

"Heal him."

Duvan breathed a sigh of relief as the searing diminished to an afterimage of the burning agony. Then he was whole and sound again. But while the reprieve from the pain was a welcome numbness, his mind flinched from the residual memory of the torment.

"Again," came Vraith's voice. "I want exact measures of his tolerances."

Duvan started to speak. He could tell them. There was no reason to keep testing him. He had no resistance. Fire and ice and dread and mind magic all worked on him. But he never got the chance to speak before the fire engulfed him a second time.

The first attack was a mere hint of the crisp, soul-searing agony that consumed him the second time. The fire erupted everywhere at once: inside his chest, all over his skin, under his fingernails. His hair burned. His skin blistered and blackened. And all of it happened in the briefest flare of the sun.

The world went dark around him, and Duvan found himself fluttering like silk in a gray wind. All around him was a flat, dark plane, only discernible in shades of gray. He could not move of his own accord, could not step through onto the plane; his presence here was insubstantial.

Against the backdrop of gray, Duvan flashed on Talfani's frail and emaciated body as he held her in those last moments. He remembered curling around her, holding her, and stroking her hair gently so it would not fall out in chunks.

"I'm sorry, I'm sorry," he repeated to her over and over, hoping that she would hear him. Hoping that she would forgive him.

Talfani never spoke a word during the days between getting sick and when she finally gave in and stopped breathing. The damage from the plaguestorm had taken away her voice so that she could just stare at him with huge, pleading eyes and try to signal that she couldn't eat or drink.

She just wanted him to hold her, to stay with her, like he should've done the entire time. If he had stayed with her, she wouldn't have gotten sick. She wouldn't have withered, her once vibrant soul wasted away and dried up.

Lying on her bed, cradling her frail figure, young Duvan cried as he felt her breath rattle to a halt. He cried as she slowly grew cold in his arms. Her spirit had left; the twin to his soul, gone. Where she had gone, he did not know.

Perhaps he could follow her.

But young Duvan lacked the will to do anything active to take his own life. He merely lay with Talfani's spiritless corpse slowly souring next to him. He blocked out the devastation of his village outside. He cried and cried that he had let this happen to her. He didn't deserve to live when she was gone. He didn't *want* to live if that meant being alone.

And Duvan might have died there too. Starvation or pestilence may have eventually taken him if the Wildhome elves hadn't come through the village.

"He's coming around." The voice was deep and male.

"Was he dead, Renfod?" Vraith asked.

"Nearly, but not quite," said the clipped voice. "I have healed him, but you might want to be more careful."

"I'll determine that."

"Of course, Commander."

The fluttering gray gave way to dim torchlight as Duvan opened his eyes. Milky, cataract-clouded eyes stared down at him, very close, seeming to look through and beyond Duvan at that same time. After a moment, the man blinked and stood up, retreating slightly.

Renfod, Duvan guessed, the cleric who so graciously brought him back to endure more torture. Renfod's thin, brown face displayed dour concern. He did not seem to be enjoying this part of his job one bit.

Next to the dark cleric, Beaugrat's wide, boyish face grinned down at him. He seemed to be relishing Duvan's torture. Duvan silently vowed to kill the big fighter, if he ever made it through this.

"Renfod, step back if he is healed," Vraith said. "Let's continue. Guraru?"

Renfod retreated to stand next to Vraith. Into Duvan's field of vision stepped the red-bearded dwarf again. Oh, this is going to hurt, Duvan thought.

Abruptly, an icy dread crystallized in his chest. The dread spread through Duvan, freezing him to his very core. The chill seized the marrow of his arms and legs. He struggled to breathe against the chill.

One breath, two breaths.

The third breath didn't come, and he felt the sharp tingle of frostbite in his fingers and toes. His skin grew numb, and the numbness spread behind advancing waves of needles, to his heart.

Duvan welcomed the numbness. He felt no pain by the end. And he welcomed the approaching death. He could just barely see the gray plane again as he wavered between worlds like a fluttering ghost.

Finally, he might be able to rest.

Slanya's head pounded with pain, sharp and pervasive. But even so she felt more integrated with her body, more whole. Her vision was no longer fragmented and split into disparate shards. In the quiet of her chambers, she was acutely aware of the persistent ringing in her ears, but she was confident that it was fading slowly. Her hearing was otherwise keen.

Almost back to normal.

Slanya's throat was thick with the taste of medicine. She scraped the top of her tongue with her teeth to try to get rid of the bitter anise flavor. Sitting on her straw cot, in the quiet of her small chamber, she took slow, deep breaths and tried to clear her mind.

The yellow light of the late-afternoon sun streamed through the small window opening and warmed her face. Some of the clerics and monks sang evening prayers in the chapel, and she smelled the smoke from the funeral pyre, but it was faint.

In the back of her mind, she knew that further challenges lay in her path—dangerous and full of peril—but for this moment in time, she sought to clear her mind and body. To bring calm and unification, and with that, health and renewed strength, so that she could meet those challenges.

After a few moments of meditation, there was a soft knock on the door, after which it cracked open admitting High Priestess Kaylinn. She wore her daily cleric's robes, and Slanya noticed that the beige fabric bore fresh bloodstains.

"It's good to see you awake," Kaylinn said. Concern was evident in her voice. "I think I've done all I can do. The rest is up to you, but you are as whole as I can make you by magic. I also gave you something for the pain. You've had a great deal more exposure to the plaguelands than most pilgrims who manage to survive."

Slanya blinked and noticed that she was absently rubbing the stub of her missing pinkie. So much for order and peace of mind.

"Your spellscar is intriguing," Kaylinn said. "It's spread throughout your body like a fishing net—concentrated knots of spellscar connected by a web of thinner, physical scars. I don't recommend you use your spellscar ability too much. Channeling that much wild magic is likely to tear your body apart."

"Thank you for the advice, High Priestess," Slanya said, her tongue still thick with the medicine. "Do you know what it . . . does??"

Kaylinn shrugged. "You will figure it out."

"Thank you, Priestess, for healing me. I am indebted."

"Not at all," Kaylinn said. "You are family. I think you should know that."

"I do," Slanya said. "Of course."

After a short pause, Kaylinn continued, "I need to speak with you about Brother Gregor. I am concerned that he has lost his way, that his pursuit of personal glory has blinded him to the harm he is causing others."

Slanya nodded.

"This . . . pact with Vraith is inappropriate, to say the least. The Order has long supported our presence in Ormpetarr, but the situation with the young man and

Gregor's elixir . . . I no longer trust they have our congregation's best interests in mind. We need to determine if something is influencing Gregor and then isolate him from it, if so. I need your help, Sister Slanya. I need the backing of all clerics and monks of our monastery, especially those loyal to him."

"I agree with you, High Priestess. I will help however I can."

There was a knock on the door, and Kaylinn's eyebrows raised in surprise. She went to the door and opened it a crack, and in the space Slanya was shocked to see the tall slender figure of Tyrangal.

"I must speak with Slanya," she said. Tyrangal was at least two heads taller than Kaylinn, her long auburn hair shining in the sunlight of the courtyard.

Kaylinn didn't budge. "She's in no condition."

Tyrangal's gaze softened, and a smile graced her young face. "You've done a wonderful job, Priestess." Her voice grew melodic and convincing. "And I am just going to talk with her. I need to tell her something very important."

Kaylinn frowned. "Do not try to charm me."

"I apologize for the attempt," Tyrangal said, "and merely plead urgency as the motivator. It's imperative that I have a few words with Sister Slanya, and what I have to say cannot wait any longer."

Kaylinn made no move to allow Tyrangal into the room. "I have no reason to trust you," she said. "This is a most unusual breach of protocol."

Slanya spoke. "It's all right, High Priestess. I will speak with her."

Kaylinn's resolve melted just a little. "Very well, but I will remain here."

Tyrangal gave a catlike smile. "Of course. What I have to say might be important for you as well." She strode into the room and looked down at Slanya. "I hope you're feeling up to some action," she said, "because we need to rescue Duvan."

Slanya sat up. "You know where he is?"

Tyrangal nodded. "I do. He is being held in the Order of Blue Fire headquarters, in one of the underground rooms."

"Is he well guarded?"

Tyrangal nodded. "Aye," she said, "but I have considerable resources. My Copper Guard is ready to assist us, but we cannot do it alone. I was hoping that you and a number of your trusted clerics and monks could help us get Duvan out of there."

Kaylinn interjected, "Why do you want to rescue Duvan? What is he to you?"

"Duvan is my ward," Tyrangal said. "He is my apprentice, and I am responsible for him. But more than that, Duvan is the only one who can shut down the Order's plan to extend the Plaguewrought Land."

"What?" Slanya asked.

"Vraith has developed a ritual that will allow her to move the border of the changelands, and I have no doubt that she's planning to expand the border until all lands are Plaguewrought Land."

Slanya remembered the horror of the unbridled Plaguewrought Land, and she shuddered.

"My Copper Guard isn't large enough to breach their defenses in two places at the same time—besides, we will need your prayers and your magic. Vraith and her inner circle of accordants will be leaving for the festival soon. That's where my guard will be. We need to get to Duvan, because his resistance to the Spellplague is the only thing that can stop them."

Slanya thought about it. She wasn't at all sure about what Tyrangal had said concerning Vraith and the Order. It sounded preposterous and overblown, but she did know that she owed Duvan her life and that she cared for the ornery rogue. She would help to save him.

"I will go with you. Duvan saved my life more than once. It's time to repay the debt."

Kaylinn looked at Slanya, her eyes wide. "I never trusted Vraith, and I've suspected Brother Gregor to be under the influence of some obsession. Ever since he became spellscarred and convinced me to move us halfway across Faerûn, I've had my doubts about his objectives."

"Does that mean you'll help us?" Tyrangal asked.

"Yes," Kaylinn responded. "And I think I can persuade a few others to join us as well."

"Excellent," Slanya said, invigorated. The pain in her head had receded. She found herself growing excited, and the impending thrill had chased away her craving for calm and balance.

Dizzy and exhausted to the point of delirium, teenage Duvan staggered toward the fluctuating prismatic veil and peered through the haze at the tall waterfall of crystal-clear water. Waves of blue fire pulsed like irregular heartbeats just inside the border here. Thirst clawed at his throat.

How long had it been since his last drink? Days? Tendays? He could not remember.

Since escaping from the Wildhome cage, Duvan had scrabbled and clawed his way across terrain straight from images of the Nine Hells. And now, he scraped his way up steep, bare rock. Pulses of spellplague washed over him, and he ignored them.

Younger Duvan pushed through the oily curtain and emerged into the light. Monochrome purple gave way to verdant fields. Dust and static and cold dissipated as he trudged out of the Plaguewrought Land. He'd made it across!

A flash of white—

The lush waterfall vanished as young Duvan dragged

himself, exhausted, across a small meadow and collapsed by the trunk of a small cypress tree. The spray that had fractured the sun into rainbow droplets vanished, leaving behind dry grass and sporadic scrubby trees.

Just a mirage. Disappointment flooded him, and he let it sap his will to go on.

Sun shone down on him, warming the chill in his bones. Compared to the excessive gusts of the Plaguewrought Land, filled with flying rocks and dust, the gentle wind felt like a caress. Maybe he could still make it. He'd made it this far through agility and determination and never giving up. He just needed to gather his strength. Then he could find water.

A flash of green—

He must have passed out. He awoke to find elf faces staring down at him. They had bronze skin and long hair adorned with forest plants to camouflage them. The elves looked at him with pity, with fear, with concern.

They had come from Wildhome, this small cadre of elven rangers and druids. They offered him food and water, and he accepted. They set up camp around him, too afraid that moving would injure him. Rhiazzshar was not among them. These were not elves he knew, although he thought he might have seen one or two when the wide-ranging scouting teams had come through the Chondalwood.

Had they come for him? How had they known to find him here? He had just made it across the changelands, crawling through the belly of the beast.

The elves were going to take him back. After the impossible trip through the most chaotic and dangerous place in Faerûn, he was just going to go back to captivity, to Rhiazzshar. To torture. He wouldn't let them. He would kill himself rather than go back. He hated them all.

A flash of red—

A few days later, the encampment came alive when sounds

of a troop of men on horseback approached. Led by a tall woman with long, auburn hair, the armed force looked well enough trained that it would give the small encampment trouble.

First, however, the tall woman spoke to them in sweet, honeyed words. Tyrangal was her name, and just listening to her gave Duvan a rush of joy. Many of the elves obviously felt the same way, and those who didn't were afraid of her. They certainly would not risk engaging the Copper Guard in combat.

Duvan watched in awe as the elves packed up and rode away, leaving him with Tyrangal and her men. He did not know what this wonderful and frightening new captor would do with him. He did not entertain hope. He'd been down that path before, and it always had led to greater disappointment.

Tyrangal sent the elves home. And after the last horse had disappeared down over the low, rolling grassland hills, the strange woman came to Duvan. She dispelled the charm she had put on him and the others, and she told him that he was free to go wherever he wished. She told him that she would like him to work for her. And that if he did, he would be paid handsomely for his efforts.

She laid out the possibility of a new life for Duvan—a life of learning and adventure, if he allowed her to guide him. But she emphasized that he was free to refuse her offer. She was not going to force him to do anything. He could walk away freely if he wanted.

Duvan didn't believe it. And over time, as he slowly came to realize that she had not been lying, he broke down and cried. He still had the nightmares every night, but now he was in charge of his own destiny. Tyrangal hoped that he would stay with her and perform the tasks she requested, but he was always asked and never forced.

A flash of blue—

Duvan awoke with a start. He opened his eyes and looked

around. Arched stone ceiling streaked with soot. He was in the same room, most likely underground. Maybe beneath the Changing House. The smell of sweat and ashes and healing balm filled the room.

He was still lying on the table where he'd been tortured. Apparently not dead yet, he thought wryly, as ghost sensations of earlier pain filtered back into this consciousness. The room was quiet and felt largely empty, except for Vraith speaking with two others on the other side of the door. He could only catch snatches of words and phrases.

His magical bonds from earlier had been replaced with leather ones. One of the absent spellcasters must've been keeping him immobile earlier.

Discreetly, he started testing the limits of his bonds, while focusing to try to understand the conversation outside the room. Vraith's northern accent was easy to recognize, but he could barely hear enough to follow what they were saying.

"—monk is working with us fully now . . . best of both worlds."

". . . believes he's free, but the . . . visions from . . . Masters of Absolute Accord." Laughter.

Then Vraith's voice rose clear and loud. "We must prepare for the festival now. Soon we shall all be part of an historic moment."

"What about our guest?"

"Continue the testing as appropriate. Jahin will stay. Push him to his limits, but don't let him die."

Duvan shuddered. More pain like he'd been through, only to be healed up for further torture? He'd rather die.

He gritted his teeth.

Duvan's hands slid free of his bonds, and he sat up quickly. Looking around, he noticed a small table on his left, upon which were several knives and a pair of iron tongs. Apparently the planned torture wasn't limited to just the magical variety.

Duvan grabbed one of the knives, palmed it, then put his hands back against the bonds. Anyone scrutinizing them would know immediately that he'd slipped out, but a casual glance might not give him away.

Hesitation would mean more pain, more and prolonged agony. And even if all that his escape attempt brought was death and an endless oblivion, it was better than writhing in pain. The door opened.

"I think he's awake again," said the genasi. "Shall we continue?"

Duvan had made his decision.

"Let's try this . . ."

And with that, dread like a dark hole in the slimy recesses of Duvan's gut penetrated his soul. He felt unclean and smelled waves of putrid spray sluicing off his body. He was being corrupted from the inside out.

There was no choice. There were no other options. This realignment of his soul felt wrong in every way that something could be wrong. If he could beg for it to stop, he would.

If he had to die to make it stop, he would.

With that thought, his reticence vanished. With practiced agility, he spun the knife in his hand, feeling the hilt lock into position in his grasp. Even if he failed to kill all of his captors, Duvan would be making his own choice at the end. He could decide his own fate.

The genasi mage, Jahin, was closest, her attention focused on the torturous spell she was casting.

Duvan sprang free of the table, leaping at the mage in a blur. He brought the knife to bear, aiming for the genasi's hands. Anything to stop the spell.

Jahin reacted too slowly. Shocked, she stumbled backward as Duvan's blade slashed with surgical precision along her arm and wrist.

Duvan's legs shook and buckled from weakness. As he collapsed to the ground, he watched as Jahin's blood sprayed from the cut in her wrist. She fell back and came down on one knee.

Pain wracked Duvan's muscles as he braced his fall with outstretched arms. Gritting his teeth against the agony, he struggled to his feet. Which of his captors would be his next victim? Looking past Jahin, clutching her gushing wrist, Duvan caught sight of Renfod's dark head.

A frown graced the cleric's face, but there was no fear there. The man seemed to be irritated, and his mouth was uttering something Duvan couldn't hear. A prayer for magic.

I need to stop him from finishing, he thought.

With all his effort, Duvan lunged across the room toward Renfod. One step. All his attention focused on the effort to get to the cleric before the spell was complete. Two steps. Duvan knew that he'd be caught again if Renfod was able to finish. Three—

A sudden, searing agony pierced Duvan's back. He went rigid as a huge blade sword slid through him as easily as if he were made of lard. Beaugrat's sword, he realized too late.

"No!" Renfod cried out.

"What?" That was Beaugrat's surprised voice. The blade pulled free, and Duvan slid to the stone floor. "He was going to kill you."

"You are such a fool," Renfod said. "Commander Vraith wanted him alive."

Thick, warm liquid spilled from Duvan's back and chest, spreading in a sticky pool under him. The thump of his heartbeat hammered in his ears, drowning out all else. Numbness, starting in his fingers and toes, spread up his arms and legs.

"So heal him," Beaugrat said.

Duvan's vision grew dim, the room darkening as if looking through a veil. This was the end, he knew. Was he ready?

"Do you think a healing spell is as simple as swinging your sword?" Renfod demanded. "He'll be dead before I can start."

No, not ready. How could anyone be ready for death? Duvan fought down panic and tried to welcome oncoming death. But his body bucked and gasped, spasmed uncontrollably, and struggled to breathe.

"I must join Commander Vraith now," Renfod said. "I will have to deal you later. Clean up this mess!"

Then all went dark.

All went silent.

Duvan's last sensation was the iron tang of his own blood in the back of his throat and its overpowering odor in his nose.

All went dead.

CHAPTER TEN

Locked inside his laboratory, Gregor felt his spellscar hum with wild magic in his skull as he focused on the cauldron in front of him. The musty tomes that lined the shelves along the walls had long since faded from his consciousness. He was no longer aware of the flickering candles in their sconces, smelling faintly of vanilla and sage.

Entranced, Gregor's head resonated with the music of alchemy. Nothing else existed except the dark green, oily concoction bubbling away before him. Nothing else mattered except the slightly sweet scent drifting up from the cauldron.

Almost perfect. Almost there.

Gregor had been cooking his potion for what seemed like hours. He had no way to be sure how much time had passed. His trance skewed his sense of time.

Just a hint more crushed plaguegrass, Gregor thought, and maybe a sprinkle of ground dragon claw. Yes, that was it. Gregor flicked these last ingredients into the pot and very carefully stirred the mixture.

Vibrating in his skull like an internal tuning fork, his spellscar knew the brew was exactly right. Tiny explosions of energy and pleasure burst in his head and cascaded down through his body. This was it; the elixir was perfect. Ready to serve.

For hours, Gregor had let his spellscar show him how to cook the potion. The scar revealed the secrets of the ingredients, helping him to predict what each component would do, what effect it would have on the mixture. And along the way, Gregor had used magic here and there, infusing the elixir with potency—just a tiny sprinkling that allowed the brew of magical and mundane elements to combine in a unique and powerful way.

Gregor delighted in his work. He rejoiced in the process of creating something potent and life-changing. Ever since he'd been a child, he had loved what alchemy could accomplish. Ever since he had seen the utility and power for himself, Gregor had wanted to master it.

Just before his seventh birthday, Gregor had been travelling with Brother Velri, his mentor. They'd been approached by thieves, and Velri had told Gregor to hide in the rocks next to the narrow road.

Too terrified to make a sound, Gregor had watched as the older monk fought the small band. Though Brother Velri's martial skills took down one of the robbers, the band managed to stab him. They robbed Velri and left him for dead. When the thieves had fled, Gregor had come out of hiding to find the elder monk bleeding and on the verge of death. Velri had been stabbed many times, and thieves had taken any poultices and bandages along with his backpack.

Gregor had been certain that the man was going to die. The two of them were far from the nearest healer.

Velri removed a small pouch of powder from his boot. He told young Gregor to find some water and fill the pouch to the mark, about halfway up. Gregor ran to the small stream that flowed near the road, filled the pouch as instructed, and returned to an ailing Velri, who was nearly dead from his wounds.

Gregor watched as the monk muttered a short incantation over the pouch, mixed it with his finger, and quaffed the entire contents. A few minutes later, Gregor had looked on in awe as Brother Velri stood up and brushed the dirt from his tunic.

Alchemy had saved Velri's life. And while Gregor eventually far surpassed Velri's skill, it was the elder monk's demonstration of alchemy's power that had inspired Gregor to pursue the arcane art.

Since he'd become spellscarred, Gregor's brewing sessions had become long and exhausting. Still, he found them exhilarating as well. As he brewed each concoction, Gregor rode a building rush of excitement and pleasure from the first ingredient to the final product. And every time, in the glowing aftermath, satisfaction overwhelmed him.

The elixir in front of him was perfect, complete, and ready for consumption. And with that realization, Gregor found himself coming out of his trance. The chamber around him coalesced into existence again. His bookshelves and walls materialized into his consciousness. He could smell the distracting mustiness of the books and the faint vanilla and sage of the candles.

Gregor blinked, and his knees nearly buckled from sudden weakness. The resonating buzz from his spellscar had faded to nothing, but in its wake came a skull-splitting headache, like the prow of a ship cleaving his skull in twain.

His vision blurry from the pain, Gregor groped toward

his potion cabinet. He opened the doors and found the proper remedy, then took a swallow. The thin liquid slid down his throat, leaving a bitter taste on the back of his tongue. In a few minutes the pain would be manageable. Which was good—he didn't have time to take his normal recovery period.

"Brother Velri!" he croaked, weakened. "Please come in now."

Gregor became aware of the metallic sound of a key in the door lock. Velri—his one-time mentor, quite elderly but still alive and healthy—had been standing guard, making sure nobody disturbed Gregor during his brewing trance. Any interruption or distraction would have meant ruin for the entire batch.

Squeezing his eyes shut against the debilitating pain, Gregor breathed, "Velri, can you gather some others to help?" Gregor's breath scratched raw against his bitter throat, each intake of air sending waves of skull-cleaving pain through his head. "We need to move this cauldron to the Festival of Blue Fire."

"Yes, Brother Gregor," came the elder monk's reply. "Are you feeling all right?"

Gregor could already sense the edge of the pain starting to recede. "I will be fine in a few moments," he said. "Now, we're in a hurry."

The elder monk did not respond, but Gregor heard him shuffle off to collect some help.

Gregor concentrated on taking slow and even breaths. With each exhalation, he visualized a portion of the debilitating agony flowing out of him with the air. In with the fresh, out with the pain. And by the time Velri returned with three younger monks, Gregor's headache had dampened to a dull throb.

Gregor took another deep breath before addressing his brethren. When he exhaled, he could think again.

"It's imperative that we move quickly, my brothers," he

said. "We cannot be late to the Festival of Blue Fire." Gregor gestured toward the cauldron full of elixir. "Many pilgrims will die if they are not protected with a dose of this potion.

"We must be quick," Gregor told them, "but also extremely careful. We cannot afford to spill the concoction."

Adept and sure, his monks wasted no time. Soon, a metal lid covered the cauldron, the edges sealed with wax to prevent leakage during transport. They wrapped the covered pot with rope, tied tightly in case of jostling.

And finally, three of them carried the heavy pot to the stables and loaded the precious elixir into a small wagon. In a matter of minutes, the wagon had been hitched to a burrow and the whole group headed toward the Festival of Blue Fire.

Shortly, history would soon be made. Soon, Gregor would be taking the first step on the path to fulfilling his vision of a world without rampant spellplague. He smiled. That was a dream worth taking a risk for. A shiver of excitement danced down his spine, as he and his helpers made slow but steady progress away from the monastery.

Despite his personal dislike for Vraith, Gregor remained optimistic that it would all be worth it. The beauteous end result would completely justify the tactics they were forced to use to get there, for that result would be a restoration of order. That result was peace.

Peace was worth substantial risk.

A chill wind slid across Slanya's skin as Tyrangal teleported her, Kaylinn, and several others whom Kaylinn had enlisted to help rescue Duvan. The light of the afternoon sun winked out as the monastery courtyard vanished. The open, fresh air gave way to a smoky and stuffy enclosed corridor that smelled of tallow and soot.

The hot air made the dark space feel tight and claustrophobic. Slanya struggled to take slow, even breaths while her eyes adjusted to the darkness. Her heart raced with anticipation, and sweat prickled on her brow from the heat. But as she focused on her breathing, balance returned, and she found herself ready for a fight.

"Duvan is in the room just down these stairs," Tyrangal whispered. "I scried him earlier. There are five or six people in the room, but Commander Accordant Vraith and her entourage have left. We should be able to overcome those remaining."

Taking a deep breath, Slanya took a firm grip on her staff. She was ready.

"Hey! What are you—?"

Slanya turned toward the sound, coming from a man in chainmail climbing up the staircase toward them.

She watched as Tyrangal gestured with her hand, her reaction extremely quick. Simultaneously, on the edge of her vision, Slanya could swear that she saw something flick out of Tyrangal's mouth, stretch out and touch the man on the forehead, then retract. But the whole thing happened in a blink of an eye, leaving Slanya wondering what she'd seen.

"We are friends," came Tyrangal's soothing contralto. "We're here to escort the prisoner to his cell."

The man's face slackened from suspicion to understanding. He nodded. "All right," he said. "Wonderful. Although I don't think you will be needed."

"We'll be the ones to judge that," Tyrangal said as she swept past the guard. She laid one hand on his head, whispered a quick spell, and the man collapsed.

They crept down the hallway to another door. Tyrangal paused here.

"There's a guard just inside," Tyrangal said. "Leave her to me."

"We'll try to find Duvan," Slanya said, looking at Kaylinn, who nodded.

Slanya entered the room behind Tyrangal, who was enshrouded now in a shifting, prismatic aura and was difficult to see. A quick glance around the room showed Slanya a torch-lit dungeon, complete with stone walls and arched ceiling, iron chains and manacles, and several tables fitted with restraints for securing and interrogating prisoners.

To Slanya's right, she caught sight of Duvan, lying slumped across the floor. He looked unconscious and there was an alarming amount of blood pooled under him. She hoped they weren't too late.

"Kaylinn," Slanya called. "There he is."

the room was mostly empty of Order members, but those remaining had converged on Duvan. There was no sign of Vraith, but Slanya counted three others in addition to the guard. Four, if she included the genasi woman wrapping a bandage around her wrist.

Slanya recognized one of the Order guards—Beaugrat.

"You again!" Beaugrat stood beside Duvan, a bloody sword in his hand. "You should have gotten out when you had the chance."

Beside Slanya, Kaylinn sent a wave of holy fire into two Order members clustering around Duvan's body. They backed away as she approached, but not fast enough to avoid the blast. The genasi wizard dodged and started toward Tyrangal

Slanya spun her staff and leveled it at Beaugrat. She advanced on the warrior, moving quickly, but careful to remain steady and aware. She knew her opponent was an accomplished swordsman and was far stronger than he looked. She'd seen that when he had fought Duvan in the ruins outside Tyrangal's mansion.

Beaugrat drew his huge sword and leveled it at Slanya. He held the weapon with both hands and swung it with surprising deftness and agility. If he but hit her once, Slanya would be out of the fight.

Best not let him hit me then, she thought wryly.

Circling him, Slanya was aware of the escalating magical battle between Tyrangal and the genasi wizard. The woman's aquamarine skin glowed, and the spellscar on her head seemed to flow with silver. She had manifested some sort of magical shield around herself—a clear bubble of power that absorbed and deflected Tyrangal's fiery blasts. Inside, the genasi appeared to be unharmed.

Tyrangal's attacks increased in power, but each one merely rolled off the protective bubble and scorched the walls and floor around her. The splash damage from their combat could easily fry everyone in the room.

Beaugrat stepped forward and brought his large sword down on Slanya—a quick strike, but one she easily dodged.

Breathe. Counterattack. Her staff glanced off his neck guard, but she followed it by stepping lightly to her left and cracking her staff against his hands. Perhaps she could loosen his grip on his weapon.

Her strike landed hard, and it was like hitting a stone wall. No give at all. Her staff vibrated in her grip, and she barely held on.

Beaugrat hardly seemed to notice.

As she sidestepped another swing, Slanya calculated her next strike. Her quickness meant that she could make several attacks to each of his. His head was the only part of him that was exposed. He was vulnerable there. She whipped her staff around and struck the big man in the side of head, just over his left ear.

Her staff was a blur, and Beaugrat had no time to dodge. The weapon shook in her hands as the blunt end thudded home. Slanya was gratified to see dark blood welling through Beaugrat's blond hair.

"Nice hit," he snarled, but his expression was of a wounded animal, cornered and more vicious than before. "Now it's your turn."

Abruptly, Beaugrat sheathed his sword. He pressed his wrists together with his palms facing Slanya.

What was he doing?

Blue fire flickered to life from the spellscar on his shoulder, rippling like ignited oil down to his elbow and encasing his whole arm.

A wave of nausea pulsed through Slanya. But as she focused on Beaugrat's spellscar, she felt something awaken inside her. Energy sparking from one point to another, prickling against her skin. Her own spellscar activated, illuminating her skin. And as the wild magic permeated her and fragmented her, she suddenly she understood how Beaugrat created the blue fire.

She understood, and she reached out to affect it. As her spellscar web attuned to Beaugrat's power, Slanya's reality split and split again until she could barely keep her mind integrated. But she found the essence of Beaugrat's ability. Slanya felt the wild magic flowing through Beaugrat's scar, and she willed it to stop. In an instant, the web of filaments that made up her spellscar closed down his power.

The blue fire on Beaugrat's arm guttered and dwindled away then died. He stared at his hands in disbelief. "How did you . . . ?"

Slanya didn't really know. When her spellscar flared to life, she simply understood how Beaugrat's own spellscar worked—and how to stop it from working.

The big man stumbled, weakened and in shock. He fell to his knees, his plate armor ringing against the tile floor.

Slanya wasted no time. The fragments of her reality made physical combat difficult and quick movements nauseating. Her staff came down hard on his head, and Beaugrat collapsed to the floor in a heap of metal and flesh.

Slanya glanced around. Tyrangal and the genasi guard

fought vigorously, each unable to do serious harm to the other. Tyrangal was clearly the more powerful wizard, but the genasi's shield made her invulnerable to attacks. On the opposite side of the room, Kaylinn and two others from the monastery had reached Duvan. They were examining him, and as much as she wanted to go to Duvan, her skills were needed elsewhere for the moment.

Can I do it again? Slanya wondered. Turning, she reached out with her ability and touched the genasi wizard fighting to a near stalemate with Tyrangal. Yes. In moments, Slanya understood the source and nature of the guard's protective shield. She saw how the shield ability worked.

Different shards of reality vied for the attention of Slanya's mind. She could not hold everything together, and part of her knew that if she didn't stop using her spellscar ability shortly, her mind would unhinge completely from the physical world around her.

She wanted to try one more thing first. Whether it was worth the risk to herself, she never considered. Watching as though from farther and farther away, Slanya tried to reverse the process. She used her spellscar ability and tried to amplify the guard's shield.

And she saw the shield double in diameter, then triple. Before her fragmenting eyes, Slanya watched as the shield grew so large that it soon encompassed Tyrangal as well. The genasi's eyes went wide in astonishment.

Astonishment turned to fear as the full power of Tyrangal's spells descended upon her. Cast from inside the bubble, Tyrangal's flames incinerated the genasi guard.

The guard's aquamarine skin blackened, charred, and blistered. In seconds, the genasi was reduced to soot hovering in the space where a fully alive being had been. The shield vanished, and the genasi's remains drifted in the air like dust.

Turning slowly, Slanya's mind sparkling like a constellation of independent stars, she became aware that Kaylinn was yelling something from where she stood over Duvan's limp body. As Slanya's spellscar waned in successive pulses, she tried to focus, tried to reintegrate herself. It seemed to take forever, but eventually she heard what Kaylinn was yelling.

"He's dead!" Kaylinn said. "Duvan is dead."

Stunned and enraged, Slanya screamed, "No!" But she could barely hear herself.

Beaugrat lay slumped at Slanya's feet, completely helpless. Anger rose up in her. Duvan was dead, and it was this man's fault. Duvan did not deserve to be dead. Duvan had saved her life several times. He was her friend.

As if watching herself from far away, from different vantage points simultaneously, Slanya reached down and took hold of Beaugrat's bruised head. She crooked his jaw into the fold of her right elbow and made sure her grip would not slip.

Anger welled up inside her. She clenched her jaw and with all her strength, jerked Beaugrat's head in a rapid, wrenching twist. The snap of his spine made a satisfying crunch, and she knew he was dead.

Part of her knew she shouldn't want revenge. She had been taught that revenge accomplished nothing. Part of her knew she'd done this before, a long time ago as a little girl. But that time it had accomplished something. That time, revenge had changed her life.

That wasn't revenge, she realized. That was escape. Survival.

Here, too, killing Beaugrat was survival. The man had proven that he would keep coming back. His continued existence was a danger to Duvan. Well, not anymore.

Slanya stood, her reality fragmented. Queasy, her awareness floating out of her body, she collapsed next to her dead victim.

Duvan stood on a featureless plane—a flat gray landscape stretching as far as he could see. The sky overhead was a lighter shade of gray. Ahead, there were no trees or rocks or hills or vegetation of any kind. He could no longer taste the intense iron tang of blood in the back of his throat, and the thick smell of blood had disappeared.

There were no other people on this vast plane, none close enough to see at least. However, he could hear something. Whispers and hissing bass voices were the only sound, an undercurrent of indistinguishable vocal droning that seemed to come from all around. Those whispers permeated his spirit, seeming to snap at his soul like dogs.

Where am I? he wondered.

Duvan examined himself. He was whole, his body sound except for a dry cut under his ribcage. No blood there, but the scar remained open. It didn't hurt. In fact he felt nothing—no pain, no joy. Nothing. Only emptiness.

He felt like an animated husk—a hollowed-out marionette.

Turning, Duvan caught sight of a small, gray bump on the horizon—a tiny blip on the flat landscape of gray. He started walking toward it, his progress marked only by the shape's fractional increase in size. But whatever it was, that dull bump on the otherwise flat plane, Duvan felt drawn to it.

Deep gray and black shadows drifted like tatters of wind-driven fog all around him as he walked. He felt no fear and no fatigue as he walked and walked. For hours he walked, and the dark bump on the horizon grew little by little. Days and tendays and even months seemed to pass as he trudged forward. He had no sense of time in this place.

Fragments of memory flitted through his mind. He'd heard tell that souls passed to the Fugue Plane, Kelemvor's home, to be judged. Perhaps that is where I am, he thought. But where is Kelemvor?

After more hours of walking, some of the whispered voices grew more distinct. One of them started talking to him, telling him that he didn't have to go to the City of Judgment. Telling him that there were better options. The gods might not want him, but there were lords elsewhere who would accept him with open arms. He would start out at the bottom, but a soul like his could rise quickly. He would have power and eventual dominion over many others.

Duvan shook his head and marched on.

You should consider the offer, the whispers murmured. You are one of the Faithless. Your fate will otherwise be an eternity of boredom and monotony. The death god will entomb you in the walls of his city, forever.

Duvan walked on, considering. The Faithless—he had heard of that legend. No god to speak for him meant spending eternity as part of the City of Judgment. Duvan felt detached from himself, but even so he knew that he did not want to end up that way.

But the alternative? An eternity in the thrall of the demons of the Abyss. Endless boredom or endless pain.

As if on cue—although it could have been hours later since Duvan had completely lost track of time—another voice came to him. "Duvan?" It was not the low hiss of the demons' voices. This was a voice he recognized. "Duvan?"

He turned to see a shimmering archway shining with blinding light, so bright he couldn't see anyone through it. "I am here," he said.

"I have come to guide you back, if you will come," the voice said. "You must decide quickly, for the spell does not last long."

Somewhere in the distant, hollow recesses of his mind, Duvan remembered his life—the struggles, the distrust, the pain.

There was also pleasure, he remembered. That had been

part of his life. And contentment. Sadness, yes, but also humor and even joy, once or twice.

"I will come," he told the voice—a voice he recognized as belonging to the High Priestess Kaylinn of Slanya's monastery. Slanya had not betrayed him after all. His friend Slanya had come to save him.

His friend. Duvan liked the thought of that.

"Step through," Kaylinn said. "Come back into the light."

And so he did.

Commander Accordant Vraith strode purposefully through the throngs of revelers who had arrived for the Festival of Blue Fire. Pilgrims young and old had come to this broad, grassy field on the boundary between the mundane and the glorious. Entire families celebrated here along the border of the Plaguewrought Land.

The pilgrims had brought their wagons full of supplies and had built huge bonfires whose flames licked the sky. Here and there, pilgrims danced to music and singing. They feasted on roasted food and drank wine and ale without restraint. Many children joined in the festivities, and Vraith noticed more than a few coming-of-age rituals under way.

They smelled of joy and intoxication. Chaos and abandonment.

Vraith felt the stirrings of her spellscar beneath her sternum, eager to pull the threads of their souls and weave them together. If her ritual worked, some part of each of these lucky volunteers would end up locked inside the new border.

Vraith's deputy—Renfod, himself a Loremaster Accordant— came up next to her, joining a handful of others here to carry out her instructions. The chaotic crowd would have to be at least minimally structured, which she knew might prove more difficult than performing the actual ritual. It was one thing to arrange five or ten people, and quite another to organize a thousand or so.

The evening sky reddened overhead as she neared the border veil. Like a sheen of oil on water, the barrier reflected an undulating rainbow, stretching like a semi-translucent curtain as far as she could see in all directions. Most of the pilgrims gave the barrier a wide berth.

"Has anyone seen Brother Gregor?" Vraith asked nobody in particular. "He'd better have brought his elixir."

Renfod nodded, then said,. "He's here, Commander. At the edge of the festivities."

Vraith smiled. "Excellent. We'll start with him. Lead on."

Renfod's dark form angled away from the border veil and through the crowds of drinking and dancing pilgrims. Vraith appreciated the man's efficiency, his obedience, and willingness to serve.

Still, there was no need to get sentimental. He was just one filament in the tapestry of her rise to authority and power. A willing filament to be sure, but nothing more. Her ascendancy would culminate, ultimately, in her rapture—her melding with the sharn. She would become one with the transcendent collective minds of the sharn; she would live in the Blue Fire and across many universes simultaneously.

Unfortunately, while Renfod bent over backward to help her further her cause, the same could not be said for Brother Gregor.

She hated that she needed him. But there was nobody else who could work the alchemical magic that he could. The man had a gift. She'd had to resort to non-magical forms of manipulation—persuasion and cunning. That was all right with Vraith, however; she was good at those talents too.

Renfod and his entourage cleared a path to the periphery

of the festival throng. They passed a wedding ceremony under-way. The tall bride was all smiles in her lace finery, while her portly groom looked nervous behind his well-clipped beard.

"There he is," Renfod said as they circumnavigated the wedding, pointing a little ways ahead at Gregor.

The monk's shock of white hair was a beacon tinged with red in the light of the waning sun. He stood with several other monks and clerics from the monastery, all surrounding a large metal cauldron. Vraith could see as she approached that the cauldron was full of dull green liquid.

"May the Blue Fire burn inside you," Vraith said.

"Pray Oghma grants you wisdom," Gregor replied, his tone icy.

Vraith pretended to ignore Gregor's cold attitude; she gestured at the cauldron with her hand. "I trust the elixir is ready?"

"It is," he said. "Now I just need to get people to drink it."

"I can help," she said. Then, turning to Renfod, "Let's get our militia to arrange everyone in a long line. Tell them that I will come by and bless them each individually with a small cut on their palms and a drink from the cauldron. The ritual can begin only when this is completed."

Renfod nodded and then strode away, barking orders.

"This thing you do," Gregor said. "I have your word that it will be used to tame and capture the spellplague in all its forms across Faerûn?"

Vraith stared hard into Gregor's gray eyes. "Don't start having second thoughts now, monk. You're in too deep to swim to the surface on your own."

Gregor refused to back down. "You didn't answer the question."

So he was going to need her to lie. That was fine with her; lies came easily to her. "Someone's word," she said, "is as fickle as the next famine or plague or war. I give you my word, for whatever that is worth to you."

Gregor's brow knitted in puzzlement.

"But," Vraith said, "nobody's word is worth what you think it is. The only thing that you have of value is your own internal compass, your own faith. Gregor, you either trust me to do what you believe needs to be done, or you do not. My word cannot change that.

"And," Vraith continued, "as I just said; you are in too deep to be having doubts now."

Gregor shook his head slowly. "I have many options," he said.

Vraith forced herself to bite back an angry retort. She smiled. "Well, you do what you need to do. But I assure you that you have nothing to worry about. The truly great have to make hard choices, and oftentimes lesser folks get caught in the way. It is the price of vision.

"We will change the world, you and I," she told Gregor. And she believed it.

Duvan came to life with a shock. His back arching in spasm, he gulped air. Again, shocks shot through his body, and his chest seemed to be filled with broken glass. A violent exhalation seized him, as though a giant invisible hand clamped down on his chest. He rolled on his side and coughed up blood and phlegm. Then the pain hit. His back burned where Beaugrat's blade had pierced him. His head felt like it had been wrenched off and then jammed back into place.

Darkness and silence surrounded him. He could see nothing, hear nothing. The iron tang of blood that filled his nostrils stank so powerfully that it blocked out all other smells.

Then, filtered through the black cotton in his head, he heard a voice he recognized. "He's alive," Kaylinn said. "Welcome back, Duvan."

Liquid against the back of his throat blazed a trail down to his chest, somewhat dulling the ache that pervaded his muscles and joints. His eyes were open, but he could not see any light. Only tiny pinpricks of light showed in the vast dark gray in front of him.

"Thank you so much, Kaylinn." That was Slanya's voice, and he heard tears in the utterance. His heart opened with the sound. Slanya had not betrayed or abandoned him. On the contrary, she had come to save him.

"Thank Kelemvor," Kaylinn said. "For he allowed Duvan back among the living."

"His time is not over," Slanya said, and her voice was not the stoic and rigid Slanya he remembered—the combat cleric who challenged him, who stood by him and fought. No, there was a deep vulnerability in that voice, a touching quality that melted Duvan.

"Where am I?" he asked, but no one seemed to hear him. He couldn't even hear himself. His mouth wasn't working right.

"He's trying to talk," Kaylinn said. "It will take a few hours for him to completely recover all his senses. But he can hear you now."

Slanya's voice was in his ear. "You rest now, Duvan," she said, and her breath smelled of almonds. "You have no cares in the world."

If the voice said rest, then that's what he would do.

Some time later, though he had no way of knowing how much, he awoke. His vision came back slowly and in patches. And he could sense that he was lying flat on his back, but the pallet that held him was soft, and the sheets under and over him were elegant and clean. He was naked, he realized then, and had been scrubbed free of dirt.

"How do you feel, Slanya?" came Kaylinn's voice.

Duvan's eyes fluttered open to see the High Priestess standing in the open doorway of the small chamber.

"I feel a little more myself," Slanya said. She sat on the foot of his cot, wearing a clean cloth robe. "After I used my spellscar power, everything fragmented. It was as though reality was crumbling around me. I couldn't trust what I saw. Your healing has helped some."

"Your spellscar has left you fragile," Kaylinn said. "And I have reached the limit of my healing abilities."

Slanya was injured, Duvan realized.

"You must be exceedingly careful to use your power in moderation," Kaylinn said.

"I understand. Thank you, High Priestess. I will be careful."

"Well, if you're stable now," Kaylinn said. "I am going to go get some rest." Duvan heard fatigue in Kaylinn's voice for the first time. "I'm exhausted."

Light came through a window, red and orange. The setting sun, Duvan guessed, from the tenor of the light. At the foot of his bed, Slanya's silhouette was limned in red, like a crimson halo. Duvan blinked; the richness of color was overwhelming after the monochromatic gray of the plane of death.

Duvan heard a door slide closed as Kaylinn left to get some rest. Late-summer birds chirped as treble accompaniment to the deep droning of chanting monks in the background. The smells were overwhelming as well. The odor of lilac soap drifted up around him, and he grew increasingly aware of the spicy scent of healing balm permeating the room.

Then the sheets around him rustled, and the smell of woman washed away everything else. Slanya nestled in next to him, her body warm against his. She wrapped her arms around him in an intimate hug.

"I thought you were gone, Duvan," she said. Her hands combed through his hair, and the feel of her caress brought tears to his eyes. Whether he was too tired or overwhelmed to fight it, he didn't know, but he realized that he cared for Slanya.

She cradled him in her arms and petted his brow. "Everything's all right now," she whispered.

He curled up in Slanya's embrace. He surrendered to the overwhelming urge to trust in her. He could be vulnerable with her, and everything would be all right. That was a gift beyond anything he'd imagined possible ever again.

"I've got you, Duvan," Slanya said. "I will take care of you."

Since Papa had died, nobody had said that. Nobody had ever rescued him. Even Rhiazzshar's pleasures had been manipulative and full of expectant reciprocity. Slayna's offer was pure generosity and selflessness. He had always been on his own, and it felt so good to let someone take care of him. Tears welled in Duvan's eyes, and his voice caught in his throat.

"Thank you," he mouthed to her through the sobs. "Thank you."

CHAPTER ELEVEN

Gregor stood in the cool air washing across the grassy fields. He shivered, chilly despite the body warmth of the masses of pilgrims gathered for the Festival of Blue Fire. His silk robe let the wind through, sending waves of goosebumps across his skin.

He clenched his teeth and hoped the events of this night went well. He hated that Order of Blue Fire bitch. Hated that he had fallen into this deal. Hated that she was right when she said he had come too far to stop.

Taking a deep breath, Gregor calmed himself. Anger would not serve him well. He needed focus. Fortitude.

The prismatic glow of the towering border veil cast an eldritch pall over the crowds and the trampled grass field. The sun had set hours earlier, and bonfires had sprung up sporadically through the field. Many revelers danced in groups around the fires, although most responded to the instructions by Vraith's small army of Peacekeepers. They had fallen quite literally into line.

Gregor was impressed with the efficiency and organization of Vraith's workforce. After only a short time, a long line of pilgrims arced out from a spot on the westernmost edge of the wide field, circumnavigated the bulk of tents and wagons, and came to a head near the eastern edge.

Vraith and a small entourage of her trusted advisors travelled along the line, while Gregor and his helpers trailed behind. "Join us in embracing the Blue Fire together," Vraith said over and over again as she moved along the line.

Gregor noticed that while most pilgrims had joined the line, quite a few had ignored the call to join in. Quite a few of those were children. He knew that once the ritual was complete, the entire field would be inside the Plaguewrought Land. All those children would be swallowed up by the advancing changelands.

"Here, I need to cut your palm," Vraith said further down the line. "It hurts but a little and will ensure that you are one with the others when we are all baptized in the light of the Blue Fire." She sliced their palms and told them not to stop the bleeding until the ritual was complete. They would know when.

Gregor and his monks followed behind her and gave each pilgrim a ladle from the cauldron. "A single swallow will protect you from overexposure to the wild magic," he told them. And mostly, he believed it. As with most things, the truth was far more complicated and could not be explained in a single sentence.

Using a hollow needle and indigo pigment, Brother Velri marked each pilgrim who received a dose of the elixir. It was important to give everyone enough and there was a limited supply; he didn't want people taking more than one drink.

Ahead of them, Vraith paused a second. "Congratulations on the wondrous occasion of your wedding," she said, speaking to a tall, dark-haired woman dressed in fine lace. "I am extremely honored you have chosen the Festival of Blue Fire to celebrate your personal union."

The woman beamed a toothy smile at Vraith, and the shorter, portly man beside her gave a respectful bow. His dark eyes showed concern as Vraith cut his new wife's palms with the ceremonial knife. The woman, for her part, demonstrated no reluctance and showed no evidence of pain.

Gregor and his crew followed, doling out doses. He too congratulated the couple, although he couldn't help but wonder as he passed them whether their wedding night would be marred by the horrific massacre of scores of children.

No, he thought. Surely, Vraith would hold off until all pilgrims were safe.

Gregor had given out over a thousand doses by the time they were nearing the end of the line. Everyone was in a festive mood, gazing up in awe at the gauzy haze of the border veil punctuated by flashes of blue-white fire behind it. It seemed that even the Plaguewrought Land was restless behind the border, eager to reach out and touch all these willing participants to history.

Gregor shivered. This minor expansion of the Plaguewrought Land was temporary. It was a necessary test to achieving his vision—a proof of concept on a grand scale. If this worked, then he would work to enforce the agreement he'd made with Vraith.

The Commander Accordant's perfected ritual would make it possible to contain rampant spellplague storms. They would be able to create borders where none existed before. And eventually all of the tumultuous changelands that existed in the world would be organized.

And yet, Gregor had grown more and more suspicious that Vraith did not share his vision. The ritual was dependent upon her. Her spellscar ability was critical, and even if the same result could be achieved without her, Gregor had no inkling of how that might be accomplished. If it turned out that Vraith was not willing or motivated to use the ritual to contain spellplague storms, then Gregor's help now was more than a waste. He was all too aware that it made him complicit in the destabilization of the Plaguewrought Land.

Tyrangal's words haunted him. *Vraith will use this ritual to move the border of the Plaguewrought Land, to expand the total area of these plaguelands. Of that I am sure. The Order wants to* increase *the blue fire's reach, and if they gain control over the border, they will eventually be able to unleash the spellplague contained within.*

As he came to the last pilgrims in the line and gave them drinks of his concoction, Gregor straightened. His work tonight was nearly done. Ironically, Vraith was right about him. He despised her, but it was too late to back out now. He'd placed his bet. The stakes were high, but the payoff would be massive. All of Faerûn would reap the profits of this gamble.

Tyrangal would see that. And if she did not, she would be left behind.

Gregor looked across the field, bathed in the gray light of the border. There were still many, many pilgrims who had ignored the call to line up. Every one of them would be exposed if they were inside the arc when the ritual started.

Bonfires provided hubs of warmth and celebration. In the glow from the changelands, and the warmth of the bonfires, the festival had managed to mutate this plain into a landscape of dancing and music. The smell of spiced meat and roasting garlic and warm bread mingled in the air, temporarily masking the lingering scent of the funeral pyres and the Plaguewrought Land—the stench of oranges and carrion.

Gregor gave over the task of distributing elixir to Brother Velri. "We need to encourage everyone to drink a dose," Gregor said. "All of these who are determined to stay inside the arc. And give it to children first. It will protect them all."

Velri nodded.

"I'm going to talk with Vraith," Gregor said. "To see how much time we have. All these folks should be outside the arc just in case, and the Order Peacekeepers can help with that."

Gregor stepped up his pace and caught up to Vraith. Surrounded by Order Peacekeepers and clerics, Vraith barked instructions to her minions to get the lined-up pilgrims to space themselves evenly and hold hands. "The blood bond must be complete for this to work!"

"Vraith," Gregor said, pushing through the Peacekeepers, who reluctantly allowed him to pass.

"Gregor," Vraith grinned at him. "Thank you for your good work. Now, you and your monks should move outside the arc."

"We're trying to get the remaining pilgrims inoculated." He gestured at the bonfires still surrounded by dancers and drunken pilgrims passed out on the ground.

Vraith shrugged. "I don't think they'll cause trouble for the ritual."

Gregor was appalled at her lack of compassion. "Yes, but that means that hundreds of pilgrims remain unprotected and will likely die."

Vraith's angular face went stone hard. "I understand that, monk. And it is not my concern. They all know what they are risking. It is their choice to make."

Momentary shock took hold of Gregor, but he quickly quelled it. He glared at her. "That doesn't excuse genocide, wizard."

Vraith's straight-chopped blonde head shook slowly back and forth. "I don't have time for this," she said. "These few stragglers," she waved at the pilgrims inside the arc, "were told the same thing as those thousand or so." She pointed at the line. "I wash my hands of the ignorant and selfish. You do what you need to do."

"At least give me time to give these folks the elixir," Gregor said.

"You can do that if you'd like, of course, but the ritual will begin as soon as the circuit is complete."

"How much time do I have?"

Vraith glanced around at the line of pilgrims. There were still places where people weren't lined up perfectly, sections where the pilgrims weren't holding bloody palms to their neighbors'. "I'd say about a half hour," she said. "An hour at most."

An hour? Gregor thought. An hour to save all these pilgrims?

An hour was no time at all.

A faint breeze tickled Duvan's skin. A dim flare of red slowly grew brighter. A burlap-covered pillow scratched against his cheek as he drowsed. The weight of Slanya's arm draped across his chest made him feel secure, reassured that he wasn't alone in the universe. Not anymore.

The red light brightened, spurring him awake. The door to the small chamber was opening. He opened his eyes and realized that he felt refreshed and alert. He should be exhausted after all that had happened. He'd only been asleep for several hours, but for the first time in years, no dream memories had haunted him.

Slanya stirred in the bed next to him. Sweet Slanya.

The sky outside the window had grown dark during their sleep, and the room was dark except for the torchlight coming through the opening door. The torch's red flicker cast sharp shadows into the room as someone entered.

"Duvan?" came Tyrangal's voice from the opening door. "Time to get up! I need your help."

He came fully awake and sat up in the bed. Despite feeling alert and rested, pain shot through him with the movement. His back itched and burned where he'd been stabbed, and the bones of his recently broken leg ached. Magical healing and resurrection were phenomenal things, but the body still remembered the trauma. Duvan's body was telling him that it was time to rest.

Hopefully, he would soon get to do so. "What do you need, mistress?" he said. "I am a little worse for wear, but I will do whatever you require of me."

Tyrangal stepped into the room, tall and radiant. Her face seemed to glow with inner fire, and her eyes were like embers. She looked at Duvan, and then at Slanya slipping out of the bed on the other side.

Duvan turned to watch as Slanya shrugged into a thin, brown robe. The colorful tattoo of Kelemvor's scales disappeared beneath the garment as it came down over her neck and back.

Slanya turned and met his gaze. Her thin lips spread into a broad smile, lighting up her whole face. Affection and gratitude welled inside him. He felt better than he'd felt in a very long time.

Tyrangal's tone grew even more urgent. "The Festival of Blue Fire is underway right now. Vraith has Gregor's elixir, and with it she can expand the changelands. She can unleash the Spellplague once more. Even with my guard, I cannot defeat the Order without help."

Duvan looked around for his combat leathers and found them on the small wooden table, clean and folded. He dressed quickly, despite residual pain throughout his body, pulling on his worn and abused pants and lacing them up. He donned his thick leather tunic, and with sure hands he arranged and tightened all his gear so that he would ready for whatever challenges lay ahead this night. "I'm not sure what I can do that you cannot," he said. "But I am with you."

"You are immune to the touch of the plaguelands," Tyrangal said. "You can destroy the Order's plans."

Duvan shook his head, remembering the torture. "They can easily kill me in other ways," he said with a harsh laugh. He remembered the searing burn of the fire and the deep soul-wrenching dread he had experienced during torture.

Glancing over at Slanya, Duvan saw that she was nearly fully dressed in her combat gear now. He didn't know how their friendship would evolve from here or if it would develop into something more. But he did know that it *was* a friendship and that was something worth keeping. Worth living for.

In fact, he had a lot to live for, not the least of which was to avoid ending up as part of Kelemvor's city wall. Duvan knew he wanted to do something good with his life. He needed his life to mean something. Right now he would help Tyrangal stop the expansion of the Plague-wrought Land.

Stop the plaguestorms from spreading. Prevent villages like his from being wiped off the map. That was worth doing.

He met Slanya's eyes. "I'm going to do this," he said. "But you don't have to go." He turned to look at Tyrangal. "She doesn't have to go, does she?"

Slanya gave a grim chuckle. "You're going, so I'm going," she said. "And I'll roust the other doomguides too."

Tyrangal's aristocratic face registered awareness at this exchange, but when she spoke, there was a deep sadness in her voice. "I need Duvan to come with me now," she said then gazed at Slanya. "If you wish to help, make all haste possible to the festival field."

Duvan finished preparing himself. He stood, feeling marginally more ready for battle but still a shadow of his normal self. Like a husk, ready to be blown aside on a gust of wind. Still, Tyrangal said it was important, and he owed her his life.

He turned to Slanya, who was fully dressed and heading for the door. He reached out for her hand, and his touch stopped her. Surprised, she turned to him. He mouthed, "Thank you," then let go.

Her smile was brief, but it was enough. And then he watched her pass through the door and disappear down the hall, calling for Kaylinn and the other monks to join her.

"Come outside with me," Tyrangal said. "I will show you my true form."

Duvan followed quickly and quietly. In the distance, he could hear Slanya calling for the monks and clerics to gather in the central courtyard, raising the alarm.

Duvan always known that Tyrangal was more than what she seemed, that she was alien to him in some primal way. But her bounty and generosity toward him was undeniable. She had never betrayed him or lied to him, so he'd never questioned her about what made her different. It had never mattered.

Outside in the courtyard, under the deep, midnight-blue sky full of stars and motes, Duvan watched as Tyrangal commanded the gathering monastery folk to give her a wide berth. When they had backed away from a Tyrangal who seemed larger and less and less human, his long-time mentor and benefactor underwent a remarkable transformation.

Duvan watched in awe and growing recognition as Tyrangal's neck elongated. Her skin grew rough and scaly. Her arms thickened and her body stretched until she had grown to fill half the courtyard. Duvan found his heart pounding, but more with pride than fear when Tyrangal sprouted a heavy tail and broad batlike wings.

Horns grew out of Tyrangal's new elongated head. Teeth as long as Duvan's forearm showed from her snout as she grinned. The torchlight reflected coppery off her shiny scales, as smooth as polished glass, and glimmered off spikes as sharp as daggers sprouting from the back of her head and neck.

Duvan took a step back as the huge beast stretched her wings and neck. Then she let out a loud, bone-shaking roar into the sky. Tyrangal was a dragon.

Duvan sucked in a breath. It made sense, he thought. It fit. He was glad he'd never tried to kiss her, though.

"Climb on," she said. "We have a date with fire."

Slanya watched in amazement as her fellow clerics and monks gasped at the massive dragon in the courtyard. Everyone took a step back as Duvan climbed up onto Tyrangal's extended front knee. Slanya felt a rush of sympathetic fear as she watched her new friend grab hold of a spike that jutted from Tyrangal's shoulder and pulled himself up to her neck.

By Kelemvor! Slanya thought. Tyrangal was full of surprises.

Was she really a dragon? Or a powerful illusionist? It hardly mattered; she was on Slanya's side. It was good to have such friends.

When Duvan had finally settled into a somewhat secure position, straddling Tyrangal's neck near the base, he leaned down against the dragon and swung a rope around her neck to help him hang on. And as he tied the rope loosely but securely, the dragon stretched her leathery wings and rose into the air in a swirl of wind and dust.

Wind buffeted Slanya as she watched the two of them fly off toward the border of the Plaguewrought Land, toward the Festival of Blue Fire. She shook her head to clear it.

Marvels like this happened. She'd been through the change-lands and come out again! No time right now to dwell on these things.

As she readied herself for combat, Slanya considered her condition. She was tired and still in a great deal of pain. She was far from completely healed and certainly not completely sound of mind and body. But she could not afford to sit this out. She didn't have time to heal up. She didn't even know if her spellscar could be healed.

Slanya tried not to think about Duvan's safety now, but she already knew that she would miss him if something happened to him. She steeled herself, focused, and tucked away her emotions as best she could.

She located Kaylinn, dragging herself from her chambers half-dressed and bleary-eyed. Slanya told her what Tyrangal had reported and what needed to be done to stop Vraith. She explained that hundreds of pilgrims could die in the festival—that the Order of Blue Fire intended to expand the border of the Plaguewrought Land.

The Order must be thwarted in this.

Kaylinn merely yawned and nodded. "Go confront Brother Gregor," she said. "He's not evil, just driven by selfish motives. Get him to help you stop Vraith. I will organize the temple complex, and we will meet you at the festival field."

"Aye, High Priestess," Slanya said. And then, overcome with gratitude, she continued, "Thank you for all you've done."

Kaylinn merely grinned and said, "When this is all over, you can take my duties for a day while I sleep."

Slanya laughed. "Deal."

"Now go!"

Slanya grabbed her staff then raced to the stables. She quickly saddled one of the mares, eased it out of the stall, and mounted. Slanya heeled the horse into motion, quickly picking her way through the scattered tents toward the Festival of Blue Fire.

Warm wind washed over her scalp, her sideknot whipping as she rode. Despite the darkness of the night, the horse made no missteps. The mare easily negotiated the proliferation of tents and scattered wagons. Then Slanya was clear of the encampment and galloped up a short hill.

Wheeling her horse around, Slanya gazed down at the sight of the Festival of Blue Fire aglow with many bonfires. The pandemonium of the festival drew her in like a moth to a funeral pyre. Part of her wanted to dive in and dance, revel with the pilgrims, and let the chaos consume her. Part of her had always been drawn to let go of her iron grip on order. Abandoning herself to randomness would be freeing.

And self-destructive.

As the pallet of colors resolved in front of her, patterns emerged. Order from chaos. She caught sight of a long line of pilgrims arcing out from the border veil, enclosing the revelers. It made sense that the line marked where Vraith's new border would be. Vraith would increase the size of the Plaguewrought Land by an area about the size of Ormpetarr.

If Vraith was successful, would everyone inside the arc be consumed? Burned alive by the chaotic changelands?

Where were Tyrangal and Duvan?

Slanya searched the skies above. Eldritch light from the border veil washed the sky in blue-gray, making it hard to see shadows. For a moment Slanya saw nothing but a flat, monochrome expanse above her—no stars or motes or clouds, although she knew all of those things were up there. A flicker of red flared low in the sky, drawing her attention.

Ah, there they were. Flying low, the burnished copper dragon breathed a stream of burning acid as she dived at a small group of what looked to be high-ranking Order of Blue Fire accordants standing amid a cadre of well-armed Order Peacekeepers.

Dragon's breath belched forth from Tyrangal's diving form, but the Order group stood their ground near the far end of the line of pilgrims, right next to the border veil. As Slanya watched, the deadly acid was absorbed by a protective sphere of energy that surrounded th group. And as the liquid ran off and hit the ground with a hiss, it became clear that nobody inside the sphere had been touched by the acid.

A few of the pilgrims scattered in fear. Most of them, however, held their formation, and those who ran were caught by roving Peacekeepers on horseback and returned to their spots. Other Peacekeepers fired arrows and cast spells at the dragon as she swooped past.

To her right, Slanya noticed the arrival of a well-armed fighting force on horseback. From the red-brown glint to their shields, she concluded that these new forces were Tyrangal's own Copper Guard riding in from Ormpetarr. They immediately engaged the Order's Peacekeepers as well. It was a full-blown battle.

Abruptly, flares of gossamer blue-white arched up from the shielded Order accordants on the ground. The flares shot out like ballista bolts encased in fire, up into the sky toward the circling dragon.

Tyrangal was wheeling around for another dive when the first of a barrage of flares struck her and Duvan. The blue fire wrapped around the dragon like tendrils of smoke and the dragon was lost in the clouds of magic.

Only for a moment, though. The fire washed over and off, like fog around the prow of a sailing ship. And in the passing wake, the blue fire swirled away and condensed, raining the stench of rotting corpses and oranges on those below, including Slanya.

She caught sight of Duvan, a tiny dark form clinging to Tyrangal's neck, his spellscar protecting her.

Vraith had to be in the group that Tyrangal was attacking.

Slanya doubted Vraith was powerful enough on her own to take on Tyrangal. But together the accordants of the Order of Blue Fire were more than a dragon's equal.

Slanya observed all this in moments, trying to determine the best course of action. She could find Gregor and try to get him to stop the ritual, but as she took in the full scope of what was happening on the field below, it quickly dawned on her that things were too far along. Gregor couldn't help her stop it now.

The line of pilgrims formed a nearly complete circuit around the field, holding hands. Accordants and others in the pale blue robes of the Order of Blue Fire scoured the line and stopped where pilgrims were jumbled. They made them get quickly back into line and link hands. And soon, if Slanya's guess was correct, the entire line of pilgrims would form a complete circuit. And once that happened, Vraith would use those souls in her ritual to move the border of the Plaguewrought Land.

Not only would all the celebrating pilgrims inside be destroyed, but—more importantly—the Order of Blue Fire would see this as a huge victory, and they would do it again. And again. They would expand the Plaguewrought Land at their whim, wreaking chaos across Faerûn.

Slanya shuddered. No, this must be stopped.

Just at that moment, Slanya registered a palpable change in the air around her. It was as though the line of pilgrims coalesced all of a sudden. Something new had arrived—the birth of a new entity. Slanya could feel it forming from the line of pilgrims down the hill.

She watched in rapt horror as the border veil spat the wild magic onto the nearest pilgrims at either end of the arc. Some power held the pilgrims in its thrall, for they did not run. They did not flinch or cry out. They did not react at all as the blue fire leaped from pilgrim to pilgrim and raced to complete the circuit.

Above them, the gauzy border veil fluttered, and Slanya felt her gut drop inside her as she watched. The solid, prismatic surface pulsed and flickered as the ritual magic increased, as the blue fire rushed along the line of pilgrim flesh and souls.

The ritual had started.

The rising screams reached Duvan's ears as he clutched the rope around Tyrangal's neck with both hands, trying to stay on. Hot wind blew foul and dusty through the border veil. Hundreds of tiny rock particles floated in the air, stinging his skin as they flew.

Duvan had never wanted to ride on a dragon's back, and now that he had, he never wanted to again. Jerky and rough, with sudden turns, drops and climbs, the ride left Duvan's stomach behind. His hands burning from the effort, Duvan's entire job seemed to be to hang on and protect Tyrangal from the spellscarred's attacks.

So he held on as tightly as he could, refusing to be dislodged despite his bruised hands and the cuts on his knees and belly from the dragon's sharp horns and spikes. He held on despite the magical attacks from below, and the arrows flying past.

Apparently dragons were unwelcome at the festival.

As they flew, Duvan caught glimpses of the scene below. Spellplague advanced along the perimeter of pilgrims, lighting up the night with white fire. They must have been in unfathomable pain as the blue fire burned their bodies, but they could not move out of it. The line was on fire from both ends now and would soon meet in the middle.

What would happen then, Duvan didn't know. But it was bound to be decidedly not good.

"I am not making much progress against Vraith's

cadre of accordants," Tyrangal said. "Together they are too powerful."

Duvan nodded. He didn't know what he could do; the scale of this battle was beyond his abilities. He did know that he wanted to survive it. He wanted to live through this to figure out what he could do with his life. How he could make a difference. It was an odd feeling; he'd never cared about making a difference before.

He'd never cared about much of anything before.

His tenure on the Fugue Plane and the prospect of spending eternity as just another brick in the wall of the City of the Dead had given him a new perspective. The boredom and futility of doing nothing forever was far scarier to Duvan than living in pain.

"Hold on, Duvan," Tyrangal said, her voice drowned out by the cacophony of screaming pilgrims. "It looks like three of them are coordinating and—"

Duvan saw three glowing spheres now floating at intervals near the border veil. He watched in fascinated awe as bolts of ice blue shot out from them. The shafts sped directly toward him and Tyrangal.

Duvan's hands yanked abruptly as, under him, Tyrangal swerved in the sky, plummeting as she tried to dodge the bolts. But even though the main shafts missed hitting them directly, the air froze and crystallized around Duvan. Tyrangal's scales iced up, and the dragon's movements grew sluggish.

Breath stopped in Duvan's chest, and his skin burned with cold. His eyelids froze open, and his hands went numb. His vision darkened, and his joints locked. The vapor in his nostrils crystallized.

From the rate of their plummet, it seemed as though Tyrangal was having similar issues. The ground approached quickly as they fell.

He'd never been afraid to die before, but now he was.

Now he wanted to live. He wanted to accomplish something, to be a force for good. Slanya had showed him that being a force for good didn't always mean pain. Sometimes it meant satisfaction and companionship and caring.

The dragon managed to shift against the magical frost, moving enough for her wings to catch the air. Tyrangal's body shuddered and lurched beneath Duvan, then rose sharply. Perhaps they'd get out of this.

As they quickly gained altitude again, Duvan felt himself sliding to his left. Inexorably and uncontrollably, he drifted nearer the point where he would fall. His ice-encrusted hands on the rope around Tyrangal's neck had grown numb. With his fingers frozen, he was unable to hang on.

Tyrangal must have sensed this and adjusted her flight to nudge him back to the center. With a slight shift of her body, she helped him regain his balance on her neck. For now.

Far below, tiny pilgrims screamed as their bodies ignited with spellplague. The line was almost entirely engulfed now, the circuit nearly complete. In the halos of the bonfires, Duvan could see scattered pilgrims who had refused to join the line. They had all stopped their dancing, stopped their revelry. They all stared, dumbfounded, at the rippling wave of blue fire that raced over their brethren.

More blue bolts slammed into Tyrangal and she faltered. Huge blocks of ice formed large encrusted masses on the dragon's wings. Beneath Duvan, Tyrangal dropped into an angled, spinning nosedive.

Completely frozen, Duvan slipped free and fell.

He could not move, but his eyes were frozen open, and he could still see. He could see the dark shadow of the ground grow larger as he fell. Beneath him, but off to the side, Tyrangal crashed into the ground. She was moving so fast that her body dug a massive furrow in the grassy earth.

In the split second before the onrushing, unyielding

ground shattered his frozen body, Duvan saw his mentor and benefactor defeated. Defeated and probably dead—a huge dragon, frozen into a monstrous block of ice, crashing like a mote to the earth, scattering a bonfire and a small group of pilgrims out of the way.

So this is the end, he thought in his last instant. If they can beat Tyrangal, they win.

Standing in the stirrups, Slanya's breath caught in her chest as she looked out across the field and watched Tyrangal fall out of the sky. Her heart wrenched as she saw the tiny figure of Duvan, a dark speck, silhouetted against the massive backdrop of the undulating prismatic border veil.

Dread swelled inside her as she watched Duvan's plummeting form break away from the dragon and fall. She lost sight of his dark form as he disappeared into the blackness of the field, crashing into the ground. Falling substantially apart, both dragon and rider had nonetheless landed inside the arc of pilgrims.

Slanya took a quick glance at the line of pilgrims. Spellplague covered about half of the arc and was marching forward rapidly on two fronts. Each successive pilgrim called out when the fire took them. And once ignited, each person seemed to glow white hot, forming the base of a high wall made of pale blue flame stretching up into the sky.

Obviously, talking to Gregor now would have no impact, but was there anything else she could do?

Abruptly, a possibility occurred to her. Perhaps there was a way to stop it. She wasn't sure if it would work, and she knew it might kill her, but it was a chance. To stop the chaos from engulfing the world, she would do whatever it took.

Spurring her horse, Slanya crouched in the saddle and

leaned forward. She pushed the mare faster and sped down the short slope and across the grassy distance toward the line of pilgrims. The blue magic advanced from pilgrim to pilgrim, inexorably approaching the apex of the arc from both sides. A small—and shrinking—section of the line remained untouched.

Slanya aimed for that opening. She needed to reach Duvan. She needed to make sure he was all right. Everything depended on it.

The mare broke into a gallop beneath her. The beat of the hooves synchronized with the rapid thumping of Slanya's heart in her ears. Wind rushed past as she rode. Heated air bristled with magic and set the hairs on her exposed skin on end.

Closer.

Slanya took shallow breaths to avoid retching from the stink of sour orange-stuffed rotting flesh. Just ahead, the line of spellplague-touched pilgrims loomed, towering above her into the sky. She focused on balance and speed, trying to ignore the massive wall of disconcerting chaos she was speeding toward.

Ahead of her, the fire continued its consumption of pilgrims. Two by two by two. The arc was almost completely engulfed now, but Slanya could see a narrowing section where the spellplague had yet to catch hold. She needed to reach the line before the circuit completed.

Closer.

Slanya caught sight of one of the Order of Blue Fire Peacekeeper guards, patrolling the line. But he was too slow to react. Slanya approached with such speed that he did not even notice her until she was upon him. He could not have been expecting a single rider moving at such velocity.

Slanya went shooting past him.

Closer.

As she raced directly toward the line, she watched in apprehension as the gap narrowed to five pilgrims. The stench and heat from the blue fire, so close, made it hard to breathe. Then the gap was only three pilgrims wide and closing rapidly. Slanya fought back the urge to retch.

The last pilgrim to ignite was a small human woman. Mousy brown hair blowing in the hot wind, but her delicate features calm. She seemed to be waiting for rapture.

Closer.

The mare leaped into the air at the last second, narrowly avoiding crashing into the pilgrim. As the horse jumped, Slanya teetered on the edge of losing her balance. Flying through the air, her training came and her quickness to her rescue,. She adjusted in time and did not fall off the leaping mare.

And then she was through, and the tendrils of spellplague snatching at her failed to gain purchase. The horse came down on level ground and did not stumble. Slanya dropped back down in the saddle and gripped tightly with her knees. She'd made it completely inside the perimeter.

Thank Kelemvor for this mare, she thought.

Behind her, the circuit was complete, and already a palpable change hung in the air. Would this whole area be inside the Plaguewrought Land soon? Not if Slanya could help it.

She aimed the mare toward the spot where she had seen Duvan fall. She needed to get to him. She needed to make sure he was all right. And more than that, she needed his help.

She just hoped there was still time to stop the ritual. If Vraith had completed her magic, perhaps it was already too late. And even if the blonde elf wizard had not finished the ritual, Slanya's plan might not work.

She needed so many things to work exactly right. Lacking any one of them would result in failure.

Duvan might be dead. She might not be strong enough. It might be too late in any case.

As she galloped ahead in the direction where she'd seen Duvan land, Slanya put doubt out of her mind. She'd know soon enough. *Everyone* would know soon if she succeeded . . .

Or if she failed.

CHAPTER TWELVE

Partially encased in ice, Duvan slammed into the ground. He felt the jolt in his skull and ribs. He heard the snap and crunch of bones breaking and frozen flesh shattering. The pain, however, seemed to be muted and far away, numbed by the cold.

The ice shattered around him, breaking away as he impacted the ground. Once, he bounced high into the air. Twice, spinning and sliding, and the bounce was lower this time. Thrice, until he finally skittered to a stop near one of the abandoned bonfires. Frozen and rigid, he skipped like a chip of crystal across the trampled grass.

As they broke free, the shards of ice peeled away the outer layer of the skin on his face and scalp. It felt like a scab being ripped away across his entire head, and he imagined huge chunks of his hair torn away in the ice.

Darkness closed in. His chest frozen, Duvan couldn't pull in any air. He desperately needed to breathe. He was drowning in ice. Flares and sparkles flickered in the closing blackness at the edges of his vision.

"Duvan! Duvan!" Slanya's voice came faintly to his ears.

He couldn't answer, couldn't move. Couldn't breathe.

"Duvan!" Horse hooves thudded next to him, growing louder by the moment. And then Slanya was on the ground, cradling his head. Her hot touch burned his raw skin.

"You're so cold," she said. "Can you breathe?"

He struggled to pull in a breath. He failed.

She pressed her mouth to his. She breathed warm air into him, and it seemed like she was filling his lungs with broken glass.

But the chill in his chest melted ever so slightly and he could move again. He gasped and sucked in a breath of crystalline air on his own power.

"Good," she said, pulling back and looking into his eyes. "Now I need you to watch over me. So don't die; I need your protection."

Duvan grimaced. "I can't even protect myself," he said.

In the field beyond the line of pilgrims burned with blue-white fire. It was a beautiful and frightening sight. The circuit was complete, Duvan saw. So bright was the fire that Duvan could hardly see the individual bodies of the pilgrims. They had become one entity. Vraith's ritual had transformed them into a wall, a new barrier of souls.

"I think you and I can fix this whole thing together," she said.

Duvan didn't know what she was talking about. Feeling was trickling into his flesh, most of it burning and painful. He looked up into her face, tried to ask her what she meant, but no words would form.

Slanya's eyes were filled with wild urgency. The thin line of her mouth was set with determination. She seemed ready to jump into the fires of chaos. In a way, she already had, he knew. By coming inside the arc, she'd risked death.

How can we stop this? he thought. We are so small.

Above him, the border veil flickered. Dark perforations formed on the oily surface, and at each hole, the fabric of the curtain weakened. The perforations spread rapidly, each one like an eruption of thousands of black ants eating away at the veil.

Soon the border would lose cohesion, and the Plague-wrought Land would claim this area. Many souls were going to be trapped inside. Stay close by me, he tried to say to Slanya, but his mouth wasn't working.

Off to his right, Duvan caught sight of Tyrangal's massive form, stirring as she lifted herself out of the deep furrow created by her impact. Melting ice sluiced off the sides of the huge dragon as she got to her feet and stretched her wings.

She was still alive, thank the gods.

But as Duvan watched, the veil behind and above Tyrangal went completely dark. The eldritch light from the massive curtain flickered one last time and was extinguished. The border shifted, snapping to its new location along the line of burning pilgrims.

Tyrangal, too, was trapped inside.

Duvan watched as the plagueland rushed out to fill the void, like water released from a broken levee. And then Tyrangal was lost behind the flood of blue fire.

Slanya stroked his hair as she concentrated. "I have the power to affect the spellscar abilities of others," she said. "When we rescued you, I discovered that I can dampen them. That's how I defeated Beaugrat. But I also learned that I can amplify others' abilities. I'm hoping I can do that to yours."

Duvan felt his stomach liquefy as the tide washed over

them. The sounds of screaming pilgrims faded as the blue fire rushed to the next barrier. But Duvan and Slanya had their own isolated and protected bubble.

Resting in Slanya's lap, Duvan felt his power grow. It swelled and expanded, the shell of protection increased in size, doubling at first, then tripling. Sweat beaded on Slanya's brow as needles of pain shot through Duvan's thawing and broken body.

By ourselves we are small. But together . . .

Together . . .

Duvan could feel Slanya tapping into his ability. She fed his power, multiplied it. Duvan felt his shell of spellplague protection expand. And he used that power, directing his protection out toward Tyrangal, toward the line of pilgrims. He fed off Slanya's ability and extended his protection as far as it would reach.

A network of fine filaments of the palest blue glowed in Slanya's flesh as the flood of spellplague retreated in a wide, darkening sphere around them. This sphere of protection was the size of four city blocks now, and still growing.

Duvan focused his attention on the line of pilgrims ablaze from Vraith's ritual. The brilliant line of pilgrims dimmed then went dark as his sphere of protection grew to engulf them. Duvan watched in satisfaction as the blue fire burning through them retreated and guttered out. The wild magic extinguished.

Many of the pilgrims fell out of the line instantly, releasing hold of their neighbors' hands and collapsing to the ground like a sack of burned bones. Others seemed to crystallize in place, standing like alabaster statues. Their skin ablated, all that remained of their flesh was the translucent blue of spellscar. From Duvan's perspective, it seemed like the solid wall of blue fire gave way to a haphazard line of white shapes—jagged quartz teeth along the ground.

Abruptly, with the perimeter circuit broken, there came

the sound of a snapping whip, only a hundred times louder. Duvan's ears broke as the border veil crashed back to its previous location. He flinched from the thunderous impact of the sound.

In the wake of the veil shift, a multitude of spellplague pockets remained outside the curtain. Loosed from the change-lands, the blazes of blue fire burned through the charred grass. Duvan watched as these pockets of wild magic, now free of the Plaguewrought Land, created chaos as they scattered into the night.

Silence descended on Duvan and Slanya. Around them people lay scattered like crystallized corpses, some of them still partially alive. Some others seemed mostly whole physically, but wandered aimlessly, traumatized. Duvan could not see Tyrangal, and he hoped she had survived.

Above him, the lines of Slanya's spellscar glowed blue white through her translucent flesh. Her wide, innocent eyes bulged with the growing activation of her spellscar. Blue lines traced her face, pulsing like magic along a web embedded into her flesh.

Ignoring the pain in his legs and chest, Duvan sat up next to her. "You did it," he said. "You stopped them!"

Slanya's spellscar was so pervasive that the natural flesh around the filaments lost its cohesion. Duvan watched in growing alarm as the muscles and skin of Slanya's face sagged and started leaking fluid. He soon realized that she was bleeding from hundreds of tiny wounds all over her body.

Slanya gasped, and Duvan felt his heart lurch as she slumped to the ground in a growing puddle of her own fluids.

For a single, glorious moment, Vraith luxuriated in sublime achievement. The line of pilgrims—no longer

254 • Jak Koke

individuals—formed a unified fabric, woven with the tendrils of their life force. These strands appeared in Vraith's vision like black and blood-red filaments superimposed over physical reality.

The glory of the moment stretched on and on.

Standing at one end of the line of pilgrims, just next to where it intersected with the border veil, Vraith was surrounded by Order Peacekeepers and her personal guard. Renfod kept a close watch on her as well, knowing that she would be vulnerable during the ritual.

Vraith did not trust Renfod, but that was only because she trusted no one. Renfod had never actually done anything to merit distrust. In his own way, the cleric cared for her. And for that, she had taken him along on her rise to power.

Wild magic pulsed through Vraith's sternum like blood through her heart. The threads of her soul formed a bridge between the huge, complex curtain that defined the border of the Plaguewrought Land and the new entity she had just created.

Red tendrils intertwined the veil with her core. Black strands weaved her spirit with the life patterns of the pilgrim entity. This fabric formed a foundation matrix for the border veil, which fluttered along the surface of Vraith's tapestry of pilgrims' souls. The border curtain would soon attach to the tapestry, Vraith knew, and become permanent.

Only then could she disentangle herself and the pilgrims. Success was mere moments away.

Already a flood of wild magic had rushed in to fill the new opening. Already the blue fire spread its spectacular chaos into the gap.

Gazing with blue-lit faces, the group of Peacekeepers and guards around her gasped in awe and wonder as the border veil settled along its new path. The prismatic curtain flickered and fluttered, still partially unstable, but solidifying by the moment. Renfod was saying, "Fantastic accomplishment! This will go down in history as a defining achievement of the Order."

Abruptly and without warning, the moment of perfection and awe passed. Amidst the blinding blue-white fire, darkness sprouted.

Making the final loops and knots in her ritual weave, Vraith pondered the black spot in the fabric of her magic. What could be wrong? she wondered. How is this possible?

Too slowly, she realized everything was over. The darkness bloomed quickly like a fetid flower. Starting out as a small black spot, the anomaly grew like a rampant plague, sapping the power of the changelands and nullifying the foundation for the border veil.

A deafening crack shattered Vraith's ears, and the ground shook under her feet.

Vraith could not move to maintain her balance, and she started to tip backward. Renfod rushed with reactive urgency to stabilize her, putting his arms around her to hold her up. She silently thanked him, noticing that many of the Peacekeepers did not fare as well. Armed men and women tumbled around her like dolls.

Doubling over as though she'd been kicked in the gut, Vraith watched in red and black as the border veil snapped back to its original position. Only the presence of Renfod's strong arms allowed her to keep her feet.

Vraith gasped as the darkness erased the glorious creation she had built. In an instant, her dreams of imminent rapture blackened and vanished into the dark. She could not believe it at first. Stunned, she reacted too slowly to avoid the collapse of the pilgrim wall tapestry she had created.

"I've got you," Renfod said.

Screams of shock and pain met her bleeding ears. Everything—and everyone—connected to the border veil split asunder as it snapped back. Vraith had woven the souls of every pilgrim through herself and into the fabric of the border curtain. All of those threads tore.

Many of the pilgrims died instantly, leaving only statues of crumbling white chalk. Others seemed to have survived, but Vraith could see that their minds and hearts had unhinged as the border veil claimed sections of their life essence.

Vraith smelled burning flesh and ashes—the odor of death and failure. She had the briefest of moments to wonder whether she would be able to survive this catastrophe. If anything, she was more interconnected with the magical fabric of the border veil than any of the pilgrims.

She was grateful, suddenly, for Renfod. He was possibly her only friend. If she could count on anyone, it was him. And she knew with certainty that if she died tonight, Renfod would not hesitate to resurrect her.

This failure would prove a huge setback, and it would no doubt be very painful. But she would be back to try it again. She would figure out what had gone wrong and what would rectify it. Eventually, she would succeed. It was just a matter of time.

Vraith felt a sharp tug. The tendrils of her own spirit, intricately intertwined with the border veil, yanked her spirit out of her flesh. A ripple of the border curtain plucked her soul from her body, leaving her lifeless corpse suddenly slumped in the hands of the faithful Renfod.

It happened so fast that Vraith hardly had time to process the tidal wave of excruciating pain. So she was going to die after all. Vraith felt her consciousness stretch and spread as the threads of her spirit dispersed across the surface of the border veil. She felt herself grow thinner and thinner.

Was she dying? She did not think so.

Neither was this the rapture she had dreamed about, the ascension into the consciousness of the sharn that she had wanted for almost all her life. Merging with the sharn, those wondrous night black creatures of wild magic, would give her eternal life and supreme knowledge. Incredible power.

This felt different. Vastly different.

With her last coherent thought, Vraith recognized the horror of her mistake. So interwoven with the border curtain, her spirit was irrevocably caught in its matrix. And as the border jerked back into its normal spot, Vraith's soul stretched across its surface—impossibly thin, she spread over the vast expanse of the border veil like a droplet of oil on a still lake.

There could be no resurrection if she was not actually dead. Renfod would no doubt try to bring her back, but she knew it would not work. She had not died, but she had failed. She had failed so utterly that the Order would never attempt such a ritual again. Her plan to expand the Plaguewrought Land was dead even if she was not, her dream to join the sharn forever gone.

For Vraith, trapped and lost across the border curtain, failure was worse than death.

A blazing halo of light shone in the darkness around Slanya. The deep rumbling of a multitude of indistinct voices murmured in the spaces beyond the light. She stood naked on a featureless, gray surface. If she stood in the center, the light gave off no heat.

Come to me, my child. And she knew it was the voice of Kelemvor.

Blink.

A shock of pain rocketed through her, and she was alive again. Sounds filtered through to her. The rumble of voices faded, replaced by screams of the dying and the clomp of hooves.

The border veil stretched up into the sky. It was back to its previous position—where it had been for a hundred years if historians were correct. The veil cast a ghostly light over the field, making the dying pilgrims look like spirits.

Slanya caught sight of Gregor's cauldron, lying overturned just beyond what had been the line of pilgrims. The ritual had left half of the pilgrims as towers of blue-tinged salt, crumbling crystalline statues whose entire beings had been dried up by Vraith's ritual. Some of the monks lay injured among the pilgrims, and others tended to the wounded and sick.

Of Gregor himself, there was no sign.

Pain rocketed through her, burning up her skin. And in the spaces between the pulses of pain, she could feel Duvan's arms cradling her. She watched him with a distant curiosity. Chunks of his long, dark hair had been pulled out, giving him the look of an abused doll.

He seemed alarmed. "Help!" he yelled. "She needs help! Cleric!" There was panic in his voice, and deep concern.

But she was wet and falling apart. Dying, she knew. Finally stepping into the fire.

Blink.

Aunt Ewesia's paddle came down hard on the backs of little Slanya's thighs. She deserved it and worse for what she had done, Aunt said. Moving the cups in the kitchen to a new cupboard was one thing, but forgetting the lye in the laundry basin was inexcusable. She'd been told more than once.

The paddle came down again. Pain radiated out from the point of impact. Despite the calluses, this beating would leave marks. Later, she was thinking. Later she will be asleep and I can have peace.

Blink.

Duvan's usual three-day beard had been stripped away, leaving exposed and bleeding skin on his face. But when he spoke, his voice was calm, showing no evidence of the pain he must be in. "Help is coming," Duvan said. "Hang on."

She shook her head. The lie in his voice was sweet, but unnecessary. "No," she mouthed. "Don't lie to me."

In response, Duvan gave a solemn nod, but she saw deep sadness in his eyes. He did not want to accept the truth of matters.

Her back itched as though a thousand beetles crawled across her skin. Then the itch turned to pain as the beetles all burrowed into her flesh simultaneously. Each gurgling breath came with great exertion, great agony.

"Duvan," she said, gritting her teeth from the pain incurred by just speaking. "I need your help to die."

"No," he said. "No. No." His head was shaking. "Kaylinn is sure to be here soon, right? Or another cleric? You just have to hang on."

He still doesn't understand, she thought. But she would try to make him. "But it is my time," she said. "Kelemvor is calling me to him."

Fear made Duvan's eyes grow wide as shook his head. Poor, dear friend, Slanya thought.

"I achieved greatness," Slanya whispered. "*We* achieved it together, and for that I am proud." A pulse of agony caused her to spasm and arch her back.

Blink.

Aunt Ewesia's snores resonated through the room, and Slanya knew it was safe now. Drunk and unconscious, Aunt would be out until morning. Hatred rose up inside Slanya, and despair. Why did she end up with this woman who didn't want her? She couldn't run away; everyone in the small town knew her and would return her to Aunt.

Little Slanya was practical enough to know that she'd never make it far enough away, and that the punishment for trying to escape would be severe. No, that wouldn't work. She must destroy her life. She might die trying, but she might escape. She might be reborn.

Very deliberately, little Slanya scooted the grate out from

its place in front of the fire. Moving quietly, she leaned the grate up against the wall. Then she dragged the basket of laundry to a spot just in front of the fire, setting it way too close.

It took far longer than it should have, but little Slanya was patient. Crouching in the shadows by the door, she watched with detachment and pragmatic calculation as the fire finally jumped into the laundry. She stayed at her vigil, breathing through laced fingers, until the room had ignited and Aunt was on fire too. She felt nothing inside at the sight.

Blink.

"Slanya?" Duvan said, wiping at his eyes with an angry, hurried motion.

She couldn't feel her legs now. "My time has come," she said flatly. "I can never be put back together. I will die here tonight, but how I die is important."

Through blurred vision, she watched the devastating realization of her seriousness wreak havoc across Duvan's face. Underneath the rough, prickly surface, he was a sweet, generous man who kept his word and would do anything for his friends. He had been so very badly mistreated for much of his life; he didn't deserve more pain.

She loved Duvan, she had come to realize, and hated to hurt him. But she needed him to do this one last difficult thing for her.

"I . . . don't know if I can," Duvan's voice broke. "It may be selfish, but I want you to stay."

"I want to stay too," Slanya said. "But that is not among the choices I now have. I can die slowly in a great deal of pain and anguish. Or—" She gurgled fluid in her throat, struggling to breathe. She spat up bloody phlegm.

Tears streamed down Duvan's dark face now, turning red in the dim light as they mingled with his bloody skin.

"Please do this, Duvan," she said, coughing. "You are a true friend. I know this is hard for you, but I'm imploring you. I have already lived a meaningful life."

"That's more than I can say," Duvan said. "I've cheated death so many times without even knowing or caring about life."

Duvan's black eyes hardened above her, his face set in stone as he accepted what she said. "I can take . . ." His voice wavered. "Take the pain away," he said. "And you will pass quickly."

"Do it," Slanya begged. "Now."

Moments passed, and she hardly noticed Duvan moving. His arms still held her to his own broken and battered body. She could not think of anywhere else she'd rather die. Slanya barely felt the dagger prick in her shoulder. But the numbing poison spread its paralytic quickly. Anesthetic chased the pain like water chasing away thirst, rapidly washing over her body and cleansing it. Calming her.

"Thank you, my good friend," she whispered with her last words.

Duvan's voice was soft and punctuated by sobs. "Good night, friend," came his words from far, far way.

Blink.

Standing naked again on the featureless, gray plane, Slanya stood encircled by the halo of fire. The deep, resonating rumble of voices murmuring in the distance felt reassuring and comforting.

Slanya forgave herself for setting the fire that had killed Aunt Ewesia. She forgave herself for wanting her aunt dead, for knowing that her aunt would probably die. It had been her only way out of an abusive and horrifying childhood, her only way to take control in a situation where she had no power.

Come to me, child. Kelemvor's voice resonated through her entire soul. *And I will calculate the balance of your spirit and set you on your next path.*

Slanya found that she could move now. She stepped out

of the center of the halo of flames and felt the infernal heat purge her as she walked into the fire. Flames consumed her, but they did not hurt.

And as she passed through, she was cleansed. Her material burdens were lifted from her. This is what she wanted, to be erased and purged, reinvented and incarnated anew.

Slanya found peace.

Sitting on the hard ground with Slanya's perforated and leaking body slumped in his lap, Duvan stared at the tip of his dagger as he pulled it slowly out of her shoulder. He had killed her to take away her pain. She'd asked him to, and she had been of sound mind. What he had done was a good thing, right?

Knowing all of that didn't make him feel any better. A deep aching pain filled his chest, making it hard to breathe.

His dagger was still in his hand, its blade glimmering oily green from the sheen of paralytic poison that coated it—the very same blade that he'd used to hasten Slanya's journey to her death.

Duvan's blade held plenty more poison to speed him along with Slanya. It would be so fast, so easy. Just a momentary jab and in moments he'd be dead too. No muss, no fuss. Painless and quick.

But she was already gone, he knew. She'd left him and passed to whatever lay beyond. He could die, but he could not follow. Kelemvor would not send him to where she had gone.

Duvan set his blade down. If he could not follow, then he would live. At least for today. For this moment in time, he would live.

Around him, the night was in pandemonium. Dead and dying pilgrims lay everywhere, scattered and bleeding, some screaming, some moaning, others passing beyond the pale in quiet anonymity. Those still alive and mobile fled the area by the hundreds, scattering as far away from the border as they could get. There was no way to know for certain that the Plaguewrought Land would stay secure behind the veil.

Duvan noticed that the only people staying to help were the clerics and monks from the monastery. The Order of Blue Fire members had fled with the others. Vraith and her inner circle of accordants seem to have disappeared. Even Tyrangal was not to be found, and her Copper Guard had dispersed.

Duvan couldn't move if he'd wanted to. Not yet, anyway. Perhaps not ever, without help. He merely cradled Slanya's body and concentrated on his next breath. He focused on his own pains and aches, of which there were plenty. His right leg was broken in at least one place, maybe two. His left leg might also be broken, but he wasn't sure.

He bled slowly from a hundred tiny abrasions and cuts, but the pain of those was like a deep, burning itch all across his body. Unconsciousness crawled like a swarm of ants at the edges of his mind, advancing then retreating and advancing again. Several times he nearly passed out from weakness and loss of blood, but he was determined not to allow the scavengers or potential poachers near Slanya. By the gods, he would defend her.

Perhaps, she could still be brought back. Kaylinn or another of her clerics could accomplish that, like they had done to him. Duvan hadn't given up hope yet. And even if Slanya could not be brought back, she deserved a proper funeral—a celebration of her life, her accomplishments and sacrifices.

"Duvan?" the voice came from behind him.

He croaked out an unintelligible reply.

"Duvan?" It was Kaylinn's voice. The cleric gasped as she noticed Slanya's dead body. But her words were soothing. "I've found you, now," she said. Her voice was both motherly and commanding. "I will take care of everything."

At Kaylinn's arrival, Duvan let Slanya's hand go. He released his embrace of his dead friend and curled up on the ground next to her body. As Kaylinn's hands passed over him, examining his injuries, more people arrived to help.

Duvan heard Kaylinn finishing an incantation as though from a great distance. He felt warmth seep into him, and he sensed Kaylinn giving instructions, but he lacked the energy to focus anymore. Duvan let the dark tide of unconsciousness wash over him. Kaylinn would take care of things. Thank the gods for her.

Some time later, Duvan awoke from a dreamless sleep. The smell of jasmine and sage filled his nostrils. The smell reminded him of his home with Papa and Talfani. His wounds had been mended, and his body had been cleaned.

Lying flat on his back, Duvan opened his eyes to a modest monastery room. Through the small window, he saw the first hints of light from the rising sun. Morning birds called and chirped outside.

It was another day. The end of the world had been avoided once more.

Duvan gave a wry chuckle. Then the full impact of Slanya's death flooded back over him, filling his chest with breath-catching pain. Duvan rolled on his side and pulled the pillow close. He wore a body-length tunic of light cotton, but the fabric felt rough against his battered skin.

Now, all he wanted to do was go back to sleep, to disappear into the oblivion. It seemed that his shell of cynicism had lost its ability to deflect pain. He understood that, and he wasn't even sad about it. He'd been living behind that shell for too long.

"You did well." The voice sounded musical and enlightening, despite being barely above a whisper. "I'm sorry I let you fall."

She emerged from the shadows by the corner away from

the door. Tall and stately, regal in her shimmering garments and coppery rain of hair.

Duvan found he was both glad to see Tyrangal and immensely sad that she wasn't Slanya.

"I am sorry about Slanya," Tyrangal said. "The clerics say they're unable to raise her."

His gut imploded as though she'd kicked him in the stomach. He gasped as the realization trampled him that he would never see Slanya again. Still, he wasn't completely surprised.

"It was because of her—and you—that we were able to negate Vraith's ritual," Tyrangal said. "You two disrupted the ritual magic and put the border back to its original location. Stopped the dam from breaking. Thank you."

Duvan hugged his pillow into the hollow of his gut, wrapping himself around it. Lonely and aching, the hole in his chest would not be filled.

"Of course it was far from a complete victory. I had to reveal my true self. I may have to move. There are those who will remember me from . . . before. You should know that I have been called by many names over the centuries— 'Gaulauntyr' most recently on this world. I fled after the rage and returned only after Mystra's death."

Duvan blinked. Tyrangal grew more interesting and strange by the minute. And yet for all her power, she had been unable to stop the Order of Blue Fire by herself. For all her age and knowledge, she had been unable to prevent Slanya's death. She could not bring Slanya back.

Tyrangal continued, "Vraith was lost to the Plague-wrought Land and is perhaps dead. But that's not certain, and if her knowledge of the ritual gets into the hands of her masters, they will certainly try the ritual again in the future. Of course, with Gregor's disappearance, it will take them a long while to find another elixir."

Duvan blinked. Gregor was gone? Not that he cared for Gregor; the man had sold him to be tortured by Vraith.

But he also had rescued Slanya after her house had burned down. He was not all bad.

Tyrangal's hand touched Duvan on the shoulder. "I am not much good at relationships, Duvan," she said. "Your lives are too short and your actions are colored by the fear of death. But you are different, my friend. It may not seem like it, but I care for you and I consider you a friend."

Duvan felt the words chase away the emptiness, if only slightly.

"I am rarely one to wax emotional, so please know that I mean it when I tell you this. I want you to stay with me at my mansion or wherever I settle. I have many lairs."

Duvan took in a breath. This offer was unexpected, and he did not know whether he trusted it. Did she truly want him? Or just his aura of protection?

"I also would like you to consider helping me to keep tabs on the Order of Blue Fire. It is extremely hard to find someone I can trust. I can trust you, Duvan."

But can I trust you? Duvan wondered. Tyrangal had kept her true nature hidden from him. Had she just saved him from the Wildhome elves to use him for his spellplague resistance? Duvan didn't know if he could trust anyone besides Slanya.

Tyrangal stood up straight. "The offer of my home is not contingent upon anything. You can come and go as you wish. You can help me combat the Order or not as you wish. However, I sense you are ready for a new journey, friend."

Duvan nodded. "I just want to rest," he said. "Just rest."

"Do that then," Tyrangal said. "Take some time to rest. Take some time to say good-bye. That is important. But know that you can come to me whenever you need me."

Duvan took a deep breath and sat up. "Thank you, Tyrangal." Duvan stood and faced his rescuer, his long-time employer, and—just perhaps—his friend. He took her into his arms and hugged her.

She returned the hug with less awkwardness than he expected. Up close she smelled of smoke and hot metal.

"Thank you for everything," he said. "I am not sure what I will do, but you have been kind and generous to me. You have treated me more like a friend than have most humans."

Yet, as much as Tyrangal's relationship was important to him, she was still alien in her thinking, still a dragon at heart. And while he respected her immensely, and he appreciated all that she had done for him, he could not really relate to her with any degree of closeness, especially when contrasted against the intimacy of the bond he had shared with Slanya.

"You are most welcome, Duvan. You are a remarkable human. Don't believe anyone who says otherwise. Despite the hardships you have endured, or perhaps because of them, you are unique and valuable."

Duvan gave her an awkward grin. All those things may be true, he thought. And part of him appreciated that Tyrangal had made a point of mentioning them. But none of those things made losing his closest friend any easier.

Sadly, nothing Tyrangal could say would make the hurt of Slanya's death go away. "I need to leave now," she said. "But I hope to see you again soon." And with that she vanished, leaving Duvan standing alone in the room.

Gregor paced the perimeter of the massive chamber one more time. There had to be a way out, just had to be. A domed, stone ceiling arched overhead, polished like red marble veined with black and green.

The floor was made of more of the same, smooth as glass except where ancient crates and piles of what looked like valuable sculptures and ceramics, embroidered pennants and crested armor drifted haphazardly. Gregor hadn't tried to move the piles yet, to see if there were any exits through the floor, but that would come in time, if necessary.

The light in here seemed to come from crystals set into the domed ceiling high above, but if there was another source, such as windows to the outside, Gregor couldn't tell. His flying abilities were lacking for the moment.

He chuckled, then caught himself. A few hours in here and he was already starting to lose his discipline. That was a bad sign.

But so far his diligent, methodical check of the room had revealed nothing. So far his adherence to order was doing him no good.

"Good to see you haven't given up."

The abrupt appearance of a very large dragon in the room startled Gregor. As it was no doubt supposed to do, he thought.

"Tyrangal?" he guessed.

Muscles rippled underneath heavy copper scales. Her batlike wings stretched for a moment before folding against her body. Her lips peeled back to reveal huge teeth. "Very good."

"I saw you fall to the ground at the ritual. And watched as the plagueland swallowed you."

"That wasn't very enjoyable," Tyrangal said. "But I survived, thanks to your elixir. I drank the rest of the cauldron just before the border broke down."

Gregor smiled, determined not to show his fear. The horns that curved from her skull were as long and sharp as swords, and the disconcerting bitter smell of acid hung over her. "You're welcome, then," he said.

"We won, actually, if you haven't heard."

"I—" Gregor considered. "The last things I remember are the ritual failing and the border snapping back into place."

"No thanks to you." Tyrangal's tone had grown mean.

Her claws scraped against the polished stone floor, the sharp sound raising the hairs on Gregor's neck.

"I was pursuing a vision," Gregor said, defensive. "The ritual could be used to reduce the size of the Plague-wrought Land and eventually contain all the remnants of the Spellplague."

Tyrangal's deep laugh rumbled through the cavern.

"You can laugh, but it is a noble vision. I thought it worth pursuing and even convinced High Priestess Kaylinn to move to Ormpetarr in pursuit of it."

Tyrangal's laughter cut abruptly off. "Yes, a noble vision, but a naive one. Your visions, my young monk, were sent to you by creatures who help shape the Order agenda."

"What?" Gregor felt like he'd been kicked in the gut.

"The Order of Blue Fire has been sending you images of what you want to see. Ultimately, they were hoping that you'd join the Order, but at a minimum they just needed your elixir. And that, you happily supplied to them."

Gregor's gasped for breath. His dreams had been fabricated? He'd been manipulated?

"The Spellplague cannot be contained," Tyrangal went on. "It is, in fact, a major feat that your elixir works at all, and that is the reason I helped you. That is the reason you are still alive."

Suddenly, Tyrangal was standing next to him in human form. Her long, auburn hair shone brightly in the light from the crystals above, and her round, golden eyes appraised him kindly. "Let me show you something." She reached out and touched him on the shoulder.

In a flash, the room disappeared. And suddenly the two of them stood side by side in a richly appointed chamber lined with bookshelves and reagent bottles. Gregor stepped back in shock; the books on the shelves were *his* books. The labels on the reagent bottles were written in *his* handwriting.

"I've brought your lab here," she said. "I want you to

continue your work, but for me this time. Here you will be shielded from the influence of the Order, from their visions."

Gregor looked around. If anything, this lab was better equipped than his own. "And if I refuse?"

Tyrangal stared into his eyes, and for a brief moment, her gold eyes became reptilian slits. Her tone, however, was matter-of-fact. "We live in dangerous times, Gregor. An epic battle is shaping. You can choose to be a part of it. Or through negligence, become a casualty. I don't have a lot of patience for apathy."

Gregor grimaced. It was clear that she would kill him in some way if he didn't agree. "Such options! What are we working on?"

Tyrangal grinned. "I suspected you would listen to reason," she said. "You are a pragmatic being. This location should be shielded enough so that you won't get any confusing visions. Vraith may still be out there, and even if she's dead, the Order of Blue Fire will replace her with another. There are big forces at work."

Gregor nodded. So she wants help, he thought. And he realized that they were mostly on the same side. Perhaps he wouldn't be compromising his ideals by helping her. Not that he had much choice.

"To begin with," Tyrangal said, "we'll need more of your elixir. And also, I think you'll be interested in taking a look at this." She indicated a thick tome lying on the table. "This is something that Duvan graciously acquired for me recently."

Gregor stepped up to the table and looked closely at the heavy book. The cover was crafted from thick hide and inlaid with gold runes. "What is it?"

"When the goddess Mystra died," Tyrangal said, "much old magic was lost. Many spells and powers that used her Weave no longer work. This tome contains some of the most powerful, and I am only able to cast a small fraction of them in the current climate." The dragon's tone grew soothing, reassuring. "You have an extraordinary ability to infuse magic into your potions, Gregor. You understand how modern magic works."

Gregor was somewhat confused, and apparently it showed on his face.

"There are some potion recipes in here," Tyrangal said. "They are yours. I want you to figure out how to make them work now. And I want you to show me your process. I think you can teach me. Perhaps I can use your methodology to adapt the other spells to the modern rules of magic."

"Ah," Gregor said. "Well, I will try." He tried to sound indifferent, but truth be told, he was quite intrigued by the tome. Perhaps this captivity would be interesting. "But I am curious . . ."

"Yes?"

"If I cooperate fully, how long do you intend to keep me prisoner here?"

"You have not shown me that you are trustworthy. You went against my counsel and aided the Order."

Gregor lowered his eyes. "I'm sorry," he said. "I can see now that I made a grievous error."

"However," Tyrangal continued, "I abhor slavery. I know what it is like to be overcome by passions and visions that compel you to do things you would otherwise not do. I have done things that I regret. For many years I was a victim of the Rage.

"I banished myself until it passed, until I could return with the ability to act as an intelligent and free creature. And that is what I hope to do for you here. Dry you out and free you of your obsession with these visions. Free you of your addiction."

Gregor nodded. He had already started missing them.

"I believe that in time, your visions will fade from your mind. You have a strong will, Gregor. You did not join the

Order when that would have been the easy path. In large part, that is why I have invested so much in you. I believe you can be rehabilitated."

Gregor took a deep breath, realizing that Tyrangal had not given him a time frame. She might never release him.

"And then, Gregor, when I have gained a measure of trust in you, I will free you."

"Well at least that's something to work toward," he said with more enthusiasm than he felt.

"I have big plans, Gregor," Tyrangal said. "You and I will make excellent partners."

Gregor wondered if he could ever believe that.

"For now, take a look through the tome that Duvan brought me; I think you will find it very engaging. Meanwhile, I must leave you for a while. I have much to do, much to prepare for." With that she teleported away, leaving him alone.

Gregor looked at the tome. Yes, he had to admit he was intrigued. But first, he started pacing the perimeter, looking for a way out. Just in case.

EPILOGUE

Duvan took a deep breath of morning air as he walked up the stone steps to the balcony. His bones ached as he took each step slowly. The healing he'd gotten from Kaylinn's personal care had been the best of his life, but there was only so much that magic could do to heal the trauma.

Some things only healed with the passage of time, and not enough time had passed. Not yet.

As he climbed the last step and approached the balcony's edge, Duvan looked out across the expansive field that separated the temple complex from Ormpetarr. Despite the events of the past tenday, the walls of the city stood seemingly unchanged. Just another day, for most of inhabitants of the city.

Life went on.

The field below was remarkably barren. The pilgrims who had come for the Festival of Blue Fire were all either dead or scattered. Duvan hadn't been back to the site of the ritual, but he suspected that it was a graveyard of pilgrims. A warning to others, perhaps.

But even as he thought this, he saw that the field was not entirely barren. A small group of new arrivals had arrived and were setting up their tents. These fresh pilgrims had come to try their chance at flirting with blue fire. When would people learn?

The aroma of sage and jasmine threatened to lull Duvan into a daze. The morning sun shining hot in the sky warmed him. And with that welcome heat, exhaustion started. Duvan shook himself, fighting the urge to sleep. It seemed like he had been sleeping constantly, and while he needed the rest, he was determined to get back on his feet. Now that he had a reason to live, he didn't want to waste one minute of those he had remaining.

Footsteps sounded behind him, and Duvan turned lazily to see the familiar sight of Kaylinn climbing the last step to the balcony. Lines of fatigue showed deep in her broad face, but she smiled when she saw Duvan. "It's good to see you up and about," she said. "I am glad you are still with us."

Duvan had to smile back. Despite the deep ache in his gut and chest, he felt connected to the world. "Thank you for healing me," he said. "I am in your debt."

"No, no." Kaylinn shook her head. "We are in your debt, Duvan. Many owe their lives to you and Slanya."

Duvan shrugged. "To Slanya, perhaps," he said. "She's the one who really made the effort, the sacrifice."

Kaylinn's face darkened. "It's all right to be humble, young man," she said. "But do not lie to a priest."

"I just wish I could have done more," Duvan said. "That I could have saved her." Like she saved me, he thought.

"She died content and fulfilled," Kaylinn said. "And part of that was due to you. It is what we do in our various lives that defines us. I can see that you grieve, Duvan. And that is natural. That is an acknowledgment that Slanya touched you." She sniffed. "Just as she touched me and many others."

Duvan remembered Slanya's barging into his room at the Jewel, interrupting his time with Moirah. He remembered how angry he was at the intrusion. How surprised he was at Slanya's determination. How much he'd grown to like her in the time since. Grown to love her.

"Don't grieve too long, however," Kaylinn said. "You've been grieving for your sister all your life—yes, Slanya told me some of that story. Let it pass. Celebrate the lives of the dead, then let them go. You must, if you're going to make your own way."

Duvan was too tired to muster any anger or even irritation at Kaylinn's lecture. Besides, she was probably right.

"In any case," Kaylinn said, "I came to tell you that Slanya's funeral ceremony will begin shortly. I knew you would want to come to honor her. And to say good-bye."

Duvan nodded. "Thank you," he said. "I need to be there."

"There are some appropriate garments on the chair in your room," Kaylinn said. "Your own leathers are acceptable, but they are somewhat . . . um, how to put it? Filthy."

Duvan laughed. "I will change." Then he started walking back down the stone steps toward his room. When he found himself off-balance, he allowed Kaylinn to help him. The cleric walked all the way back to his room with him, steadying his balance with her reassuring hand.

Dressing took three times longer than it should have, but eventually with a great deal of help from Kaylinn, Duvan was clad in simple, black, linen pants and a tunic cinched at the waist with a white rope.

"Thank you, Kaylinn," he said. "Lead on."

Duvan slipped on the sandals they had laid out for him and walked out of the room, leaning on Kaylinn when he needed it.

A special funeral pyre had been built in the center of the courtyard, and Slanya's body lay on it. Draped over her body was cloth embroidered with Kelemvor's scale. About thirty clerics and monks had gathered to pay their respects.

"Sister Slanya had no family," Kaylinn said, raising her voice to address the entire group. "We were her family, and she was family to us.

"Of all the many sisters I have had, Slanya was my favorite. Resolute and ethical, she held to her code. She believed in order and in doing the right thing, despite the consequences.

"I shall miss her."

Duvan stopped listening. He too would miss her. He too loved her.

Since Talfani had died, nobody had reached his heart the way Slanya had. It hurt so much. Worse than a penetrating wound that would not stop bleeding, the agony of loss was an injury that magic could not heal.

Several others spoke, but Duvan did not hear them. He reflected on his brief experiences with Slanya. He'd only known her a few days, but in that time she'd taught him to care again. She'd saved him from a life of cynical detachment and reckless self-pity. She'd rescued him from an eternity of boredom as a brick in the wall of Kelemvor's city.

He'd hated her. He'd loved her. And now she was gone, and he would miss her so.

As he looked on, Kaylinn put a torch to the pyre. The kindling caught fire and soon was ablaze in flames licking the sky above the temple complex. Through the veil of heat and light, Duvan watched as Slanya's corpse burned away.

A small group of monks sang a lament, the tune haunting against the rumble of the fire. The song seemed to reach into his heart and touch the most painful places, reminding him of the beauty and vivaciousness of his lost friend, of his lost sister. Of all his losses.

Duvan knew of only one way to make the pain in his chest stop hurting. Stop living, and the pain would cease. But that was not an option for him. He wanted to live, pain or no pain. He would accept Tyrangal's invitation. Helping her was something he could believe in. Something that Slanya would approve of.

Duvan took a deep breath. Having a goal—a purpose—filled his aching void. The pain was still there, the loss still acute. But he could go on. He could let her go, let both Slanya and Talfani go.

"Good-bye, my friend," he whispered, staring into the flames. "May you find peace and contentment on your next journey." Tears streamed down his cheeks as he watched her body burn.

"Good-bye."

AN EXCERPT FROM
ED GREENWOOD
PRESENTS
WATERDEEP

THE
GOD CATCHER

ERIN M. EVANS

THE
GOD CATCHER

Andareunarthex watched sullenly as his scrying pool
reflected a band of men and women in borrowed
armor, the last handful of whom were trying to
fight off an unusually well-equipped group of orcs.
At least a score of the humans lay on the ground,
their blood seeping into the early frost.

He waved a claw over the water and the image
vanished. A waste, an utter waste, he thought.

A slight ringing in his mind precipitated the
flutey tones of another dragon.

Your army has fallen, said Magaolonereth, the
clutch-mate of Andareunarthex's sire. Dareun
growled a warning trill.

I do not know what you mean, he sent back.

Don't pretend to be stupid. The Claw Test, Magaolonereth said. *Those humans were yours. Everyone*

suspects. Dareun drummed his claws on the stone floor of his cave.

It was a magnificent cave—dry and wide and sparkling. Even if he hadn't amassed a goodly amount of treasure for his young age it would be a cave to marvel at. A fomorian cavern, until he'd chased those ugly brutes away and made it his. The walls were scalloped and sparkling with mosa-ics of crystals, their exposed edges polished with time. The ceiling was high and dramatic, a cathedral of earth spangled with stalactites. A wyrm twice Dareun's age would be lucky to have the cavern for a lair, he thought. Not that they'd admit it.

I know the move was yours, Magaolonereth went on, and Dareun could almost see the old green dragon, sneering down at his own scrying glass, watching the orcs tear the last of the humans apart. *No one else would be so forward.*

You see forwardness, I see an aggressive move.

You forget yourself and play another game. Xorvintaal *is not for the rash.*

I was not rash! Dareun snapped. The silence that followed was full of his father's clutch-mate's smugness.

I was careful, he amended in calmer tones. *The humans thought they were helping a village at the base of the mountains, who in turn thought they were avoiding the fate some travelers convinced them would fall upon them in a few tendays. I was ready for Karshinevin's orcs.*

Magaolonereth snorted. *Not near ready enough. Everyone knew you had sent your* lovacs *out in rags to play as travelers. Do you wonder that no one staked his or her treasure on your winning? Everyone knew your move, knew you would fail.*

But only Dareun had known Karshinevin had maneuvered through her minions to put a band of orcs into play. No one would mention that. They would only say what a clever move Karshinevin had made. Dareun would be forced to agree. He had grudgingly staked a casket of gold on the bronze dragon's success—but thrice that on his own. The orcs were a clever move, but he'd been hoping Karshinevin would pull back when she realized the orcs were going to attack humans. Knowing Karshinevin, she'd managed to find the single tribe of orcs who had a good reason to raid the village.

It is not about winning every encounter, Dareun said.

Magaolonereth fell silent for a moment, and Dareun suspected he'd caught the old green off-guard. He lashed his tail against the ledge of the scrying pool. They all assumed he was too young to be patient, too young to play the game. But with every loss, he was learning, gaining on their graying hides, finding holes in the restrictive rules of *xorvintaal*.

He turned his attention briefly to the other voice that whispered in his mind—a dark, distant voice. Cold and alien and full of magic, the voice he'd lured to him by painstaking ritual, and tricked into imbuing him with the magic of a dying star.

Learning to play *xorvintaal* had stripped away what magic he'd had—what magic all his fellow players, the *taaldarax,* had. One of the oldest rules of *xorvintaal:* to gain, first you must lose.

Every opponent Dareun knew had hatched and grown to adulthood before the Year of Blue Fire. Every one still puzzled and fumbled occasionally over the new ways of magic. In time, they'd relearned the focus of the wizard, the control of the sorcerer.

But only Dareun wielded the star's powers. He had an edge.

It's also not about throwing away the Claw Test. You should be cautious, Magaolonereth said. *You're angering other* taaldarax. *You'll draw their eyes to you. I say this not as a rival, but as your sire's clutch-mate.*

Everything you say is as a rival, Dareun thought. There were good reasons Dareun had not accepted the tutelage of Magaolonereth. But after a contemplative pause, he said,

Perhaps you are right. Perhaps I will step back and observe. Plan my next move more carefully.

With luck Magaolonereth would spread that information. The old ones would be distracted, sending their *lovacs*, their minions, after his minor hoards and holdings—or more likely still, point unsuspecting, greedy fools toward them. All in the hopes of crippling him and forcing him to yield.

He would keep them busy—his own *lovacs* had been warned of possible attacks.

Which left plenty of time for Andareunarthex to make a move no other player would expect. He stirred the water of the scrying pool with a claw.

Most prudent, Mageolonereth replied. *We'll await your return to the game.*

When the ripples settled, the image of a city by the sea surrounded by a high wall and crowned by the peaks of many towers appeared. He thrashed his tail again.

I promise you won't be waiting long, Dareun said too sweetly and then bade his uncle farewell. It was time to move pieces into Waterdeep.

"Heavens to Hells," Lady Aowena Hedare cried. She leaned out of the window that overlooked the square of the God Catcher. "What sort of neighborhood is this?"

"A good one," Tennora assured her aunt, though it was hardly a neighborhood—more the accidental square created where Sul met a funny little jog off Market that to Tennora's knowledge had no agreed upon name. There was a hearth-house, a dry goods store, and a few far-shippers tucked into the surrounding buildings, but the tenement the locals called 'the God Catcher' *was* the neighborhood.

"Doesn't look that way to me," Tennora's uncle Eckhart

said, peering over his wife's rounded shoulder. He snorted through his thick moustache. *"Or* sound like it."

"I promise," Tennora said, "this isn't normal."

But of course, the one day she'd managed to set aside for her aunt and uncle, to prove to them once and for all that she wasn't living in the midst of criminals and coin lasses, everything had to fall apart. Tennora had planned everything carefully, she always planned carefully—but even Tennora couldn't have planned for the madwoman standing in the street and screaming up at her apartment.

"What is she saying?" Aunt Aowena asked. " 'Plaque Clock'? 'Brack Rock'?"

"I believe it's 'Blacklock,' " Tennora said, stifling a sigh. "Aundra Blacklock. The landlady." She pointed up at the arm of the God Catcher, stretched out above them.

Long ago, Tennora's apartment had been part of a glorious statue, controlled by the Lords of Waterdeep. It fought off the invasion of the sahuagin and crushed the leading edge of the invaders itself. Then the Spellplague erupted and drove the statues mad. The God Catcher had been headed to crush the market, the very heart of its city, when a wizard—the Blackstaff, they said—turned the ground beneath it into mud. Its leg sank, and the statue collapsed. The leg remained, a passage into the sewers below. The body curled over its other knee had been built over with new construction. But the side of its face looking out into the city and an arm that reached up to the heavens as if grasping for the hand of a god both remained untouched.

Twenty feet above the statue's open palm, a sphere without visible door floated—the home of Aundra Blacklock, proprietor and sorceress, and source of the madwoman's ire.

"She could at least *enunciate.*" Aunt Aowena sniffed.

Or, Tennora thought, she could shut her mouth and let us get highsunfeast over with.

"If *that* is the sort of person your landlady is acquainted with," Uncle Eckhart said, "I shudder to think of the sort of ruffians she's rented to."

"No offense, dear," Aunt Aowena added.

"I don't believe they're acquainted," Tennora said. The woman had the red-faced, uncomprehending look of pure rage that mysterious Aundra Blacklock frequently inspired in people who didn't know better. Aundra kept to herself, unapologetically so. Tennora could count on one hand the number of times she'd spoken to the raptoran landlady— once when she'd rented the apartment in the God Catcher's shoulder, and twice when Aundra had flown down to Tennora's window to pick up the rent payments in the early evening hours. If the woman wanted Aundra's attention, she was going to have to wait.

The madwoman scooped up a piece of broken pavement from the street and hurled it at the God Catcher. It hit Tennora's neighbor's shuttered window. Aunt Aowena squealed, and Tennora fought the urge to scream.

"Why don't we just sit back—," she started to say.

"Ah!" her uncle interrupted. "There's the Watch. About time."

A carefully prepared highsunfeast lay forgotten on the table, the expensive roast growing cold on its platter while it waited to be carved. But, Tennora thought, perhaps things weren't all bad. The disturbance outside had interrupted her aunt's latest attempt to convince Tennora to return home with them to the North Ward.

"You're not *truly* happy here," Aunt Aowena had said, ignoring the cashew soup Tennora had spent most of the morning preparing. "How could you be? Shabby, shabby place. The air has to be terrible on your poor lungs."

"I'm certain the air is quite the same here as in the North Ward," Tennora said.

Aowena ignored her. "I'll tell you what—Eckhart and I are looking for a tutor for your cousins. You can move back in with us and we'll even give you spending coin, like a little salary. How does that sound?"

"It's very kind," Tennora replied, even though it wasn't kind in the least. It was an easy way for her aunt to educate Tennora's four cousins and an easier way to slip her back into the house. "I know I can always count on you Aunt Aowena, but—"

Her aunt clapped gleefully. "You can move into the Griffon Room! And we'll introduce you to all the *best* young men— don't want to be a tutor forever, do we now?"

Tennora's thoughts unavoidably slid to the last young man she had been introduced to. He was the Marchenors' second son, an officer of the Guard who spent the better part of the last evenfeast she'd attended regaling her with the geography of the sewers he patrolled. He had been very eager and sweet and called her "Lady Hedare" as he was supposed to and taken her hand with an earnestness that suggested he didn't do that often. Tennora had found it too cruel to tell him while she was sure he had many nice qualities, he was an utter bore and that he smelled still of the sewers.

She concentrated very hard on not making a face. "That is kind of you as well. But I'm afraid my studies—"

"Tut! There's no point to a lovely young girl wasting her time with wizardry. I always told your mother—"

That was when the madwoman started screaming, saving Tennora the unbearable chore of explaining to Aunt Aowena that she didn't *want* to live in the North Ward and teach arithmetic to her snotty cousins, while empty-headed young men squired her around ballrooms. That she wanted to continue studying wizardry in her apprenticeship at the House of Wonder.

It also saved her the embarrassment of admitting she wasn't studying wizardry anymore, that her apprenticeship had been ended.

"They're not going to—" Aowena broke off with a squeal. "Oh Eckhart, they've got their swords out!"

"There, there, my dear. They won't do anything upsetting."

Judging by the way Aowena squealed again and covered her eyes, Tennora suspected the Watch couldn't cross the square without being "upsetting" to her aunt.

Add it to the list of things that upset her, Tennora thought, along with me moving away, learning something useful, having friends I wasn't introduced to at a party at the Roaringhorns', and wearing my hair like this. Ever since Tennora's parents had died of a featherlung epidemic when she was fifteen, she had been struggling to find a way to please her aunt and uncle without making herself miserable. The idea of telling Aunt Aowena about losing her place at the House of Wonder, a school for wizards, made Tennora wish she could trade places with the madwoman.

She leaned over Aowena's shoulder to look out the window. Tennora was just tall enough to prompt her uncle to tell her to stop growing every time he saw her, but not so much for anyone else to notice. It was a grayish, drizzly day, and the silvery armor of the Watch seemed faded and insubstantial in the gloom. The captain of the patrol was inching toward the woman. She slung another pebble up at the God Catcher.

"All right, mistress," the captain called. "Put your hands on top of your head and come along quietly. No need to disturb the God Catcher further."

The woman turned to him with contemptuous grace and looked the captain over as if sizing him up. She was too far away and spoke too softly for Tennora to hear what she said next, but the captain stepped back as if jolted and shouted an order to surround and subdue the madwoman.

"Oh!" Aowena cried, her eyes riveted on the advancing guards. "It's just too terrible to watch!"

The Watchmen slipped through the crowd, ordering the bystanders to step back and clear a path. The woman seemed to coil, preparing for the attack, relishing it—though Tennora suspected that was only her imagination. Who would relish such a thing?

The patrolman behind the woman sprang forward and twisted her arm behind her back. The woman slipped from his grasp, fluid as an eel. A second patrolman with ginger hair peeking out from his helmet snatched her around the waist and tried to lift her off her feet—and got a heel to each knee for his trouble. He dropped her but managed to hold tight to her waist.

"She ought to be ashamed of herself!" Uncle Eckhart said. "Making such a scene! Didn't her mother ever teach her to respect her betters?"

It would be more useful, Tennora thought as the madwoman twisted against her captor, if her mother had taught her to fight off an attacker. The guard holding the madwoman had positioned himself perfectly for a sharp punch to the kidney—

She caught herself in the midst of the thought.

I would never do that, she reminded herself. Just because she'd made a point of learning to protect herself when she'd moved deeper into the city and away from her family's guardsmen didn't mean she fantasized about using those skills.

Except, a little part of her said, you just did.

The first guard and one of his comrades—a woman with a brown braid down her back—grabbed the madwoman by the wrists. The captain shouted for her to stop resisting and come along. The madwoman's laughter rang through the courtyard.

And then, she vanished.

The Watchmen all fell back, staring at the empty space. Something powerful had just happened, to be sure.

Tennora leaned out the window, scanning the crowd for any sign of the woman—there were spells that let a body move through the air with a thought, but not too far. The Watch seemed to be thinking the same thing. They spread through the crowd, searching the bystanders. She might have been invisible. A disturbance in the air, a phantom brush against an arm, the sound of fabric sliding against itself—there were clues, to be sure, but no one seemed to notice anything amiss.

Only that the woman was gone—no trace, no trail, no aftereffects.

A shiver ran up Tennora's spine. Powerful magic, indeed.

"Well," Aowena said, "I do hope she's learned her lesson. Now, what were you saying about your studies, dear?"

An hour later, after the street had calmed down and the Timehands chimed tharsun, Aowena and Eckhart finally went home to the North Ward, thanking Tennora for the visit and reminding her that the position of tutor was still available.

"But don't count on it forever, dove," Aowena said, handing the coachman her handbag. "I do need to fill it soon."

"Never mind her," Eckhart said once Aowena had stepped into the coach. "You're always welcome to come home, tutor or not."

"Oh!" Aowena cried, sticking her head out of the window. "I nearly forgot! We have a trunk for you. I told them to send it this morning, but you *know* how the servants can be."

"What trunk?"

"Oh, they found it tidying up the Phoenix Room—that was your mother's room, remember dear?" Aowena's tones had not, to the casual observer, changed, but to Tennora's practiced ear, the enmity Aowena felt for her sister-in-law rang clear. "It was pushed back under the bed, behind *all* her boxes of clothes."

"What trunk?" Tennora asked again.

"Just some things of your mother's," Aowena said. "I thought you might like to have them. It should come by this evening."

Tennora tried not to look too surprised. Those things of her parents' that hadn't been destroyed to ward off the disease were kept at the Hedare family manor—where they belonged, according to her aunt and uncle. She had some few relics of their lives: a portrait of her mother, her father's silk handkerchief, the quilt that had lain on their marriage bed. The trunk was likely full of odds and ends, bits of junk that her mother had wanted out of sight and out of mind.

Still, it had been hers.

Tennora agreed to watch for the errand boy and no, she wouldn't let anyone else into her home. She kissed her aunt and uncle on the cheeks, went back to her apartment, locked the door behind her, and sat down in front of the window to watch the rain that had started pouring down in earnest. A fitting complement, she thought, to the past two days. She tugged at a loose thread on the hem of her skirt.

All of her worries came back to her in a rush: There would be no more lessons. There would be no more chances. She closed her eyes, the afternoon that had ruined her life running through her mind.

She had been in the library of Master Rhinzen Halnian's tower, researching for a test on enchanted objects. Carefully balancing on a wobbly step stool, she scanned the shelves for a book she'd found mentioned in a footnote—*Ritual Development and Magical Restraint.* Not a book she *needed,* to be fair, but the footnote—itself in a book she had not strictly needed to be studying—implied intriguing information about how imbuing magic in items often created drawbacks if the ritual was more powerful than the caster intended. Master Halnian's test wouldn't ask anything about magic item creation, she was sure, but Tennora's curiosity begged to be sated.

Behind her someone cleared his throat. Startled, Tennora looked down at a handsome young man wearing blue robes similar to her own.

Cassian Lafornan was a fellow apprentice to Rhinzen Halnian, and if there was a better-looking young man anywhere in Faerûn, Tennora hoped they kept him locked away somewhere to avoid riots. He had soft brown hair and hazel eyes so bright and warm, Tennora felt as if she were melting when he looked at her.

She had not—of course—told Cassian any of this.

"Coins bright, Cassian. You scared me. Can I help you?"

At that moment the stool wobbled. The young man reached out to steady her, grabbing her hands. Warmth flooded Tennora.

"All right there?" Cassian asked, giving her a charming smile.

"Yes!" Tennora said. "I mean, thank you. This old stool is . . . They should replace it."

Cassian gave her a curious look, and Tennora blushed as he helped her down.

"I was just looking for a book," she said, mentally kicking herself. What else would she have been doing up there? Bird-watching?

"Do you really need another?" Cassian asked, casting an eye at the table Tennora had been using for her research. Books lay open on still more open books, hanging over every edge. "You have nearly the whole library there."

Tennora smiled nervously. "Well, there are a lot of references and . . . I just like books?"

He smiled back. "You certainly do. Master Halnian sent me. He wants to have a word with you. He's in his study." He looked at the mountain of books. "He sounded urgent."

"I'll just . . . clean them up later," Tennora said. "Thank you. For telling me." Before he could answer, Tennora rushed out of the library.

Bloody Sune's spit, she thought, pressing a cool hand against her face. Why did he make her act like she had all the social graces of an orc? Tennora knew she was pretty enough, knew she had plenty of interesting things to say—yet when faced with Cassian . . . She might as well *be* an orc.

The door to Master Halnian's study was open. Her master stood in front of a row of windows that faced the sea and was high enough in the tower to spy the gray edge of the water and catch the smell of the salt breeze if the windows were open. Shelves of books and strange artifacts lined two walls. Behind Master Halnian's divan, he kept an array of particularly precious items behind glass—a sword with an amethyst carved like a sleeping face in the hilt; a crown made of silver bones; a collar set with a moonstone the size of Tennora's fist Master Halnian had said was a piece of the Songdragon's armor. They all scintillated with waiting magic.

On the wall farthest from the windows, the symbol of the dead goddess still traced the stones—a ring of seven stars around a plume of red. As she often did, Tennora took a moment to study it, reverence in her memorization of the fading paint and chipped stones.

"Master Halnian?" Tennora said. "You wanted to see me?"

The eladrin wizard turned abruptly. "Tennora. Please sit," he said. She slid into the chair opposite him.

"Tennora," he said, taking a seat behind his desk. He said her name like a sigh. Tennora's heart squeezed—she was in trouble. She ran through the last tenday—nothing stood out. But the look of concern on Master Halnian's face was unmistakable.

"Tennora, there's no easy way to say this. I'm afraid I'm going to have to release you from your term of study," he said.

The words struck her like a slap to the face. "I-I'm sorry?"

"I don't believe this is the proper . . . path for you. I know you are very passionate about learning the Art," he said. "But I simply cannot condone keeping you here. You see, when Lord and Lady Hedare first brought you to me, I had thought . . . well, my dear, you have a certain grace in your physical movement. It does not translate to your casting."

"What do you mean?"

"I mean that the practice of the Art should be like a dance, an opera, a synergy of motion and sound and magic. What we have left is fragile and fickle. It deserves care and focus. You, my dear—how shall I put it? You *yank* on the threads of the Weave as if they were leashes and the spells errant hounds."

"But . . . ," Tennora said. "But isn't there anything I can do? I mean, I'm studying very hard—"

"Yes, yes," Rhinzen said. "You're a very intelligent girl. Very quick. But being clever is only a *part* of mastering the Weave."

"Isn't that what you're supposed to be teaching me?" Tennora asked. "I can sense it—I can—it's just sometimes the spells don't quite work right. That happens to everyone."

"You more than most," Rhinzen had said. "I am glad to see your eyebrows have grown back, by the by."

Tennora blushed. "It wasn't so bad as all that."

Rhinzen stood and paced behind her, studied his artifacts. "The matter is simple, my dear: Some of us are gifted with understanding of the Weave. And some of us are not. That is the way things are, and neither you nor I can change that any more than we can make ourselves dwarves!"

"But I . . . I know I can. I just need—"

"Waterdeep needs quality wizards. What would we have done if Ahghairon's spells didn't work quite right? Where would we be if the Songdragon's armor had been enchanted by mere amateurs?"

Exactly where we are now, a small voice in the back of Tennora's mind said. The Spellplague came, with or without you.

Out loud, she had said, "Master Halnian, I promise you I do not take this lightly. Give me another chance. Please. I have wanted to be a wizard all of my life."

"Tennora, please." The eladrin set a hand on hers. "Make certain you tidy the library before you leave."

And that had been that. She was unsuited to the Art. She had wasted whole years trying. It didn't matter how much she wanted or tried or studied, she would never be able to work spells reliably. Master Halnian wouldn't take her back. Everything she'd loved, everything she'd studied for so long, had been pointless.

She thought of her fellow students—especially handsome Cassian. He'd go on to great things, probably marry some elf girl with no hips, Tennora thought bitterly. One who can cast a fire spell without burning anyone's eyebrows off.

She watched the rain fall and the clouds drift by, becoming darker and stormier with each passing sigh. It was as if her life had stopped.

Her stomach gurgled as if to remind Tennora that her life had not stopped and that she still had to figure out what she was going to do next. A meal, a pint, and some sympathy seemed like an excellent plan to start with, and Tennora rose from her seat to look out the window.

The view encompassed the square and its jumble of ancient and rebuilt architecture. People tended to forget anything was even there, sandwiched as it was between busier streets. Tennora adored it. The history of Waterdeep peeked out of every corner. Where other areas of the city had been rebuilt with care, the street of the God Catcher made do with what it could, picking up bits and baubles off the ruins. A section of cobbles made from a fallen tower, the window arch still intact. A wall that jutted proudly between two buildings, surpassing and supporting them both. An ornate streetlamp, just in front of the hearth-house, that hadn't been lit in a century.

Tennora squinted into the rain.

Under the streetlamp, the madwoman waited.

Something about her made Tennora want to close the shutters and crawl back into bed. If Tennora went out, the madwoman would seize her, she felt sure. She might scream, a banshee's scream, and then rip her—

Tennora shook her head. What in the Nine Hells was getting into her? She looked at the woman standing in the rain. Just a woman—she didn't even seem to carry a weapon. Though whatever she'd done earlier had clearly been some sort of a spell . . .

The hearth-house—and a hope for capping off this dreary day with a better evening—waited beyond the dark streetlamp and its mad sentinel. If Tennora moved quickly and kept her distance, she could probably avoid speaking to the woman at all. She was quick. She knew how to avoid people, how to slip by with a demure smile and be on her way. It wouldn't be difficult at all. She buckled her stormcloak and snuffed out the candles and with them the concern lingering in the back of her mind.

Her staff rested in the corner by the door. Tennora let her fingers trace the hard lines of the wood grain, eager to take it up.

She left it and slammed the door shut behind her.

Every step of the four flights it took to reach the street level was punctuated by the sounds of children shouting, women and men laughing and arguing, the smells of a dozen suppers—and here and there, conversations between neighbors about the madwoman screaming in the street.

Once she was out the door, Tennora crossed the square quickly, trying to keep her head down so the woman wouldn't make eye contact with her.

Her curiosity gnawed at her. At the gutter she stopped and risked a glance.

The woman was still staring at the hemisphere that hovered over the statue's outstretched hand. She was watching for Aundra Blacklock.

The woman was soaked to the skin, her dark hair plastered against her back and shoulders like a shroud. Up close, Tennora could see her aquiline nose, her skin the color of burnt sugar, the sharp outlines of sinewy muscles wrapping up the woman's arms. The woman's hands were clenched at her sides. She wore nothing but a linen sheath with a belt and a pouch on a leather string around her neck. Just looking at her made Tennora want to shiver.

Tennora clearly made no impression on the woman. Nor did the rain, the children watching from the windows of the God Catcher, or anything else, it seemed.

Tennora felt a twinge of pity. After all, trying to deal with Aundra Blacklock could make anyone a little mad.

And, too much like Tennora, the woman seemed to be at the end of her rope.

"Excuse me," Tennora said, before her fear could stop her. "Do you need some help?"

The woman kept staring at the God Catcher.

"Excuse me?" Tennora tried again. "Coins bright? Are you a friend of Mistress Blacklock's?"

Silence.

"Would you like to come in while you wait for her? To the hearth-house here?" Tennora paused. "I'd rather not dine alone."

"Dokaal," the woman said, "what makes you think I need or even wish for your assistance?" The woman's voice was coldly musical, and it made the hair on Tennora's arms stand on end. Tennora's mouth felt dry, and she swallowed.

"Perhaps," Tennora said, hesitantly, "because you are standing in the rain with no stormcloak."

The woman looked down at her arms and the state of her tattered dress—which was rapidly becoming translucent—as if she hadn't noticed this turn.

"I will survive it," she said.

"The Watch will be back."

"And I will remind them why they fled the last time."

"They didn't exactly flee."

The woman's gaze was suddenly on Tennora, her eyes bright blue against the cold gray of the rain. "What did you say?"

"They didn't exactly flee," Tennora said. "They just gave up."

"It is the same," the woman snorted. She looked back up at the God Catcher.

Tennora pulled her hood down. If the woman wanted to stand in the rain and skulk like a lunatic until the Watch came back and dragged her off, that wasn't Tennora's concern. She'd tried her best. If the woman died of damp lungs, she couldn't fault herself.

"Well, good evening then."

As she turned, an iron grip closed around her forearm and yanked her back. The woman was looking down at her again. She wore a strange, biting perfume that Tennora hadn't noticed before.

"You came from the statue."

"Yes."

"Do you know Blacklock?"

Tennora frowned. "Aundra?" She tried to pull free and failed. "She owns the God Catcher."

"Do you *know* her?"

"I don't think anyone *knows* Aundra, whatever you mean. Can I be on my way?"

The woman let go, and Tennora stumbled backward. "You know Aundra Blacklock," the woman said, "so I would like to have that meal you offered. I need information."

"I only offered a meal and company. I don't know what you want from Aundra—"

"I need . . . help." The woman drew herself up—she was very tall—and held her chin a little higher. "I have a problem to discuss with her."

Tennora hesitated—she wasn't about to give some madwoman a map to Aundra. But what was to stop this woman from following Tennora into the hearth-house and harassing her there? Besides, there wasn't much information she could give about Aundra Blacklock. Nothing the woman didn't already seem to know.

Call it, she thought as she entered the hearth-house, my good deed for the day, and hope the gods are paying attention.

The hearth-house was warm and anything but gray and wet. Aunt Aowena would have pressed her handkerchief to her nose and never lowered it, if she'd set foot inside, but Tennora thought the place had a certain irrepressible charm. Mardin, the owner, watched from behind the bar as Tennora came in and hung her stormcloak by the fire. Aunt Aowena would also have had a few things to say about Tennora carrying on a friendship with the owner of a hearth-house, but Mardin Eftnacost had been a friend of her mother's—from before she had married Tennora's pleasant and respectable father and settled down.

Mardin had visited a few times when Liferna was still alive, always bringing little Tennora a gift and a story. And when Tennora'd moved to the God Catcher, he made a point of watching out for her. He was a better uncle, she was sorry to admit, than Uncle Eckhart—a friendly ear to bend, a shoulder to cry on, and a free meal if her rent was due. He'd been the one to teach Tennora how to handle herself if some tough tried to roll her—including the trick with the kidneys. He'd been in far worse scrapes and far more interesting adventures than anything Tennora had weathered. There was nothing like hearing stories of Mardin escaping from a tribe of gnolls in the middle of the night, while he was still tied up, to put embarrassing herself in front of her classmates into proper perspective.

Mardin raised an eyebrow at the woman dripping on the floor and glaring at the ceiling. Tennora shook her head as if to say, "Don't ask," and held up two fingers for ale and whatever smelled so deliciously of rosemary. She sat down at a table close to the fire. This time of day, Mardin's hearthhouse wasn't crowded.

The woman sat down across from her, where she could look out the cracked window at the God Catcher. "Where is Aundra Blacklock?"

"I have no idea," Tennora said.

"When will she return?"

"I don't know that either."

A grin that was more frustration than joy curved the woman's mouth. "Well, *dokaal*, what do you know?"

"I know you're chasing a very difficult person to pin down." One of the serving girls set two mugs on the table. "And my name's Tennora. Tennora Hedare. What's yours?"

The woman smile fluttered, as if she might laugh or maybe cry.

"Clytemorrenestrix," she said, speaking each syllable as if it were a pearl she was laying down before Tennora, with care and precision.

"It's pretty," Tennora said and meant it. "Is it Tethyrian?"

"No," the woman said.

"It's very unique," Tennora said, sensing she'd hit a nerve. "You just . . . you looked as if you might be Tethyrian. I feel as if I know it though. It almost sounds like a name out of a storybook. Like an ancient queen."

She laughed—a brittle, strange laugh that made Tennora shiver. "Not a queen."

Tennora frowned. "Does it . . . mean something?"

" 'She Will Thunder in the Sky' "

"That would be an interesting name for a queen," Tennora said with a tentative smile. "Or perhaps some sort of folk heroine, like in the old stories . . ."

Her voice failed her. She felt her mouth dry up again, and the pages of history books flew by her mind's eye. She knew where she'd heard a name like that before.

"No," she heard herself whisper. "It's not for a queen, is it? Not a heroine. It's a dragon's name."

Clytemmorrenestrix slowly looked up at Tennora through dark lashes, and this time Tennora could see that her eyes glowed like caged spellplague. The look they gave her was not merely speculative but predatory. The woman's perfume smelled like nothing so much as the air in summer when the sky was full of lightning, so much so that Tennora felt as if it crackled in her lungs.

"A dragon?" the woman said. That cruel grin curled across her lips again, and Tennora's blood ran cold. "Is that what I look like?"

"No," Tennora said. "A little. You just—"

"Just what?"

Tennora swallowed. "Mistress, if you told me you were a dragon . . . I wouldn't doubt you."

"Well I'm not," the woman said, sitting back from the table.

All at once, whatever strange power had gripped Tennora fell away. Clytemorrenestrix was once again an ordinary woman.

"What . . . what are you then?"

Clytemorrenestrix glowered up at the God Catcher again. "I don't know. But I'm not a dragon. Not anymore."

"How could that happen?" Tennora asked.

"Spellplague," she spat, and then she drank from her mug as if to rinse the taste of the word from her mouth.

Boren Angalen had entered Waterdeep by the South Gate, tired and hungry and looking for an inn to spend the night and sort his thoughts out in. Instead, what he'd found was a dark-haired woman looking up at the towers of Waterdeep, a woman he'd been hunting for the last fourteen months.

That had been a day and a half ago. Sitting in the corner of a hearth-house, cooling his heels and picking the last strings of meat from the bones of his dinner, Boren walked himself through what had gone wrong, and what could easily go wrong when he found her again.

He pushed his plate back, and picked the saltcellar up from the table, setting it down carefully. If he was the salt-cellar, then she had been as close as the knot in the woodgrain of the table—in reality, perhaps the length of three carts. There had been plenty of carts to measure against—he laid several squab bones out to represent these. His knife he laid on the edge of the table—the South Gate he'd entered by.

He shifted the saltcellar. He had ducked behind a passing cart and watched her, hardly believing his eyes. The same features, the same height and build. If he called out her name, there was no doubt in his mind she would turn. He had known she was in Waterdeep, he just hadn't expected to find her as soon as he crossed into the city gates. City of Splendors, indeed. She was distracted, staring up at the towers—he could capture her and take her back to Cormyr, collect his payment, and find another target.

He slid the saltcellar around the knob of a leg bone, so that it stood, partially shielded by the rib-cage water wagon. Behind the knot that stood for the woman by a bare inch. It had been perhaps five feet. It would have been so simple.

But the Gate had been crowded—scores of hawkers, farmers, pick-pockets, servants, patrolmen. There was nothing on his plate or in his pockets that he could use to represent all the people who had been milling between him and the woman.

In Cormyr, Boren had seen the body—the wizard on the floor with his throat cut in a jagged line. Not by a knife. A shard of glass the size of his palm with a trim of dried blood as thick as his thumb lay discarded and cracked in half beside the dead man. Pieces of arcane equipment had been smashed to pieces. Scorch marks on the floor and the pages of tomes thrown open.

The servants all attested that the woman had been *invited* into the wizard, Ardusk Nagaenil's study and that he'd asked not to be disturbed. They had been there for the better part of an hour.

Brace, the older hunter who employed Boren, hadn't believed it. "Servants will say a lot of things when their master's dead."

But if they had been telling the truth, they had called for the war wizards when they heard their master shouting. Which meant the chaos that had ended with another man dead had taken all of a few minutes.

If she snapped in a crowd of people, who knew how many would end up dead.

Boren was inclined to believe the servants. He'd found the wizard's notes. Ardusk had been interested in her. Spell-scarred, the wizard had posited. Loss of memory. Erratic behaviors. Possibly violent.

And thinks she's a dragon, of all things, Boren added, studying the knot in the wood. The woman was madder than a mouther.

Boren didn't know why she'd cut the wizard's throat, or why the wizard hadn't managed to stop her. He didn't know why the wizard had brought the woman up into his study in the first place—all of which bothered him.

What Boren did know was that she was dangerous. That if he didn't capture her, his reputation would crumble. That he was very tired of hunting this woman, who had managed for the past year, to be a village ahead, a kingdom away. Easier than catching the murderer unawares would be killing her and calling it done with. But the wizard's family wanted her captured alive, and he had agreed.

He'd slipped out from behind the cart, intending to trail her until they were out of the rush of the gate. But by then, she was gone. He'd missed his chance.

So, he had spent the better part of two days wandering the city and looking for a sign of her. Nothing. In a city as large as Waterdeep, it was easy to lose oneself. Everywhere he looked, the crowds offered up dark-haired, tawny-skinned women, none of them the killer from Cormyr.

He dropped the pigeon bones one by one back onto the plate, and knew there was nothing he could do but wait a little longer, listen a little closer. Boren had toyed with the idea of going to the Watch shortly after he'd lost her.

But no. No. it would be a waste of time. As soon as he said "I'm looking for a woman who thinks she's a dragon," they'd be laughing and teasing. He knew the wizard's family doubted him, eyeing his beardless chin. He'd had a string of lucky captures—but he knew they were due more to Tymora's blessing than his skill—and when he'd heard about the wizard's murder, he'd seen a chance to increase his renown. Brace had spoken highly enough of him, that the Nagaenils, and the war wizards besides, had come around and hired him. No doubt in addition to half a dozen other hunters.

But as far as Boren could tell, no one had tracked her as far or as long as he had.

In the last year of pursuing her, Boren had learned a great deal about the woman, but important questions—Why did she kill the wizard? What might provoke her to lash out again?—still troubled him. He sipped his ale.

If—no, *when* he found her again, he would have to be cautious. Careful. But confident. He would need help, that was for certain.

Down by the water, where the dank chill of Mistshore hung heavily on the air and the occasional body in the alley gathered no notice until it started to smell, a well-appointed if carefully nondescript carriage waited.

Standing in the doorway of an establishment he'd rather not be connected to, a man in a mask frowned. The carriage was meant to draw little notice, but in this place, anything undecayed by moisture and hard life stood out like a torch in the night. Even through the pouring rain, it was clear the carriage didn't belong. As it had been sitting there by the water for the better part of a day, it had—no doubt—drawn plenty of notice.

The carriage couldn't be helped, he decided—it was the carriage or he would have to walk to this dreadful neighborhood.

Besides, while it might have stood out in Mistshore, he thought, it did not connect *him* in any way to the drug den. Provided he wasn't followed. He watched the carriage and the street for several moments, feeling the lethargy in his bones acutely. He was alone.

The drug in his system—a rare and special treat imported from the shores of Returned Abeir solely by the establishment behind him—made his already-sensitive eyes ache from the lamplight. He pulled the mask a little lower, so the eyeholes shaded his sight, and strode briskly to his carriage. His groom scrambled down to open the door and help him in.

With a contented sigh, he sank down into the plush seat and pulled the mask from his face, revealing the fine-boned features of an eladrin. He rubbed his reddened almond eyes, thankful the magical lamps were shaded and the curtains drawn. The dark carriage smelled faintly of musk and vinestar blossoms. He frowned.

"Master Halnian," a smooth voice said.

Rhinzen Halnian nearly leaped out of his seat. He pulled the shade from the lamp, squinting in the sudden light of the glowballs. There was another man sitting opposite him. His hair was oiled back, sleek as an otter's, and the faint hint of rouge stained his cheeks. Virulent yellow lace dripped from the sleeves and collar peeking out of his black stormcloak. His muted red leggings were tucked into bright green, thick-heeled boots. He smiled, revealing two copper-capped canines.

"Enjoying your haepthum?"

"Son of a barghest, Magli," Rhinzen swore. The haepthum, the drug pulsing in his veins, made his heart race and thrust vicious spells to the front of Rhinzen's mind. He ran a hand through his fine, blond hair, as if to push those thoughts back where they belonged.

"What are you doing here?"

"My patron is in the city," Ferremo Magli said, "and I am not looking forward to discussing how you've crossed me."

"Crossed you? Magli, I've done no such thing. Have you told—"

"I haven't said anything. Yet." He pulled a thin stiletto from under his jacket.

Fire, Rhinzen thought, the spell coming easily to mind, more easily than it would have that morning. But the man merely began cleaning his fingernails. Rhinzen cleared his throat to cover his nerves.

"What can I do for you then?"

"When," Ferremo asked, "were you planning on delivering the information my patron paid you for?"

"Soon," Rhinzen said. "It isn't as if the spells are all the same. You can't underestimate what a delicate process it is."

"That's funny," Ferremo said, not looking up from his nails. "I believe you told us you knew these particular . . . spells. Had set them up, in fact."

"I did."

"Seems to me if you're worth even the half you've been paid, you would be finished by now." He looked up at the eladrin. "And I would be out of your hair, instead of watching you spend my coin on your filthy habit, trying to build up enough magic to impress anyone."

Rhinzen sneered. "It's a pleasure, not a crutch."

"So you say. I suppose you could also quit whenever you like." The blade flashed in the cold light. "Just like any dreamkisser."

The eladrin's anger boiled spells through his thoughts. "Who are you to speak to me like that? I am Rhinzen Halnian of the Court of Summer's End, Master of Wizardry, Head of Ritual Studies." The haepthum hummed in his blood, and Rhinzen felt as if the threads of the Weave were becoming his very veins. "I have warded the noblest of Waterdeep. I have cut down mages whose simplest spells would make you weep like a babe. I have culled the weak-willed from the mighty and raised the clever above the meek. Do you think I'm *afraid* of a thug in lady's boots?"

Thunk!

Rhinzen heard the stiletto sink into the seat beside him before he felt the knife pierce the back of his hand and slide between the bones. The haepthum dulled the pain, but Rhinzen still cried out as what the drug left untouched burned up his arm. His eyes watered. He tried to pull away, but the stiletto stuck, and Ferremo didn't loosen his grip. His eyes never left Rhinzen's as he leaned in close.

"First, I do know who you are," Ferremo whispered. His breath smelled like lemon peel. "I know exactly who you are. You shouldn't doubt yourself: plenty of people know.

"Plenty of people who would also love to know what it is you're doing down in Mistshore in the evening hours. Think those noblest families would like to know what their scions' mentor is addicted to? I'll bet my whole purse I can tell you how well that would go. Especially when we get to discussing side effects."

Blood pooled beneath Rhinzen's palm, soaking into the velvet seats. His breath shuddered in and out of his lungs. His ears were ringing, but he heard every word Ferremo said. The man wasn't lying. He wouldn't hesitate to ruin Rhinzen's life.

"Second," Ferremo continued, "you've been paid. I want to see results. If I have to go to my patron empty-handed, I'm going to make certain you take the brunt of what comes next. And I'm sure you can guess how painful that would be for you."

He pulled the stiletto from Rhinzen's hand. Rhinzen cried out in relief and swaddled his bleeding hand in the hem of this robes.

"Third," Ferremo said, pulling a handkerchief from his pocket and wiping the knife clean, "you should be lucky enough to have these boots. Hydra scale. Hand-stitched. They're worth a small fortune." He lifted his foot to show the gold embroidery running up the green-dyed, scaly leather. "And I think they're cunning. So I'd like to hear an apology."

"Sorry," Rhinzen said, trying not to scream.

Ferremo smiled, flashing his copper teeth. "Thank you." He slid his stiletto back into its hidden sheath. "I expect to hear from you in the next few days. Or we'll have to have another conversation."

Rhinzen nodded. Bastard human thought he was so clever.

The man smiled wider and opened the door of the carriage.

"A good evening to you, Maister Halnian," he said as he descended into Mistshore.

That, Ferremo thought as he walked away, was terribly fun. He seldom got the chance to do the dirty work anymore. The look on that puffed-up eladrin's face when the knife went in had been worth a dozen dragons in his coinpurse. He didn't look back as the carriage clattered into the night— Rhinzen would take care of himself now. Time to get out of this cesspool and back to a nice warm—

Ferremo? The voice slapped Ferremo Magli's well-coiffed head with exquisite vertigo.

"Master?" he asked softly.

Have you gotten it? the voice rumbled through his thoughts, deep as a cavern—the voice of his master's true form.

"Soon. The mage is running scared. He won't fail us."

Never underestimate the cowardice of the fey, his master said. *Keep after him. The dragonward is more than I expected.*

"Of course, master." Ferremo pulled the hood of his storm-cloak lower as he passed a group of sharpjaws lurking in an alley, looking rough and reckless. "And the . . . next step?"

I am preoccupied. You will do it for me. Go to her home.

Ferremo winced inwardly. He was cold and drenched and his boots were getting muddy—but he could not disappoint, not at this stage. "Yes, master."

I will send a carriage to meet you outside the docks. Hurry now. You show yourself too late and they'll suspect. We can't have that.

No indeed, Ferremo thought to himself. All his master's plans hinged on the next step and a single woman.

Read the rest of Tennora's adventures in The God Catcher, releasing February 2010!

ONE DROW · TWO SWORDS · TWENTY YEARS

A READER'S GUIDE TO
R.A. SALVATORE'S
THE LEGEND OF DRIZZT®

"There's a good reason this saga is one of the most popular—and beloved—fantasy series of all time: breakneck pacing, deeply complex characters and nonstop action. If you read just one adventure fantasy saga in your lifetime, let it be this one."

—Paul Goat Allen, B&N Explorations on *Streams of Silver*.

Full color illustrations and maps in a handsome keepsake edition.

FORGOTTEN REALMS

The New York Times BEST-SELLING AUTHOR

RICHARD BAKER

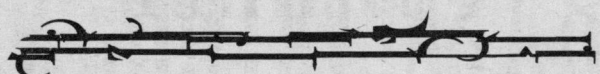

BLADES OF THE MOONSEA

"... it was so good that the bar has been raised.
Few other fantasy novels will hold up to it, I fear."
—Kevin Mathis, d20zines.com on *Forsaken House*

Book I	Book II	Book III
Swordmage	**Corsair**	**Avenger** March 2010

Enter the Year of the Ageless One!

Award-winning Game Designer

BRUCE R. CORDELL

Abolethic Sovereignty

There are things that we were not meant to know.

Book I
Plague of Spells

Book II
City of Torment
September 2009

Book III
Key of Stars
September 2010

". . . he weaves a tale that adds depth and
breadth to the FORGOTTEN REALMS history."
—Grasping for the Wind, on *Stardeep*

FORGOTTEN REALMS

Ed Greenwood
Presents
Waterdeep

BLACKSTAFF TOWER
STEVEN SCHEND

CITY OF THE DEAD
ROSEMARY JONES

MISTSHORE
JALEIGH JOHNSON

THE GOD CATCHER
ERIN M. EVANS
FEBRUARY 2010

DOWNSHADOW
ERIK SCOTT DE BIE

CIRCLE OF SKULLS
JAMES P. DAVIS
JUNE 2010

Explore the City of Splendors through the eyes of authors
hand-picked by FORGOTTEN REALMS® world creator Ed Greenwood.

TRACY HICKMAN
Presents

The Anvil of Time

The Sellsword
Cam Banks

The Survivors
Dan Willis

Renegade Wizards
Lucien Soulban

The Forest King
Paul B. Thompson

The lost stories of Krynn's history are coming to light.

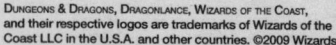